A MESSAGE
TO THE CHARNWOOD READER
FROM THE PUBLISHER

Since the introduction of Ulverscroft Large Print Books, countless readers around the world have confirmed that the larger and clearer print has brought back the pleasure of reading to an ever-widening audience, thus enabling readers to once again enjoy the companionship of books which had previously been denied to them due to their inability to read normal small print.

It is obvious that to cater for this ever-widening audience of readers a new series was necessary. The Charnwood Series embraces the widest possible variety of literature from the traditional classics to the most recently published bestsellers, and includes many authors considered too contemporary both in subject and style to be suitable for the many elderly readers for whom the original Ulverscroft Large Print Books were designed.

The newly developed typeface of the Charnwood Series has been subjected to extensive and exhaustive tests amongst the international family of large print readers, and unanimously acclaimed and preferred as a smoother and easier read. Another benefit of this new typeface is that it allows the publication in one volume of longer novels which previously could only be published in two large print volumes: a constant source of frustration for readers when one volume is not available for one reason or another.

The Charnwood Series is designed to increase the titles available to those readers in this ever-widening audience who are unable to read and enjoy the range of popular titles at present only available in normal small print.

PATRICIA MACDONALD

THE UNFORGIVEN

Complete and Unabridged

CHARNWOOD
Leicester

First published in Great Britain in 1981 by
Fontana Paperbacks
London

First Charnwood Edition
published December 1986
by arrangement with
William Collins Sons & Co. Ltd.,
London
and
Dell Publishing Co., Inc.,
New York.

British Library CIP Data

Macdonald, Patricia
    The unforgiven.—Large print ed.—
Charnwood library series
I. Title
813'.54[F]   PS3563.A28/

ISBN 0-7089-8375-8

Published by
F. A. Thorpe (Publishing) Ltd.
Anstey, Leicestershire
Set by Rowland Phototypesetting Ltd.
Bury St. Edmunds, Suffolk
Printed and bound in Great Britain by
T. J. Press (Padstow) Ltd., Padstow, Cornwall

Prologue

THE chill light of the moon cast the shadow of bars across the face of the young woman lying rigid on the steel frame bunk. She could hear the steady drip of a tap, and the uneasy noises of restless women trapped in their own nightmares, echoing through the concrete caverns of the prison. It was almost peaceful now.

Tonight, as every night, her fellow inmates lay writhing in the straitjackets of their own dreams. But knowing this brought her little comfort. With the dawn they would be released from their private fears. Ghoul-like, they would glide from their cells, seeking her out. Female vampires who stalked by day. "Maggie, honey, whatsa matter? Too good for a little fun with us? Fuck you, bitch. We'll kick your ass, bitch." Alternately crooning and cursing, they pursued her, mocked her. She had tried to keep apart from them. That was enough to make them want to destroy her.

A feeling of bitterness coupled with relief stole over her. Tomorrow, when they called out to her, she would not be there. By then, she would be gone. She thought, for a moment, that they would probably miss her. They would have to find another victim.

Stealthily, Maggie slid down to the end of the bunk and then crouched beside it. She lifted up the thin mattress and groped beneath it, being careful not to rattle the webbed metal of the frame. After a minute she found what she wanted. She grasped the plastic bottle, and pulled it towards her, half rolling it along the frame. When she had manoeuvred it almost to the edge she lowered the mattress on it and stood up unsteadily.

In the corner of her cell under the narrow, barred window was a metal, folding chair. She lifted up the chair and placed it so that it faced the bed. On the shelf above the sink she found her metal cup. She brought the cup over and placed it on the seat of the chair. Then she reached under the mattress again and pulled out the bottle. A harsh cough from across the tier startled her, and she froze where she was. But the sleeper cleared her throat and did not awaken.

Maggie clasped the bottle to her chest. It had not been easy to procure. She had stolen it after supper from a cart outside the shower rooms. Sooner or later, someone would notice it was missing. She had to act quickly. Holding it up to the light of the moon, she could see the label which said "disinfectant". She read the grim warning beneath it with a studied detachment. Then she unscrewed the cap.

The smell of the caustic liquid assailed her nostrils and caused her stomach to turn. Quickly she poured the liquid into the cup and placed the bottle beside it on the chair seat. She sat as if mesmerized, staring at it.

The configuration of the objects on the chair seat struck an odd, long-forgotten chord in her. She was reminded of an altar, or a table prepared for the Last Supper. An anguished laugh rose to her throat. This was certainly her Last Supper, she thought. She was about to commit a mortal sin. It didn't matter. She was damned anyway. That was what Sister Dolorita always reminded her when she came to visit.

Her visit this morning was unexpected, but that was not unusual. She brought no message from Maggie's mother, and that, of course, was also as usual. Maggie realized that she no longer even hoped for a word from her.

The guard had come by at the start of the lock-out, as the others were filing off to the exercise yard, to tell her that the nun was waiting for her in the visitors' room. After nearly two years of these intermittent visits, Maggie knew what to expect. She had nearly refused to go, but she felt herself propelled to the audience by some misplaced weight of obligation. Sister Dolorita had stood throughout the interview, her black eyes like rosary beads in her pasty face boring into Maggie's. She ordered Maggie to confess, as she always did, and Maggie insisted wearily, as she had time and again, that she had not killed Roger. That crime was not among her sins.

When she returned to her cell she found the journal she had been keeping lying exposed on her pillow. It was soggy, soaked in urine. They had been busy while she was gone. The ink blotched and ran on the pages as if a million tears had been cried over it. The smell of the befouled diary was revolting.

Maggie looked from the cup and the bottle on the chair, to the sodden book which lay in the corner of her cell. She was twenty-two years old and she had endured this hell for nearly two years. She had another ten ahead of her if she was lucky. She could not survive it. She was sure of that. The irony was that if Roger were alive, if she only knew that he was there, on the outside, and that he believed in her, she might be able to make it. Tears sprang to her eyes. She ignored them. She did not want to feel sad. She did not want to feel anything. The thought sprang to her mind that her mother would feel utterly vindicated when she heard.

Maggie sat up straight and gazed at the chair in front of her. Then she reached down and picked up the cup. She brought it to her lips. The smell made her want to vomit, but she forced her stomach to relax. She looked away for a moment, and drew in a deep breath. She held it, and then she drank, gulping down the vile liquid.

Almost instantly, she froze. Her eyes bulged, and the cup fell from her hand, clattering to the floor near her feet. Maggie clapped her hand to her mouth, and a few dark streams ran out over her fingers. She stood halfway up, and lurched forward, grabbing for the chair. Then, both she and the chair crashed to the floor. The liquid disinfectant ran from the bottle in rapid trails out through the cell and into the corridor.

The crash of the chair reverberated through the silent tiers. In a moment the sounds of angry unrest began to stir through the cell block.

1

THE sea-gulls beat their wings in a steady rhythm that kept them floating just a few feet ahead of the prow. They led the ship through the fog towards the island which had just come into view. Alone on the deck, Maggie Fraser pulled her light raincoat tightly around her and leaned over the rail, straining to see the outline of Heron's Neck. It looked larger than she had expected, forming in the distance like a long, charcoal smudge. It was too misty to see any buildings yet, and the only visible point was the lighthouse at one end, sticking up like a bony finger.

The ferry boat churned through the grey-green ocean, spewing white foam to either side of the bow. Maggie narrowed her eyes and attempted to bring into focus the contours of her new home.

Home. After twelve years the word seemed foreign to Maggie. She tried to align it in her mind with this island in the Atlantic, over an hour from the New England coast. It was the first time in her life that she would be living near the sea.

A blast of wind blew the rain into Maggie's face, and she shivered. For the tenth time that day she wished she had worn something warmer than her unlined raincoat. It was only October, but the air already had a bite to it. It made her feel unsettled, as if she had come in answer to an invitation, only to find she had the wrong address.

The thought of being unprepared for the weather struck her as being a bad beginning. She had made such painstaking preparations for this arrival in every other way. She tried to remember when she had started imagining it. It seemed to her now that the idea had been conceived when she received that first, perfunctory note from the publisher over a year ago. It was only a brief word of congratulation which came shortly after she received her college diploma in a prison ceremony. A busy man had taken time for a thoughtful gesture, meant to encourage someone like her. But between the lines she had deciphered the glimmer of a possibility for herself. Now, when she thought about it, she realized that the idea for her arrival today had come to her when she was carefully composing that first reply.

The correspondence which began between her and William Emmett had a journalistic flavour to it. She satisfied his curiosity about prison life, while he provided details about the small newspaper which he ran in his retirement. And finally, it had yielded the results she had hardly dared to hope for. Maggie reached instinctively

2

into her coat pocket. The envelope rested reassuringly in its spot. As if it were a talisman, she patted it. Today she would assume her job at Emmett's newspaper.

The clang of a metal door opening interrupted her thoughts. Maggie turned, and saw a man emerging from the stairwell to the lower deck, his hands grasping the calves of a pudgy child who was riding on his shoulders. The child squealed with delight and bounced up and down, her yellow anorak glistening with the spray from the sea.

"Upsa daisy," cried the man, hoisting the child from his neck and grabbing her around the waist. He pressed a slice of bread into her tiny hands. "Crumble it in pieces," he ordered.

The child did as she was told, giggling all the while, and then held up a corner of bread in her outstretched hand while her father held her aloft. "Here seagull," she chirped.

"Hold it up there," the man instructed the child.

"Will he come for it today?" she asked.

"Sure he'll come for it," said the man.

What a dangerous game, Maggie thought uneasily. The child could slip from his arms, and fall into the sea. Maggie glanced back at the pair, the child wriggling and laughing in the man's arms. But she loves it, Maggie thought.

"Are we almost there, Daddy?" asked the child.

3

"Almost there," the man assured her.

Almost there. Despite the misting rain, Maggie's mouth felt dry at the prospect. What would the others think of her? She smoothed out the dress she was wearing anxiously under her coat. It was apricot-coloured, and had looked so well on her in the store, fitting closely to her body, and showing off her white skin. For years she had not been allowed to dress like a woman. She had felt a moment of lightheartedness, when she had first put the dress on. It had made her look attractive. Even pretty. Now, all at once, it seemed like too much.

The child on the deck shrieked with pleasure as a gull swooped down and picked the bread from her little fingers. She quickly held up another piece and a second gull hovered briefly, and then dived for the crust. The child clapped her hands, and then turned, throwing her arms around her father's neck and covering him with wet kisses. "He took it," she crowed.

The man held her fast, his hand gripping her chubby thigh beneath her anorak, his lips puckered to receive her kisses.

Maggie scowled at the pair on the deck. What a reckless thing to do, she thought. She wanted to walk over to them and cry out, be careful don't do that. But she turned her back on them instead. It was none of her business what they did. She had her own concerns.

She stared out over the water, thinking again

4

of her dress. It was too short. Maybe she still had time to change. She closed her eyes and tried to visualize the contents of her suitcase, but another image flashed across her mind. For a moment she could picture the face of Sister Dolorita, glaring at her, the glittering eyes full of imprecations.

No, she thought angrily, shaking her head to dispel the unwelcome image. I'll wear what I like. She realized sadly that even though Sister Dolorita had been dead for years now, she could not yet escape her memory. With an effort she banished the painful thoughts and tried to concentrate on what was ahead of her. She was going to a completely new life, where no one would know her and her past would be a secret she could guard against all intruders. She wondered if it would show on her, like welts after a whipping. Maggie turned the idea over, and then rejected it. *Even those, she reminded herself, fade without a trace.* She rubbed her chilled hands together, and chided herself for her expectations. Soon enough she would know.

"Raw day for the deck," a voice broke into her ruminations.

Maggie turned abruptly and saw a young deck-hand in a khaki rubber raincoat holding a length of rope. "I don't mind it," she said defensively.

"Well," he shrugged, "you better get below soon. We're almost in."

Maggie looked around and realized it was true.

She had been so preoccupied with her thoughts that she had hardly noticed their rapid approach to the island. She could see the dock now, and a number of neat, grey-shingled houses edged in white surrounding it. The pale, chalky sand stretched away from the dock in every direction.

As the engine died away and the boat glided towards the wharf, Maggie noticed two children playing together on its weatherbeaten boards. They crouched side by side in their matching windbreakers, the wind lifting the flaxen hair of the larger boy and tousling the black curls of the smaller. She felt an unfamiliar pang of pleasure mingled with regret at the sight of them. It had been a long time since she had enjoyed the simple sight of children playing. In truth, she had hardly ever noticed such innocent moments years ago.

The boat slid slowly into its berth, and Maggie leaned over the rail to get a better look at the children. Suddenly she paled at what she saw.

Between the two boys, on the boards of the dock, lay a large turtle turned on its back. The beast flailed the air with its horny feet, struggling to right itself. The older, blond-haired boy grasped a stick, sharpened at the end to a point. He poked at the legs of the helpless animal, and when the turtle withdrew its injured limbs into its shell, the boy jammed the stick into the turtle's sanctuary, poking and probing mercilessly, while the smaller boy cried out in glee.

6

The older boy poked at each orifice, finally reaching the hole where the turtle had withdrawn its head. Gently he probed the opening, and then he drew back the pointed poker and thrust it in as hard as he could.

Maggie gasped, her stomach churning. She began to shake, as if she could feel the agony of the dumb beast. Probably a few moments ago it had been crawling peacefully along the sand, she thought. Now it was being tortured.

"Hey, you kids, get the hell out of there. And leave that goddamn animal alone." Maggie looked up to see the young man in the khaki raingear brandishing a fist at the boys over the rail. The older boy kicked the turtle hard, and it flew into the water, the poker still protruding from its shell. The two children turned and scampered down the dock.

"Hey, lady, you better get going. You think we stay here all day?" he asked, turning to her.

Maggie shook her head, and ran a trembling hand over her hair. "Steady," she told herself. A wave of apprehension surged up within her. She forced herself to inhale lungfuls of the damp, salt air, until she felt calmer. Everything will be fine, she told herself. She picked up her suitcases, and headed for the top of the stairs.

The man and his daughter were already descending. The child clung to his neck. The father murmured to her, his face buried in her yellow anorak. Maggie watched them disappear, and then on rubbery legs she followed, into the darkness of the deck below.

The offices of the *Cove News* were in a white frame house, in need of painting, on a cobbled side street. On one side of it was a large private house which looked dark and untended, and on the other was a small building housing a well-lit and fragrant bakery, advertising all-natural fresh-baked bread in the window.

Maggie went up the walk to the peeling white house past the little sign announcing the *News*. She pushed open the door and walked in. Once inside, she found herself in a gloomy hall with faded wallpaper, facing a wooden staircase. On her right was a coat rack with black, cast-iron hooks. Maggie slipped off her soggy raincoat and hung it up, removing the letter from the pocket. She placed her bags beside the coat rack, and then, smoothing down the slightly damp dress, which clung to her body, she walked down the hall to the first open door and walked in.

It was a large, light room with small-paned windows almost completely covered over by the dense trees outside. There were three desks in the room, although only one was occupied at the moment. A plain-looking woman of about forty with a short cap of brown hair streaked dirty blonde, and silver-rimmed glasses, sat pounding away on an ancient Royal typewriter.

Maggie stood uncertainly just inside the

doorway, as the woman seemed to ignore her, absorbed in what she was doing.

"Excuse me," she said finally.

The woman looked up and peered at her from behind her glasses, but she did not smile, or get up.

"I'm here to see the editor."

The woman wiped her hands on her muted tweed skirt, and slowly rose from her seat. She folded back the sleeves of her mud-coloured cardigan and walked over to where Maggie stood.

"I don't believe I know you," she said.

The woman's tone nettled Maggie, but she maintained a very neutral expression. This was a small place. This woman probably knew everyone on the island.

"I just arrived," Maggie replied evenly.

"That's what I thought," said the woman, satisfied with herself.

Maggie spoke in a voice that sounded strained to her own ears. "I'm here on business."

The woman said nothing, but she ran her eyes critically over Maggie's silky dress and high-heeled shoes.

Maggie felt her face start to burn. "Mr. Emmett sent for me. I wish you would tell the editor I'm here. Margaret Fraser."

"What about?" the woman said, eyes narrowed.

Maggie returned her stare. "A job."

"Come with me," said the woman.

Maggie followed her down the draughty hall, to another large room at the back of the house. There were several desks in this room also, littered with papers and newspapers. A man of about thirty-five in a plaid flannel shirt and tie sat on the edge of one of the desks, earnestly explaining something on a piece of paper to a thin, boyish-looking girl of about eighteen. The girl had hair the colour of dead leaves, and light eyes that looked like the pale blue birds' eggs Maggie had seen once in the barn at home. The girl seemed more intent on studying the contours of the man's lean, expressive face than on listening to what he was saying.

"Jess," said the woman beside Maggie, and the man looked up.

"Yeah, Grace."

"This girl wants to see you. What's your name again?"

"Margaret Fraser."

The man looked up at her with a distracted expression in his eyes. Then, as he took in the tense but attractive face and figure of the woman before him, a smile formed on his lips and spread to his eyes. A flicker of pleasure and challenge enlivened his expression as he leaned forward and extended his hand to the stranger. "Hello," he said warmly. "It's a pleasure to meet you."

Perplexed, Maggie took the proffered hand. "Are you Jess Herlie?"

He nodded, holding her hand longer than he had to.

"Aren't you expecting me?" she asked. "I'm here to start the job."

Reluctantly, Jess released her hand. His smile faded into a frown. Maggie looked in confusion from the man to the girl he had been talking to. The girl stared at her curiously.

"What job?" Grace demanded.

"Editor's Assistant. Didn't Mr. Emmett tell you?"

"That's my job," Grace yelped. "What's she doing here?"

Jess put a soothing hand on Grace's arm. "Back up here," he said. "Start over."

Maggie tried to keep her voice cool and deliberate. "I was hired by Mr. Emmett to work for the paper. I'm supposed to start right away."

"Mr. Emmett's not here. He's away on business," Jess explained.

"I know that," Maggie said impatiently. "He told me to come and get started. Here's the letter."

Jess reached out and took the envelope. He pulled out the folded sheet and opened it. Grace crowded up beside him and peered angrily at the letter which he made no effort to conceal as he read. The girl continued to scrutinize Maggie.

Jess finished reading and ran his hand rapidly through his thick hair. "How about that? The

11

old man never said a thing to me about you, never mentioned it."

Maggie felt herself vibrating with anger and alarm. "Well, you can see for yourself I'm expected," she insisted weakly, pointing to the letter in his hand.

Jess nodded, watching Maggie's stricken face with concern. "Evy," he said finally. "Get Miss Fraser a glass of water."

Intent on their exchange, the girl did not seem to notice right away that she was being addressed. "Oh," she said, as if she had been suddenly awakened. "Sure." She went to the sink in the corner and filled a paper cup. At arm's length she offered the cup to Maggie.

Maggie took a sip and steadied herself. She looked directly into the kind, worried gaze of the director. "It seems to me," she said, "that you could just call him and check."

Jess sighed. "I'm afraid we can't do that. He went away rather abruptly and left word that he was going off island to do some business. We're not even sure when to expect him back. We could try his Boston office, I guess . . ." Jess's voice trailed off.

"Well, she can't just walk in here and take my job," Grace protested.

"Look. I don't know what the problem is here," Maggie said grimly, "but I have come a long way for this job."

"Where did you say you came from?" asked Jess.

Maggie was instantly on her guard. "Pennsylvania," she lied.

"Oh, did you work on Emmett's old paper down there in Harrisburg?" Jess enquired.

"Harrisburg? No." Their eyes felt like bright lamps trained on her face.

"I don't know." Jess sighed again, and shook his head. "Who knows what Bill had in mind. He's a little forgetful these days."

Maggie stared at him. Her thoughts would not arrange themselves into the words she needed.

"Maybe you should just start," Jess continued, "and we'll see what he wants to do when he gets back."

"She can't take my job," Grace repeated adamantly.

"Don't worry, Grace," Jess reassured her. "No one's going to take your job from you. There's plenty of work around here to be done."

Grace glared at him, unconvinced.

"Besides," he laughed, "we could always do with another pretty face. I think Miss Fraser would really brighten up the place."

Evy turned and looked sharply at him. For a second her eyes flared. Then she looked down at her shoes.

Maggie let her breath out slowly. She could feel the colour returning to her face, "That's fine," she said. "Thank you. What shall I do?"

13

Jess waved her off. "Go get yourself settled," he said. "Do you have a place to live?"

"Not yet," Maggie admitted.

"Well, take care of that. Then come in when you're all set."

"Fine," said Maggie awkwardly, backing off. "I'll do that."

"Don't forget your coat on the way out," said Grace sarcastically. "You'll freeze to death in that dress."

There were only a few customers in the dank, oak-panelled dining-room of the Four Winds Inn. Maggie took a table by the window, far from the others who were scattered around the room. She asked for a muffin and tea from the waitress, a girl with a crown of braided hair, who took her order and glided away.

From where she sat Maggie could see the few lights of the stores that were open on Main Street. She brooded over the scene in the newspaper office. Somehow, things had so quickly gone wrong. The older woman, Grace, already resented her arrival. She would probably give her no end of hassle. If only Mr. Emmett had told them she was coming. She had asked him to keep her past a secret, but she hadn't expected him to leave her in such an awkward position. She could also sense that the young girl did not like the way the editor greeted her. She must have a crush on him, Maggie thought. Great.

Well, he is good-looking. Immediately she chided herself for the thought. That was absolutely the last thing she wanted.

Despite all her planning, it had gone awry. She had wanted to slip in, unobtrusively, like a diver slipping into a lake, with the surface closing up tranquilly around her, leaving no ripple of where she had entered. Instead, she had drawn unwanted attention to herself.

Maggie looked out towards the dock. A few lights winked on around it in the gathering dusk, but otherwise it was deserted. She wondered where the boys were who had played their vicious game there this afternoon. Home eating cookies, no doubt, their windburned faces angelic in the lavender, fluorescent glow of television cartoons. The thought of them made Maggie shudder.

The waitress returned and put Maggie's order down in front of her. Maggie stared at the plate with no appetite.

Maybe you should get out now, she thought. Run, before things get any more complicated. The realization stabbed through her that she had nowhere else to go. This was her only option, and she had come this far. She had to face the fact that she was bound to feel ill-at-ease around normal people. She would have to learn to adjust. Anywhere you go, she scolded herself, there's going to be some problems. "You have to try," Maggie said aloud, and then looked around

15

embarrassed. This was not the kind of place where you could talk out loud to yourself and not be noticed. This was not prison.

Maggie closed her eyes and rested her face in her hands. Wearily she massaged her temples with her fingertips. They had all looked at her so suspiciously. As if they could sense something wrong about her.

"Pardon me."

Maggie bolted upright.

Evy, the pale girl from the office, stood beside the table, holding a bundle of books and papers. "I didn't mean to startle you."

"You didn't," Maggie lied.

"Figured you'd be over here. It's really the only hotel in town that's open, now that the season's over."

"Do you want to sit down?" Maggie asked.

"Can't," said Evy.

Maggie could not imagine what the girl wanted with her, but her stare made Maggie feel awkward. She wished the girl would go away.

"Jess sent me over," Evy explained, as if in answer to Maggie's unspoken question.

Maggie picked up her knife and began buttering her muffin. "Oh?" she said politely.

"He thought you might want to look at these. Some back issues, books about the island and stuff."

"Thank you. That's very nice," said Maggie,

16

reaching for the papers and placing them on the chair beside her. "I'll enjoy looking at them." Maggie cringed inwardly at the hollowness with which the words came out.

"You're welcome." Maggie looked up at Evy to see if she could read any sarcasm in the girl's face, but Evy had delivered her message with Western Union-like detachment.

"I hope it won't be a problem, my being there, at the paper," Maggie stammered on, in the face of the girl's silence.

"No," said Evy surprised. "Why should it?"

Maggie forced a smile. "I got the feeling that Grace wasn't too happy to see me."

A ghost of a smile hovered on Evy's lips, and deep in her eyes. "Oh, Grace. She can be a drag sometimes."

For a moment Maggie felt absurdly grateful to the girl for her remark. "Why don't you have some tea?" she asked.

Evy hesitated, as if considering the invitation. Then she shook her head. "No. I have to go back." Still, she did not move. Maggie looked in confusion at the pale, oval face.

"What's wrong?" said Evy.

"Nothing," said Maggie, looking away. "Thank you for the books. I appreciate your bringing them to me."

The girl fixed Maggie with her curious,

appraising gaze and then, quite unexpectedly, she smiled. "I thought you would."

Maggie drew back, surprised by the smile. But as suddenly as it appeared, it was gone.

18

2

BELLS tinkled faintly as Maggie opened the door of the estate agent's office and stepped inside. The narrow, stuffy room was filled to bursting with oversized chairs, a sofa, and an assortment of tables. On each table was a vase filled with dusty plastic geraniums and tulips. At the end of the room was a large desk, piled high with papers and folders. Behind the desk an old man in a sea captain's cap sat eating a sandwich and studying a chart. He looked up at the sound of the bell and peered at Maggie, wiping yellow mustard off his white moustache with the back of his hand.

Maggie glanced down at the signs which rested on the edge of his desk. One read, "Plan Ahead," with the letters dribbling down the margin of the plaque. The other read, "Henry Blair."

"Mr. Blair?" she asked.

"At your service," replied the old man jauntily, placing the half-eaten cheese sandwich atop a pile of papers.

"I'm interrupting your lunch," she apologized.

"No problem," he insisted. "What can I do for you? Sit down, Miss . . . ?"

19

"Fraser," Maggie said, taking a seat. "I'm looking for a place to rent. An apartment. Or a small cottage, here in town."

"How long do you want it for?" asked the old man in a gravelly voice.

Maggie shrugged. "Indefinitely."

"You moving here, to the island?" asked Henry Blair.

"I have a job at the paper," Maggie admitted.

"Well, well, okay," said the agent, shifting some of his papers around and knocking over his sandwich in the process. "Where you staying now?" he asked.

"Well, I spent the night at the Four Winds."

"So, you need something right away."

"As soon as possible," Maggie replied.

"Can't stay in hotels. Too expensive. You need a place."

Maggie smiled wanly in agreement.

The old man stood up and shuffled over to an army-green file cabinet in the corner. "You know the island?" he asked.

Maggie shook her head.

"Mmmmm," he murmured, extracting a folder, and resuming his seat. He put on a pair of bifocals, and squinted at the papers inside. "I haven't got too much right here in town. Nothing that's really comfortable, you know."

"Nothing?" she asked worriedly.

The old man made a clucking noise. "Not

20

much. There's a little apartment above the café, but that's not very nice for a lady like you."

Maggie glanced mournfully out the front window at the rain, which the wind was sweeping down Main Street. "It might be all right," she said.

"You'd do a lot better out of town," the old man advised her. "Lots of houses sitting empty. There's folks with homes here who have two or three houses around the country. Only spend a week or two here in the summer. You can rent one of them for a song. Just take your vacation somewhere the same time these folks come back to their houses. Works out perfect. We've got a lot of folks here who do that."

Maggie sighed. "It sounds very nice, but I imagine you need a car to live out there. I can't. I don't have a car."

"No car. That's a problem," the old man muttered. "You don't drive, you say?"

"Oh, I can drive," Maggie said, wondering anxiously to herself how soon the licence she had applied for would come through. "I just don't have a car."

"Wait a minute," said the old man, tugging on his moustache. "I might just have something for you." He stood up and shuffled back to the file cabinet, replacing the folder he had and pulling out another. "Just one darn minute here. Aha!" He smiled cheerfully at her revealing two missing lower teeth.

"What is it?" Maggie worked her hands in her lap.

"The Thornhill place," Blair exulted. "It's way out there. On Liberty Road. Out past the cemetery. Nice house. Very nice. Not too big, but very comfortable. A lot of property around it, so it's private. And," he paused for effect, "there's an old Buick in the garage which they let with the place."

"It sounds good," Maggie said doubtfully.

"You want to see it?" Blair asked. "We'll take a run out there." He was already wrestling his coat off a hanger in the cupboard.

Maggie stood up. "What about the people who own it? Do they come in the summer?"

"Thornhills? Maybe a week or two. They're off on a cruise now. We'll figure it out when they get back, if you like the place."

"I'd like to see it," Maggie ventured.

The old man was already opening the door of the office and stepping out on the porch. "Rain's letting up a bit," he observed. "It's just misting now."

Maggie joined him on the porch.

"My car's over there," he said, pointing to a battered old station wagon parked by the kerb. "You don't want that apartment," he said, jerking his chin towards the café up the block. "This'll suit you much better."

Silently hoping that he was right, Maggie

22

followed Mr. Blair down the steps to the car.

The Thornhill place was set far back from the road. Its weathered clapboards were barely visible through the fir trees as Henry Blair turned up the driveway. The nearest neighbours were not even in sight of the house, Maggie noted with satisfaction. It was away from any other people. It was just what she wanted.

"This is it," Blair announced, pulling his car up in front of the garage. Maggie looked over towards the house. The outside of it looked worn, but it still retained a kind of stark charm with its grey paint and black trim. Skeletons of rose bushes twined around the front door.

Blair got out of the car and motioned for Maggie to follow. "I better see if this car still runs, before we even look inside. No point in looking if the car don't work, right?" He grinned pleasantly at Maggie, who nodded in agreement.

The old agent began tugging on the iron handle which opened the garage. "Have a look around the place," he suggested, "while I fiddle with this."

Maggie did as she was bidden, passing by the back porch steps and looking up at the screen door and the darkened windows. The quietness of the house seemed oddly comforting, as if it stood ready to protect her solitude. Maggie continued on around to the back of the house and looked out.

It was a rugged, disorderly piece of property. Directly behind the house was a field of long grass, now turning silver, and a thick grove of pine trees hedged the left side of the land. The weak, grey light of the day was not strong enough to penetrate the grove, and illuminate its dark recesses. The faint rustle of pine needles and waving grass softened the hardy landscape.

Maggie scanned the field and the rise behind it, covered with scrubby bushes of bittersweet. Her eyes rested on the naked, upper branches of a clump of crabapple trees, just visible over the rise. A few wizened apples still clung to the thin, grey branches. Maggie headed towards the trees, wading through the tall grass and climbing up the rise. She saw that it fell off steeply on the other side, to the bank of a brook below.

Maggie stood on a flat rock, and surveyed the area. The icy water burbled over the stream's rocky bed. Across the brook, Maggie spotted a tree frog squatting gingerly on a slick-surfaced stone, staring at her with lazy, black eyes. She held her breath, so as not to scare it off. A sense of peace, tinged with loneliness settled over her. She felt at ease here. The land was an undreamed-of luxury.

The sudden roar of an engine broke the spell. The frog leapt off the rock, and into the rushing stream. Maggie turned, and started back towards

24

the garage, picking her way through the grasses.

"Got her going," said Blair, beaming, as Maggie entered the garage.

"Great," Maggie assured him.

"Let's have a look through the house now," he said, getting out of the car and switching off the engine.

It was not a large house by island standards, but it was clean and well-kept. All of the living area was on the ground floor with an attic above and a cellar below. Blair guided Maggie through the rooms, pointing out the genuine antiques among the odd assortment of furniture which appeared mismatched but comfortable.

"Everything you need here," he said, opening the door to a linen cupboard off the bedroom. "Bathroom's a little old-fashioned, but everything works." Maggie looked in and noted the deep, claw-footed bathtub, and the pull-chain toilet.

"Fireplace works," Blair observed, as he passed through the living-room. "And the kitchen has all the utensils you'll need."

"It's perfect," Maggie interrupted his inventory. "I'd like to rent it."

"Sure you won't be too lonely out here?" asked the old man.

Maggie pursed her lips and looked away from him. "No. This is fine."

"Well, a pretty gal like you is sure to make

25

friends before too long. Now, I'll just need some references, and we're all set."

Maggie stared at him, "References?"

"Where you lived before, something like that?"

Maggie could feel beads of sweat popping out at her hairline. She groped around for an answer. "I'd give you my parents, but they've passed away."

"An employer, anyone like that," Blair replied patiently.

There is no one, Maggie thought, squeezing her eyes shut.

"Anything wrong?" asked the old man.

"No," said Maggie sharply. "No. How about Mr. Emmett? He can give me a reference."

"Bill Emmett? Oh sure, that'd be fine."

Maggie sighed with relief. "He's out of town right now on business, but when he gets back?"

"That's soon enough," Blair agreed. "Now come on back to town, and you'll sign some papers, we'll have the lights turned on, and you can move in today if you like."

Maggie nodded gratefully. "Thank you," she said. "You've made this so very easy."

"My pleasure," said the old man, tipping his captain's hat. He headed for the back door. Maggie took a hopeful look back at the darkened rooms of her new home, before she followed him.

That evening, Maggie stared down at the contents of the worn leather suitcase which lay open on the chenille bedspread.

What a collection, she thought, shaking her head. I really need some clothes. One by one she lifted the few faded blouses and threadbare sweaters from the bottom of the bag. She carried them over to the dresser and placed them in the open drawer of the bureau which was lined with white shelf paper.

She ran a finger over the collar of a cotton blouse with blue flowers on it that had been her favourite in high school. She had found it in the boxes of her belongings salvaged by a neighbour, Mrs. Bellotti, when the farm house was sold for back taxes, three years after her mothers death. At first, Maggie had not wanted to keep any of the clothes she had found there. They were too young for her, long out of style, and most of them had unhappy associations which clung to them, like a musty scent. But common sense had won out. She had very little money, and she was starting a job. She had to wear something.

Maggie closed the drawer slowly and opened the one above it. Then she returned to the bed, and the other smaller suitcase, which held her underwear, a few scarves and some gloves. In less than twenty minutes, she had unpacked both suitcases, and organized the bedroom just as she wanted it. She closed the empty suitcases, and shoved them on the top shelf of the cupboard. Then she sat down on the edge of the sagging double bed. All moved in, she thought.

The lamp beside the dresser threw a warm light over the room as Maggie looked around. She had a real bed to sleep in. Her own kitchen. A living-room, with a fireplace. A job to go to in the morning. As she counted up these assets, she felt a flurry of happiness. The estate agent had been amiable this morning, and the rental had gone smoothly. Everything except that part about the references. Maggie grimaced, remembering how it had thrown her. Things that were so natural for other people seemed like insurmountable obstacles for her.

Enough, she thought. Everything has worked out fine, and you're settled in here. You have a home now.

Abruptly, Maggie stood up and went towards the kitchen, leaving the lamp burning. Damn the electric bill, she thought. She wanted light around her. Light and comfort. She had spent so long in the dark.

She opened the refrigerator and pulled out a bottle of juice. She poured it into a glass and drank from it, revelling in the luxury of having her own refrigerator which she could fill with whatever she pleased. She leaned back against the sink and thought about tomorrow, her first day on the job. It will be all right, she told herself. You'll do fine. Just don't panic. Keep your head. She glanced up at the kitchen clock. It was getting late.

Her neck felt stiff from the tension of the day. "A shower," she said aloud, "and then to bed." With a purposeful nod of her head, she put the empty glass in the sink, and returned to her bedroom for a bathrobe. Then she went into the bathroom and turned on the water in the tub.

At first the perforated metal disc on the ancient showerhead let out only a trickle, but gradually the pressure worked up to a breezy shower. Maggie hoisted herself over the high rim of the tub, pushing aside the shower curtain which crackled with age. She pulled it closed again, and put her face up to the showerhead. Torrents of water soaked her hair, and plunged down over her body. She could feel all her muscles relaxing under its steady pressure. For a few moments she just stood there, luxuriating in the heat of the water and the privacy. Then she groped for the soap in the clam shell on the windowsill and began to languidly work up a lather.

Suddenly, she gasped, and dropped the bar of soap as if it had burned her. She gazed first at her lathered hands, and then down at the frothy bar, which had slithered and skipped down the side of the tub, and now rested inches from her toes. She had forgotten to check. For the first time in years she had not remembered to examine the soap.

Maggie stared down at her body. In the bright bathroom light, the network of thin, hairline scars, intersecting diagonally on her sides, were clearly visible. Her mind drifted helplessly back to that awful night. She could feel a weakness in her knees as she remembered.

She had removed the soap as usual from her meagre grooming kit, and stepped under the lukewarm prison showers in the group stall that smelled of mildew and lysol. She was late, having worked an extra shift as punishment for the fist fight she'd had with one of her tormentors. The matron stood outside, waiting impatiently for her to finish. Maggie closed her eyes and let the water rain down on her aching body. Slowly she began to soap herself on her sides, and under her arms.

"Hurry up in there," the matron barked.

The water seemed to sting her all over. For a moment she thought it might be a rash of some kind. Then she looked down.

Blood streamed down her sides. Scarlet rivulets ran where the water trickled. Bloody orange scallops billowed where the shower blasted.

Too horrified to even scream, she was transfixed by the sight of her mutilated body. Her eyes darted to the soap, which she grasped in her trembling hand. As she moved, she saw a glint. She looked again. The razor's edge was shining now, the menacing blade glaring out at her from where it hid, embedded in the bar of soap.

Despite the heat of the shower, Maggie shivered at the memory. Then she bent over and gingerly retrieved the sticky cake of soap. Sprays of water bounced haphazardly off her back as she picked it up. Slowly she began to work up a lather again. You don't have to check it any more, she reminded herself. You're safe. She rubbed the bar of soap thoughtfully between her palms. There's nothing to be afraid of now.

Outside, the storm had fled, chased by a wind which still gusted, rattling the panes in the desiccated window frames of the Thornhill house. Lengths of clouds, like grey rags, trailed over the moon. A few scattered stars pierced the sky. The air was infected by a damp, autumn chill.

The light from the lamps inside the Thornhill house shone through the windows and threw squares of weak, lemon-yellow light on the brown, matted grass below the sills. Inside the house, the solitary figure of a woman was visible, seated on a bed, then moving through the rooms to the kitchen for a drink, and finally to the bathroom, where she pulled off her robe, preparing for a shower.

Behind the dense cover of a fir tree, just beyond the strip of light-patched lawn, a pair of eyes watched Maggie's progress from room to room. Their gaze did not waver. One might have thought that those eyes could see through the

31

walls themselves, incinerating beams and clapboards with their fierce intensity.

The hands of the watcher curled around a low-lying branch of the shielding tree, gripping it so tightly that the knuckles seemed to glow in the darkness, like bare bone.

The breathing of the rigid figure came in short, feverish pants, almost like a wolf's, as the eyes, hooded and unblinking, followed their object. The only other sound, made virtually inaudible by the gusting wind, was the relentless grinding and grinding of the watcher's teeth.

3

MAGGIE hesitated, standing in the dim, draughty hallway outside the editor's office. The door was slightly ajar, and she could hear the murmur of voices coming from the lighted room. She felt like a prowler at a window, shivering there, the papers rattling in her hand. After two days she was still overcome by a sense of awkwardness whenever she entered a room, as if her limbs might suddenly splay out, betraying her discomfiture which she tried to hide.

She had not made an exceptional number of mistakes for the first few days on a job. She had misjudged the length of a headline, misfiled the mayor's speeches, and called the printer several times more than was necessary. Maggie reflected that her work on the prison newsletter had served her well. Even Grace, who made it plain that she was watching for slip-ups, had been forced to inflate her complaints with bluster. But this did not quell Maggie's uneasiness. On the inside she had learned that errors, even small ones, incurred punishment. It was a simple code, really. And it had a way of keeping her off balance, even now, when the gates were locked behind her.

Maggie strained her ears to listen for a lull in the conversation. She was reluctant to interrupt. But there was no good time. Tentatively, she knocked.

"Come on in," Jess called out.

As she entered, Jess and Evy looked up. Jess leaned forward on his desk, folded his hands and smiled at her. Evy hunched down in the chair which was pushed up close to the desk. She screwed her mouth up and began to chew the inside of her cheek absent-mindedly.

"I'm sorry to interrupt," Maggie apologized. "I just finished editing this fishing column, and I thought you'd want to take a look at it." She handed the manuscript to Jess.

"Do you want to sit down?" Evy asked, rising halfway out of her chair.

Maggie shook her head and motioned Evy to stay seated.

Jess riffled the pages of the manuscript. "Everything you ever wanted to know about quahogs," he said wryly.

"And more," Maggie conceded.

He laughed, and shook his head. He began to peruse the typed pages, nodding and making an occasional mark on them as he did so. Maggie tried to think of something to say to Evy in the silence. Before she had a chance to speak, Evy glanced up at her.

"Do you know what time it is?" the girl asked.

Maggie showed her empty wrists. "I don't have a watch."

"Quarter to twelve," said Jess, looking up. "Nice work, Maggie. You've managed to make Billy Silva's nautical prose resemble English."

Maggie flushed with pleasure at the compliment. "He has a rather unusual style," she said, smiling at her feet.

"Barnacle Bill's Chronicles," Jess added.

"Jess," said Evy, "I need to know how many columns for letters this week."

He looked at her in vague surprise. "Oh, I guess the usual, three above the fold." He picked up the fishing column on his desk distractedly. "Here you go, Maggie."

Maggie reached for the papers which the editor had placed on the edge of his desk.

All at once, Jess leaned over and grasped her hand in his. "What a lovely ring," he said, peering at the glimmering violet stone on her finger. Maggie looked up at him, startled by his touch.

"Thank you."

"Where did you get it?" he asked, without releasing her hand.

"Jess," Evy interrupted. "Do you want to tell me about these changes?"

Jess frowned. "Let's do it later, okay?"

Evy barely nodded, and stood up. "Let me know when you're ready," she said stiffly.

"After lunch," he promised. "Maggie, sit for a minute."

Maggie could tell that Evy was offended. She hesitated, not wanting to take the seat the girl had just vacated.

"You don't mind," Jess said to Evy. It was a statement.

Evy shook her head, but Maggie could see the tension in the unnatural lift of her chin. The girl left the room without another look at either of them. Maggie sat down.

"May I see it?" Jess enquired politely.

Maggie looked at him in confusion. "What?"

"The ring. It looks like an antique."

"Oh!" Maggie twisted the ring off her finger and handed it to him. For a moment she felt disappointed at his genuine interest in the ring. She realized suddenly that she had hoped it might just be a ruse to detain her.

Jess examined the ring curiously, holding it up to the light from the window and squinting at it. "Amethyst," he pronounced.

"Yes. It belonged to my grandmother," she offered. "My father gave it to me. Shortly before he died . . ." Maggie's voice trailed away.

"Is that right?" he murmured. "My mother had quite a collection of antique jewellery. Her enthusiasm was sort of infectious. My father could never pass a shop window without going inside to look. As a matter of fact I can

36

remember an amethyst pendant that he had his eye on for her for quite a while . . ."

Maggie tried to concentrate on his words, but she found her attention slipping away. As she watched the ring turning in his fingers, anxiety began to rise in her chest and engorge her throat, as a long-buried memory bubbled up from within. Her eyes remained riveted to the ring, but her mind travelled back in time.

"What is that you have there?" Her mother's sharp question startled her as she sat, playing with her treasure on the floor of the parlour.

Quickly she cupped her hand over it and squeezed it shut. "Nothing," she whispered.

"Don't lie to me. I saw something," her mother insisted, grabbing her arm and prying at the clenched little fingers.

"No, it's mine," she cried, trying to wrest her hand from her mother's grasp. With a sharp crack to her knuckles her mother forced her fingers open, and the ring flew out landing at her mother's feet. Slowly the woman bent over and picked up the ring. She stared, ashen-faced, at the child.

"Where did you get this?" she demanded in a shaking voice.

"I found it," she insisted tearfully, avoiding her mother's eyes.

"You couldn't have found it. It was in your father's dresser."

The child curled herself up, crossing her arms protectively over her chest.

"You took it from him," the mother cried, as if trying to convince herself. "You took it, after he died. Admit it." She shook the child in desperation.

"No," Maggie cried defiantly. "He gave it to me."

Suddenly she heard the sound, familiar and ominous to her ears, of heavy fabric dragging across the carpet. The dark figure of her mother's visitor came to a halt just above her, blocking out the patch of sunlight on the carpet where she crouched. The child cringed, and did not look up.

"We know how you got it. You're a sinful, evil girl," said Sister Dolorita, glowering down at her. "You are worse than a thief." She spat the words out.

The child began to shiver but she refused to look up at the Sister's accusing eyes. "No," she whimpered, shaking her head. Then she saw, from the corner of her downcast eyes, a flash. And then again. It was the silver cross, swinging on a chain clenched in Sister's fist.

"Maggie."

The woman started, and stared at Jess, who was holding the ring out to her, a puzzled look on his face. "Anything wrong?" he asked.

"No, I was just . . . it was nothing." She took the ring and forced it back on her finger.

38

"It's lovely," he commented.

"Thank you," she said. For a minute his eyes held hers. "So," he asked abruptly. "How are you finding it here?"

"The job?" Maggie asked faintly.

"Well, the job, the island. Did you find a place to live?"

"Oh yes," Maggie assured him hastily. "I'm renting the Thornhill Place, on Liberty Road. It even includes the use of their old Buick."

"It's comfortable?"

"Very," Maggie agreed. "All that room. And the property is beautiful. So far from everything."

"That's what I love about this island. Gives you room to breathe. Privacy. Were you a city dweller before this?"

Maggie avoided his eyes. "Yes. That is, I'm not used to . . . I'm used to a much smaller space. I grew up on a farm though," she added.

"In Pennsylvania?"

"Yes," she said. He seemed about to ask another question. Hurriedly, she changed the subject. "I'm enjoying the work."

Jess nodded. "You seem to be catching right on."

"I'm doing my best."

"Any problems with Grace?"

"Grace? No." The false note hung in the air. Jess spoke reassuringly. "It will all work out.

39

We'll get things straightened out when Emmett gets back."

"Well, whenever," said Maggie lightly. "I guess I should be getting back to work." She stood up.

"Maggie," Jess said, looking at his watch. "I was just about to knock off for lunch. I was wondering if you'd like to join me?"

Flustered, Maggie bit her lip. "Oh, thank you. No, I can't . . ." Jess looked at her expectantly.

"Well, I need to do some shopping, you know," she mumbled.

"That's all right," he said. "I understand. Maybe another time."

"Yes, maybe," she said, getting up and backing out of the office door. "I'm sorry." She closed the door behind her.

"Watch where you're going," Grace whined.

In the dimness of the hallway Maggie had not seen Grace coming. "I'm sorry, Grace."

The older woman assumed a long-suffering expression. "While you're busy chatting there's work piling up on your desk."

Without a word Maggie followed Grace back into their office. She walked to the chair by the window, picked up her pocketbook and started for the door. As she crossed in front of Grace's desk she could feel the older woman glaring at her. Ignoring the butterflies in her stomach, she spoke calmly.

"I'll do it after lunch." Maggie left without glancing back.

You idiot, she berated herself, as she turned on to Main Street and started up the block. Refusing his invitation like a bashful schoolgirl. He's your boss. He didn't mean anything by it. But the combination of elation and apprehension which was making her stomach churn belied the lecture that Maggie was giving herself.

Carefully she made her way along the cobblestones to the pavement, where she began looking into the merchants' windows. Through the sparse foliage on the trees between shops, she caught an occasional glimpse of white caps and waves.

It wasn't just business, she thought. He was being friendly. But that, she reminded herself, was the point. She couldn't even consider a flirtation with him that might lead somewhere. Unless she wanted to tell him about how she had spent the last twelve years. And that was impossible.

That melancholy realization stifled her appetite. With a sigh she decided that a walk might do her more good than lunch. Maggie paused at the darkened window of the gift shop and saw the child-sized sweatshirts with Heron's Neck printed on them, placemats with a map of the island and a rack of post cards forming a dusty display. She gazed wistfully along the deserted sidewalks and tried to imagine what it would be like in the summer, thronged with vacationers in sneakers and sailors' hats, teenagers eating ice-cream and music blaring on the street. What she saw before her was a wide street, nearly empty of people, with a few cars and pick-up trucks parked outside the scattered shops which were open.

A little further up the block she stopped outside the ice-cream parlour and peered through the unilluminated window. Inside, the imposing mahogany fountain, the marble-topped tables and wrought-iron chairs formed a curious scene to her eyes, like the stage setting for some Victorian drama, waiting there in the gloom for the actors to appear and the lights to come up. Waiting in vain, Maggie thought.

"There's nobody in there."

Maggie straightened up to see a man in a plaid lumberman's jacket carrying a roll of barbed wire. "I was just looking," she protested.

The man eyed her suspiciously. Maggie noticed that his right hand was bleeding slightly where he grasped the wire. "Closed for the winter," he said balefully.

Maggie nodded, and slipped past him. She could feel his eyes on her as she hurried away. At the next corner she spied a sign for Croddick's Dress Shop. She was about to pass it by, assuming that it too was closed, when she saw a woman emerge from the store carrying a

42

large shopping bag with "Croddick's" printed on it with a flourish. Curious, Maggie pushed the door open and went in.

The store was softly lit, and redolent of bayberry. A few women were browsing among the clothes, and in one corner a man was arranging a display of belts and scarves. He turned and gave Maggie a wan smile. "Hello," he said.

Maggie returned his greeting, and turned towards a nearby rack of skirts.

"I'm Tom Croddick," he said, coming over to her. "I don't believe we've met."

Maggie felt a pinprick of annoyance at the intrusion on her anonymity. However she answered him politely. "My name is Maggie Fraser."

"Are you new to the island?" he asked.

"Yes," she replied.

The shopkeeper looked at her expectantly.

"I work at the paper," said Maggie grudgingly.

"Is that right?" he asked. "Well, welcome, welcome. Have a look around."

"I was surprised to find you open."

"Oh yes. Winter or summer, the ladies always like something new to wear," Tom said philosophically. "Go ahead. See what you like." He waved Maggie off, and returned to his display.

Maggie began to pick through the clothes, sliding the hangers by her on the rack, and occasionally holding up a skirt or blouse against herself to see how it looked. She noticed, to her surprise, that the clothes in Croddick's store seemed quite fashionable and well-tailored. They also seemed terribly expensive, although she realized that she was still getting used to the prices of things, which seemed to have tripled while she was away.

She knew about changing fashions on the inside. In the news magazines she was allowed to read were occasional articles about fashion. And she could also tell by the ads, and the things people wore on television. But she still felt overwhelmed by it all. Getting out, and buying clothes, she felt like an alien from another planet, trying to assemble a costume so that she could pass, unnoticed, through human society.

Maggie turned away from the racks of skirts and blouses, and drifted over to a table which displayed trays of jewellery and hair ornaments. Using the gold-rimmed, oval mirror which stood on the counter, she tried on several necklaces, feeling silly and yet pleased at the game. Then she removed each one and carefully replaced it on the display rack. Slipping a bracelet on each of her narrow wrists, she turned them over, admiring them. Then she wriggled them off, and put them back on their velvet tray. She was about to walk away from the counter when she spied two matching silver combs with blooming irises engraved on the top. Lifting them up with a smile, she drew back the sides of her mass of hair, and inserted one on each side. She liked the way they looked. The style seemed to draw her face up, making her look less tired, more carefree. She decided to leave them in for a little while, although she reminded herself that she could not afford to spend money on such a frivolous item.

Yet something about wearing the combs lightened her spirits. She wandered through the racks of clothes, giving a desultory glance to the businesslike clothes which she needed, and being drawn, instead, to the array of play-clothes and lacy lingerie. She ran her fingers over the soft fabrics of sheer nightgowns, and wondered who on Heron's Neck would ever wear the peek-a-boo camisole which Tom Croddick had hung at a rakish angle above the shelves of underwear.

She thought she had about exhausted the store's stock, when she suddenly discovered a rack of evening gowns, hanging at the back, near the dressing-room. Maggie began to flip through the rack of floor-length dresses, to the clacking of bugle beads and the rustling of taffeta, when all at once she came upon a dress that captured her whole attention.

It was slate-blue and satiny, a simple, low-cut bodice that looked like it would cling to every curve of a woman's frame. Maggie grasped the hanger, and pulled it out. She looked at the price tag and whistled under her breath. She felt grateful that she had utterly no need for such a dress. Put it back, she thought. But it was so tempting.

Humming to herself, she waltzed discreetly to the mirrored door of the dressing-room, relieved that no one seemed to notice her. Removing the dress from the hanger, she held it up against herself, covering her dowdy skirt and blouse. Turning this way and that, Maggie admired herself furtively. The colour of the dress whitened her skin, and complemented her grey eyes. Her reddish hair glowed by contrast. She was grateful that it had not turned grey. She was only thirty-two, but she had seen women of twenty-five go completely grey in a year on the inside.

And she was still slim. Slimmer, in fact, than when she had gone in. But of course one did not expect to gain weight in prison. She noted that her complexion was slightly pallid, and resolved to get some fresh air. She wanted to look attractive.

For a moment she imagined herself dancing in the dress. Her partner was Jess Herlie. She could picture him smiling at her, his eyes travelling down the neckline, admiring her. She shivered with pleasure, and smiled at herself in the mirror.

Suddenly, she stiffened. The mirror caught the murky image of another face, staring at her, eyes narrowed, as she preened.

Maggie blushed furiously, caught in her posing. She could see without turning around, that whoever was watching her was outside the store, looking at her through the window. The noon light made the figure dark and amorphous, but there was no doubt that the eyes were trained on her as she cavorted before the mirror.

Feeling ridiculous, and angry with herself, Maggie grabbed the hanger from the nearby chair and forced the dress back on it with trembling hands. She must have looked a sight, she thought, puckering her lips, her face aglow with her romantic fantasy. She should never have been thinking that way about Jess. Never. It was exactly what she had promised herself not to do. Just the kind of fantasies she had to avoid. And to be caught at it. It served her right.

Clutching the dress in both hands, Maggie hurried over to the rack and shoved the dress haphazardly back into line. Then, with her head down, to avoid the eyes of any other shopper who might have noticed her antics, she headed for the front door of the shop. Just as she put her hand on the brass door handle, a hand clamped down on her upper arm.

"Where do you think you're going?" Maggie jerked sharply around to face the bespectacled glare of the white-haired shopkeeper.

For a moment she gazed at him, perplexed. He was staring at her hair with a grim expression on his face.

"Did you intend to pay for them?" the man asked, a hard edge to his voice.

A light of recognition came into Maggie's eyes. She reached up her free hand and felt the comb. "Oh, the combs." She winced in embarrassment. "I'm sorry," she blurted out.

She had not intended to buy the combs. They were too expensive for her fragile budget. But it seemed futile to try to explain that to the angry shopkeeper.

"I forgot I was wearing them. I'm really sorry. Of course I'll pay for them," Maggie conceded nervously.

The shopkeeper went around behind the counter to the cash register and Maggie reached for her purse. She avoided meeting the offended look in his eyes. Resigned to the fact that she would have to pay for her impulsiveness, she opened her bag and fumbled inside it. At least she would be able to wear the combs. At the moment, that thought was no comfort.

"That's nineteen ninety-five," the man said.

Maggie realized that it was almost half of the cash she had. The thought of asking Jess for an advance was humiliating. She thought of telling the shopkeeper that she simply could not afford it, but the look in his eyes was forbidding. Maggie groped in the bag for her wallet. Through her confusion, she realized that she could not put her hands on it. She pulled open the top of the bag and stared inside.

"My wallet is gone," she said quietly.

The shopkeeper shifted his weight and said nothing.

"Someone must have taken it," Maggie protested. "It's not here."

The man glared at her. "Then I suggest you remove those combs right now."

Maggie stared at him, and he returned her look without flinching. A muscle worked in his cheek, but he did not avert his gaze.

"Someone must have taken it," she repeated.

Then, her cheeks aflame, she reached up and loosened the combs from the tangle of her hair. She laid them on the counter, and turned to leave the store, not meeting Croddick's gaze. As she reached for the door handle she could feel his eyes on her, disbelieving, like a cold spot on her spine.

There she was.

Smiling at herself in a mirror. Picturing herself in that party dress she was holding. Probably thinking she was some kind of fairy princess.

The lips of the watcher curved into a hideous parody of a smile. The stony eyes flickered, as they observed Maggie before the looking glass. Unaware. It was fascinating.

But it would not do to stand there too long, on the sidewalk in front of the dress shop on a sunny, wind-blown street. Someone might stop. Say something. It was better to move on.

One last look. The gown that Maggie held was blue-grey and cut low. The watcher imagined the white shoulders, the white throat, splotched with bruises, purple and red, where the vessels burst. Ragged fingernails dug into the watcher's palms. The fingertips tingled.

Maggie was looking up.

Their eyes met.

Then Maggie began to fumble with the dress.

Quickly, silently, the watcher moved from the window, and started down the street.

4

"HAVE you got everything?" Grace asked, brushing by Maggie, who stood in the doorway of the *News* building, looking out towards the street.

Instinctively Maggie reached into her bag, although she had already checked twice for her wallet before she got up from her desk. The day before, when she returned from Croddick's still smarting from the humiliating incident in the dress shop, she had blurted out to the disinterested Grace that someone had taken her wallet, only to see her glance across the room at Maggie's desk.

"What's that over there?" Grace had drawled.

It was on the desk. She could hear Grace snort and mutter to herself before the typewriter's clacking resumed. Maggie had stared at the wallet for a long time before she picked it up and put it in her purse. They hadn't mentioned it for the rest of the day.

Maggie looked out at the street and sighed. She had only to get through this afternoon and the week would be over. She thought longingly of the house on Liberty Road, where she escaped from the strains of this new job. Two whole days

51

of peace and solitude. Maggie pushed the door open and stepped outside. The Island Luncheonette was out. It would mean passing by Croddick's and she wanted to avoid that today. Maggie decided to head down towards the dock. She remembered passing a sea-food place there the day she arrived. The wind snapped at her, and she put her head down against it as she started towards the water.

"Maggie."

She stopped and looked up. The shout fell short of her, like a rope thrown across a canyon. Figuring it was only the wind, she kept walking. Suddenly Maggie heard steps behind her and, as she turned, Jess jogged up beside her.

"I thought you heard me," he panted.

"I wasn't sure."

"Have you eaten?"

"No," she admitted.

"Me neither," he said. "Will you join me? If you're not doing something else, I mean."

Maggie studied his face for a moment. He was smiling at her, his eyes guileless and dark as forest pools. His angular face, although young, was already deeply lined. She repressed a sudden urge to reach up and trace the hard outline of his cheekbone into the shadowy hollow of his cheek. It's only lunch, she argued recklessly with the warning voice inside her.

"Okay," she agreed.

52

"You sure you're not from New England?" Jess asked in a wheedling tone.

Maggie shook her head and gripped her menu.

"You're so reserved," he said. "Real Yankee trait."

She allowed herself to smile. "Are you sure you *are*?" she chided him.

Jess nodded. "Born here, grew up, married . . ."

"Married?" Maggie exclaimed, immediately regretting her tone.

"Let me finish," he admonished. "Got divorced here. About five years ago. The only substantial amount of time I spent off this island was when I went to college. After graduation I worked in Boston for a few years, but I really missed this place. So, I came back."

Maggie hesitated, reluctant to verbalize the question that was on her mind. "Does your family still live here?" she compromised.

"No. Sorry to say. My parents moved down to Sanibel, an island off the Florida coast, when my dad retired. Winters just got to be too much for them. I had one brother, but he was killed in Viet Nam."

"I'm sorry," said Maggie, biting her lip.

Jess shrugged. "He's buried here on the island. Otherwise it's just me."

"And your wife?" she ventured.

Jess smiled at her. "My ex? No. Sharon

always blamed this place for all our problems. She was a summer person when I met her. Her folks have a house out here and used to come in July. Their place is not far from Thornhill's, as a matter of fact. Anyway, after we got married I wanted to live here year round, but she began to hate it. Said it was too bleak and lonely. She was depressed eight months of the year."

"But you wouldn't leave?" Maggie asked, an accusatory note in her voice.

Jess paled slightly and licked his lips. At once Maggie realized that he had been trying to dismiss a painful subject as lightly as possible. She felt a stab of remorse as she watched the distress surface in his eyes.

"It's true that I wanted to stay," he admitted. "I love this island. It's my home. But I don't think it was entirely my fault."

"You don't have to explain," she interrupted him.

"We had our problems," he concluded lamely, "like most couples."

"I didn't mean to pry," she said. "It was none of my business." She began studying the menu. She could feel his eyes on her as she pretended to debate her selection.

"It's all right," he said, smiling at her. "I don't mind."

Alarmed by the warmth in his voice, Maggie avoided his eyes. "How's the food here?" she asked.

"Try the lobster salad," he said. An awkward silence fell between them. "How about you?" he asked finally. "Have you ever been married?"

Maggie lowered the menu and faced him. "No," she replied.

"Never?" He seemed surprised.

Feeling uncomfortably as if she owed him a confidence, Maggie groped for a simple explanation. "There was one man," she admitted cautiously. "I loved him, but it didn't work out."

"Why not?" Jess persisted.

"It just didn't," Maggie said firmly.

"Do you ever see him?" Jess enquired.

Maggie stared at him. "No. Never," she said. "He's dead."

Shaken by her blunt response, Jess hurried to apologize. "I'm really a clod sometimes. It's just that I wanted to know more about you. I didn't mean to tread on sensitive ground . . ."

"It doesn't matter," said Maggie, returning to her menu. "I'm over it."

The words on the menu wavered, and started to dissolve before her eyes. She could feel Jess's worried eyes on her, but for a moment she had the uncanny sensation that if she looked up she would see Roger sitting across from her. She pictured him vividly in her mind's eye, with his gentle eyes which always looked sad, despite the laugh lines around them.

"I could sit here and look at you forever, Maggie." She could still hear his voice.

"I wish you would," she said earnestly.

Roger smiled. "It's so simple for you, isn't it?"

Maggie shrugged. "I love you. That's simple."

Roger sighed and turned his head to stare out the window.

"What's wrong?" she asked, squeezing his hand which held hers below the tabletop.

He turned his troubled gaze on her. "This is all so unfair for you. You deserve a young man. A fellow who could take you out openly. Spend all your evenings, every free moment together."

"I don't want any other man," she protested stubbornly.

"But you can't be happy this way," he insisted.

"I'm happy with you," she said, her eyes lowered. "I don't mind the rest." The last was a lie, but she did not want to complain to him. The prospect of losing him was worse than any loneliness or shame she might endure as a result of their affair.

"We've got to get back to the office," he said quietly, putting his napkin beside his plate.

She looked up at him and smiled bravely. But she could see that he was not fooled by her protests. He knew that it was not all right, but he was helpless to change it.

"Do you know what you want?" Jess asked kindly.

Maggie started, and looked at him blankly for a moment. Then smiled. "I'll try that lobster salad," she said, hoping it would please him.

Jess leaned back in his chair and signalled the waitress. As he turned, Maggie noted, with an unfamiliar longing, the line of his jaw, the breadth of his chest. It had been years since a man held her. The last time was the night of Roger's death. Jess turned back to her and was adjusting the flower vase on the table so that he would have a clearer view of her.

"Cheer up," he said pleasantly. "If you don't like the lobster you can send it back, and get something else."

Maggie regarded his open countenance pensively. A weight descended on her heart. Change the subject, she thought.

"I've been thinking about getting a puppy," she said.

"For lunch?" Jess feigned indignation.

Maggie laughed. "I thought you could tell me where to look for one. I'm kind of rattling around in that house."

"Not off-hand," he said. "But I'll nose around for you."

"I'd appreciate it," Maggie said. Determinedly, she smiled at him. "Now, tell me about growing up here."

57

Maggie waited on the steps outside while Jess paid the bill. It went pretty well, she thought, with some satisfaction. The conversation, after the initial awkwardness, had been surprisingly easy.

"Seems to have warmed up a bit," Jess observed, joining her on the steps. The door banged behind him.

"It's much nicer now," Maggie agreed.

"I really rattled on, didn't I," he said, shaking his head. "Motor mouth."

Maggie laughed. "I enjoyed it," she insisted.

"I'm usually the tall, dark, handsome, strong and silent type," he protested. "Not a magpie."

"You were just answering the questions."

"Okay, this time, lady," he said. "But you're going to get your turn."

Maggie frowned, and turned away from him. She had not considered another time. Or the prospect of her turn. She started down the steps. "We'd better be getting back, I guess."

"Hey, what's the rush?" he asked, catching up to her. "You're with the boss."

"I know," she said. "I've just got a lot to do this afternoon."

"You're trying to make me look bad?" he teased.

"No, of course not."

"I'm kidding," he said.

They fell silent as they walked along, Maggie setting a brisk pace. The confidence she had felt

58

in the restaurant ebbed away. She wanted to sneak a glance at his face, to see if he was bored, or annoyed with her. Instead, she kept her eyes trained on the cobbled street in front of her. I've forgotten how to act around a man. All those years of sly women. I must seem ridiculous to him.

As they turned the corner on to Main Street he broke the silence. "You know, I like being with you," he said thoughtfully. "It's been a long time."

It felt like being jabbed with a pin. She looked up at him, her eyes wide with surprise. Just then the heel of her shoe caught in the space between two cobblestones, and she stumbled.

Jess grabbed her before she could fall, and pulled her arm securely through his. "You all right?" he asked. "Did you hurt yourself?"

Maggie flushed with relief and embarrassment.

"Just my pride," she admitted.

Jess started to laugh. After a moment, Maggie began to giggle. They stood in the street, her arm locked in his, laughing. Maggie's eyes softened as she looked at him.

"Let's go," he said at last.

They turned together, and started to walk. All at once, Maggie stopped short. Standing on the opposite side of the street, her face white, her eyes wide, was Evy. The girl stared at Jess and Maggie, her eyes fixed on the spot where Jess held Maggie's arm. Her thin body trembled in the fawn-coloured jacket that she wore, and her spiky hair was wild, dishevelled by the wind.

"Hey, there's Evy," Jess spotted the girl and began to wave vigorously at her. "Come on," he said, starting to drag Maggie across the street. "We can all walk back together."

Maggie disengaged her arm from his. "No," she said uneasily. "You go ahead."

Jess looked at her, perplexed. "Is anything wrong?"

"No," she insisted. "I just forgot. I have to stop in at the drugstore." She made a vague gesture behind her.

Jess shrugged. "Okay. See you there."

Maggie watched as he crossed the road to Evy. The girl greeted him coolly. The two exchanged a few words, and then Maggie saw Evy smile shyly at him. The two turned and started towards the office. Evy had her face up towards Jess. His large body seemed to shield her from the ocean breeze. Next to Jess, Evy looked fragile, and very young.

With a start, Maggie realized that she had been about Evy's age when she had fallen in love with Roger. For a moment she recalled the pleasure of the first time he had lifted her from her desk chair and drawn her to him. After months of imagining just such a moment. She had been so blissfully happy, and ignored all the guilty feelings that the stolen kiss aroused. If only she had known how it would all end.

Maggie shook herself out of the memory and watched Jess and Evy disappearing up the street. She wondered if there was anything between them. The girl was clearly infatuated with Jess. Perhaps something had happened at one time. A flirtation, or an affair. It might still be going on. The thought caused a stab of jealousy which Maggie had not expected. Disturbed, Maggie started for the drugstore.

Whatever it is, or was, she thought, you don't want to be in the middle of it. It was obvious that Evy wanted him and cared for him. It was just another good reason to stay away from Jess.

It was twenty minutes before Maggie was able to get back to the office. An old woman in a tattered sealskin coat was discussing the merits of various indigestion remedies with the chemist and would not be hurried. Maggie considered leaving the few items she had found to buy behind, but then she remembered that it was Friday, and she didn't want to come to town over the weekend if she could help it.

She glanced at her watch apprehensively as she hurried up the path to the *Cove News* building. As quietly as possible she opened the front door and went in, pulling the door gently shut behind her. She was relieved to see that there was no one in the hall. Maggie slipped off her jacket and hung it on one of the hooks of the coat rack. As she approached the office door she heard voices drifting out. She composed her face, preparing

61

to walk in and interrupt the conversation. Suddenly the sound of her own name jumped out at her from the rise and fall of the voices. She stepped back against the wall.

"I don't know where she is," said Grace querulously. "She should have been back half an hour ago."

"Finish the story, Tom." Maggie recognized Evy's flat tones.

The man cleared his throat and spoke in a voice that sounded vaguely familiar to Maggie. "So," he said indignantly. "I look up and there she is, walking out the door wearing two of my silver combs in her hair just as brazen as you please."

"Get out," Grace breathed.

"That's so," he affirmed. "And I chase after her. And when I ask her if she means to pay for it, she gives me this song and dance that she doesn't have her wallet."

"She left it here," Evy volunteered.

The sound of their incredulous laughter floated out into the corridor.

"I'll tell you something," the man went on soberly. "I was thinking about telling Jack Schmale about this."

"Why?" Evy asked. "She gave them back, didn't she?"

"That's not the point, young lady," Tom barked. "Is it, Grace? The point is that she's new

62

around here and right off the bat she's lifting something out of my store."

"Jack's off island until Monday," Grace volunteered. "Meeting of the state police chiefs."

"I don't see what the big deal is," said Evy. "If she gave them back and she offered to pay for them, I don't see why you'd want to go ratting on her. Anybody can make a mistake . . ."

"Hey," Grace bridled, "whose side are you on, anyway?"

"Nobody's side," Evy insisted. "I'm just saying . . ."

"Well now, Grace, maybe the girl has a point. Maybe I shouldn't be bothering Jack with this. But you can bet I'll keep an eye on her. After all, you can't be too careful with new people . . ."

Grace and Evy shifted abruptly in their chairs and Grace cleared her throat. Aware that he had lost his audience, Tom Croddick looked behind him. Maggie stood in the doorway, her eyes carefully devoid of expression.

"Oh," he squeaked. "Hello."

Maggie ignored him and walked over to her desk. She picked up a manuscript and focused her eyes on it.

Tom raised his eyebrows over the black frames of his glasses and rolled his eyes meaningfully at the other two. "Well," he said heartily to Grace and Evy. "I guess you girls are busy. I'd better be getting back too."

Grace nodded. "See ya, Tom."

The shopkeeper started for the door. "Bye, girls."

As he passed through the doorway he nearly collided with a large man with a grey beard who was barrelling through, a camera swinging from a strap around his neck.

"Hey, Tom."

"Owen," Tom said. "How are you?"

"Good, good." The big man pumped the hand of the departing storekeeper and then turned to the others. "Hello, Grace, Evy." He looked over at Maggie, and then looked again, a puzzled expression on his face.

Grace spoke up. "She's new. Emmett hired her."

"I'm Owen Duggan," he said to Maggie. "Wildlife photographer extraordinaire and sometimes free-lance paparazzo for the *Cove News*."

Maggie took his extended hand. "How do you do," she said softly. "I'm Maggie Fraser."

"Nice to meet you, Maggie. Although you're looking a little pale there. You should get out more. Breathe the salt air." He thumped on his barrel chest with a flat palm. Maggie forced a smile.

He looked at her sharply for a second. From the first moment he saw her he was struck by the thought that there was something oddly familiar about her. He felt certain that he had seen her face before. He was just about to say so, and

64

then he dismissed it, with a shrug. Owen seated himself on the edge of Grace's desk and leaned towards the older woman with a wicked smile. "Charley keeping you happy, Grace?"

"He sure is," Grace trilled, with a flirtatious toss of her head. "How are things with you?"

"Just fine," Owen announced, clapping his hands and rubbing them together. "I'm going to be making another trip to New York in a few weeks. An editor over at *Life* magazine may run a whole feature on the series of wild birds that I did. So, I'm here to pick up the negatives. Did Jess use any of them?"

"He used one," Grace said, "but we've got the whole lot back now. Maggie," Grace called out imperiously, "get Owen's negatives for him. I think they're over on the file cabinet."

"I was up to the firehouse just now," Owen said conversationally to Grace. "They just delivered the new ambulance."

"Oh, yes," said Grace. "Charley was mentioning something about that to me last night."

Maggie was only dimly aware of their conversation as she moved towards the file cabinet. She tried to concentrate on the simple errand which she had to accomplish, but her mind was still reeling from what she had heard from the hallway. She should have known that it would get back. On an island like this, gossip would travel in no time. She was grateful that Jess hadn't been in the room to hear it. Sooner or later, he probably would.

At least Evy had defended her. She tried to hold on to that fact, knowing it should make her feel better. But it was not enough. She was trying so hard to be inconspicuous, but it seemed as if everything she did left the wrong impression.

Right at her eye level, atop the cabinet, she saw the black strips of film, poking out of a tissue paper sleeve. Grateful that she would not have to hunt for them, Maggie grabbed the handful of negatives.

It was not until she was in the act of jerking them off the cabinet that Maggie saw the coffee mug. It was resting atop the cabinet, steam issuing over the rim, and its lower edge overlapping the negatives. Even as Maggie yanked at the film strips, she helplessly watched the cup spin, spill, and begin to roll. The burning hot liquid splashed over her hand and she heard the crash of the cup on the floor.

"Ahhh." Maggie cried out and clutched her throbbing hand. The negatives fell to the floor and began to curl from the heat of the coffee.

"Shit," Owen yelled. "My film."

Owen scrambled for the negatives while Maggie squeezed and shook her aching hand.

"What'd you do?" Grace asked angrily, coming over to them. Evy stood behind her, peering down. Grace reached for Maggie's hand.

66

"Don't touch me," Maggie hissed at her, drawing back.

"Don't worry," said Grace. "I don't intend to." She began to mutter as she bent down to gather up the chips of the mug beside Owen, who was moaning and squinting up at the transparent strips in the light.

Maggie clenched her teeth and tried to will the pain away. She looked up and saw Evy watching her, the faintest suggestion of a smile on her face.

Maggie stared at her. "What's so funny?" she asked angrily, shaking her injured hand.

"Nothing," said Evy in an injured tone. "You should put some cold water on that."

Maggie turned her back on the girl.

"Come on," said Evy. "Let me help you." She took a hold of Maggie's arm, and steered her over to the sink.

5

YOU'RE taking a chance, Jess thought to himself as he eased the car into a parking space on Main Street. Maybe she'd rather not spend her Saturday with you. He switched off the engine and sat behind the wheel, staring at the dashboard for a while. He knew he should probably call her first, but he figured it would be harder for her to refuse him face to face. It had been a long time, he reflected, since he had felt so inept. For a moment he wondered if it wouldn't be better to just spend the day alone, as usual. Then, purposefully, he clambered out of the car and slammed the door.

As he walked up Main Street, glancing in windows, he tried to think about Sharon, and what she had liked. All he was able to remember was the scrimshaw necklace he had brought home to her one day after she had been feeling low for weeks. She had lifted the lid of the box and stared at the pendant with a dull look in her eyes. The carving on it was of a ship, fully rigged, and Jess had thought it quite handsome. He waited for her to smile. Instead, she had picked up the necklace, and rolled it around in her fingers. Then she had turned abruptly, and hurled it across the room. It smashed against one of the kitchen cabinets and dropped into the salad bowl. Without another word she had turned and walked away from him.

Jess sighed and peered intently, unseeing, into the window nearest him, until the prickling behind his eyes subsided. Then he continued up the street.

Physically, he thought, the two women were not at all alike. Sharon had been blonde, and diminutive, her skin brown in the summer, when he first knew her. In the winter her colour had faded into a sallow, yellowed hue. Maggie's white skin reminded him of a polished stone, and he liked her red hair. Maybe he would get her a scarf, to drape loosely around her white throat. He remembered Sharon, seated at her mirror, saying she was glad she was not a redhead. There were so few colours they could wear. Jess frowned, and wondered if it were true. It seemed to him that Maggie would look good in any shade he could think of. Still, perhaps he should avoid colours.

He thought of flowers, realizing that it would mean driving out to the nursery on Eagle Rock Road. But flowers died so quickly and had to be thrown away. He wanted to give her something she would keep. Something that would make her think of him each time she used it. For a moment Jess stood on the kerb, tapping his foot impatiently. "Perfume, maybe," he said aloud.

He looked up and down the street, and then crossed over, in a loping gait, to the drugstore.

Jess turned up the Thornhill driveway, and pulled up beside the old black Buick. He chuckled, remembering Maggie's description of it over lunch. "One automobile wreck included, no extra charge."

The house seemed unusually quiet, and he wondered if Maggie could possibly still be asleep. He looked at his watch. It was almost noon. Nobody slept that late, he reasoned, and he got out of his car and ran up the porch steps. He opened the screen door, and pounded on the wooden door frame.

There was no answer. Jess knocked again, and then called out, but no one came to the door. Leaning over the porch railing he craned his neck to see into the kitchen window. Everything was neatly in place, but there was no sign of Maggie.

I should have called first, he thought in annoyance. He turned and descended the steps. Just then he saw her, standing with her back to him, pulling shut the side door to the garage. She was wearing a bandanna on her head, and her hands and forearms were smudged with black grease.

Jess grinned, and called out to her. "Hello there."

Maggie jumped and turned, staring at him in surprise.

70

"Hi," he said. "Didn't you hear me drive up?"

Maggie shook her head.

"Looking over your estate?" he asked with a nervous laugh, starting towards her.

She met him halfway between the house and the garage. "I just wanted to see what was in there," she explained.

"Find anything interesting?"

Maggie glanced down at her greasy hands and then looked up at him, her face flushed. "Well, there's a bike. It needs fixing though. How long have you been here?"

"Just a few minutes. When you didn't answer the door I was afraid I'd missed you."

"Do you want to come in?" she said, avoiding his eyes.

"You're not angry that I came, are you?" he asked uncertainly.

Maggie met his apprehensive eyes. She could not tell him that she had found herself thinking about him all morning. But now that he was here, she felt troubled. She had vowed to herself that she would try to steer clear of him. She could see that her silence was making him uncomfortable. "I'm glad you're here," she told him, pushing back a strand of hair which had flopped on her forehead with the side of her hand. "It's just that I'm a mess."

"You look great," he said eagerly.

She tried to smile, but it resembled a grimace.

71

"Come on in," she said. She turned away and started up the steps towards the house. Jess followed her through the back door. "This is a great house," he said, looking around the living-room.

"It is," Maggie agreed. "Make yourself comfortable. I have to clean up." Jess sat down. He heard the water running in the kitchen. Suddenly he remembered the package in his coat pocket. Maggie entered the living-room wiping her hands on a tea towel. She had taken off the bandanna and her hair tumbled free around her face. Jess fished out the package and offered it to her.

"I brought you something."

Maggie looked down at it, and then looked up at him questioningly.

"Open it," he urged.

He noticed that her fingers trembled as she unwrapped the paper, and that the sun streaming through the windows glinted gold through the coppery hair which fell around her face. She held up the small, pear-shaped bottle, tied with a gold string.

"Perfume," he said. For one moment he remembered Sharon, silently fingering the necklace.

Maggie chewed on her lower lip. Maggie looked up and smiled at him, her eyes guarded but pleased. "Thank you," she said. "That was so nice of you."

Relieved, Jess shrugged it off. "I thought you might like to take a look at some puppies. Some people I know have a new litter of mutts."

Maggie hesitated. "I don't know."

"Oh, come on," he said. "At least take a look. You don't have to get one right away if you don't want it."

"Well," she said softly, "I do want a puppy."

"Get yourself a jacket," he ordered. "It's windy today. I'll wait in the car."

Maggie stood at the door and watched him thoughtfully as he walked to the car. His step was springy and boyish, and the aimless tune he hummed drifted back to her on the breeze. She looked down at the bottle he had given her. It glistened in her palm, like an enormous teardrop, trembling there. When she looked up again, he was already at the car, leaning on the open door. He waved to her to hurry up. A cloud passed over the sun, casting a shadow on his gentle face, and causing her to shiver.

She walked over to the mantel of the fireplace, and placed the bottle of perfume there, admiring its amber glow in the streaks of sunlight. She removed the top and smelled it. The scent was delicious. Then she replaced the stopper and arranged the bottle between two candlesticks. It's almost too pretty to use, she thought. With a happy sigh she headed for her bedroom and her dresser, in search of a sweater.

Five fuzzy white and nut-brown rumps protruded from the side of the sad-eyed mother. The dog and her pups lay in a large, low-sided cardboard box, atop a dirty, faded quilt. The squealing and sucking of the newborns did not seem to worry the bitch, who stared at her visitors with languid eyes.

"How old are they, Ned?" Jess asked the farmer, who was leaning against the door jamb of the musty shed where the puppies were kept.

The dark-haired man rubbed his stubbled jaw and squinted at the beams of the small, peaked roof. "Nearly six weeks now, I guess."

"What do you think, Maggie?" Jess asked.

Maggie watched in rapt attention as, one by one, the pups disengaged themselves from their mother's teats and began to stagger around the quilt-lined box. The two largest ones curled up on top of one another in a heap in the corner and began to snooze. One of the others remained, suckling at the mother, and a fourth sniffed blindly around the side of the box. The smallest wandered gamely towards the opening of the box, leaned over, and tumbled off the quilt on to the warped, straw-covered floorboards of the shed.

Ned Wilson reached down and scooped up the

tiny adventurer, and replaced him by his mother's side. "There you go," he said.

"I love them," said Maggie. "Especially that little one."

"That's the runt," Ned informed her.

"That's the one I want," she said.

"Ned," said Jess. "Seems my friend here wants a dog. What's the going price on one of these pups?"

"Well," said the farmer, "that I don't know about. I'm gonna have to talk to Sadie about that. Livvy here is her dog, really."

"Livvy?" Maggie asked.

"Yup," said Ned. "Named after Olivia de Havilland in *Gone with the Wind*. Sadie's upstairs vacuuming. Let me just run up and get her," said Ned. "I'll be right back."

As the farmer departed, Jess and Maggie crouched down to have a closer look at the pups. "Sadie'll probably just give him to you," Jess said, running a forefinger over the puppy's delicate skull. "Nobody ever buys these mutts. Especially not the runt."

"Hey," Maggie protested. "He's the cutest one of them all. Besides, he's going to be my watchdog one of these days. Aren't you," she murmured to the little animal.

"Kind of a puny watchdog," Jess observed.

"He'll grow," she said. Then she looked up at Jess and smiled. "They're perfect," she said. "Thanks for bringing me here."

75

"I figured you'd like them," he said. "Besides, I was glad of an excuse to come and see you."

Maggie shook her head. "Don't say that." She scrambled to her feet.

Jess straightened up beside her. "Why not?" he asked. "It's true." A darkening in the doorway interrupted him.

Ned cleared his throat. "Excuse me folks. I brought Sadie." A thin woman who only came up to Ned's shoulder stood in front of him in the doorway. She wore sneakers, baggy grey pants and a cherry-coloured cardigan. Her greying hair was pinned in a shapeless topknot. The woman peered suspiciously into the unlit shed.

"Sadie," Ned went on. "You know Jess. And this here's his friend, Maggie. They come up to see the pups."

Maggie anxiously extended her hand to the older woman. Sadie gave her a perfunctory grip with her thin, muscled hand, and then wiped her hand on her trousers.

"The puppies are beautiful," Maggie said. "I'd like to buy that little one from you."

"I'm not selling 'em," said Sadie.

"I don't understand," Maggie stammered. "I thought . . ."

"I'm glad to get rid of 'em," said Sadie. "You can just take it."

With a beaming smile, Maggie bent down towards the pups.

"Not yet," Sadie yelped. "Didn't Ned tell you they're too young to leave their mother?"

"Aw, Sadie," Ned protested. "It's just a matter of a couple of days."

"I said 'not yet'," the old woman insisted. "When they're ready."

"I can wait a few days," Maggie soothed her. "I've waited this long. I'll come back whenever you say."

Sadie sniffed, but seemed satisfied with this compromise. "You got to take care of it," she warned.

"I will," Maggie promised.

"Did you ever have a dog before?" Sadie asked.

"No, I haven't," Maggie admitted.

"Why not?" the old woman demanded.

Maggie looked at her guiltily. "Well, I . . ."

"Maggie never had the space before," Jess interceded. "She used to live in an apartment."

Surprised by his response, Maggie suddenly remembered that that was the lie she had told him. Sadie chewed over the piece of information suspiciously.

"Well, I guess we better be going," said Maggie. "Let you get back to your cleaning." She edged past the couple in the doorway and down the path. "Thank you so much."

"That dirt's not going away on its own. That's for sure," Sadie complained.

Jess caught up to Maggie in the Wilson

driveway. "Hey, you were in an awful hurry to get out of there."

"I didn't want to give Sadie a chance to change her mind," she said.

"She's a slippery customer, all right," Jess laughed.

"I got a puppy," Maggie exulted.

"Keep it down," Jess warned her. "You're not safe until we're out of the driveway."

"Weren't they adorable?" Maggie cried.

"They were. Yours especially."

Maggie threw her arms around his neck and squeezed him. "Thank you, thank you."

Jess wrapped his arms around her and pulled her close to him. "I'm glad you're happy," he whispered.

Maggie pulled back, embarrassed by the impulsive embrace. Jess held on to her. His lips followed and met hers. His kiss was short, but insistent. When he drew back her lips felt as if they had been stung. They wanted to be stung again. Instead, she pushed his shoulders away lightly with her palms. "We'd better go," she said softly.

"That kiss will be all over the island," he agreed wryly, glancing back at the Wilson farmhouse.

Jess charted a meandering route back to Maggie's, which included a stop for clam rolls down by the Clearview landing, and a tour of some of the narrow, dirt roads which wound surreptitiously through the island forests. The sun was already sinking into the ocean as they wended their way back towards Liberty Road.

The salt breeze ran through Maggie's hair like fingers and the rays of the sun, although weak, warmed her elbow as the car sped along. She turned her face from the window and studied Jess. He smiled at her.

"Glad you came?" he asked.

"Very."

"I was thinking about you last night."

"You were?"

"Well, I was thinking about asking you to come look at the puppies today, go for a ride, and I was worried that you'd had enough of the office for one week, and maybe that included me."

"No," she admitted. "Not you."

"Owen Duggan called me this morning, by the way. He printed up those negatives last night, and he only lost about three shots. He asked me to tell you not to be concerned about it."

"That was thoughtful of him," said Maggie, recalling for an instant the quizzical look on his face as he had shaken her hand, as if he were trying to place her. She tried to shake off the disturbing impression.

"The first week is always a little rough, Maggie."

"I know," she said, after a pause.

"How's the hand?"

Maggie flexed her fingers gingerly. "Better. It's okay."

"I still don't know how that happened," he said.

"I just wasn't paying attention to what I was doing." For a moment she remembered Tom and Grace's scornful laughter as she stood in the corridor, and Evy's fleeting look of amusement. Nothing was going as it should, she thought. She could picture Owen Duggan's negatives curling under the heat of the coffee. A defeated sigh escaped her.

"There's Evy's house, on the left," said Jess, gesticulating out the window. Maggie turned and saw the flash of grey, and a sign reading Barrington Street, as they slowed at the corner. "What's the sigh for?" he asked.

"Nothing," said Maggie firmly. "That's where Evy lives?"

"Are you sure?" Jess asked, frowning at her.

"Positive. What do her parents do?"

"Oh, it's just Evy and her grandmother. Her grandmother's an invalid. She's totally incapacitated. It's a sad thing. Evy takes good care of her though. It's hard on her."

Maggie recalled the look of dismay on Evy's face when she saw Maggie and Jess walking back arm in arm from lunch. She looked over at Jess's angular, sensitive face, and wondered what role that handsome face might play in the lonely life of a girl stuck taking care of her grandmother. Once again she was overcome by the sense that she should not intrude in their lives. She had been there. She knew what it felt like. For a moment Roger was vivid to her again. Her fantasy come true, and the beginning of her long nightmare.

"I'd better be getting back," reality struck her like a slap.

"We're almost there," he said ruefully. He glanced over at her. "Are you in a hurry?"

"Well, it's my first weekend, you know. I have a lot of things I want to do around the house."

"Okay," he interrupted her. "I understand."

They drove in silence for the next five minutes, until they reached the Thornhill house. They pulled in the driveway and Jess shut off the engine.

"I'd ask you in," Maggie said hurriedly, "but I didn't have a chance to go shopping and I don't really have anything . . ."

"Never mind," said Jess. "You do what you have to do."

Maggie put her fingers on the door handle, and bit her lip. Then she turned back to him. "I had a lovely time," she said. "Thank you again."

Jess leaned over and cupped his hand lightly under her face. He drew her to him and gave her a gentle kiss which she felt singing all through her body in spite of herself. "So did I," he said, letting her go.

Maggie opened the door and got out, without looking back at him. When she reached the steps she turned back to see the car backing down the driveway. She waved briefly, and then rushed through the door and into the house.

She could hear the faint sound of the motor as the car departed. For a few moments she stood there, her back to the door, her eyes closed. She ran the day through her mind again, like a home movie, his face and his eyes disturbing and exciting her. Then she shook her head. Wondering how she would ever get out of this. Wondering if she wanted to get out of it.

She flopped down in a living-room chair. All right, all right, she thought. You do like him. You are attracted to him. That doesn't mean you have to get involved with him. She winced, remembering her lie which he had repeated so ingenuously to Sadie about the apartment. He was such an honest man. How could she ever tell him the truth? If she did, he probably wouldn't even want her.

But her mind kept running back over the things he'd said, the way he'd looked at her. He had even brought her a present. She could not help but smile when she thought of how shy he had seemed in offering it to her. She glanced up at the mantelpiece to admire his gift.

Then she looked again. The bottle was gone.

Maggie leaped from her chair and approached the mantelpiece. She ran her hands over its smooth surface, even though she could see clearly that the amber vial was not there. "I put it here," she said aloud. Then she wheeled around, and her eyes searched the room, as if she expected to see someone behind her.

The room was in perfect order, just as she left it. She turned back to the mantel and stared at her fingers, curved tensely around its edge. Someone had been in the house. That was the only possible explanation. Thieves, she wondered? She scanned the room sharply. All of the Thornhills' ornaments were in their place. She walked over and lifted up a sterling silver candy dish on the bookcase. There was a faint ring of dust around its base. It had not even been touched.

It didn't make sense. Why would someone take a bottle of perfume and leave a sterling silver plate? Maggie hurried to her bedroom. As she came through the door, she half expected to see all her belongings strewn on the floor. She steeled herself.

The room was neat, and undisturbed. She rushed to her closet and threw open the door, her heart pounding in her ears. Everything was there, all in order. No one would come into a house and take just a bottle of perfume. As she turned away from the closet, and switched on the bedroom lamp, an unfamiliar shape seemed to wink at her in the mirror across the room.

Her eyes darted to the dresser top. There sat the bottle of perfume.

Maggie stared at it a minute. Then she walked over and picked it up. Now, how did this get in here, she thought. She retraced her steps of the morning. She had put the perfume on the mantel, and then . . . "And then I came in here and got a sweater," she said aloud. Relief made her laugh aloud.

It must be prison. Still, it made her realize how jumpy her nerves were. She looked down at the bottle, safely in her hand. Either that or you're lovesick.

Then she banished the thought.

6

MAGGIE glanced up as Evy entered the office and sat down at the desk across from hers. All day she had barely seen the girl, who had been delegated by Jess to a job on the art room. Evy inserted a piece of paper into her typewriter and studied the roller as she turned it. She looked up abruptly to find Maggie watching her.

Maggie quickly lowered her head and began shuffling through the papers on her desk. Then she opened her desk drawer, pulled out a pencil and closed it again.

"How was your weekend?"

The question took Maggie by surprise. She met Evy's gaze diffidently. "Fine, thank you," she replied.

The girl nodded, and seemed to cast about for a way to begin a conversation. "Did you do anything special?" she asked.

Maggie contemplated the girl for a moment without replying. Taking the initiative in a conversation seemed to be beyond Evy's usual scope. It occurred to Maggie as she looked at her that Evy must have been a scrawny, unattractive child. The kind of child that people forget to

85

fondle. The thought made her feel a wave of protective feelings for the girl.

"I went up to see some puppies," she offered. "I think I found one."

"That's nice," said Evy. "What kind?"

"Just a mutt. Mostly beagle."

"Where'd you get it?" the girl asked.

"Well, I don't have it yet. It can't leave its mother for a few days."

"Oh, I know them," said Evy. She was silent for a moment. Then she asked, "How did you know they had puppies there?"

Maggie squirmed slightly.

"I was just driving by," she said. "I saw a sign, so I stopped in." She began an exaggerated motion of making an erasure on the paper in front of her.

"Well, that was lucky," said Evy. She hesitated. Then she asked casually. "Did you go by yourself?"

Maggie stopped short, and then slowly continued her erasing with hard, deliberate strokes. She heard the anxious catch in the girl's voice. Jess. That was what this sudden interest in her weekend activities was all about. Maggie sighed. "Yes," she lied. "I was just out exploring."

"That's nice," said Evy enthusiastically. "You should have called me. I would have come with you."

Maggie called her a grateful smile. The

friendly overture made the lie seem worthwhile. "Thanks," she said. "Next time I will."

Just then, they heard the outer door slam. In a moment Grace trudged into the office and dumped several packages down on her desk by the door. "How's everything?" Grace addressed herself to Evy.

"Okay," said Evy, and returned to her type-writer.

"Grace, have you got that . . ." Jess rushed in and met Grace's irritated glance. "Sorry, take your coat off. I'm looking for the column on fishhook injuries."

"I don't know where it is," said Grace. "She had it."

"It's right here," said Maggie, ignoring Grace.

"Thanks," said Jess absently, and began running his forefinger down the page.

"Honestly, I'm so disgusted," Grace announced. "Friday is my mother-in-law's birthday, and I went up to Croddick's to get her a sweater she wanted, and it was gone. Now I don't know what to get."

Jess looked up from his reading. "Try the drugstore. He's got lots of nice perfumes and soaps and things."

"Since when are you the expert on ladies' toiletries?" Grace asked him, bemused.

Jess shrugged, but his eyes held a guilty, laughing look, and he shot a brief glance at Maggie. "I get around, you know," he said.

Maggie could feel Evy's eyes on her, but she did not look up.

"Well, why don't you get her a book," Jess suggested.

Grace stared at him. "What?"

"Your mother-in-law. Get her a book on gardening."

"A book!" said Grace incredulously. "She's half blind." She shook her head. "I don't know. I'll think of something," she muttered as she unbuttoned her black coat and shrugged it off. Then she draped it over her arm and headed for the coat rack in the hall.

Jess smiled at Maggie conspiratorially. Evy began to type. "Just trying to be helpful," he said.

Maggie forced a smile.

"You okay?" he asked.

Maggie nodded. Jess came over to her desk and sat down beside it. "What'd you do yesterday?" he asked.

"Nothing much," she said. "Things around the house. Cleaning. I did some reading."

Jess toyed with the letter opener near the edge of her desk. He picked it up, ran it down his palm, and then replaced it. "I had a nice time with you on Saturday," he said. "I guess you'll be glad to get that puppy home."

Maggie shifted uneasily in her chair. From Evy's direction the typing faltered, then stopped.

"Yeah," she replied softly.

"I'm glad I could show you a little bit of the island. There are a lot of other beautiful spots I'd like you to see."

"I'm sure there are," said Maggie grimly.

"Listen," said Jess, "I know it's short notice, but I was wondering if you'd have dinner with me tonight."

"Tonight," she repeated, staring at him. "I can't." She could feel her face burning and was acutely conscious of the silence from Evy's direction. She was conscious that she was trying to say as little as possible, although she realized that Evy had already heard more than enough.

"Well," he said, "that's too bad." He got up from the chair as Grace reappeared in the doorway.

"Thank you anyway," she whispered. Surreptitiously, Maggie glanced over at Evy. The girl sat facing her typewriter, her hands clenched in her lap. Maggie could see the muscles in her dead white face working as she stared straight in front of her.

"Evy," Grace broke in. "Are you done with those paste-ups?"

"They're on your desk," Evy snapped.

"Pardon me," Grace sniffed, and then flipped through the sheaf of dummy sheets. "Well, these are all right," she pronounced. "Now why don't you work on those new subscriptions for the rest of the day."

Evy pushed back her chair and stood up. "No, I can't. I'm going home."

"Home?" Grace yelped. "It's only four o'clock."

"Well, I feel sick, and I'm leaving," Evy muttered, shoving the chair into the desk.

The older woman was immediately concerned. "What is it, honey?" she said, coming over and placing a hand on Evy's forehead. "Do you have a fever?"

Evy shook off her hand and stared at Maggie. "I feel like throwing up," she said.

"Uh, oh," Grace clucked. "Well, all right. You get on home."

Evy picked up her purse and started for the door.

Maggie spoke up in a strained voice. "Do you need a ride?" she asked.

"No," the girl retorted.

Grace wrapped an arm around Evy's stiff shoulders, and accompanied her out of the office, murmuring words of advice.

At five-fifteen, after an afternoon of silence save for a few razor-sharp exchanges between them, Maggie watched Grace retrieve her black coat, put it on and gather up her packages. With a brusque "Good night", she left, slamming the front door behind her.

Maggie sat back in her chair, and stared over at Evy's empty desk. In the silent room Maggie

90

had the eerie sense that the battered old antique accused her for the absence of its occupant. Slowly, she rose to her feet and crossed over to it. Everything on the chipped and gouged-out desk top was neatly in place. There were piles of papers, and a group of pencils, all sharpened and carefully aligned on the sides of the blotter. A box of rubber bands, paper clips and a stack of typing paper sat on the right. Nothing on the desk betrayed anything of the girl who sat there, except for a round, crystal paperweight with a blue, black and golden-winged butterfly inside of it which rested on a stack of papers. Maggie ran her fingers over the object, and then picked it up to examine it. She frowned as she inspected the fragile creature, trapped in its crystal orb. It was beautiful, suspended there. Beautiful and lifeless. Maggie replaced it on the papers, and then noticed that her fingers had left smudges, clouding the glass. Guiltily, she picked it up and tried to wipe it clean with a tissue in her pocket. The smudges lengthened into smears.

"Maggie."

She started, and looked up. Jess stood in the doorway in his coat. "If anyone calls, I had to run over to the health food store and pick up their ad copy. Last minute amendments from the counterculture."

She tried to conceal the paperweight. "Okay," she said, without looking at him, "but I'm just about to leave."

"All right." He seemed about to add something, but then he thought better of it, and left.

As he disappeared out the door, Maggie replaced the paperweight on Evy's desk. She didn't want to hurt his feelings, but it was better this way. The memory of Evy's stricken face recurred, as it had all afternoon. She sat down heavily in the girl's chair. A feeling of shame overcame Maggie as she recalled the girl's awkward attempt to find out the truth, and her own lies, now exposed, that she had given in response. I was only trying to protect her, she thought. Whatever the motive, it had done more harm than good.

The girl's infatuation with Jess was so apparent. Naturally she'd resent any attention he showed to another woman. Maggie realized that she had come, unwelcome, into Evy's life and disrupted her fantasy. Evy was very young, and in love with her boss, and it was painful. Stinging memories of Roger recurred as she sat in Evy's seat. She too had been young, alone in a strange town. She had fled her home, and the years of silent recrimination from her mother, whispered imprecations from Sister Dolorita. She had settled in a new place, and promptly fallen in love with her boss. For months she would go home to her lonely rented room at night and think of him. And at work her stomach would churn with jealousy when she heard the familiar, disembodied voice of his wife on the phone.

And then, unbelievably, she found her love returned. That was when the guilt, and the pain, had begun in earnest. But she had been vulnerable, like Evy, and she needed him.

Maggie rubbed her eyes, as if to banish a disquieting vision. Then her glance fell on a bag under Evy's desk. Glad for any distraction, she reached down and picked up the package which had a pharmacy's mortar and pestle insignia on the front. She looked inside, and found that the bag contained two bars of soap, a tube of toothpaste, and two vials of prescription pills. The labels indicated that the pills were for Harriet Robinson, to be taken three times a day.

Maggie rolled the plastic containers around in her hand. She read the labels again. Harriet Robinson. The pills were obviously for Evy's grandmother. In her anger, Evy must have forgotten them. Maggie dropped the vials back in the bag, and rolled the top closed. Then she wedged the bag under her arm, and went to gather up her purse and coat.

Setting out, Maggie felt confident that she could find the way. But the dusk was gathering rapidly, and the roads, once she was out of town, looked confusingly similar. She crept along in the old Buick, craning her neck to see the street signs which the headlights dimly illuminated.

93

The old car coughed and rattled. Maggie gripped the wheel, and glanced apprehensively at the gauge as she made her way down the country roads. Through the bare branches of the trees she spied an occasional light from a farmhouse like a beacon in the purple dusk. The further along she drove, the fewer the isolated glimmers became.

Just as she began to feel certain that she had lost her way, she came up on a traffic island in the road. She slowed the car and strained to make out the street signs, partially obscured by branches which drooped down from the trees like tangled strands of grey hair.

Barrington Street. The old car groaned in protest as she turned the wheel and accelerated. This is it, she thought.

The Robinson mailbox, clearly lettered, jutted out at her about half a mile along Barrington. Maggie turned up the long driveway, the gravel crunching under the tyres of the car, and came to a halt beside the house. She turned off the engine, and the car sighed.

The old house must have been beautiful at one time, Maggie thought, but the garden out front was now strangled by rampant weeds, and the painted trim was peeling off in strips around the windows. Maggie grabbed the pharmacy bag, and approached the back door. She opened the outer door, and her coat snagged on the ragged edges of a hole in the screen. She jerked the fabric free, and then rapped lightly on the wooden door.

Through the dusty windowpanes and the limp, net curtains she could see into the kitchen. There was a light on, and the table appeared to be set for dinner. Maggie knocked again, but there was no answer. Tentatively, she tried the doorknob. The door opened. Maggie stuck her head into the room. The strong smell of cooking fish assaulted her nostrils.

"Hello," she called out.

From the next room she could hear the sound of a voice, or maybe two voices, speaking in low, insistent tones. She considered placing the bag on the table and just leaving quietly, but instead she forced herself to call out again. "Anybody home?"

Abruptly the speaking stopped. Maggie stepped into the room and turned to close the door behind her. When she looked back, Evy was standing in the doorway. She wore a blue chenille bathrobe which had lost most of its nub, and scuffed slippers. Her hair was mussed, as if she had been lying down, and her pale eyes widened at the sight of Maggie in her kitchen.

"Hi," said Maggie uncomfortably.

Evy stared at her. "What are you doing here?" she asked flatly.

Maggie held out the chemist's bag to her. "I brought you this. You forgot it when you left

95

the office. I thought you might need something in it. The pills, or something."

"I didn't need it," said the girl, ignoring the bag in Maggie's extended hand. "Where'd you find it anyway?"

Maggie put the bag down on the table. "It was under your desk."

"What were you doing looking under my desk?"

"I was passing by it. Look Evy, I didn't have to bring it all the way out here . . ."

"Nobody asked you to," the girl snapped.

"But," Maggie continued, ignoring the rebuke. "I wanted to. I wanted to see how you were feeling."

"I'm beginning to feel sick again," said the girl. "I think you should go."

Maggie eyed her steadily, but the girl tossed her head. Maggie plunged on. "Evy, I also came because I thought we should have a talk. Away from the office. Maybe we could clear up a few things . . ."

"I don't want to talk," the girl replied. "I don't feel well."

"Look, I know this might not be the best day, but I just wanted you to know something. I'm sorry about what happened this afternoon." She paused, but Evy did not respond. Maggie stumbled on. "I think you probably misunderstood what you overheard today . . ." Maggie corrected herself, "*if* you overheard . . ." She stopped in mid-sentence, her attention suddenly diverted by a whirring sound which emanated from another room and was coming towards them.

Evy broke in impatiently. "I don't know what you're talking about, and I don't really care. I just think you better go."

Evy was staring at her defiantly. Maggie shook her head, and groped around for another approach to her. "I just think . . ."

"Will you please go," the girl whispered angrily, a vein in her temple throbbing visibly.

The whirring sound came closer to the kitchen and then stopped. Maggie looked curiously around Evy's shoulder and saw that an old woman in an electric wheelchair had just entered the room.

Evy addressed herself to the old woman without turning to look at her. "It's okay, Grandma. It's nothing. Just go back to the parlour."

"Is this your grandmother?" Maggie asked.

"Of course it's my grandmother," the girl said angrily.

"Couldn't I just say hello to her?" Maggie asked.

"She's sick," said Evy.

Maggie felt a growing anger at Evy's insolent tone. She could see the woman in the wheelchair was feeble, her frame bent and her head dropping on her chest. "Is that any reason to ignore her?" Maggie asked.

Evy glared at her, but did not reply.

Maggie approached the woman and put her fingertips lightly on the knotty hand curved around the chair arm. "Mrs. Robinson?" she whispered.

"That's enough," Evy insisted. "Let her be."

Maggie could see the purple veins, thick and close to the surface of the woman's faded, wrinkled skin. Her grey and white hair was sparse and wispy, and she stared at a spot on the floor a few feet from Maggie, her large, but fragile-looking head nodding of its own volition. She wore a pink bed jacket, its ruffled neckline tied in a neat bow around her scrawny neck, and there was a multi-coloured rug wrapped around her legs.

"Mrs. Robinson," Maggie repeated, leaning closer to her face. "I work with Evy. My name is Maggie Fraser, and I've just come here to work on the newspaper. Maybe Evy's told you."

"She doesn't know a thing you're saying," Evy interrupted scornfully. "What are you talking her ear off for? Leave her alone."

The old woman blinked, and then slowly lifted her shaking head. Her rheumy eyes were pale, blue like Evy's. She focused them with difficulty on Maggie's face, as if she were trying to understand an explanation, but had forgotten how to concentrate. Maggie stifled her feelings of revul-

98

sion, and smiled encouragingly at her. She was about to straighten up when she saw the old woman's lower lip begin to tremble. Then, deep within the aged eyes, Maggie saw an expression of clarity flutter, and then drop into place, like a tumbler snapping back at the insertion of the right key.

She stared at Maggie, her eyes widening grotesquely, and then a look of terror surfaced from their depths and contorted her whole face. Her crippled fingers clawed impotently at the arms of her chair, and she worked her mouth violently, as if straining to speak. Suddenly, a cry, harsh, and piercing, burst from her throat, and her cracked lips formed a string of unintelligible words.

Maggie's heart pounded in her ears, but she could not tear her eyes from the old woman's horrified gaze. Suddenly Evy, who was temporarily immobilized by the exchange, jerked to alertness. "All right," she shouted at Maggie. "That's enough."

Maggie looked helplessly from her to the old woman. "What's wrong?"

"You've upset her," Evy accused her.

Bewildered, Maggie began to protest. "But I didn't do anything . . ."

Evy turned on her, enraged. "I told you this would happen. I told you to go before."

"I don't understand," Maggie sputtered. "I didn't . . ."

"Get out," Evy commanded shrilly, over the cries of the old woman which had begun again.

Maggie hesitated a moment, and then backed out the door, slamming it behind her as she fled towards the car.

"And don't come back," she heard Evy shrieking after her.

For a while Maggie drove aimlessly, barely aware of the roads, trying to still the racing of her heart which had resulted from the scene at Evy's. She did not want to go home. She knew that. She could not bear to face the empty house. Her feeling of total isolation would only be intensified by those silent rooms.

Even as she drove along the deserted country roads she felt exposed and humiliated. It seemed as if everything she did alienated her from these people. And Evy. Evy was so furious with her. The one person, besides Jess, who had been relatively friendly to her.

Before she was conscious of what she was doing, Maggie had driven back to town. I'll just go back to the office, she thought. I'll just stay there for a while. She parked the car outside *News* Building. There won't be anyone there. Maybe I can get some work done. But as she got out of the car and walked up the street, she knew what she was really hoping for.

The light from Jess's office spilled out into the hallway. Her heart caught in her throat as she spied it, when she opened the front door. She knew she should be avoiding him. But she needed someone to talk to. Someone who would not look at her with suspicion and hostility. She stood in the vestibule, her hand clutching the doorknob, an aerialist about to go out on the wire.

A moving shadow blotted out the light on the floor. Jess stood in the doorway, a pencil behind his ear. He squinted into the darkened hallway. "Who is it?"

"It's me," Maggie breathed.

"Maggie?"

"Yes."

His face relaxed into a smile. "What are you doing here?" He came towards her.

She was about to lie. A forgotten folder. An unfinished column. The excuses formed in her mind, and then dissolved. She looked up at him helplessly. "I was hoping to find you here," she said.

He reached out a hand and grasped her elbow. "You found me," he said.

7

"**M**ORE coffee?"

Maggie agreed, and the waitress poured the steaming amber liquid into her china cup. Maggie raised it to her lips, and then balanced its ribbed surface between her fingertips, examining the delicate, flower-sprigged pattern in the flickering candlelight.

It tasted different, she thought, when you had to plead for it, like a beggar, holding out a dented metal mug. She took another sip. The day she was sprung they had all pressed up against their cell doors to jeer as she walked down the tier. Then, one of them had started with the cup. In a minute they all caught on, rolling and banging them against the bars, metal on metal. The clangour attacked her. She could feel it everywhere—in her armpits, behind her knees, in her genitals. She wanted to clap her hands over her ears, but she couldn't give them the satisfaction.

"You'll be back," they screamed over the din. Her eyes iced over at the memory.

Never, she thought.

"This place is a find, isn't it?" Jess asked, gesturing around the intimate dining-room. "A little out of the way, but it's always good."

"It's perfect," Maggie murmured, recovering quickly.

"Our waitress is one of the owners. She and her husband keep the place open all winter because they love good food, and there's nowhere better to eat."

Maggie cocked her head and smiled at him. "You know, you're really quite a guide."

"Quite a guy, did you say?" he asked, pretending to have misunderstood.

"That too," she said quietly.

"I fished for that," he admitted, pleased. He crumpled up his napkin and tossed it on the table. "Well," he said, "I feel as if this dinner has been a great success.

Maggie raised her eyebrows. "Oh?"

"I finally know a little more than you."

Maggie smiled ruefully. The conversation had run a perilous course. But despite two glasses of wine, and the fact that she was still shaken by the encounter at Evy's, she had managed to steer it away from sensitive areas. Safe anecdotes about growing up on the farm, and some stories from high school seemed to content him. He listened with pleasure, interrupting her with an occasional question. His interest, and the sound of her own voice were reassuring. The need to tell him about the incident at Evy's receded. Just being near him made it seem unimportant.

"However," he went on, "I still haven't heard what I came here for."

103

Maggie looked at him sharply.

"There was something on your mind when you came looking for me," he said. "What was the problem?"

Maggie shook her head. "It was nothing much, really. I guess I was just feeling a little lonely, a little down. It's much better now."

"Well, that's good," he said. He knew she was evading the question, but he was letting her get away with it.

Deliberately, Maggie took a sip of coffee and sat back. She could feel the warmth of his gaze on her. The intimacy between them was making her uncomfortable. She searched for a neutral subject.

"That's a very nice sweater you have on. It's a good colour on you," she said pleasantly.

"Oh, thanks," said Jess, plucking at an invisible pull on the sleeve.

"It looks handmade. A great-aunt, perhaps?" she teased him.

"It is," Jess agreed shyly. "As a matter of fact, Evy made it for me."

"Evy?" Maggie drew in a sharp breath.

Jess regarded her quizzically. "Yes. Why?"

Maggie felt a stab in her stomach. Was there something between them after all, she wondered. Perhaps that explained why Evy was so angry with her. Maggie chose her words carefully, trying to keep her voice even. "It just seems like a rather personal gift. That's all. I mean, more

104

like something one would give a close friend, than a boss."

Jess sucked reflectively on the stem of his pipe. "I suppose we are friends. I've known her for years, long before she worked at the paper. She was still a little girl when I first knew her."

Maggie chewed over this explanation in her mind. Drop it, she thought to herself. But she could not dispel the image of Evy's furiously ordering her out of the house over her grandmother's inchoate wailing. "She seems to be very attached to you," Maggie said finally.

"I guess she is," he said.

"I mean in other than a friendly way," Maggie persisted. "I was beginning to get the impression that you two . . . That there was more to it than friendship."

"Between me and Evy," he asked incredulously. "Oh, maybe she's got a little crush on me. That's not unusual for girls her age," he dismissed it.

"She's not exactly a child. She must be over eighteen."

"Just barely," said Jess.

"She's a woman, really."

"So?"

"So, I just wondered if the two of you might be involved in some way."

"What gives, Maggie?" Jess asked impatiently. "Did Evy tell you that?"

"No," Maggie admitted. "It was just a feeling I had."

"Did you have a falling out with Evy?"

Maggie sat silently for a moment. "I don't know if you'd call it a falling out," she said, at last.

Jess watched her expectantly.

"I think she's pretty angry with me."

"Why?"

"Well, I think it has to do with you," Maggie replied, trying to speak calmly. "I went over to her house after work, to bring her a package she left behind, and she ordered me out."

Jess waited for her to continue, but Maggie fell silent. "Is that all?" he asked.

"It was awful," Maggie insisted. He frowned at her. "I saw her grandmother. She was terribly upset," Maggie blurted out.

Jess shook his head sadly, as if he finally understood. "It's an awful thing, isn't it? A person struck down like that. I remember when Harriet was a strong, vital woman. But she's had a hard time."

"What's wrong with her?" Maggie asked.

"A couple of years ago she had a series of strokes. Three of them, boom, boom, boom. They didn't think she was going to make it, but she hung on. Poor Evy was so scared. That's all she's got in the world. Her grandmother. Harriet's been a mother to her, really, since her own mother got sick. Her mother's been hospitalized for years, on the mainland."

"And her father?" Maggie asked.

"He's dead, I'm afraid. So poor Harriet had to cope with a growing girl, and all those worries. I guess it was just too much for her. It's a shame."

Maggie recalled the old woman's pale, terror-filled eyes, and the hand clawing frenziedly at the arm of the wheelchair. "Is she always like that?" Maggie asked.

"I'm sure she has her good and bad days. But, more or less, yeah."

Maggie did not speak for a moment. "It is too bad," she conceded, "but I don't see what that has to do with Evy's being so rude to me!"

"Come on, Maggie. The poor kid was probably ashamed to have you see her grandmother like that. Evy's a sensitive girl."

For a moment Maggie remembered overhearing Evy's defence of her to Grace and Croddick, the shopkeeper. She felt guilty for having complained of her behaviour to Jess.

"Give her a chance," he suggested.

"You're right," said Maggie. "I will."

Jess turned the doorknob on the A-frame house, which stood on the crest of a hill. "I've been looking forward to showing you my house," he said. "I did most of the work myself."

"The ocean sounds so close by," Maggie exclaimed, pausing to listen.

"I've got a dock right at the bottom of the hill. I keep my boat down there during the summer. It's a little inlet that leads right out to the sea."

"What a soothing sound," she observed.

"Come on in," said Jess, making way for her.

It was chilly in the house. Maggie shivered in the doorway as Jess went around turning on the lamps. The living-room where they stood had a vaulted ceiling, and a Franklin stove at one end. The room was full of large windows, but Jess drew the curtains over them and began to straighten some of the pillows on the furniture.

"Don't fuss with that," Maggie reassured him. "It all looks wonderful." The room, although slightly untidy, had a cosy, comfortable feeling to it. Maggie looked around approvingly. "Did you really do all the work on this house yourself?" she asked.

Jess placed his hands on his hips and scanned the room. "Most of it," he said. "Except the curtains," he added thoughtfully. "Sharon made the curtains." He waved towards the door. "The rest of it is back that way. Kitchen's right through that door. My den, two bedrooms upstairs. I've even got a back porch."

Maggie smiled. "It's wonderful."

"I think we need a little fire," he said, crouching down in front of the stove. He began to arrange the crumpled newspaper and kindling.

Maggie perched on the edge of the sofa which faced the stove, and watched him lay the fire.

"When I was a little girl," Maggie mused, "I liked to sit right up against the screen of the fireplace. I didn't care how hot it was. I remember once my mother told me that someday I'd go up in flames."

Jess struck a match and it flared brightly. Then he lit a torch of newspaper and eased it into the fireplace. "That's a funny thing to say to a kid," he observed. He rocked back on his heels and watched the kindling catch. Then he looked over his shoulder and smiled at Maggie. "Did your dad used to do this?" he asked.

"What?" Maggie asked guardedly.

"Light a fire for you. Since you liked it so much."

"Why do you ask that?"

"I don't know," said Jess, selecting a narrow piece of wood and placing it deftly in among the flaming kindling. "From different things you said I got the idea that you and he were close. That he liked making you happy."

Maggie cocked her head and stared at the flames. "My mother said he would do anything for me."

"You mentioned he's dead," Jess asked, tossing a few more hunks of wood into the blaze.

"Yes. He died years ago. When I was a child."

"Was he ill for long?" Jess asked.

Maggie shook her head slowly. "He had a

heart attack." She hesitated, and then she continued. "He was out working on the roof of the shed. He fell off the ladder."

"Were you at home when it happened?" Jess asked, sitting back on his heels.

"I was sitting on the roof of the shed, holding the nails for him."

Jess whistled. "That's terrible. It must have been tough for you. Particularly for a little girl. They say that daddy's her first love."

The first, yes, Maggie thought.

Jess put on one more log and stood up. "How's that?" he asked, joining her on the couch. He sank down beside her, and the weight of his body caused her to roll slightly into him. "Maybe we should talk about more cheerful things," he said, slipping his arm around her and studying her face. Tenderly he lifted a lock of hair from her forehead and smoothed it back. Maggie rested stiffly in the crook of his arm.

"What are you thinking?" he asked.

Maggie shrugged but did not reply. She was seeing her father, clutching his arm, his face ashen, the ladder falling. Falling away from her.

Maggie started as Jess ran one rough hand down the side of her face. "You seem so tense. I'm afraid I upset you."

Her cheek felt as if it were pulsing where he had touched it. "Well, I'm just not . . . I may be a little edgy tonight," she said, squirming slightly.

110

"What can I do to cheer you up?" he asked. "You want to hear an elephant joke?"

"No." Maggie's laugh was more like a cough. His fingers on her arm felt electrically charged. She heard her own breathing becoming shallow.

Jess looked down and sat silently for a moment. She was aware of his body next to hers. She felt as if her whole body was throbbing. "Maggie," he said softly. "Listen. It's hard for me to talk about my feelings."

"You shouldn't," she said quickly.

"I want to," he said. "It's just that I've been alone a lot since my . . . since Sharon. You get kind of rusty." He took a deep breath and went on. "There's something about you. I noticed it right away. You let people know that you can take care of yourself. But you seem very uncertain too. Shy, kind of. Right away I felt something for you. I was touched by you. I'm not saying this very well. I felt," he said carefully, "that there was something between us. Do you know what I mean?"

Tell him "no", Maggie thought. Stop this right now, before it starts. But at the same time her heart, and her senses were clamouring for him. She sat in silence, avoiding his eyes.

"Was I wrong?" The gentle anguish in his voice caught her off guard. Impulsively, she reached up and touched his face. Jess turned his lips to her hand and kissed her fingers. Maggie caught her breath at the caress, which brought back feelings long kept in check.

Tentatively, Jess pulled her towards him, and pressed his mouth to hers. Every muscle in her body responded to his kiss, softening into silken cords which strained to wrap themselves around him. She breathed in the scent of his hair, the faint, sweet smell of pipe tobacco and the rich smell of his body as his arms encircled her in an urgent clasp. She found herself being sucked: into the vortex of conflicting currents. She struggled, and then pushed him away.

"No, Jess," she said. "I can't." Ignoring the pain in his eyes, she freed herself from his embrace and drew herself up. Without a word she stood up and walked towards the door to the kitchen, leaving him seated there on the sofa, staring ahead of him.

In the kitchen she leaned against the sink, her arms wound tightly around her, and gazed out the window at the inky sky. Her heart was still pounding, as if she had just made a narrow escape.

She blinked away the tears which were forming in her eyes. The last time she had been with a man, the night of Roger's murder, it had been snowing—the beginning of a blizzard, in fact. They had watched it start, lying amidst the scratchy, rumpled sheets of the motel bed. The sky was that deep blue it is just before nightfall.

"We have to go," Roger said wearily. "That

snow is really starting to come down there. Look at it. I have to get home. She'll be worrying."

Reluctantly Maggie released him from her embrace. She pulled the sheets up to her chin, and watched the snow already piling up on the windowsill. Then her eyes moved to her lover as he slowly retrieved his trousers from the floor beside the bed.

"Maybe," she said softly, "you should tell her tonight."

With a look of consternation in his eyes, Roger turned to face her. "Tell her?" he asked.

"About us," she said boldly. "That you love someone else. Maybe she would give you a divorce."

Roger's forehead was ridged with pain. He turned away from her and stared out the window. His trousers dangled from his hand.

Maggie leaned up on one elbow and reached out to touch his thigh. "Why not tell her and get it over with. She may agree to the divorce. You won't know unless you try."

"I can't do that," he said quietly, avoiding her eyes.

Maggie drew back her hand. "Why not? Roger, we love each other."

He was silent for a moment. Then he turned to look at her sadly. "I told you a long time ago that it wasn't fair. Maggie, I have to be honest with you. I have a family. A kid in school, a house, a mortgage. I have responsibilities. They need me."

Maggie stared at him blankly. "I need you too," she whispered.

"We have to go," he said. "I'm sorry."

Slowly she rolled over and buried her face in her arms. He began to dress in silence.

"Maggie," Jess said softly. "Can we talk about it?"

Maggie turned and saw him looking down at her, his eyes dark and troubled.

"Whatever it is," he said, "why don't we talk it over? I wasn't trying to pressure you. Honestly."

Maggie sighed, and shook her head. "I know you weren't. It's not you. It's me. Really. But I can't help it. I should never have spent this time with you. I knew this would happen. It was a mistake. I just can't. There's too much in the way. Oh, I'm not making any sense," she said.

"I thought you liked being with me," he said.

"I do," she said. "That's the whole thing."

"Look," he said. "It's not the easiest thing for me, either."

She looked at him sadly. "Believe me," she said. "It's best this way. For you too."

"Maggie, what are you . . ."

"Jess, I can't. Don't ask me."

"Tell me why," he pressed her.

"No, I . . . I have to go." She pushed past

him. "I have my car," she said, grabbing her coat from a chair in the living-room. "I can find my way out."

You're a fool, she thought, slamming the car door shut. Do you want to tell him about yourself? Do you want to see his face when you tell him you spent the last twelve years in prison? Stay away from him. Do your job, live quietly, mind your puppy. That's what you came here to do. Stay away from him. You are not like other people. You can't live like other people. Stop pretending that you can.

Tears blurred her vision as she drove through the dark country roads. No feelings, she thought. That was how she had planned it. Just peace, and solitude, and a gradual subsiding of the painful memories. Maybe, after a while, a few friends, carefully chosen. That was how she had envisioned it. Not the emotional turmoil of a love affair. That was the last thing she needed. She wasn't strong enough now. Safety. Anonymity. That was what she really wanted.

But even as she thought all these things, his face was crowding her resolve. Her skin felt as if it had been restored to life by his touch. Her heavy heart kept being pierced by the persistent thought, you'll see him again tomorrow. She wanted to stop it. She did. But she knew she couldn't.

The old woman shivered with the cold that

seemed to emanate from the pit of her stomach. Her knobby fingers were stiff, like icicles. Beneath the thin flannel nightgown, her spindly legs trembled from the chill. But she was unable to retrieve the rug which lay on the floor beside her chair, like a heap of funeral flowers on a new grave. She opened her mouth. A harsh noise came from her throat. Her granddaughter, who sat brooding in a chair across the room, finally looked up and glared at her.

"What do you want?" Evy demanded. The old woman tried to incline her head towards the blanket on the floor.

"Don't look at me like that," Evy snarled. "I'm tired of you." Evy snatched the long-handled wooden spoon from where it was hanging beside the refrigerator and began to smack it lightly against the sole of her slipper. The steady thwacking, and the ticking of the clock above the stove were the only sounds in the kitchen. The old woman stared at her grand-daughter, the limp muscles in her face twitching involuntarily.

"I don't know why you had to make a fuss like that," Evy said at last, pointing the spoon at her grandmother across the room. "I didn't invite her here. I certainly did not. She wanted to talk to me," Evy said, in a scornful, sing-song voice. "Talk to me?"

With a concentrated effort, the old woman pushed her emaciated forearm off the armrest of

116

her chair until it fell, dangling beside the chair, grazing the wheels with her knuckles. The tips of her gnarled fingers could almost reach the peak of the heap of crocheted flowers. She strained to touch it.

"She found the package under my desk. What was she doing snooping around my desk?" the girl cried. "She should have kept her hands to herself."

The old woman snagged a strand of wool on two fingertips. She let out a groan.

"Stop it," Evy cried. She leaped from her chair, the wooden spoon in her fist. With a vicious smack she brought it across the old woman's brittle fingers.

The old woman's head and shoulders shot back at the shock of the impact. Evy grabbed a handful of the wispy hairs and drew back her grandmother's head.

"I'm telling you something," Evy said slowly. "I want you to listen. I listened to you all those years. You bet I did." The paper-thin skin of the scalp stood away from the skull in tiny peaks. Evy gave the woman's head a shake, and let it go. A few grey hairs stuck to her damp fingers.

"The first thing she did when she showed up here was to throw herself at Jess. Jess! And she keeps right on doing it. She thinks I don't know. This morning she tried to fool me about it. Ha!" Evy began to laugh, a mirthless, gasping sound issuing from her throat. The laugh distorted her face into a leer. "She thinks I don't know." The girl's laugh was an incredulous scream.

Suddenly she stopped, interrupted by another sound. It was a moan, faint but agonized, issuing from the direction of the basement. Evy glanced over at the cellar door. The moaning rose and fell. No words. Just a plaintive, incoherent wail of suffering, with little strength behind it.

Evy fixed her narrowed eyes on her grandmother's face as the old woman listened to the piteous cries. Tears began to trickle down the creases of the old woman's withered cheeks, and her frail chest heaved as she struggled to catch a breath.

Evy returned calmly to her seat beside the refrigerator and threw her grandmother an unctuous smile. "She'll be sorry," said the girl. Then, she crossed her legs, and resumed tapping the spoon against the sole of her slipper.

8

MAGGIE placed her pocketbook in her desk drawer and pulled her chair up to her desk. Then she looked down in surprise. Waiting for her was a flaky, cherry-studded pastry sitting on a piece of waxed paper. She studied it quizzically for a moment, and then looked up. Grace sat typing with her back to her. There was no one else in sight. Maggie pulled off a piece of the pastry and put it in her mouth. She began to chew it thoughtfully.

Just then Evy came into the office, carrying a pile of manuscripts. She smiled sheepishly at Maggie. "I hope you like cherry," she said.

Maggie swallowed the morsel she was eating and looked at the girl in surprise.

Evy shrugged. "I got it at the health food bakery." She waved her thumb in the general direction of the building next door.

"I just tried it. It's good."

Evy took a few steps closer to Maggie's desk and began to fidget.

"That was nice of you," said Maggie.

"I wanted to apologize to you about . . . you know. What happened last night. My grandmother is sick and sometimes . . . Well, I never

119

know how she's going to act. It was really nice of you to bring the pills over."

"Forget it," said Maggie. "I understand."

"I guess I just worry about her, and I don't want her to get all worked up. Sometimes with strangers, you know."

"I'm sorry I upset her," said Maggie. "Let's just forget it."

Evy smiled at her. "Okay. Thanks." Then she turned and went over to her desk to sit down.

An unfamiliar feeling of well-being lightened Maggie's glum mood. Evy was a good kid, really. It took a lot of courage to apologize that way. She was having a hard time, and Maggie could certainly sympathize with that. She took another bite of the pastry so that Evy could see she was enjoying it. Then she pulled out the file of photographs she had been working on the day before. Maybe Jess was right about her, she thought.

The day passed for Maggie with hardly a glimpse of Jess, who spent his time in his own office. Their brief exchanges were businesslike. He made no reference to the night before. Although it made her feel slightly melancholy, Maggie told herself firmly that it was best that way. At about three o'clock Jess came into the office with Owen Duggan at his side.

"Maggie," he called out.

She looked up.

"I want you to try your hand at a little reporting today. Owen's going over to take some pictures of one of our local legends, Ben McGuffey, who's retiring next week on his nine-tieth birthday. Ben's a sailmaker, used to ship out on whalers in his younger days. It'll make a kind of a nice story, I think."

"Okay," Maggie gathered up her pen and pencil. "I'm ready to go."

"Owen," Jess went on, "you know what to do. The usual stuff. Kind of help Maggie out if she gets stuck on anything." He smiled at her reassuringly. Flustered, Maggie avoided Jess's eyes.

Owen gave Jess a ragged salute, and started for the door. "Looks like rain," he muttered squinting up at the sky from the front doorstep. "Come on." A distant fork of lightning cracked the sky as he motioned to Maggie.

A little while later, Jess entered the office and walked over to Grace's desk. He dropped a stapled manuscript on her blotter. Grace picked it up and looked at it.

"What's this?" she demanded.

"First instalment of that series on island land-marks," said Jess. "Give it a thorough going-over."

"Are we running this?" she asked.

"Next week."

"I thought you were going to wait on this until Mr. Emmett gets back."

"Changed my mind," Jess shrugged.

"When is he coming back?" Grace asked petulantly.

"I dunno. I haven't heard from him yet."

"I wish he'd hurry up," she whined. "So we can get things settled around here." She looked significantly in the direction of Maggie's desk.

"Why, Grace? What's the problem?" Jess asked politely.

The older woman looked at him in surprise. Across the room Evy chewed on her pencil, pretending to be concentrating on the proof sheets in front of her.

"Well," Grace went on indignantly. "I just think there's some unfinished business that can't be settled until he gets back."

"You mean Maggie?" Jess said patiently.

"I didn't say that," Grace protested. "I was just saying that I'll be glad when Mr. Emmett gets back."

"It seems to me," said Jess firmly, "that we're a lot better off with the extra help around here. That's what I intend to tell Mr. Emmett when he gets back. You have to admit, Grace, that your load has been a lot more manageable since she came."

Grace sniffed, and raised her eyebrows. "Whatever you say," she agreed sarcastically.

Jess paused, as if he were going to say something else, and then thought better of it. He did not want to start an argument over Maggie. That would not make Grace any more favourably disposed to her. With a shrug, he left the room.

Grace turned to Evy, who looked up from her proof sheets. Grace rolled her eyeballs and shook her head. "How do you like that?" she demanded.

"I wasn't really paying attention," Evy claimed innocently.

"Looks like if he has anything to say about it we're going to have Miss Forgetful Butterfingers with us forever." Grace heaved a sigh of disgust.

"Maybe not," said Evy.

"Well, didn't you hear that? She's got him so he can't see straight already. We don't need her here."

"Oh well. What's the difference," said Evy. "She's not that bad."

Grace snorted indignantly, annoyed that the girl was not supporting her view. Suspecting Evy's weakness she threw the girl a sly glance. "I think he's got kind of a crush on her, don't you?"

Evy lowered her eyes to the pages in her hand. Grace could see her whitening. "I don't know," she said.

"That's what I think," Grace announced. "I wonder if they're up to no good together. I'll bet. He sure looks at her that way."

Evy stood up abruptly and stuck her chin out in the air. "Who cares?" she said. "I have to get some new pencils in the art room."

123

"Go ahead," said Grace. "I'm not stopping you."

A crack of thunder greeted Maggie and Owen as they emerged from the sailmaker's shop.

"We'd better hurry," said Maggie.

"Oh, it won't rain for a while yet," the photographer assured her. "I've become a semi-pro forecaster since I've lived here."

"Well, I have work to do."

Owen glanced at his watch. "It's nearly five."

Maggie shrugged, and started walking. The photographer made her uncomfortable. All during their talk with the old sailor she felt his eyes on her. It was not a lascivious look. It was more like he was studying her, trying to place her. She was eager to get away from him. However, Owen kept pace with her as she hurried along.

"That was kind of fun," he said. "Ben's quite a character. Did you notice his hands? Brown as an Indian's. And those long fingers. Really beautiful hands. They tell a whole life's story."

"He's had an interesting life," she agreed. "A regular Conrad character."

"You did very well with him. He really opened up to you. That story about him falling out the boat and the swordfish towing him in the tangled line was great.

"It should be a good story," she said.

124

"Were you a reporter on the papers you worked for before?"

Maggie stiffened, and answered him curtly. "No."

"Where'd you work? Big dailies? Small town papers?"

"Small papers. Why?" she countered.

Owen was taken aback. "Just curious. I thought maybe you came here to escape the rat race. It's the perfect place for it. I used to work in New York myself, years ago."

Maggie backed down. "Just small papers," she said.

"I just keep having this nagging feeling," he went on, "that I know you from somewhere. That's why I wondered if you ever worked in New York."

Maggie's stomach tightened into a knot. A photographer from New York. Maybe he had even been at her trial upstate. A vivid memory came back to her of flashbulbs and floodlights bursting through the darkened corridors of the courthouse. No matter how she tried to hide her face, they swarmed over her, mosquito-like, devouring her with their cameras. In the grainy black-and-whites she looked stunned and ghostly. "I'm sure we've never met," she said coldly.

A flash of lightning was accompanied by a tremendous thunderclap.

125

"Uh oh," said Owen sheepishly. "Here it comes."

The words were hardly out of his mouth before the rain started, pouring down on them. Owen drew his jacket over his camera equipment. "There's my jeep," he yelled to her. "I'm going to make a run for it. Tell Jess I'll bring the pictures in a day or two."

Before she could reply he was sprinting across the street. Sheets of grey, chilling rain drove down the sidewalks and the street. Maggie ran for the *Cove News* building, but it was already too late to preserve an inch of dryness. She threw open the door and stood panting in the front hallway, water dripping down her face and hair, seeping all the way to her soggy shoes.

Jess came out of his office and stared at her. "God, you're soaked," he observed.

She glanced down at her dripping garments and shrugged. "I'm afraid so."

"You better go home. It's nearly five anyway."

Maggie nodded, still panting.

Grace and Evy came out and stood in the doorway of the office. Grace shook her head and clucked her tongue.

"Where's Owen?" Jess asked.

"He's gone home. We got a nice story from Ben."

"Tell me about it tomorrow," Jess urged her. "Go on home now. Get out of those wet clothes."

By the time she reached the door of her house, the downpour had become a steady drizzle. Maggie was chilled through by the cold, wet garments plastered to her body. Wearily she sank into a chair in the dank, cheerless living-room. Almost immediately she jumped up again, conscious of the spreading stain from her wet clothes. The oncoming grey twilight gave the house a gloomy aspect. Maggie could feel a vague depression settling over her.

Jess had made no further advances, no mention of seeing her. Perhaps she had been successful in convincing him last night. So, there she was, just as she should be, alone in her damp, empty house. That's just what you wanted, wasn't it, she thought. Listlessly she paced the living-room floor, not even bothering to turn on a light. At last she stopped in front of the fireplace, and stared into the ash-filled grate. She realized she should try to pull herself out of it. There was no point to just sinking further into her depression.

Bending over, she began to build a fire, deftly adding wood to kindling, until a small fire burned energetically in the fireplace. She stared into it for a few minutes. Her wet clothes felt like they were beginning to steam in front of her.

All right, she told herself. A hot shower, dry clothes, and you'll feel better. Forcing herself wearily to her feet, she trudged into the bedroom and dropped her clothes in a sodden pile on the floor. Then she headed for the bathroom, stopping on her way to poke her head into the living-room. The fire was crackling cheerfully. The chill was beginning to leave the room.

Maggie closed the bathroom door halfway.

Then she walked over to the tub, leaned over it and turned on the water. She adjusted the hot and cold taps until the water ran hot. She wanted to make it hot enough to banish the chill. Then she turned on the tap for the shower. Standing up again, she was about to step into the shower when she paused to glance at herself in the mirror above the medicine chest. Grey circles were beginning to form under her eyes. She had slept so little the night before, tormented by familiar, troubling dreams. She was weary, and wondered if she would sleep more soundly tonight.

With a sigh she stepped up over the high rim of the tub, and stood squarely beneath the cascade of hot water. It felt soothing, heating up her chilled flesh, and dousing the cold, rubbery strands of her damp hair. She let it fall over her, drinking in the heat. Then she turned, and began to grope for the bar of soap in the clamshell.

Suddenly she stopped. Through the loud rain of the shower she heard a noise outside the bathroom. She stood very still, listening. The house was silent, except for the steady beat of the water on the floor of the tub.

Stop it, she thought. Don't be ridiculous. Shaking her head, she stepped back under the full blast of the water, rubbing a knubby flannel over her skin. With grim determination, she began to hum.

From just outside the bathroom door, she heard a dull thud. Instantly she grabbed for the taps and turned them off. Wet and trembling, she stood naked in the tub, goose-flesh rising on her bare arms. Once again there was silence outside. She stood uncertainly behind the curtain, her heart thudding. She had left her robe in the bedroom, she realized with a sickening sensation in her stomach. What if she pulled back the curtain and someone was there? She could not step out naked.

After what seemed an interminable amount of time Maggie remembered the towel hanging on a hook outside the shower. Hand shaking, she reached outside the curtain and fumbled for the towel, half expecting a hand to clamp down on her wrist. Her fingers grasped the soft terrycloth. She snatched it roughly from the hook and pulled it behind the curtain. With a shuddering sigh of relief, she wrapped the towel around her and tucked it in. Then she threw back the shower curtain.

There, facing her in the doorway, stood Evy, grinning.

Maggie let out a cry, and clutched the towel tightly to herself.

"Did I frighten you?" the girl asked. She lifted up her hand and pulled out Maggie's bathrobe. "I didn't mean to. I thought you might need this."

"What are you doing here?" Maggie snapped, stepping out of the tub, and grabbing the robe from the girl's outstretched hand.

"I'm sorry," Evy apologized, a hurt expression on her face. "I just came by to visit, and I heard the shower running, so I came in. I called out but you didn't answer."

Maggie turned her back to the girl and pulled on the robe, pulling off the towel, and tying the robe securely around her. Her heart was still hammering from the shock of seeing Evy in the doorway. She tried to calm the hysterical tremor in her voice. It was innocent enough, she thought.

"You shouldn't just creep up on people like that," Maggie said angrily, turning back to face her.

Evy shrugged helplessly. "I just came by to be friendly. I didn't know you'd get so mad."

The steam and the damp heavy air in the bathroom were suffocating. Maggie felt almost irrationally cornered by the way the girl stood in the doorway, blocking her path with an expression of wounded innocence on her face. "Excuse me," she muttered, pushing by the girl's thin frame.

The cool air in the hallway hit her with a rush

that seemed to revive her and calm her temper. She turned back to face Evy. She put up a hand in a gesture of reconciliation. "You just startled me, that's all. You may as well come in and sit down."

"I'll leave if you want," said the girl. "I just thought you wanted to be friends."

Maggie was conscious of a tiny headache which was beginning to throb over her left eye. "I do," she said. "Of course I do. Would you like something from the kitchen?"

"No, I'm fine," said Evy.

"Have a seat." Maggie indicated the sofa which faced the fireplace. Maggie sat down in the rocker beside the hearth and began to rock absently, back and forth, staring into the fire. The heat from the fire felt soothing on her face, as if she were lying in the sun. The girl settled herself into the corner of the couch.

"I can't wait until next summer," Maggie sighed.

"Next summer?" Evy asked.

Maggie shook her head. "Don't mind me. I was thinking of the sun. That's all."

"Oh," said Evy flatly. She leaned back against the throw pillow in the corner of the sofa. "Summer's a long way off."

Maggie nodded, moodily, and continued to rock.

"Winters aren't so bad," Evy offered. "Doesn't snow that much. It has to do with

131

being so near the ocean. I remember one time though, when my mother and I first came here, there was this big ice storm. All the trees, everything was covered with ice. You could hear the branches creaking as you passed by. And then every so often one would just break from the weight. Crack," said Evy, smacking her palm with her bony hand, "just like that."

Maggie started at the girl's demonstration. She looked up at Evy, who shifted in her seat, adjusting the pillow behind her. "I hope we don't get one of those," Maggie said.

"Oh, it really looked neat," said Evy. A silence fell between them. Maggie felt weary from the day's events and the tension of Evy's appearance. The heat of the fire was making her drowsy. She wished the girl would go, but Evy seemed content to sit on the sofa, watching her. Feeling obliged to make conversation, Maggie searched for something to say,

"Did you get much done at the office after I left?" she asked at last.

"Not much," said the girl.

"I had a good time meeting that old sailmaker today."

"Ben?" Evy asked.

"Yes. He's had a fascinating life."

"He's really old," Evy observed, rearranging herself in her seat again.

Maggie stifled a yawn. It seemed as if the girl was incapable of making conversation. And yet

132

she made no move to leave. Maggie gave it another stab.

"I've been reading these notices we're putting in the paper about a fair on Sunday. Is this an annual event?"

Evy nodded. "Every year." She squirmed in her seat again. "There's something under here," she complained.

Maggie screwed up her mouth impatiently. "I could make some tea if you'd like," she said, hoping Evy would refuse, and take the signal to leave.

Evy stuck her hand behind the pillow, and rooted around. "No thanks," she said. She stopped fumbling and seemed to grasp something. "What's this?" she asked, dislodging the object from between the cushion and the sofa back. She held it up and scrutinized it. Instantly, Maggie recognized Jess's pipe. She tried to imagine how it had got there. Then she remembered that he had sat there on Saturday, when he came with the perfume. It must have fallen out of his pocket.

"How about that," Maggie said, careful to keep her tone indifferent. "Must be Thornhill's." She extended her hand to Evy, indicating a desire to look at it.

Evy did not look at Maggie, but continued to examine the pipe in her hands. "Why do you say that?" she asked softly.

"It must be," said Maggie, insisting on her own fabrication. "It's certainly not mine."

Evy's eyes met Maggie's. Her face was drained of all colour. "Actually, it's Jess's pipe." Evy placed it carefully on the low table in front of her, as if jarring it even slightly might cause it to explode.

"Jess's?" Maggie's attempt to show surprise resounded unconvincingly in the room.

"Mr. Emmett gave it to him last year, on his birthday," said Evy slowly.

"Well," said Maggie weakly. She rose from her seat and walked over to the fire, avoiding the girl's stare. She crouched in front of the fire and rubbed her hands together. All the while, she was casting about in her mind for a way to explain. "It might be Jess's. Come to think of it. He was here to pick me up. I had some car trouble the other day . . ."

Evy spoke coldly from behind her. "Why'd you lie about it? You knew it was Jess's."

Maggie reached out angrily and disengaged the poker from the stand which held the fireplace tools. She grasped the metal rod tightly, and began thrusting it into the glowing logs. "I didn't lie," Maggie insisted defensively. "I didn't recognize it at first. I have no reason to lie, Evy. I told you, Jess was here the other day. That old car of the Thornhills' seems to be a lemon. And I needed to get out and do some errands so I asked Jess for a ride. That's all there was to it. He came by, and stayed for a few minutes . . ."

"Stop it," said Evy. "I don't want to hear it."

Maggie clutched the poker tightly in one hand. Evy's words began to break across her back like lashes from a whip.

"What's the matter with you?" said Evy. "Do you think I'm so stupid that I don't know what you're doing? With Jess. Throwing yourself at him. It's disgusting. You're doing something disgusting and trying to pretend you're not."

"That's not true," Maggie whispered into the fire.

"Who do you think you're fooling with your lies," the girl railed at Maggie's back. She stood up and inched towards the crouching woman, squeezing and unfurling her fingers. "I know what you're doing. I know all about it. But Jess. How did you ever lure him into it?"

Maggie wheeled around and stood up, the poker clutched tightly in her trembling hand, her eyes wild. "Stop it," she cried. "Stop it. I won't listen to it."

Evy drew back in alarm at the sight of Maggie's fury. The poker bobbed a few feet from her breastbone. "All right," said Evy. "All right." Her eyes were riveted on the menacing poker.

"You don't know what you're saying," Maggie breathed.

135

"I take it back," Evy placated her. "Maybe you're right. Just don't hit me."

"Hit you?" Maggie looked down at the poker on which Evy's eyes were fixed. She looked genuinely perplexed, as if she had forgotten she was holding it. Her eyes travelled back to Evy's frightened face. "Hit you?" she repeated. Then she groaned. "Oh God." She threw the iron rod back among the collection of fireplace implements, and rested her forehead against the mantelpiece. "I'm sorry," she moaned.

Evy's eyes glittered as they moved from the fallen poker to Maggie's face, hidden in the crook of her elbow. She took a step towards her. Just then an impatient knocking sounded at the back door. Both women looked up, startled, at the door.

"Open up," cried Jess's voice. "I can't hold this thing."

9

MAGGIE opened the door to see a smiling Jess, cradling a fluffy brown and white puppy that squirmed in his arms. His smile faded as he looked at her.

"What's the matter?" he asked. "You look awful. "You're as white as a ghost."

"I'm okay," she said. She reached out to touch the whimpering ball of fur. "You brought my puppy."

"Can I bring him in?" he asked. "I think he's gonna pee on me any minute."

"Evy's here," said Maggie.

"Well," said Jess, "I hate to interrupt, but this guy ain't gonna wait."

Maggie nodded and stood aside, letting Jess and his tiny bundle through the door.

Evy was putting on her jacket as he came in.

"Hey, Evy," he said pleasantly, "you want to meet Maggie's new pup?"

"Cute," the girl muttered, avoiding his eyes. "I'm just going."

"Don't run off," he said. "I think this guy wants us to play with him a little. Hey, will you hand me that newspaper in the log basket." Evy handed him the paper without a word, and then walked around him as he bent down and put the puppy on the paper.

She continued on past Maggie and out of the door.

"Evy," Maggie pleaded, as the girl walked by with her head bowed. Evy stopped, but did not look at her. "I'm sorry," she said.

"Goodbye," the girl muttered, and started down the porch steps into the misty evening.

Maggie turned back into the room and saw Jess sitting beside the little dog, his forefinger in the puppy's tiny jaws. He looked up at her apologetically. "I guess I came at a bad time. I thought you might be cheered up by having your puppy. You seemed so blue last night."

Maggie smiled wanly. "I'm glad you brought him." She knelt down beside him, and ran a finger over the puppy's damp fur. "I didn't think you'd want to see me," she said.

"I don't give up without a fight," he said. "What was Evy doing here?"

Maggie shrugged. "She just came by to be friendly."

"That was nice," said Jess hopefully.

"We ended up having an argument."

"About what?"

Maggie glanced at him. "About you. I told you before. She's very attached to you. She's very jealous of the time I've spent with you."

"Well, she'll just have to learn to get used to it," said Jess firmly.

"Jess . . ." Maggie began, and then stopped.

"Yeah?"

"Does she have any reason to be so jealous? I mean, is there, was there ever anything . . ."

"Oh, Maggie," Jess protested, "for heaven's sake, I told you. I'm her friend. She's like a kid sister to me. How often do I have to say it?"

Maggie shook her head. "I don't want to be in the middle of anything. I can't tell you how much it bothers me."

"I don't know why this is such a problem for you. She's just a kid. You're a woman, who knows a lot more about the world than her. You have to try with her. Why do you let her drag you into these arguments? You can handle this. She's making an effort. Why don't you meet her halfway? She's a nice kid when you get to know her."

"You're angry at me," Maggie said.

"I'm not," he insisted. "I just want there to be peace between you. I don't understand how these arguments get started."

Guiltily, Maggie remembered her lies about the weekend, and the pipe. Maybe it was the lies, more than anything else, that angered the girl. Silently, Maggie resolved to try harder.

"Meanwhile," said Jess, "you're hardly paying any attention to this little fella."

Maggie picked up the little animal and drew it up to her cheek. The puppy made soft breathing sounds near her ear. "Hello. Oh yes."

139

Jess sat back and folded his arms. "Have you decided yet what you're going to call him?"

Maggie nodded. "I've been thinking about it and I think I'll call him Willy."

"Don't tell me," Jess pouted. "There's another man."

Maggie laughed. "I had a great-uncle once named Willy," she explained.

"All right," said Jess, reaching over and pulling the dog's ear gently. "Willy it is. Hey Willy," he said. "Tell this lady to go put some clothes on so we can go buy you some food and take you for a walk."

"You don't have to do that," Maggie protested quickly.

Jess looked at her with a wry smile. "I want to. You must know that by now."

Maggie smiled in spite of herself. "I'll be ready in a few minutes," she said.

"No hurry," said Jess, placing the puppy back on the floor. "Just give us an old sock to chew on and we'll be fine."

Maggie went into her bedroom and opened the top drawer of her bureau. Inside, underneath a pile of scarves, were a pair of grey woollen gloves she had worn in high school. She pulled them out and looked at them for a moment. Then she brought them back to the living-room. Crouching down, she held one in front of the puppy. Immediately the little dog bit down on it and began to work it between his tiny teeth.

"You want one too?" she asked, holding the other glove up to Jess.

"Not now," he said. "Maybe after dinner."

Laughing, and shaking her head, Maggie went back into the bedroom to dress.

It had taken Owen Duggan all of about twenty minutes to eat the chicken and dumplings which his housekeeper, Mirelle, had left simmering on the stove top for him. After his dinner and the nightly news, he was still restless, and disinterested in getting started on the day's pictures. So, an hour later he found himself enveloped in a smoky haze on a barstool at the Sloop John B, nursing a Heineken, and chatting intermittently with Roy Galaeta, who tended the bar. The colour TV droned on at the end of the bar, and the laughter and murmurings of patrons scattered around the room provided the noisy, masculine atmosphere which Owen found soothing and restorative in some indefinable way.

Owen glanced over his beefy shoulder at the other patrons of the John B. He knew most of them by now. Fishermen, men who worked the odd farms on the island, shopkeepers. It had taken him a long time to become familiar with these grizzled, clannish islanders. When he had first come to the island and began frequenting the John B, he often bellied up to the bar alone, drank alone, and left without exchanging more than a nod. It had not bothered him particularly.

141

It suited his solitary temperament. Nowadays though, he could expect to have a few conversations, and occasionally a hand of poker on an evening like this, which was all right too.

"Hey, Owen."

Owen swivelled around to see Charley Cullum slide on to the barstool next to him. "Charley," said Owen, raising his glass an inch off the bar in greeting. "How ya doin'?"

"Give me a beer, Roy. Fine."

"I'm surprised to see you out."

"I get out," Charley protested. "Not as much as you bachelors of course." Then he leaned over and spoke confidentially to the big man. "Grace has her Garden Club tonight. So I left the kids with my mother."

Owen nodded sagely. "I saw Grace today," he said.

Charley, a balding man with an open, bland face, took a sip from the beer which Roy Galaeta placed in front of him. "You were over at the paper?"

"Jess needed a story on Ben McGuffey. He's retiring, you know. He'll be ninety next month."

"Is that right? Ninety. God bless him." Both men drank a silent tribute to the resilient sailmaker.

"Did you meet the new girl while you were over there?" Charley asked.

"Yeah," Owen replied. "As a matter of fact, she did the story with me."

142

"Whew," said Charley, shaking his head. "Gracie sure doesn't like her. She's been crabbing about her ever since she showed up. She's just hoping and praying that Emmett will fire her when he gets back."

Owen shrugged. "She seems all right."

"I don't know her myself," Charley protested. "She's pretty enough though. I got a look at her the other day. She was over at the drugstore while I was there."

Owen finished his beer and motioned to Roy for a refill. "Jess seems to like her," he observed.

"I know it," said Charley gleefully, nudging him in the side. "I think that's what's got Grace so riled up."

Owen smiled thinly. The peculiarities of the female temperament were not his speciality. He had never wanted to be a married man. Thinking about Maggie, though, he was struck again by the nagging feeling that he had met her before. Somewhere. He just wished he could remember where it had been.

"Hey, look at that," Charley cried, pointing at the television at the end of the bar. "There's a Bob Hope special on tonight. That's great. I love that guy. He played for my outfit when I was in Korea. Oh man, I'm gonna stick around for that."

Owen nodded politely. "I photographed him once," he admitted, knowing the reaction this piece of information would elicit.

143

"No kidding," Charley cried. "Didja really? When was that?"

"Oh, that was some years ago. When I worked for UPI in New York. They sent me off to some fund-raiser he was doing in Poughkeepsie. There were a lot of stars there, but he was the biggest."

"Oh yeah? What was he like?" Charley asked earnestly.

Knowing what his drinking companion wanted to hear, Charley obliged. "He seemed like a very nice man. A real gentleman."

"That's what I thought," said Charley, satisfied. "I guess you've taken pictures of a lot of important people."

"Important people, not so important people, more than I'd care to remember," Owen observed. "More than I'm able to remember." Then, for an instant, his thoughts flashed back to Maggie. A little pinpoint of recognition flashed in his brain, like a shooting star. Then it was gone again. Had he photographed her somewhere? The sensation left him with the vaguely troubling idea that it was important to remember.

"Hey, Owen," said Charley. "You want to play some cards before the show?"

Owen frowned into his beer glass.

"What about it?" Charley nudged him.

The bearded man looked up. After a pause he said, "Sure." He lifted his glass off the bar, and followed Charley over to a nearby table to join the game.

"Well, I think we got everything you need, Willy," said Jess, examining the contents of the paper bag by the light of the open car door. "Collar, leash, dog food, bowl. You're all set."

"Good thing the dry goods store was open late," Maggie said, cradling the puppy in her arms on the front seat. She slid out her side, and closed the door behind her. She walked around the car and started towards the porch steps where Jess had preceded her.

"Hey," he said, placing the paper bag on the porch and turning to face her. "Let's not go in yet. Now that it's cleared up, the sky is really beautiful. You want to take a walk?"

Maggie looked up. The stars were brilliant in the blue-black heavens, as if the rain had polished and wiped the skies clean. "It is beautiful," she said.

"Come on," said Jess, taking her elbow. "We can take Willy down by the stream back there. After all, he has to get to know his new home."

"It's so dark," Maggie protested.

Jess smiled. "I'll protect you," he said. "I won't let the bears get you."

"Are there bears?" she asked, backing away from him.

Jess laughed. "Oh brother," he said. "Take my hand."

Obediently, Maggie grasped his hand, and, holding the puppy in her other arm, followed his lead through the long grass of the field behind the house. In the moonlight, the field looked enchanted, waving soft and silver. They passed by the tangled branches of the crabapple trees and found themselves on the bank of the stream. Jess sat down on a large, flat stone, and motioned for Maggie to sit beside him. They could hear the water gurgling, not far from their feet. Maggie placed the puppy gently on the bank beside her and the dog began to stumble around, sniffing hesitantly at the rocks and shrubs on the bank.

"If I remember it right," said Jess, "there's an old root cellar down that way. Maybe Willy likes apples." He slipped his arm around Maggie's waist.

She kept her eyes trained on Willy's explorations.

"He likes it here. See?" Jess asked.

"Yes, he seems to," she said.

"Do you?"

Maggie nodded, but kept her eyes on the puppy. "I like it. But I have this funny feeling like we're not alone out here." She glanced over her shoulder into the darkness.

Jess laughed. "It's just the bears," he said.

"There are no bears," she informed him primly. She picked up a nearby twig and began poking it absently into the ground around her feet.

146

"That's true," he said, running his hand gently down her bent back. "It's just us."

The touch of his hand on her back sent a thrill through her body that made her shiver.

"Are you cold?" he asked softly. "I can fix that." He pulled her back and encircled her in his arms. He spoke into her hair as he held her. "Is that better?"

She felt swollen with desire for him, and at the same time plagued by a sense of uneasiness. "It's better," she said, "but . . ."

Jess lowered his head against her cheek. "But what?" he asked, reaching for her fingers and kneading them gently in his.

Maggie wondered if he could feel the pulse throbbing in her neck. "I told you," she said weakly. "Last night."

"Last night," he repeated, and then fell silent. He brought her fingers to his lips and kissed them. She watched his thoughtful face. She knew she was trembling, but she could not control it.

"After you left," he said, "I didn't know what to think. At first my pride was hurt, I guess. I thought maybe I should just do as you said. Stay away. But the more I thought about it the more I was sure that wasn't the answer. I could feel that you wanted me. I knew it. It's just that you seem to have some reservations about me . . ."

"Not about you," Maggie interrupted him, squeezing his hand.

147

"About what then?" Jess asked, as she pulled away from him.

Maggie sighed, and sat silently for a moment, unable to answer. Jess waited. Finally, she said. "About . . . myself. Jess, you don't know anything about me."

"Tell me," he said.

"No," she said, standing up and walking away from him. The puppy yelped happily as she came closer to it. "It's better just to leave it this way. Believe me."

"That doesn't make sense," he protested.

"Believe me," she pleaded with him.

Jess got to his feet slowly and walked over to where she stood, looking down at Willy. "The man you loved before," he said. "You told me he died."

"That's right," she whispered.

"Maybe you're afraid to try again," he said. "I don't know. But what happened before has nothing to do with us."

Maggie looked at him sadly, wishing she could tell the truth. Knowing that she couldn't.

"I want to ask you one question," he said. "And I want an honest answer."

"I'll try," she said, knowing she might have to lie.

"Do you want me?" he asked. "Do you want to make love with me?"

His question caught her off guard. She did not reply, but her eyes answered truthfully.

148

Jess put his arms around her and drew her to him. "All right then," he whispered. "Then what I think is that you have to trust me. You have to believe that I won't hurt you, or leave you. That nothing bad will happen." He began to kiss her on the neck.

The kiss pierced her. She was stirred, and feverish in his arms.

"Let me love you, Maggie," he said, as his lips moved to her mouth. "Let me."

She did not want to resist him. She wanted to believe him. It had been so long. His hands were moving over her body.

"You're so soft." She found his lips again. Still holding her with one arm, he bent down and picked up the puppy. Then they started back towards the house, stumbling through the grass, clutching each other.

When they reached the back door he opened it and put the puppy inside. Then he turned to her. "I want to make love to you," he said. "Come inside."

She kissed him in passionate agreement. A warning rang inside her, futilely, like a phone beneath a pillow. It will be all right, she told herself as the fears tried to surface. It's all different this time. It will be all right. Desperately, she embraced him.

Hidden by the darkness, flattened against a tree, Evy watched them go into the house.

In a while, she saw a dim light illuminated in the bedroom at the back of the house. She waited a few moments and then moved closer. Through the curtains she could see him kneeling over her, taking off her clothes, his naked back and buttocks to the window. She watched him bend over her, covering her with his body. Then Evy turned away.

Her pale eyes stared into the night, dull and expressionless. There was no mistaking what she had seen. No question now of what must be done.

She stood motionless, like a marble statue in the moonlight. The only movement in her passive face was a slight motion of her jaw. She ground her teeth together, as if she would turn them to powder. Inside her clenched fists, her ragged fingernails gouged purple welts into her palms.

With a last, lingering kiss, Maggie pulled away from Jess, and leaned back against the pillows of her bed. She turned her head and stared out the bedroom door towards the living-room, where Willy made the noises of a puppy dreaming. Jess drew himself up on one elbow and watched her pensive face. Finally, he touched her shoulder lightly. She turned around to face him.

"Anything wrong?"

"No," she said, smiling at him. "Everything's fine. I was just thinking."

"Thinking what?" he asked.

"Stupid things," she demurred. "You'd laugh."

"Bet I won't."

She regarded his face solemnly. There was tenderness in his eyes, as well as a hint of pride. He had pleased her, and he knew it. He was satisfied with himself, and with her, and with the world. His expression did not offend her. In fact, she wished she could just live for a while in that simple, perfect feeling. But it seemed as elusive as a fragrance, slipping away at the very moment that she breathed it in.

"I was just thinking," she sighed, "that for a minute there I felt so secure. You and I, here together, Willy sleeping out in the living-room. I felt . . . safe."

"You are," Jess exclaimed. "What are you talking about?"

"You see," she said ruefully. "You think it's strange."

"No," he said. But even as he shook his head, she knew he didn't understand. He didn't, but he accepted it. "I told you I was good for you," he said.

She arched herself up and held him fiercely for a moment. Then she sank back on the pillow, and he kissed her lightly.

"Hey, I'm hungry," he said. "Have you got anything to eat in this house?"

She gestured vaguely towards the kitchen.

151

"There's some cheese. Some bread. I don't know."

"Cookies?" he asked eagerly.

She laughed, and he kissed her again. "Hold that smile," he said. "I'll be right back."

Her eyes caressed him as she watched him go. But once he had left the room, she felt a chill come over her. She lay alone in the bed, remembering her last night with Roger. If they had not gone to that motel, it would never have happened. If they had not been driving along that lonely highway, on that snowy night, the killer would have found another victim. She remembered the days after Roger's murder in a kind of blur. Numbed by her loss, alone and friendless, she had accepted her arrest, almost embraced it, as her punishment. The one person she had really loved was dead. The only one who had ever believed in her since her father. Maggie flopped over on her stomach and held the pillow tightly to her. It was so dangerous, she thought. Loving someone. It frightened her. "Jess," she cried softly.

The bed dipped to one side. "What's the matter?" he asked, lying down beside her. "What is it, Maggie?"

She turned over and faced him tearfully. She swallowed hard before she spoke. "Did you eat?" she asked.

He smiled, relieved by the ordinary query. "I brought you an apple," he said.

She smiled wryly. "Keeps the doctor away."

"Keeps all those guys away. I want you all to myself." He embraced her gently. She curled up in his arms.

"I thought you were crying before," he said in a husky voice.

Maggie shook her head. "I never cry," she told him.

"Are you worried about something?" he asked.

She hesitated a moment, and then shook her head. "Do you know," she asked with a forced buoyancy, "how many years in purgatory we could get for this? Fornication is a very serious offence. It's probably about a thousand years."

Jess laughed, relieved. "Oh, is that it? Well, I just hope we can do our time together."

"Mmmmmm, maybe," she murmured distractedly.

"Hey," he said, grabbing her fingers and curling them under his own, "you don't mean that seriously, do you?"

"No," she said.

He looked at her thoughtfully. "I didn't know you're a Catholic."

"I'm not. Any more. I was brought up a Catholic, but I don't believe." Even as she uttered the blasphemy, the eyes of Sister Dolorita rose up unbidden in her mind, glittering black beads boring into her, the pasty face distorted with rage.

"So was I," he said. "I still believe."

There was a silence between them.

"But," he murmured soothingly, kissing her damp temples and arranging strands of her hair, "I don't think I'll go to hell for making love to you, if that's what you mean. No, I don't. This can't be wrong. How could it be?" he whispered.

He rolled towards her, and rested his head on her breast. She could feel all her senses stirring again. Desire was returning, impatient to sweep away all anxious thoughts, the fears whispering inside her. Perhaps, she thought, I'll think of some way to keep the truth about the past from him. There's no need for him to know, she rationalized. Not right away. The rising and falling of his breath accelerated with her own. She stroked his hair. Her body began to hum. She ran her fingers down the smooth skin of his back. Aroused by the awaited signal, he moved his mouth to hers. It's too late to stop it, she thought. It's already too late.

10

MAGGIE lay in her bed, in the darkness, listening. The only light in the room came from the bone-white cross that glowed on the wall opposite her bed. She was waiting for the familiar sound of his steps on the stairs. It was just the two of them, alone in the house. Her mother was not home. But she could not remember where she had gone. Maggie was waiting for her father to come and tuck her in. As he always did.

Then, she heard him coming. But she felt a vague sense that something was not right. His tread was heavy on the stairs. He pushed her door open and stood in the doorway, looking at her. For a moment she felt scared. But she didn't know why. He knelt sadly beside her bed. "No story," he breathed in the darkness, ignoring her whispered pleas. She was surprised. He never could resist her childish requests. She fell silent. She was aware of their breathing, hers quick and light, his heavy and shuddering. He kissed her cheek, and then he put his face on her chest. She could not see him clearly in the darkness. She grabbed at his red curls, and twisted them. He did not push her hand away. Instead, he

155

climbed up on her bed, and lay in the dark beside her.

She felt a tiny surge of fear, but mainly she was happy. He had never done that before. His breath came in sad sighs now. He put his hand on her leg, beneath her nightgown and stroked it gently. "Oh, my little girl," he said. Then he let out a sob.

"Don't cry, Daddy," she told him. She began to pepper his face with kisses.

Suddenly, something she did not understand began to happen. His hands began to move over her, his weight felt as if he were going to crush her. He guided her hand with his own. She squirmed, and whimpered a little, but at the same time she felt a giddy delight. He was calling her name, kissing her. She looked up. Beyond his vast shoulder, the cross pierced the darkness, and she could see nothing else. From downstairs, like a rifle shot, the front door slammed.

He jerked himself free of her little arms. By the light of the glowing cross she could see the naked terror on his face. There were footsteps on the stairs.

"Oh, my God," he whispered, fumbling with the buttons of his shirt.

"Daddy," she was wailing now.

Ignoring her, he bolted from her bed, stuffing his shirt in his pants with trembling hands and zippering them up. He smoothed down his curls with his hands and threw open the door of the room. Weeping and rubbing her eyes, she trailed behind him, pulling down her nightgown. Through the balustrade she saw them. Her mother, standing on the stairs, staring into her father's florid, guilty face. On the step below her stood Sister Dolorita.

Her mother's face was a frozen mask as she stared at her father.

Maggie looked from her mother's face, to the awful face of Sister Dolorita. She did not want to look. But her eyes felt as if they were being drawn by a magnet to the blazing black eyes.

"No," she cried out. "No, please."

"Maggie, wake up!"

Struggling to the surface of consciousness, she saw Jess leaning over her, holding her wrists, and frowning with deep concern.

She relaxed in his grasp, and fell back, tossing her head from side to side on the pillow. Jess let go of her wrists. Her heart was pounding madly in her chest. She could feel the tears running down her face.

"You almost gave me a shiner," he said pointing to her clenched fists. "What was the dream?"

For a moment she stared at him, uncomprehendingly. She could not remember what she was doing there with him, so disconcerting was the dream.

"Don't you want to tell me?" he asked.

"Tell you what?"

"The dream."

"Oh, God." She stared off to one side. Outside the rays of the morning sun were shining weakly through the window. She wiped the dribbling tears away with her fingers.

"I thought you didn't cry," he said, sitting up against the headboard of the bed.

"It was about my father," she said.

He did not say anything in response. She lay there, thinking about the dream. She felt as if the dream was forcing its way out of her, as if she had no will to control it. That she finally had to tell someone about it. She began to speak. "I was a child again in the dream. And he came up to my bedroom. To tuck me in. He just meant to say good night to me. But instead, something happened . . ."

The room was silent. Jess watched her without speaking.

"Instead, he got into bed with me. He began to do things to me. Things he shouldn't have . . ."

"Sexual things," Jess said quietly.

Gratefully she accepted the words which he had supplied. She would not have been able to say it. "Yes. My mother came home. My mother and Sister Dolorita, one of the nuns from the church. They could tell what had happened."

158

Maggie's voice was flat, deadened by the memory.

For a while, Jess did not speak. When he did his voice was low. "That really happened, didn't it." It was a statement.

Maggie could not look at his face. "They didn't actually catch us," she said. "But they knew."

"I see," he said. Then, after a brief silence, he spoke again. Her face, rigid with tension, was still turned away from him. "What a terrible burden," he said.

The lack of judgement in his voice shocked her. She turned to face him. He gazed at her sympathetically. All at once, she felt anxious to explain.

"He didn't want to hurt me," she said. "He really didn't. I know that. But it was terrible anyway. The way my mother would look at me. And Sister Dolorita. They blamed me. Then he had his heart attack not long after that. I was left alone with them."

"You must have been relieved though, in a way," he said. "What an impossible situation for a child to be in."

"I don't know," she said miserably. "I guess so. But it wasn't any better afterwards. They never forgave me."

"And you missed him," Jess said quietly.

Maggie sat up and stared him in the eye. "Yes. Yes, I did. I know what he did was wrong. But

159

he loved me. He was the only one who did. I did miss him. Does that sound sick to you? Could you ever understand that?"

Jess nodded, and put one hand over hers.

She hung her head. "I didn't want him to die."

"Of course not," he said simply. He drew her to him.

They sat quietly for a moment. She shivered in his arms. Finally, she spoke. "Thank you," she said.

"For what?" he asked.

"For letting me tell you that. For making it possible to say it."

"I'm glad you told me. Actually, it helps me to understand something. About you."

She pulled out of his arms and looked at him in surprise. "What about me?"

"Well," he said. "Why you've been so reluctant. Why this has all been so difficult for you. I mean, you don't have to be Dr. Freud to figure out that sex is kind of a loaded issue for you. After an experience like that, you must have felt a lot of guilt."

Maggie looked away from him, thinking of all that he didn't know. "I suppose," she said.

"Listen Maggie," he said. "You should know that you can tell me anything. Really. Anything at all. You don't need to be afraid of what I'll think."

She looked into his eyes. He gazed back with

a grave sincerity. For a moment, she was tempted. He knew she had secrets. But he didn't judge her. Maybe she could just tell him about Roger, and the prison, and all of it. Maybe he would understand that too. He wouldn't flinch. Then she looked away. It was impossible. It was too much to expect. "That's good to know," she said.

Sensing that she had been on the verge of an admission and then stopped, Jess frowned briefly. "Well," he said, getting up from the bed, and tossing her bathrobe over to Maggie. "We'd better get ready to go."

She watched him as he headed out the bedroom door to the bathroom. She knew he was vaguely hurt, but she had to keep silent. It was for his own good.

Evy trudged up the cellar stairs, and put the latch on the door behind her. She turned, and started at the sight of her grandmother, seated in her wheelchair a few feet from the door.

"What are you looking at?" she yelled crossly at the old woman. "Get away from here."

She walked over behind the chair and began to push it towards the kitchen. The old woman's bruised hand rested limply on the arm of her wheel chair as her granddaughter pushed.

Evy brought the chair to a halt beside the sink, and lifted the tray off the arms of the chair. She removed the plate and began to scrape the lumpy mass of creamed corn and runny eggs into the garbage can. "What's the matter with the food now?" Evy demanded. "All right," she said. "Have it your own way. If you don't like the food, you can go hungry." She tossed the plate into the sink where it landed with a clatter. Then she turned back to the old woman. "Where's it going to be today? The bed or the chair? The chair, I think." She pushed the chair over by the kitchen window, and locked it.

Then she wiped off her grandmother's face with a dishrag and gave the bent shoulder a perfunctory pat. "I have a busy day today," she said, as she walked to the hall closet and pulled out her coat. "I doubt I'll be back for lunch. I told you you should have eaten your breakfast." She slammed the closet door, and began buttoning her jacket.

"I have a little invitation to extend today. I'm planning a surprise, you might say. For you know who." Evy opened the refrigerator door and pulled out her lunch bag. "So you just stay there. I'll see you when I feel like coming home."

With that the girl opened the door and walked out. She went over to her car which was sitting in the driveway. The gravel crunched beneath her feet. She slid into the front seat and put her lunch on the seat beside her. Then she turned on the ignition and began to back down the driveway.

Inside the house, the old woman watched her granddaughter disappearing down Barrington Street. Then the road was empty. It remained that way, except for the rare passage of a whizzing car.

The old house was quiet now that Evy was gone. The clock above the stove ticked, and there was the hum of the refrigerator turning on and off. For a while it was just those sounds.

Then it started again. The faint, almost inaudible moaning that came, intermittently, from the direction of the basement. Each time it came, the old woman in the chair shuddered uncontrollably. In between the moans were long silences. Lulls. As if it would not start again. And then it would begin anew, anguished and inchoate, reaching her ears which she could not cover.

She stared out at the road for a long time, as if she were watching for someone to come. Her head rested, immobile, against the pane. Her eyes were so deep and lifeless that they looked like empty sockets in her skull-like head.

"You go in. I'll be right along," said Maggie, sorting through the contents of her pocketbook with exaggerated curiosity.

"Did you lose something?" Jess asked, making no move to get out of the parked automobile.

"I had a comb in here. I just wanted to fix my hair," she explained, not meeting his gaze.

"You look fine," he said gently. "Come on."

"It won't take me long," she insisted. "You go ahead."

"Maggie."

She raised her eyes ingenuously to his.

"Sooner or later they're going to know," he said.

She chewed on her lower lip. "I'm aware of that," she said. A frown creased her forehead. "I just don't think we should flaunt it by showing up together at work."

"Is it my fault that heap of yours wouldn't start?" he protested. "Come on now. We're adults. We don't have to sneak in different doorways."

He was right of course. He had tried patiently, repeatedly, to coax the old Buick engine into turning over, while she stood in the driveway, watching with a sinking heart. The engine made grinding noises and refused to leap. Finally, Jess went into the house to call the Shell station, while Maggie stared under the hood. She slammed it down as hard as she could, and kicked the front tyre. The car sat, useless as a lump of wet coal, in the driveway.

Jess got out and came around the car to open her door. "Let's go," he ordered, holding out a hand to her. "You'll be late."

"Good morning Evy, Grace." Jess waved jauntily to the two women and continued down the hall to his office.

Grace glanced up at Maggie as she entered the room.

"My car broke down," Maggie explained. "He had to give me a ride." Grace grunted, and returned to the newspaper which she was clipping.

Maggie's face flamed as she took her seat. She wished she had not made an excuse. It was none of their business anyway. She looked over at Evy who continued to sharpen the bunch of pencils which she held in her hand. More lies, Maggie thought, and shook her head.

"There's a bunch of stuff on your desk needs filing," Grace announced. "This morning."

"I've got that story on Ben McGuffey to do. I guess I can do it after lunch," said Maggie.

"I don't care when you do that," said Grace. "Just clean up that filing. That's your job. Your little story can wait."

Maggie resisted the temptation to salute her, and picked up the piles of clippings and pictures. With a glance at Evy, who continued sharpening the pencils without looking up, Maggie retreated to the file room down the hall. It was a narrow room, filled with cabinets and shelves of newspapers. Maggie had decided that it must have been the pantry in this house at one time. It was obvious from the fixtures that the art room on the other side had been the kitchen.

Maggie settled herself behind the desk and placed the piles of photographs on top of it. She knew that Grace meant to punish her, but in truth she was glad to be alone.

At noontime, the file room door opened and Evy looked in. Maggie was seated behind a counter, a sandwich in one hand, perusing an old copy of the newspaper.

"'Scuse me," the girl murmured, and started to back out.

"No, no, please come in," Maggie urged her, putting the paper aside. "Don't rush off because of me."

Evy shrugged, and came in, closing the door behind her. She was wearing her jacket and carrying her lunch bag. Her pale skin was mottled from the cold.

"How is it out?" Maggie asked her.

"Cold. I wasn't out for long. I just had an errand to do."

"Why don't you join me?" Maggie said, indicating Evy's lunch bag.

Evy sat down on a stool, and laid the jacket across her lap. Then she took out her sandwich and slowly unwrapped it on the counter. She took a bite, her eyes focused on a point on the table just to the right of Maggie's elbow. A silence fell between them. Maggie blushed at the memory of their encounter the day before and the image of herself, waving a poker at the girl.

"Evy . . ."

"You know . . ." They both spoke at once.

"What?" asked Evy.

"No, go ahead," Maggie demurred.

"It was nothing," the girl insisted.

Maggie cleared her throat. "I was just thinking about yesterday. At my house. I was wondering if you were still angry with me. I'm so sorry that happened . . ."

"You already apologized for that," the girl observed.

"So I did," Maggie sighed. "I've just . . . just been so edgy."

"Forget it," said Evy. "It doesn't matter."

"Thanks."

"You still have more to file back here?" Evy asked.

"Just a few things," Maggie said, although she had finished her filing an hour before. She had been scouring the files with a kind of morbid curiosity, looking for any evidence of her own sordid story, just moments before the girl had arrived. She had found nothing. "These archives are quite impressive," she said. "Where do you get all these clips?"

Evy's eyes scanned the room impassively. "We get a lot of different papers. And services send us clips. Grace and I try to keep up to date on them, but we get behind a lot. There's so much else to do."

"Well, it's interesting," said Maggie.

"You can find out a lot of interesting things, if you have the time to read them."

167

"I'm sure you can," Maggie replied. A long silence fell between them. Evy took a last bite of her sandwich and brushed the crumbs off her fingers. Then she spoke casually.

"You going to the fair on Sunday?"

Maggie raised her eyebrows. "I don't know. I hadn't thought about it."

"It's a lot of fun," said Evy. "Last thing we do before winter sets in. Over at the grammar school. They have tents, and there are rides and contests and stuff."

"Sounds nice," said Maggie listlessly. "It's probably great for the kids."

"Everybody likes it," Evy assured her.

"Well, maybe," said Maggie. "I'd probably feel funny. I don't really know anybody."

"You don't need to know people," Evy protested.

"I don't know," said Maggie. "I guess I'm just feeling a little shy."

"You could always help out," said Evy. "That would be one way of getting to know people."

Maggie watched the girl as she ate a cookie which she had fished out of her bag, wiping her mouth methodically and thoroughly chewing every bit. Maggie doubted that the fair was fun for the girl, despite what she said. She could not imagine Evy having fun. Still, she felt a sudden warmth towards the colourless girl for her suggestion.

"What sort of help do they need?" Maggie asked gently.

"Well," said Evy, "I'm working in the bakery stall. They can always use baked goods."

"I guess I could bake a pie or something," Maggie offered.

"You can help me sell in the afternoon," Evy said.

Maggie smiled at her. "That sounds like a good idea. I think I'd enjoy that. Thanks."

"That's all right," said Evy. "Well, I guess I'll get back," she said, throwing her lunch bag into a bin under the counter. "I'll see you later."

"I'll be out soon," Maggie agreed.

Satisfied, Evy picked up her jacket and gave Maggie a wave as she left.

A few hours later, Evy stepped through the door to Jess's office and gently closed it behind her. She stared fixedly at Jess, who was running his hand absently through his hair as he scribbled on a sheet of paper. He looked up to see her standing there.

"Hey, I didn't hear you come in."

She kept her eyes fastened to his face. "Grace said you wanted to see me."

Jess motioned towards the chair by his desk. "Well, don't look so alarmed. I just wanted to talk to you."

Evy stood beside the chair. "I thought I must have done something wrong."

Jess smiled at her. "You're a real worry wart sometimes, you know it?" he teased her gently.

A pleased smile tugged at the corners of Evy's mouth. She dropped into the chair.

"Actually," he said, "I called you in here to compliment you."

"You did?" Evy raised her eyes to his. Their cool blueness had dissolved into a smoky grey haze.

Jess nodded.

She smiled at him. "I knew you weren't mad at me."

"Mad at you? My dear young woman," said Jess, with a briskness that made Evy giggle. "On the contrary, I am your servant."

"You are?" Evy asked, trying to stifle her giggle by putting her fist in front of her mouth.

"I certainly am," he said sternly, and then directed a menacing glower at her which made her laugh more uncontrollably.

"Get a hold of yourself, girl," he ordered, as tears of laughter gathered in her eyes. He extricated his handkerchief from his pocket and waved it at her. "Here you go," he said. "You're awfully silly today."

"I'm sorry," Evy gasped. "I don't know what was so funny."

Jess grinned, and accepted the balled-up cotton square back from her. "It's good to see you laugh. Sometimes you seem so worried."

After a pause he spoke gently. "How's Grandma?"

Evy shrugged, and lowered her eyes. "She's okay."

"Listen, Evy, if I can ever help you out in that department, I want you to let me know, okay?"

"Okay," she said softly.

"Like I said I owe you one."

"No, you don't."

"Well, yes I do," Jess insisted. "I heard from Maggie how nice you were to her today. How you invited her to help out with the fair and all."

"Was that what you meant?" the girl asked, stricken.

"Well," Jess floundered, seeing her disappointment, "I think it's a wonderful thing to help someone out when they need you. I've always known that you were that kind of person. Now Maggie's new here, and she's had a hard time adjusting. I just wanted you to know that I think you did a very kind thing."

"Thank you," said Evy flatly, the joy vanished from her face and voice.

Jess bit his lip and waited a moment before he spoke. Finally he said, "Did I say something wrong?"

Evy stared at him, wounded but defiant. "I don't know why you like her so much," she said. "You don't really know her. There's something wrong with her. Anyone can see that."

171

Jess frowned as he answered her. "Evy, I had kind of thought, after what Maggie told me today, that you two might be becoming better friends. I mean, the way you helped her, and tried to bring her in on the fair and all. I just assumed . . ."

The girl looked at him steadily. Behind her eyes Jess could see her furiously debating what she wanted to say. When at last she spoke, her voice was harsh. "I didn't do it for her. I did it for you," she said.

The girl's words stung and surprised him, but he tried to mask his uneasiness. "I see," he said.

When he looked up at Evy he could see that she was pale, as if horrified by her own words.

"Evy," he said gently. "Whatever your reasons, it was a nice thing to do anyway. I hope," he added lamely, "one of these days you two will become friends."

Evy nodded dumbly. "Can I go now?" she asked.

"Sure, of course." Jess watched silently as the girl got up and left his office. Then he leaned back in his chair and looked out the window. The day's end was upon him suddenly. Unnoticed, unobserved, the afternoon light had vanished, and the town was darkening unexpectedly, like a Kansas pirate, when out of nowhere, a twister appeared on the horizon and loomed over the land. Jess knew what it meant. It meant that the winter was coming, when the darkness

172

sneaked up on you like that. Still frowning, he slipped on the sweater hanging behind his chair. He felt chilly and unprepared.

11

IN honour of the Harvest Fair, the red brick façade of the Heron's Neck Elementary School was temporarily divested of its sober, academic aspect. A jauntily-lettered banner announcing the Fair hung suspended between two far-flung classroom windows. At one of the flat, tree-studded lawns, a green and white striped tent billowed in the autumn breeze. Under the canvas peaks of the tent, tables from the children's dining-hall were lined up and festooned with crêpe paper. The table tops were scarcely visible beneath the colourful collections of chipped china, potted plants, piles of books and used clothes. Several women clustered around each cache of goods, sorting and arranging, and consulting one another about the visual appeal of the displays they settled on.

Children on bicycles wheeled through the congested parking lot beside the school, while a group of older men in checked lumbermen's jackets surveyed the scene from their folding chairs at the lawn's edge. The fineness of the day was the observation most frequently exchanged. Wives supervised their aproned husbands in the preparation of steamer clams and cauldrons of lobsters while they shucked the last good ears of the late corn for the boiling pots.

A small Ferris wheel and several games of chance were set apart on the field-like lawn, operated by a group of swarthy strangers who had arrived on the morning ferry as they did each year. The teen-aged girls giggled flirtatiously as they loitered nearby, but the men only flashed polite smiles, and kept their distance. By sundown they would be packed up and gone again, their metal wheel dismantled despite the dismayed protests of the children—the same children who now screamed in terror at its climb.

Holding her pie plate aloft, Maggie threaded her way through the noisy crowd. Children with their faces painted like goblins darted past her, shrieking at one another. Some of the people whom she passed looked familiar to her, although they did not acknowledge her when they accidentally caught her glance.

The spirited bustle of the fair made her feel lonely. Jess had left the house early, to help set up the firemen's booth, while she set about baking her pie. It had taken longer to brown than the recipe indicated, and Maggie wondered now how it had turned out. She longed for the sight of a friendly face, and she looked about for Jess, or even Evy. A group of glass vases and china tableware under the tent top caught her eye as she passed by. Maggie stepped over the supporting rope and began to sort through the collection of ancient knicknacks with her free hand. As she shifted her pie from her hand to the corner of the table, she felt all at once that she was being observed. Maggie looked up and saw Tom Croddick, peering at her suspiciously. The shopkeeper turned his back on her. Maggie replaced the teacup she was holding on the table and quickly escaped from the shadow of the tent.

She did not know in which direction to turn as she stood in the sunlight, blinking to adjust her eyes. Hazarding a guess, she walked towards the parking lot. Almost immediately she spotted the sign for baked goods. Maggie clutched her pie resolutely, and headed in the direction of the banner. As she got closer she could see the table, covered in a faded blue tablecloth. The trays and tins of cakes, biscuits and buns were wrapped in plastic and aluminium. Above the table the sign floated, held aloft by two tomato sticks which had been nailed to the back of the table. Evy stood behind the display, arranging the baked goods the way she arranged her desk at work. The sight of her was oddly reassuring. Maggie smiled with relief as she approached the booth.

"Hi there," she said.

Evy started slightly, and then greeted her with a broad smile. "Hi," she said. Evy was not alone at the booth. Behind her a woman was bending over, writing prices on a note pad.

"I made a pie," said Maggie, holding out the results of her morning in the kitchen.

"Good," said Evy. "Just put it down on the table. Wherever it'll fit."

Maggie coughed uneasily and watched Evy resume her methodical ordering of goodies. "How's it going?" she asked.

"Pretty good," said the girl, indicating a metal cash box filled with change.

"Actually," Maggie spoke up, "I came by now because you said you might need some help."

"Oh," said Evy.

"Do you still?" Maggie asked, fearing a dismissal.

"Yes. Sure." She gestured for Maggie to come around behind the table. Relieved, Maggie quickly complied. "Alice," said Evy, addressing the woman behind her who was busily stacking cookies on a plate. "Why don't you take a break? I've got some help here now."

The woman straightened up and rubbed her back with a grimace. "I could use a break," she admitted. "Thanks." She addressed her smile to Maggie.

Nonplussed, Maggie smiled back. "You're welcome," she said.

"This is Maggie Fraser," said Evy. "She works at the paper."

"Nice to meet you," said the chunky woman pleasantly, as she untied her apron and handed it to Maggie. "I'm Alice Murphy. Here, you better wear this."

Maggie donned the apron, as Alice departed

her post to plunge into the festivities. Maggie looked around at the piles of confections and spoke to Evy. "What shall I do?" she asked.

"Finish fixing those biscuits, and then you can make price tags. Alice has the list on that pad." Obediently Maggie knelt down and set about her task, while Evy waited on the people who approached the booth. For the most part, Maggie kept to her work. Evy's conversation with the customers flowed comfortably over her bent shoulders. She paid little attention to what was said, until her attention was caught by a familiar voice. She looked up and saw Jess chatting amiably with Evy.

"Which one of these is yours?" he asked the girl, eyeing the array of baked goods.

Evy hesitated, and then pointed to a mound of chewy-looking bars on a plate. "I made the apricot bars," she admitted.

"Let me try one," said Jess, putting a quarter down beside the plate. Evy handed him a bar wrapped in a napkin.

"Mmmmm . . . They're wonderful," he told her. "Apricot's my favourite."

Evy's shy smile and awkward stance betrayed her pleasure. "You really like them?" she asked.

"They're great," he assured her.

Maggie straightened up from behind the table and smiled at him. "Hi," she said.

"Hey, I didn't even see you there," he said. "How ya doing?"

178

Evy's face tightened as Maggie returned his smile, and nodded.

"Hey, Maggie, you should try one of these. They're great," he told her, indicating the apricot bars.

"I couldn't," Maggie groaned. "I've been sampling the cookies. They look delicious," she said to Evy.

The girl shrugged off the compliment, looking away from her.

"Well, I'll buy a couple and we can have them for dessert tonight," said Jess, putting a dollar down beside the plate. And then without thinking, "Or breakfast even."

Evy stiffened as if she had been slapped at Jess's remark. Maggie felt her own face begin to burn. The awkward camaraderie between her and Evy seemed to have vanished.

"I've got to get back to the firemen's booth," said Jess. "I'll see you girls later."

"I've finished those prices," said Maggie. "What do you want me to do now?"

"I don't know," said Evy coldly.

Just then Grace came waddling up to the bakery booth, breaking the silence between them with her greeting.

"How's business?" she said to Evy.

"Okay," said Evy.

"Bobby make her lemon soup this year?"

Evy laughed thinly. Grace launched into a retelling of the story of an ill-fated lemon

179

meringue pie filling which had not set, and which swamped the pie plate every time a slice was cut. "She'll never live that down," Grace concluded about the unfortunate baker.

Maggie forced a smile, but was acutely conscious that Evy was ignoring her. She shifted her weight from foot to foot, feeling excluded from the conversation.

"Oh, look who's coming," Grace cried.

Maggie followed Grace's pointing finger. She saw Sadie Wilson approaching the table, holding the hands of two boys, one dark and one fair-haired.

"These two belong to anybody here?" Sadie joked, stopping in front of Grace.

Grace put a protective hand on each of their shoulders. "What have they been up to?" she asked.

"No good," said Sadie with a laugh as she turned to go. "They were looking for ya."

"What's the rush," Grace asked her friend. "Have some cake."

"Ned's selling squash out of the truck. I gotta help him," Sadie explained as she started off into the crowd.

"Hi, Mom," said the older, blond-haired boy.

"Hi," echoed the younger.

Grace turned to Maggie. "These are my big boys," she announced proudly. "This is Raymond," she said, pointing to the larger, blond-haired boy. "And this is Martin."

Maggie stared down at the two children before her. For a moment she squinted, struggling to place them. Then it came back to her. The children on the dock. The boys who were tormenting the turtle. She looked again in amazement at their innocent faces.

"This is Miss Fraser," Grace informed them. "Say hello," she prodded.

Maggie forced a smile. She ran a hand nervously over the mounds of baked goods. "You boys hungry? You want something?"

"Never mind that," Grace said sharply, hoping too late to douse the eager lights in their eyes.

"Sorry," said Maggie. "I just thought . . ."

"Maggie baked a pie," Evy offered.

"We want a pie," the younger, Martin, began to whine.

"What kind of pie?" Grace asked curiously.

"Apple," said Maggie.

"I want an apple pie," cried the boy and tugged on Grace's sleeve.

Grace rolled her eyeballs and sighed. "You two won't want a thing for dinner."

Maggie wiped her hands nervously on her apron and then lifted up the server to cut into her pie. She remembered the story of the lemon soup, and fervently hoped that her filling held together. Carefully she lifted the two slices out on to paper plates.

"They need forks," said Evy, nodding towards

a box of plastic utensils under the adjoining table.

Grace fumbled in her purse and came up with two quarters. "These kids never eat dinner anyway the night of the fair," she said with a shrug, as Maggie searched under the counter for the forks. "They're always full up on junk," Grace continued.

Thanks, Maggie thought ruefully as she pawed through the box under the table. She located the forks under a pile of paper bags and brought out two of them. She stood up and placed them unsteadily on the fluted edges of the plates. Then she pushed the plates towards Raymond and Martin. The two boys grabbed them, and began to shove forkfuls of the pie into their mouths.

Grace examined the other items on the table. "I'd love to have some of this," she said to Evy, "but Charley says I'm getting a spare tyre."

"Sponge cake's not fattening," said Evy.

"I don't know," said Grace. "Whose is it?"

"Carla's."

Maggie's attention wandered, and her eyes drifted back to the boys, who were noisily chewing on her pie. Suddenly, as she watched, the younger, Martin's face assumed a curiously disturbed expression. He brought his hand up hesitantly towards his mouth. Just then, the older boy started, and let out a guttural noise.

"What's the matter?" asked Grace, turning to them.

Maggie looked at Martin's face. The little face was pale, his large eyes staring up fearfully. His mouth worked automatically, like a machine which he couldn't stop. As Maggie watched in horror, a little speck of foamy blood appeared under his lower lip. At the same instant, a gash seemed to open spontaneously in his tender lower lip, and a rivulet of blood began to seep down the shiny chin.

Grace shrieked, and ran to the boy. Maggie's eye darted to Raymond, who had dropped his blood-spattered plate, and was bringing his hands up to his own face. He parted his lips, and she could see the blood, outlining his teeth in scarlet. Slowly it began to stream out of each corner of his mouth.

"Martin," Grace cried.

"Raymond too," screamed Alice Murphy who had materialized out of the crowd that was gathering.

"Spit it out," Grace screamed at her son. "Don't swallow it." Forcibly she opened the child's mouth with her fingers. The pulpy mass of apples and pastry was stained through with blood. Grace reached in and scraped out what she could with her fingers. The curly-headed child began to gag violently.

A man in a flannel shirt had Raymond pressed up against his knee, and was thumping on his back. "Spit it out," he commanded. "Whatever it is, boy, get rid of it." The older child's eyes seemed to bug out of his head, as he spat out the pie filling, and then began to vomit.

Grace clutched her youngest's pale, sweaty forehead through to her breast, and tried to shake the offending apples congealed in blood off her fingers. As she rubbed her fingers she cried out, and then looked closer.

"Glass," she whispered. She looked up slowly at Maggie who had watched the scene from where she stood, rooted to the ground behind the table. "There's glass in this pie," she muttered, her eyes widening first in horror, and then in a gathering fury.

The man in the flannel shirt lifted Raymond up in his arms and spoke sharply to Grace, and the people in the crowd who were watching help-lessly. "We've got to take these boys to the hospital. Somebody help Gracie there with Martin."

Urgent hands pried the swooning child free from his mother's vice-like grasp, and helped the woman to her feet. "Come on, Grace," said Evy, who had joined the group surrounding her.

Grace looked at Maggie in uncomprehending, unspeakable fury. "Come along with your boys," insisted Alice Martin soothingly.

Grace tore her wrath-filled eyes away from Maggie's. "Martin," she cried out plaintively. "Raymond."

A tide of people bore the mother away, close

behind the men who were hurrying towards a nearby station wagon, carrying her sons.

Pale and stiff, Maggie watched as the commotion obscured the injured boys. Her head felt light and dizzy. Slowly she noticed that several of the people who remained had turned on her and were directing at her menacing glances.

"What kind of a monster would put glass in a pie," cried a woman with frizzled hair, glaring at Maggie.

Maggie brought her hand to her chest, as if to shield her heart from their penetrating stares.

"I don't know," Maggie murmured.

The frizzled blonde jabbed a finger near Maggie's face. "You made that pie. I heard you telling them."

Maggie shook her head in dumb protest, as more people in the crowd turned to look at her.

"Didn't you make it?" the woman demanded.

A party of people were shepherding Grace and her injured boys towards a waiting car. Maggie watched their movement as if she were a statue, with a living brain. She struggled to make her mouth work. Sweat beaded on her upper lip, and at her hairline.

"Didn't you?" shrieked the woman.

Among the people in the crowd, Maggie's eyes suddenly focused on Evy, who stood to the side of the people hovering over the boys. Evy seemed to sense that she was being watched, and she looked up. She returned the stare for a moment and then turned her back. In that moment Maggie discerned a flicker of scorn in her eye that galvanized her.

Maggie's hand shot out in front of her like a bayonet. She poked at the red-faced woman who was blocking her path and shoved her away. A hand reached out for her but she shook it off. Eyes blazing, Maggie advanced on the knot of people who were arranging the boys in the back seat of the car. Peripherally, she could see a weeping Grace being forced into the front seat, and the door slamming. Maggie trained her eyes on Evy, and strode towards her. She could hear shouts coming from behind her, but she could not make out the words through the pounding in her ears.

A hail of dirt and gravel shot out behind the tyres as the car started, and shot away from the kerb. The bystanders watched it go, distress etched in their faces. Evy turned and saw Maggie barrelling towards her, wild-eyed. Quickly she pivoted, and began to hurry away from the approaching woman.

Maggie broke into a run and overtook the girl. She grabbed Evy's thin upper arm with a force that jerked the girl back to a position where they were facing each other.

"Let go of me," Evy insisted, avoiding Maggie's maddened stare.

"You did this," Maggie cried out hoarsely, tightening her grip on Evy's arm.

Evy's eyes widened. Her pale skin was like tissue paper, and a blue vein throbbed in her forehead. Fear rose like a vapour in her eyes. "You're crazy," she said.

Maggie shook the girl, grabbing her other arm and drawing her face up close to her own infuriated visage. "Don't play the innocent with me. You told me to bake that pie. Then you put something in it. You wanted to get back at me because of Jess. Because you're jealous. Admit it. I won't let you go until you do."

Evy squirmed to free herself from Maggie's grip, but the older woman only shook her harder. The stunned silence of the bystanders who had heard Maggie's shouted accusations began to dissolve into an angry buzz. "Let her alone," one man called out.

Evy's head lolled back and forth as Maggie shook her. "Tell them. Tell them what you did. I'm not letting go until you tell them." The girl suddenly went limp in Maggie's grasp. Maggie gave Evy's unresisting form one last jerk, and then stared, still clutching her arms, into Evy's pale eyes. For a moment their eyes met, Maggie's furious, Evy's vague and stunned. Then, as Maggie watched, the girl's blue irises rolled back, and the lids came down to almost cover them. A thin, crimson drop appeared in

187

Evy's left nostril, and then a trickle of blood began trailing down her upper lip.

Maggie released her immediately, as if her flesh burned, and the girl slumped over. Another stream of blood, scarlet against her white skin, rolled from Evy's right nostril.

"Somebody help her."

Maggie jumped back as two men came forward, and put their arms around the fainting girl. Maggie trembled uncontrollably.

"She'll be okay. It's a nosebleed," said one of the men who held Evy. "Okay, Evy?"

Maggie watched as Jess supported the frail girl and tried to cajole a sign of understanding from her. She could feel the angry eyes which bored into her from every direction.

"I didn't mean to," Maggie whispered. "I just . . ."

"Why'd you grab her like that," the woman with the blonde frizzy hair began castigating her. "She didn't do anything to you."

"It wasn't my fault," Maggie said. "I didn't want to hurt her . . ." Her voice became a cry, choked by the tears she was swallowing.

Jess looked up at her for a moment.

"Tell them I didn't do it, Jess," she pleaded.

The sadness and confusion in his eyes undid her. He shook his head helplessly and turned back to Evy.

Maggie wheeled around and began to push through the crowd. A few people reached out to

188

restrain her, but she shook herself free of their grasp. She began to run, tripping and staggering away from the circle around Evy.

"You're sick," a woman called out angrily, as Maggie staggered away. The sound of the voice reached her, but the words were blurred, and held no meaning for her as she ran.

12

JESS opened the passenger door of his car and looked in worriedly at the girl who rested limply there, her head angled back against the top of the seat. "We're home," he said softly.

Evy's bluish, translucent eyelids fluttered, and she gazed up silently at him.

"You think you can make it?"

Evy nodded, and swung her legs out on to the gravel in the driveway. Jess offered her his arm, and Evy stood up. She took a few tentative steps, and then they slowly began to make their way towards the back door of her grandmother's house. They had gone about fifteen feet when the girl's knees buckled, and she sagged against Jess, who was holding her arm.

"I've got you," Jess breathed. Slipping an arm behind her knees, and another under her back, he lifted her up and began to carry her across the high brown grass of the untended lawn. Evy's head drooped against his shoulder, and she clasped him tightly as he steered them towards the house.

"You're light," he said in mild astonishment, as he easily took the back steps and opened the door with the use of one free finger and his foot.

"I'm too skinny," she stated sadly.

Jess smiled at her. "You're just right," he said, entering the kitchen. "Where's Grandma?"

"Back in her room, probably. In bed."

"Well, let's get you to bed, and then I'll talk to her," he said.

"To the left and up the stairs," said Evy, pointing to the kitchen door. "I can walk if you want."

"No," said Jess, shifting her weight slightly in his arms. "I'll take you up."

Jess carried the girl through the gloomy living-room, which was crowded with heavy mahogany furniture, and a faded, stuffed sofa and chairs. The house smelled spoiled and musty to Jess, but he tried not to wrinkle his nose, for fear that the girl would be hurt by his show of distaste.

Evy seemed to sense his thoughts. "I guess I should open a window in here. It's just that Grandma gets a chill so easily."

"It's fine," Jess assured her. He began to climb the stairs towards Evy's room.

"Over there," she pointed, as they reached the top step. In the dark hall, Jess could see the open door slightly ajar to which she pointed. He pushed it open further with his foot, and carried her in. He tried to conceal his surprise at the sight of the room, which was that of a much younger girl, complete with a doll, perched on a nearby skirted chair. As he set Evy down gently

191

on the quilted bedspread and sat down beside her, he felt protective of the girl, like a parent, carrying a child to a sickroom. He arranged the pillow beneath her head, and then looked down at her wan face.

"Just like a bride," Evy said thoughtfully. "Being carried over the doorstep."

Startled, Jess stared at Evy. "Do you need a blanket?" he asked abruptly. "Are you cold?"

"No," she said solemnly. "I'm okay."

"Good," said Jess gruffly. "Now, you know what the doctor said. You just rest, and take it easy . . ."

"You've never been here before . . ." the girl observed.

"In this house? Why, sure I have," Jess protested. "Several times."

"In my room," said Evy, looking down at her hand, which still rested on his taut forearm.

With a feigned casualness Jess crossed his arms in front of his chest, and squinted in an exaggerated display of concentration. Evy's hand dropped to the coverlet. "I guess you're right," he said. "I don't think I have."

"Is this how you thought it would look?" she asked.

Taken aback, Jess hesitated for a moment. He was about to say that he had never thought about it, but the expectant look in her eyes made him stop. "It's very nice," he said kindly. "It has a lot of you in it."

"I've imagined you here," she said earnestly. She raised herself up on one elbow. "Sitting here with me, just like this."

"Well," said Jess heartily. "You should have invited me." Instantly he regretted the remark, but Evy did not seem to have noticed it, intent as she was on what she wanted to say.

"And now, all of a sudden, you're here."

Jess studied the serious, intense expression of her pinched face and felt a twinge of sadness for her. The girl's loneliness seemed to whisper through the walls of the shabby room. A room which preserved the relics of a childhood she had never really enjoyed. "You've had a lot to contend with," he said quietly. He reached over impulsively and smoothed down her dishevelled hair. "Now you should rest."

Instead of lying back, the girl suddenly sat up and slipped her arms around Jess's neck. She clung to him, her damp cheek pressed to his rough one, her arms locked awkwardly around him. "Please don't leave," she whispered. "Stay here with me."

Jess felt his heart constrict with alarm. He resisted the urge to push her away, and instead, patted her gently on the back in a rotating motion, as if she were a child.

"It's all right now," he murmured, although the tightening of her arms made it difficult to speak. "Lie down now. You have to take it easy. You heard the doctor." As he spoke he rubbed her forearms, gently prying them off his neck. "You need to get some rest. You'll feel much better when you do."

"No," she croaked, still clinging to him. "I love you, Jess. I need you to stay here with me. You can do whatever you want with me. It's all right. Just please stay."

"That's enough now," Jess interrupted her. "You're very upset. You have to rest."

"No," Evy cried. "I mean it. I need you."

Shaken by her outburst, Jess groped for a soothing answer. "Listen," he began. "We're friends, right? We're good friends. And you're very tired, and you're upset, by all that's happened. So you're saying these things, but you're not yourself . . ." He hesitated.

Evy slowly loosened her grip and fell back to the pillow. She did not look at Jess. Her face was white and still. The room was silent.

"Are you okay?" Jess asked softly.

"Yes," she said, staring at the wall.

"Can I get anything for you?"

"No. Nothing."

"Okay." Jess sighed unintentionally, and tried to cover it with a cough. "I'm going over to the hospital now, see how the boys are getting along."

Evy did not respond to his words.

"I'm sure they'll be anxious to hear how you are. Can I tell them you're feeling better?" he asked.

Evy shrugged, but didn't reply.

"Evy," said Jess earnestly, taking her frail, unresponsive hand between his own. "This has been a terrible day for you. You'll feel more like yourself tomorrow. And we can talk, if you want. I think it would be good for us to talk . . ."

He watched her face, but it remained expressionless. He hesitated for a moment, before continuing. Finally, he plunged on. "What happened today at the Fair. Well, that was very painful, but I know the kind of person you are. You realize that Maggie didn't mean to hurt you. I know you'll be able to forgive and forget . . ."

Evy stared at him, her face an icy mask. "Are you still going back to her? Even after all that happened today?" she asked.

Jess frowned, and looked down at their entwined fingers. Then Evy jerked her hand from between his. "I'm tired," she said, and rolled over on her side, with her back to him.

With another sigh, which he made no effort to conceal, Jess squeezed her shoulder and got up from the bed. Evy did not turn around.

Jess closed the door to her room behind him, and descended the stairs. Snorting once again at the distasteful smell of the house, he poked through the rooms on the ground floor until he found the bedroom of Evy's grandmother. The old woman was lying in her bed, swathed in rumpled sheets and blankets. All the shades were drawn and the room had a dark, unpleasant odour all its own. One lamp burned dimly on a table near the bed. Jess approached the bedside and leaned over.

"Harriet," he said softly.

The woman's feeble eyes moved to his face. She opened her mouth with great effort and tried, unsuccessfully, to speak.

"Harriet," Jess continued. "I've just brought Evy home. She's up in bed. She got in a little accident at the Fair today and she had a nosebleed, but she's fine now. Dr. Sorensen looked at her," he said, speaking in loud, slow tones so that the woman could follow his words, "and he says she'll be fine. She just has to rest."

The old woman stared beseechingly into Jess's face, and her dry, cracked lips twitched spasmodically. Jess could see that she was trying to lift her disabled hand to grab at his shirt. "It's all right," he insisted, patting the withered hand. "Really. She'll be okay. She'll probably be down here in no time to take care of you. Is there anything I can get for you now? Tea or something?"

Oblivious to his reassurances, the woman's eyes continued to plead silently with him, her hand clawing helplessly at the bedcovers.

"What is it?" Jess asked, his eyes filled with pity. "I wish I could help you. I guess your

196

granddaughter is the only one who can really understand."

The young man straightened up and gave the old woman's hand a squeeze.

"Don't worry," he said, as he started for the door. "Evy will be fine. Really." As he reached the door frame to go out, he turned around and waved. The old woman made a last, desperate effort to lift her hand to call him back, but he was already gone.

The effort to try to speak had left her nearly breathless, and her bird-like chest heaved as she lay, bound up in her wadded bedclothes. She heard the back door of the house slam shut. A few moments later she heard the sound of the engine starting up in the driveway, as Jess's car pulled out.

For a moment, throughout the house, all was silent. The old woman raised her eyes to the ceiling where, on the floor above, her grand-daughter rested. Then, all her useless muscles drooping, she closed them again, as if in surrender. As if to shut out everything she knew.

The tapping of his own footsteps echoed in Jess's ears as he walked briskly down the hushed hospital corridor. He had checked first in casualty, but the sister had directed him to the second floor of the small but efficient new hospital which was the pride of Heron's Neck. The pea-green rooms flashed by him as he strode along, offering brief glimpses of the sick, vulnerable in their white dressing-gowns, huddled by the glow of their TV sets like pioneers near a campfire warding off the dangers of the night.

Jess turned a corner and came upon the visitors' lounge. He looked in and saw Grace seated on a low couch, her pocketbook dangling off her arm. Beside her Charley Cullum sat, absently twirling his cap in his hands, and whistling in a low, tuneless song.

"Grace," said Jess. Charley stood up as Jess entered the room and extended his hand. Jess shook it, and looked down at Grace who raised her tear-stained cheek for a kiss. "How are the kids?" Jess asked them both.

"Not too bad," said Charley gruffly, although Grace looked up at him with tragic eyes.

"They have to spend the night. The nurses are getting them ready now," she said.

"For observation," said Charley authoritatively. "They're going to be okay. They just have to be sure they didn't swallow any of the glass."

"Did they have X-rays?" Jess asked.

Charley nodded. "Everything looks okay. No real harm done," he said nervously.

"No harm done," Grace scoffed, and then began weeping again.

"Gracie, stop now," Charley cajoled. Then he turned to Jess. "She's been like this," he said helplessly, "ever since she found out they were okay."

Grace took a tissue out of her pocketbook and blew her nose loudly. Then she stood up. "I'm all right now, Charley," she said grimly.

Charley put his arm around her and patted her soothingly. Grace spoke to Jess.

"How's Evy doing? I heard she got a dose of it too."

"She had a nosebleed," said Jess. "She'll be fine. I took her home. She's resting."

"Quite a day," said Charley, shaking his head.

Grace glared at Jess. "And we all know why," she said ominously.

Jess looked away.

"That woman put glass in a pie and served it to children."

"Come on, Grace," said Jess.

"What do you mean, 'Come on, Grace'?" she shouted. "You know she did."

"I'm sure it was an accident, however it happened," said Jess quietly.

Tears rose again to Grace's eyes. "You're still defending her? You saw what happened to my boys."

"Grace," said Jess. "I don't want to argue with you about this. I just came to check up on the boys."

Grace sniffed, and wiped her eyes. "I guess it's not your fault. I'm sorry, Jess. But you've got to realize there's something wrong with that woman. Things haven't been right since she came here. Maybe it was an accident," she said scornfully, "but that's not the only thing. I don't like it, Jess. The sooner you realize it the better."

"Grace," Jess pleaded, and then stopped. "Listen, I hope the boys feel better tomorrow. Don't come in if you don't feel like it."

"I'll be in," Grace said stoically.

"Okay," said Jess. "You two get some rest. Don't stay here all night."

"We will," Charley assured him, tightening his grip on his wife's shoulders. "Thanks for coming by, Jess."

Jess nodded, and left the room. As he reached the hall he glanced back in and saw them seated on the sofa. Charley was holding his wife's hand. Grace appeared to be crying again.

Although darkness had already fallen, the Thornhill house was unlit when Jess arrived. The only sound was the rustle of dried grass and dead leaves. Jess hurried to the door and knocked.

"Maggie?" he called out. There was no reply. He knocked again, but there was still no answer. He tried the knob, and the door opened. Tentatively, he stepped in. "Maggie? It's me."

A mewling cry caught his attention. He peered into the darkness and saw the shiny, fearful eyes of Willy poking in from the entrance to the kitchen.

"Hey, Willy," Jess called out softly. He

walked over to the puppy and picked him up. "Where's Maggie?" he whispered into the dog's silken ear.

"Over here."

Jess jumped, startled by the voice in the darkness. Adjusting his eyes to the gloom, he looked in the direction of the voice and saw her silhouette in one of the living-room chairs.

"You scared me," he said.

"I'm sorry."

"Do you mind if I turn on a light?"

"I don't care," she said.

Jess leaned over and switched on a lamp. Then he sat down on the edge of the sofa, and placed Willy on the floor by his feet. Finally, he looked up at Maggie.

She sat very still in her chair, gripping the armrests. Her face was devoid of colour, careless smudges of mascara on her pale cheeks. The wretchedness of her expression wrenched his heart, but he made no move towards her.

"How do you feel?" he asked.

"All right."

"That's good." He reached down and patted the cowering Willy distractedly.

"Where have you been?" she asked, the question snagging in her throat.

"I took Evy home, and then I stopped by the hospital for a minute. Everything's okay."

Maggie stared intently at him until he lifted

his eyes to meet hers. He met her look briefly and sadly, and then looked away.

They sat in silence for a few minutes. Finally, she spoke. "I don't know what to do," she said.

"Do about what?"

For a moment her eyes flashed angrily at the evasion, but when she spoke it was in the same flat voice. "They all blame me," she said. "They all think I put glass in that pie and served it to those kids. As if I were some kind of monster."

"Don't get carried away, Maggie," he said.

"You know it's true."

"I don't know any such thing," he said. "You're letting your imagination get the best of you."

"I am not," Maggie insisted, bolting from her chair so abruptly that it startled him. "Why are you lying to me? You know it's true." Her eyes burned with anger.

"Stop it," he said wearily. "Please, calm down. We can talk about it."

"I won't calm down," she cried, and began stalking up and down the narrow room. "Don't treat me like a child. I didn't imagine this. It is real. I'm afraid to show my face. I don't know what to do."

"Maggie, please," he said. "Hysterics aren't going to solve anything."

Maggie turned to him and stared, tears springing to her eyes. "Oh, I'm so sorry," she said.

"Sarcasm won't help either," he sighed.

"Well, what will help?" she asked, her voice shaking with fury. "Will you tell me that?"

"Well, I'll tell you what didn't help," Jess replied testily. "It didn't help for you to turn around and blame the whole ugly thing on Evy, who was just trying to be nice in inviting you over there."

Maggie stared at him. "Oh, I see," she said. "You don't think that Evy had anything to do with it."

"No," he said firmly, meeting her gaze. "I don't."

"Well then, how do you think it happened?"

"I don't know," he admitted tiredly. "It was probably an accident. Something in the pie dish. I don't know."

"There was nothing in the pie dish. Nothing in any of the ingredients. I tore my kitchen apart when I got back here. I tell you there was nothing."

"You must have missed it somehow."

"I did not miss it," she cried. "It was no accident. Someone put that glass in there."

"Maggie, stop it." He shook his head.

"I mean it, Jess," she cried. "Somebody did it. And if you're so damn sure it wasn't Evy, I'd like to know who it was then."

Jess covered his face with his hands for a moment, and then he looked up at her. "I don't know," he said softly. "Why don't you tell me?"

The words brought her up short. Maggie stared at the face of her lover. A terrible understanding began to dawn on her.

Finally, she spoke. Her voice was nearly inaudible. "You think I did it," she said.

Jess shook his head and sighed.

"You think that?" she asked, in an anguished voice.

"No, I don't think that," he protested. "I'm tired, and I'm confused, and I just think we ought to let this be for a while."

"You think I'm capable of that?" she cried. "Why would I do that?"

"Maggie," he said seriously, reaching for her hand. "Don't keep this up. I told you. I think it was an accident."

"Oh my God," she moaned.

Jess stood up and tried to put his arms around her, but she shook off his embrace as if it were a net.

"Maggie," he pleaded. "Let's not talk about this any more. Let's go to bed, and get some rest, and in the morning we'll face this thing together. It won't be as bad as you think. I promise you it won't."

She looked at him uncomprehendingly. "Bed?" she whispered.

"I'm tired. You're tired," he went on. "Whatever happened, we'll be able to sort it out better in the morning."

Maggie walked to the front door and opened it. "I want you to go home," she said.

"No," he protested. "We should be together tonight. Don't send me away. We have to see this through."

"You don't believe me," she said.

"I've explained myself to you," he said angrily.

"Yes, you have," she said. "Now leave me alone." She indicated the door with her hand.

Jess was about to speak again, but thought better of it. He walked towards the door. "I'll see you in the morning," he said sadly. "I love you."

He walked out into the night. She closed the door behind him.

13

IN five minutes, Maggie thought, I am going to get up and go to the kitchen and have some food. Then I'm going to take a hot bath, and drink a shot of whisky and go to bed.

Maggie looked at the clock for the hundredth time that night. It was ten minutes to twelve. It's too late, she thought. Then she corrected herself. It was not too late. And if she didn't eat, and take her clothes off and have some whisky she was going to lie there until morning, shivering, fully dressed, between the quilt and the bedspread. And the headache, which was already tormenting her, would only get worse. She thought of all these things, but she did not move.

After Jess left she had gone into her bedroom and crawled on top of the bed like a wounded animal. For hours she had lain there, her body trembling, her brain feverishly reliving the day's events. The more she mulled it over, the more impossible it became. Jess had asked, if not Evy, who? A shudder of fear ran through her as she realized that she could not be certain that it was the girl. Blaming it on Evy was her anchor. She had been clinging to it, not wanting to be cut adrift in the shifting ties of questions, the darkness which yawned around her. There was a hideous familiarity to it. Not me, she had cried. Cold, implacable eyes stared back at her. Eyes like mirrors, that merely reflected her confusion, her pitiful protests of innocence which spun in the face of logic.

A weak cry suddenly caught her attention. Maggie looked down to see Willy stumbling into the room. The puppy approached the bed and began to claw at the bedspread, attempting to climb up to where Maggie lay. Maggie reached down tenderly with one hand and scooped up the little animal. She rested the puppy on her chest, and began to stroke it. The animal's warmth had a calming effect on her. She held him close.

"You're hungry, aren't you, Willy. I should feed you." But still she did not move. She put the dog on the bed beside her. He teetered across the spread to the pillow, and flopped down. Jess would laugh, she thought, to see Willy on his pillow. Jess. Her mind began to race again. He wanted to believe her. But he couldn't. She was alone again. Accused, with no one to believe her.

The last time too she had been completely alone. We haven't got a case, the lawyer said. If we plead guilty to a lesser charge at least you won't face the death penalty. Her mother refused to see her, but Sister Dolorita had come to the prison to try and convince her to confess. When she closed her eyes she could see all their staring, unsmiling faces. Tell the truth, they said. God knows all your sins. He sees through your flimsy lies. Everyone does. Confess.

But she *had* told the truth.

Even now, she remembered every moment of that night. The snow was flurrying as they left the office. By the time they were finished making love at the motel it was already piling up.

He had to get home, he told her, before it got any worse. He would always have to get home. That was the meaning of what he had just told her.

She had dressed in silence, shielding herself against the cold, each layer she donned putting distance between them.

"Are you ready, Maggie?" he asked her gently.

Once he had got the car started and backed out of the forming drifts they seemed to relax a little. He reached for her across the seat and pulled her towards him. "Don't look so sad. We always manage to be together somehow."

She felt wounded and angry. She wanted to pull away from him, call him a name and jump out of the car. But at the same time she wanted to cling to him. The heat from his body felt like the only warm thing in her frozen life. She needed him, and she needed to let him go.

On the highway, Roger tensed up again. The snow whirled around the car, and the road beneath them was slick with the crystallizing ice.

He reclaimed his arm and grasped the wheel tightly with both hands. Maggie retreated to her side of the seat and watched him as he concentrated on the road. Outside, the twilight sky was lightened by the falling snow. The light from the dashboard mingled with the grey sky made him look ghastly, she thought. Old, and unhealthy. She looked down at her own smooth hands, which were clenched tightly in her lap. If I could just stop loving him, she thought.

"This storm is terrible," he muttered, and he bobbed his head around, looking out for other cars on the road ahead. The highway was virtually deserted, other travellers kept in by snow warnings.

As he concentrated on the road, she concentrated on him. Her heart felt twisted by her passion for him, and her anguish at the thought of losing him. And her guilt. She knew what they were doing was wrong. They should break it off. She studied him intently, wondering how she could bear to see him day after day, and not be lovers. Finally, she asked in a small voice, "Roger, do you think I should leave? Find another job?"

Roger continued to peer through the windscreen, a pained expression in his eyes. "I don't know," he said.

"As long as we're seeing each other day after day," she said, "I don't think I can stop . . ."

Roger did not look at her. "We could try," he

said. "If that's what you want. I don't want you to go."

"I can't do it," she said. "I'm not strong enough."

"Do what?" he asked. "Stay or go?"

"Either one," she said hopelessly.

"No more tonight," he told her. "Please. We both need time to think about it."

Maggie did not reply, but stared ahead at the icy windscreen. It was her decision. She knew it. But she couldn't bear to make it. She could not imagine the emptiness of her life without him.

"Oh my God," Roger cried out, jamming on the brakes so abruptly that the car skidded sideways before bumping to a stop on the shoulder.

"What's the matter?" she asked.

"There's somebody in the road up ahead."

Maggie peered out. She could see a light waving back and forth, and a bulky figure signalling them to stop.

"Oh no," said Roger.

Maggie looked wonderingly at him.

"I'd better go see what the problem is." He shook his head. "You'd better stay here."

Before she had a chance to reply he had hopped out of the car. He slammed the door behind him and trudged off through the snow towards the figure up ahead. She was able to watch him for a few moments, his head down against the howling wind, before the falling snow covered over the windscreen with layer after layer of flakes. Maggie sat shivering in the front seat.

With the engine turned off, the car cooled down like a refrigerator. Maggie considered turning it on again, but then decided to wait. He would be coming right back.

The time seemed to drag on endlessly as she waited. She wished that she had a watch so she could tell how long she had been sitting there. Probably not that long, she thought. It just seemed that way. Her teeth began to chatter, and she squeezed herself tightly for warmth. Finally, she could not endure the discomfort any longer. She reached over and switched on the engine. The car started with a comforting roar. He'll probably think I'm leaving without him, she thought. Not much chance of that, love.

But he didn't return. Five more minutes, she thought to herself. She tried to count off the minutes in seconds, but her mind wandered. What was he doing, she wondered. He had been so anxious to get home. It was just like him to be a Good Samaritan. But what could possibly be taking so long?

After a few more minutes, Maggie turned off the engine, and slid over to the driver's seat. She opened the door, knocking a layer of snow to the ground and stepped out. Her boots sank into the snow several inches. She had never seen it come down so hard.

It was darker now, the twilight closing in on the deserted, snow-covered highway flanked by inky fir trees, their boughs already laden. Maggie peered into the road ahead. There was no one there.

Her heart constricted with alarm. Then she began to reason with herself. The dense trees and hill to her right served as an expansive divider to the highway. The motorist's car might have broken down on the other side. Perhaps he had crossed over to find help. That was probably where Roger was now. Helping out. Maggie repeated the senseless explanation to herself like a rosary as she walked towards the spot where she had last seen Roger. His footprints were gone, obliterated by the falling snow. There was no trace of him.

Helplessly she walked along the highway's edge. Occasionally the dark form of a car would hurtle by, but the storm would immediately close up the space where it had been, leaving only the pinkish glow of receding tail-lights. With a sinking heart Maggie faced the fact that there was nothing ahead but miles of highway. She looked back towards the car, but there was no comfort in sitting there. She thought of driving away, but she couldn't just leave him there. What if he were lost in the snow? Or been hit by a car? Desperately she turned towards the wooded hill and plunged into the trees. Perhaps he *was* on the other side.

Her eyes stung from the pelting of the snow, and the strain of looking into the unnatural whiteness. The dark treetops enshrouded the hill as she stumbled along. The wind howled around her, and the tree branches moaned and creaked from their new weight. She wandered, without apparent direction, up the hill.

Suddenly her glance was caught by a wide furrow in the snow's surface, streaked dark, and filling rapidly. Shielding her eyes with one hand, she followed the trail that it made. She looked up once, as she walked, to get her bearings, and nearly tripped over a dark, inert form, sprawled in the space between two trees.

Fear flooded through her as she bent down, and crouched near the form. She reached out a gloved hand and touched it. Roger.

She grabbed his shoulder and began tugging frantically at him. Then she saw the dark stain beneath him, melting the snow with its pulsing heat.

Her anguished wail was caught up and exploded by the wind. For a long time she knelt there, staring uncomprehendingly at the body of her lover. No, no, she thought numbly. Her lips kept forming his name. She looked up, but there was no one else on the darkening hillside.

She had to get him back. She couldn't leave him there, to be buried in the snow. She began tugging at him with all her strength, trying to drag him down the hill. But the weight, which had rested so comfortably on top of her in bed, was now ponderous, immovable. "Come on," she cried furiously. Then she heard herself.

The absurdity of her cry struck her forcibly, and she sat down for a moment in the snow. Then, slowly, she scrambled to her feet, and began to make her way back down the hillside towards the car. "Help," she whispered feebly. "Somebody help."

Running and stumbling, she finally reached the shoulder. In the distance she could see the outline of Roger's car. There was something else as well, flashing pale blue and ghostly through the veil of snow. She lurched forward, calling out, but the words were sticking in her throat. Finally she reached the car, and fell heavily against the hood.

The state trooper straightened up, and turned the flashlight on her with which he had just been examining the inside of the car. "Having some trouble here, Ma'am?" he asked politely.

The tears stinging her eyes were indistinguishable from the glancing, icy bits of flakes. She struggled to speak, but she was breathless from running, and the shock. She had to tell him what happened. He would help her. Maggie reached towards him with one blood-soaked woollen glove. Slowly, the expression on the trooper's face changed. He ran the flashlight up and down her form, noting the dark stains which covered her coat and skirt.

"Roger," she blurted out, pointing to the hill. "He's bleeding. I think he's dead." Haltingly, she began to spill out her story, pleading with him to understand. The trooper watched her guardedly. When she finished she looked up into the young man's eyes. She saw there the expression which she already knew so well. Suspicion and disbelief. It was not the last time she would see it.

But I didn't do it, Maggie said to herself. She opened her eyes and looked at the clock again. It was one o'clock. There's still time, she thought. Willy whined and curled up beside her. She put a protective hand around him, and stared into the darkness.

Cautiously, Evy raised herself up from the bed and sat on the edge. She patted her upper lip with her fingertips. The warm streams of blood which had poured out of her nostrils this afternoon seemed to have been effectively dammed up. She thought it was strange that you could bleed, and feel no pain. It worried her.

She stood up, and walked to the window. She pushed back the limp, dotted swiss curtain, and looked out. There was no sign of Jess now. He had gone to her. He shouldn't have done that, Evy thought. If only he had not done that. Everything could be different.

A wave of lightheadedness overcame her, and she reached for the back of the rocker by the window. Removing the doll on the seat, Evy sat down, and took the doll in her lap. For a while she sat, staring vacantly ahead of her, her mind turning over the events of the day, again and again.

Finally she looked down at the doll that she held. Its black eyes were empty and shiny in the dim light of the darkened room. Its smooth, china arms reached up, extended as if expecting an embrace. Idly, Evy grasped the doll's head with her right hand and began to twist it. The neck swivelled with some difficulty, but Evy pressed against it firmly, and at last the head was completely turned around. The doll's head faced her knees, while the torso still faced hers, the arms reaching out helplessly.

Evy looked at it thoughtfully for a while. Then she got up, tossed the doll on the chair seat, and walked to the cupboard. Her meagre wardrobe hung neatly from the bar. Her two pairs of shoes and her slippers were arranged in a row along the floor of the cupboard. Across the top shelf were two knitted hats, and a row of shoe boxes. On top of the shoe boxes was a large album, bound in a blue plastic cover. Evy wrested it from its berth on the shelf. She carried the album to her bed, and sat down with it. She opened the cover and pressed it back. Then she began to examine the contents of the album.

The ritual was a familiar one, but it never failed to totally engage her. On the first few pages were the yellowed, brittle clippings which she had purloined from her grandmother's dresser after she had the first stroke. The old headlines blared the word "murderess", and "lovers' quarrel ends in death". Some of the articles had pictures of her father smiling pleasantly at the camera. Beside his picture news photos of the woman who had killed him.

Evy stared at the pale, frantic face of a much younger Maggie. It pleased Evy to see how scared she looked, beside the calm, unsuspecting face of her father. In one of the clippings there was even a picture of Evy herself, being held by her mother. They were in a police car. Evy noted that she was wearing the green snowsuit which her grandmother Robinson had sent her for her birthday. She started to read the stories, but finally she decided to turn to the other pages. She knew all the clippings by heart. Her grandmother read them all to her when she was younger, after her mother had to go away to the hospital. "This is why," her grandmother would interrupt her own recitation of the clips. "This is why your mother has to live in that hospital now. Because of all of this that happened."

Evy looked up from the clipping, a faraway look in her eyes. She remembered that when they first came to live with Grandma, they never seemed to talk about what happened to her father. After a while though, her grandmother told her about it all the time. And then her mother got sick. After that, Grandma took to reading her the clippings.

Returning to the album, Evy turned over to the next group of clippings. These were more recent, although there were only a few of them. "Murderess receives college diploma," read one. "Mistress-murderess due for release," announced another. She had found them in the bundle sent by the clipping service to the paper. Evy smoothed them down tenderly on the page. She was proud of finding them. They had helped her to make her plans. She read these short clippings over carefully, surprised to note that they had a new significance for her now. Now that the phantom who had haunted her dreams had taken flesh. The woman who murdered her father. She turned the page, and sighed with pleasure. The letters.

Each letter was addressed to William Emmett and each bore the return address of a state penitentiary. She opened one at random and read it. "Dear Mr. Emmett," it began. "You can't imagine how much hope and courage I derive from your interest in me, and my accomplishments behind these walls. I look forward, more than I can tell you, to the day of our meeting . . ."

Evy read through several of the letters, and then replaced them in their envelopes. A satisfied smile spread across the girl's pinched face. It had been easy, she thought. But even as she decided

218

hat, she recalled the excuses she had made to stay after work so she could use Emmett's stationery and typewriter, the furtive interception of his mail, the diligence with which she had composed her replies. And then, of course, she had had to get rid of Mr. Emmett. He was not a mean man, but there was nothing else she could do. It had not been too hard, because he was old, but still . . .

No, she decided. It had not been easy. It had worked out well though. And it had been worth it. The day the spectre had taken human form, walking in the door and announcing herself, it had all seemed worthwhile. Evy frowned. The memory of the triumphant day was clouded by the recollection of Jess, appreciatively appraising the stranger. Flirting with her. That was the one thing she had not foreseen.

Well, several things, she reminded herself, remembering the interference of Tom Croddick. He could easily have spoiled her plan by running off to the police chief with that silly shoplifting story. One word from him and the whole town would have known who their new resident was. And that would have been the end of her plan. No, she had worked too hard to let him ruin everything like that. This was her secret. Fortunately, she had talked him out of it. Made him feel foolish.

Her mind wandered back to Jess. Jess. Why did he have to take her side like that? Now Jess was a problem too. If she had any regrets about the whole beautiful plan, it was that Jess had inadvertently got in the way. It saddened her to realize what that meant now. She had tried to make him see Maggie for what she was. Tried to get him to stop hanging around her. But even today, after the glass in the pie, he still went running back to her.

Evy flushed, remembering how he had rejected her that afternoon. Rejected her, to run to that murdering whore. The memory of it hardened her heart against him. She could not carry out her plan with him always hovering around Maggie. He was in the way. He would have to suffer the consequences. She had given him every chance to escape. But no one, not even Jess, would stand between her and her plan. Evy turned another page.

The page she looked at now was empty. There would be a few more clippings to insert, probably from the *Cove News*, after it was all over, and then that would be it. Everything would be complete. In a way, she hated to see it coming to an end. She had almost enjoyed it, in a funny way, watching her, studying her movements, figuring out the final plans. Except for the part about Jess. In her mind's eye she saw him again, his naked, muscled back, as he bent over Maggie. Evy began to grind her teeth, baring her teeth like fangs.

A bumping noise from the floor below shook

her out of her reverie. "Grandma," she breathed, suddenly recalling the invalid who waited helplessly for her ministrations. Evy closed the album and hurriedly replaced it on the cupboard shelf.

She did not mind having to look after the old woman. After all, it had been Grandma who had told her the story. Grandma who had made her want to do this. Although she could see now that Grandma didn't like it. Evy could not understand why. It had practically been her idea.

Tomorrow then, she would begin with the final steps. Jess first, and then the woman. Carefully. No mistakes.

14

THREE sharp raps on the door were followed by a woman's voice bawling "It's for you."

Owen Duggan rolled his eyeballs and mouthed the words, "Of course it's for me," and then continued to slide his photographic paper through the tray of chemicals. He could envision his housekeeper, Mirelle Faria, standing just outside the door, eyes narrowed, ear to the doorframe, holding the receiver in one hand. "Just a minute, Mirelle," he called out.

"It's Jess Herlie," Mirelle informed him through the door, having learned not to incur his wrath by opening the door while he was working.

"Ask him if I can call him back," yelled Owen, scrutinizing the page he had just lifted from the bath.

"He says not," Mirelle announced with satisfaction. "He says it's important. Oh!"

Mirelle's plump figure nearly toppled over as Owen threw open the darkroom door and lifted the receiver from her hand. "Thank you, Mirelle," he said, dismissing her. She smiled, and began to dust, with great diligence, the banister next to the telephone table.

Owen turned his back to her, and spoke into the phone. "Yeah, Jess."

Owen listened for a moment and then replied, "Yeah, it's at eight-thirty."

He listened again, his lips pursing into an expression of mild annoyance. Then he spoke. "Can't she drive over herself? What kind of trouble? Car trouble?" Owen sighed.

"I suppose I could. Okay. Tell her I'll swing by at seven-forty-five. That's all right, Jess." Owen hung up.

"What's going on?" Mirelle asked cheerfully.

"Mirelle, I wish I found my life half as interesting as you do," Owen grumbled.

"What'd he want?" she persisted. At home, at her dinner table every night, Mirelle faithfully reported the activities of her employer to her husband, Frank, who worked at the filling station on the dock, and her two teenage daughters, who were showing less and less interest in Owen's comings and goings as they moved into the emotionally teeming atmosphere of adolescence. Owen suffered Mirelle's interest with little grace, but he had become, over the years, somewhat resigned to it.

Owen sighed. "He wants me to pick up someone and take them to the meeting at the school tonight."

"That new one at the paper," said Mirelle.

Owen shook his head in weary amusement.

"That's the one," he conceded. "How did you know?"

"I guessed," she said, scarcely able to conceal her self-satisfaction. "How come you have to pick her up?"

"I don't know. She had some trouble with her car. Some such thing."

"She had some trouble, all right," Mirelle said suggestively.

"I see little justification for scepticism in this instance," Owen replied disinterested.

"I know it," said Mirelle. "But I'm just repeating what I heard."

Marvelling at the obtuseness of this remark, Owen stared at his housekeeper. "What, may I ask, are you talking about, Mirelle?"

The housekeeper smiled benignly. "I'm talking about what happened at the Fair. With that new one that you're driving tonight. I heard about it at the fish market this morning. Everybody was talking."

Owen snorted in exasperation. "Are you going to tell me, or am I going back in there to work?"

"Usually you say you don't like my gossip," said Mirelle coyly, unable to resist the unusual position she found herself in.

"I'll count to three," said Owen grimly.

"Okay," Mirelle said breathlessly. "Well, you know that the Fair was yesterday, and the new girl was working at the bakery booth . . ."

In spite of himself, Owen found himself listening with interest to his housekeeper's tale.

"It's all set," Jess said, replacing the receiver on the hook and turning to Maggie. "Owen will pick you up in half an hour and take you to the meeting."

Maggie was seated at the kitchen table, staring out the window, and absently stroking Willy, who had flopped down quietly in her lap. At Jess's words she looked up and shook her head. "I can't go," she said.

Jess pulled up another chair and sat down in front of her. "Maggie, you have to go. You can't just hole up in this house. I let you get away with staying home from work today, but I can't keep that up. Neither can you. You have to get out there and face people. This meeting tonight will be a good opportunity. You can go and listen. Write a little story on it. Owen will be with you, taking pictures. It'll be fine. You'll see."

Maggie looked at him doubtfully. "Will you come?"

Jess shook his head. "You don't need to hide behind me. You didn't do anything wrong. There's nothing to be ashamed of."

She searched his face. "Do you believe that?"

Jess nodded solemnly. "Of course." His eyes held hers and seemed to repeat the apology he had offered her earlier on in the day. She

225

accepted it now, as she had then, not because she was convinced of his faith in her, but because she could not bear the rift between them. He wanted to believe in her. That much she was sure of, and it would have to be enough. It was more than she was accustomed to.

She turned her face away from his, and bit her lip. "It's all those people," she explained helplessly.

"That's exactly why you have to do it," he insisted.

"You don't know how it makes me feel. What terrible feelings it stirs up."

"Maybe it's time you told me," he said quietly, squeezing her hands.

Maggie stared into his anxious eyes steadily for a moment, and then she bowed her head. "No. Not now," she said. "I'll go to the meeting."

"That's my girl," he murmured. For a few moments they sat facing each other in silence hand in hand. Then Maggie sighed. "I guess I'd better get ready," she said.

Jess nodded his approval. "You get ready, and I'll head home."

"What are you going to do tonight?" she asked him.

"Not much," he said. "Read. Maybe watch a movie. Maybe I'll go out for a beer if I get lonely," he said with a grin. He pulled on his jacket and zipped it.

Maggie stood up, placing Willy on the floor by his bowl. Immediately he began lapping up the milk. She put her arms around Jess, unwilling to let him go. "I'll miss you," she said. "I feel so shaky."

Jess embraced her, and then held her at arms' length. "You'll be fine," he assured her.

"Will I?" she asked.

A tiny yelp from the vicinity of their feet distracted them. "Sure you will," said Jess, bending down and scooping up the puppy who had waddled over and was nibbling the cuff of his pants hungrily. "Willy says so too, don't you, Willy?" He kissed the puppy on the top of the head, and then replaced him on the floor. Then he turned to Maggie. "Go get ready," he said. "Everything will be okay."

Maggie turned uncertainly, and started for her room. She stopped, and looked back at Jess, who was heading for the kitchen door. He looked boyish and innocent in his plaid jacket, his hair standing out in unruly curls. She knew that up close there were many strands of grey in his thick hair, and that lines and creases surrounded his gentle eyes. But from across the room he looked young, like the farm boys she used to know, safe in the familiar fields and pastures that circumscribed their world. As she watched him he seemed unbearably distant from her. The secrets of her life whirled in the gulf between them. She stretched out her hand towards him.

"I'll let myself out," he said, reaching the door and returning the gesture he mistook for a wave. She raised a hand, as if to stop him, but he closed the door behind him, and was gone.

The night was cold, and uncommonly clear. Jess breathed in the pure air hungrily as he climbed the hill to his house. He paused on the doorstep and listened to the loud, insistent murmur of the nearby sea for a few moments before he unlocked the door and let himself in. It's a good place to live, he thought, as he had many times before. Even the dark silence of the house seemed welcoming to him.

Expertly skirting the furniture in the familiar darkness, Jess went directly to the kitchen and turned on the lights. He put some water in a kettle on the stove and returned to the refrigerator to find himself something for dinner. On the second shelf was a small dish of stew, the remains of a meal he had shared with Maggie several nights before. He smiled, as he remembered her observing him as he carefully picked out the peas before he ate it.

"If you don't like peas, why do you put them in?" she asked.

He looked up at her in surprise. "That's the way my mother always made it," he explained earnestly.

"In other words, it's not stew without peas?" Her incredulity dissolved into a giggling fit that resulted in his vowing "Nevermore" to the empty pea can he retrieved from the garbage bag.

The kettle whistled, recalling Jess to his preparations. He poured the water into the filter he had prepared. While he waited for it to drip he set the pot of stew into the oven which had been preheating. In the time it took for the stew to heat he drank a cup of coffee. Then he sat alone at the kitchen table and ate his meal. The dripping of the tap and the whir of the wall clock were the only sounds that accompanied his brief repast. When he was done he put the dishes into the sink and ran some water over them. The kitchen normally felt cosy to him, but tonight it seemed empty. He decided to have his pipe in the den.

Jess switched on the lamp beside his favourite chair in the den, and gazed around the book-lined room. During his marriage it had gradually become his favourite room in the house. Its utter stillness, save for the muffled roar of the ocean, was soothing to him, a relief from the distressing regularity of Sharon's complaints. She never bothered him when he was in the den, put off by its introverted atmosphere, and resentful of the volumes which provided Jess with an escape hatch from her discontentment. It was his haven. Even after the divorce he retained a special fondness for the room.

Jess looked around at the books and papers on

his desk, lying carelessly unshelved. I've got to pick this up one of these days, he thought, and then he began to peruse the titles lying neglected where he had dropped them. He picked up a conservation report he had started, but put it down again, lacking enthusiasm for its dry pronouncements. Beside it were two volumes on home repair he had been studying in preparation for the patching job he planned to do on the roof of the house. On the windowsill was a paperback copy of a spy novel. Jess mused over it for a moment, and then restlessly put it down.

With a feeling of surprise, Jess realized that the stillness of the room, which he had always savoured, seemed tinged with loneliness. He had quickly become use to Maggie in the house, her voice calling him from another room, her presence in the doorway. He found himself looking up, expecting her.

He tapped the bowl of his pipe impatiently against the ashtray and glanced over at the clock beside the television set. She's not home yet, he thought. I'll try her later. He stared blankly at the grey-green screen of the TV, planning his call. Then, with a feeling of pleasant relief he remembered that it was Monday night, and nearly time for the football game. He walked over to the TV, snapped it on, and then settled back in his chair.

The noisy laugh track of a sit-com drawing to a close filled the room. Jess consulted his TV guide, and then settled back to let the colourful, meaningless images on the screen fill his head. He was already looking forward to the irritating, nasal voice of the football announcer which would signal the beginning of the game. He was halfway through a commercial for a breakfast cereal when he became aware of a tapping sound, unsynchronized to the enthusiastic voice of the pitch man. Jess leaned forward and turned down the volume on the TV set. He listened intently for a few moments, but the house was silent. He turned the volume up again, just as the opening credits for the football show was coming on the screen, and the announcers were beginning their spiel over the racket of band music. After a few moments the tapping sound started again. Jess frowned, and snapped off the set. Leaving the study, he walked towards the front hallway, through the darkened rooms.

He reached the front door and opened it, peering out into the night. There was no one in sight. Jess frowned, and was about to close the door, when a movement in the bushes near the foot of the steps caught his eye. "Who's there?" he demanded.

A figure emerged from the darkness.

"Evy," he exclaimed. "Hello!"

The dim light from the foyer cast shadows on the girl's pale, pinched face. In the gloom of the night her eyes were like dark holes. "I wasn't

231

sure you were here," she said. "You didn't answer the door."

"I had the TV on," Jess explained. "I couldn't tell if someone was knocking. Come on in."

"No," she said. "I can't stay. I just came over to borrow something."

"Well, you can come in for a minute. What do you need?" Jess asked.

"There's a pipe leaking in the cellar, and I need a wrench to fix it," said the girl.

"Fix it? Do you know how?"

Evy shrugged. "I guess I can figure it out."

Jess gave her a wry smile. "You'll probably end up with a flood."

"It can't be that hard to do," she protested.

Jess shook his head. "You're stubborn," he said. "I'll say that for you. Come on in and wait for me. I'll get the wrench and go over and have a look at that pipe for you."

"You don't have to," she said.

Jess smiled to himself, suspecting that she had come calling in the hope that he would offer his help. "I don't mind," he said. "Just let me get my keys."

"No, you don't need them," she objected. "I'll drive you."

"How will I get home?" he asked.

"I'll bring you back. I'm glad to get out of the house," the girl assured him. "I'd like to."

Jess smiled ruefully, suspecting that the ride home would necessitate his inviting her in for a soda. Oh well, he thought. It's company. "Okay," he agreed, opening the door to the hallway cupboard and pulling his jacket off a hanger. "Let's go. The tools are out in the garage."

Evy followed him to the garage and held the flashlight on him which he handed to her as they went in the side door. "I've got to put a light in here," he grumbled as he ransacked the toolbox, extracting two different wrenches. "These ought to do us," he said, straightening up.

On the ride to Evy's house she gripped the wheel and drove cautiously, keeping her distance from the few other cars on the road, and answering Jess's attempts at conversation in monosyllables. She pulled into the Robinson driveway and sat rigidly, staring ahead of her after she turned off the ignition. Jess glanced at her immobile face before opening the car door. He wished, briefly and guiltily, that he was back in his quiet den. The prospect of spending the evening in her moody, laconic company suddenly seemed wearisome.

He stretched up towards the stars and forced out a cheerful groan. "What a night," he said. "Look at those stars!"

Evy slid out of the car and slammed the door. "Come on," she said impatiently.

Jess looked at her in surprise. "What's the hurry?" he asked.

She stared blankly at him for a second. Then

she spoke. "It's the leak," she said. "It'll get bigger."

Jess followed her up the path to the house and into the front door. The girl looked straight ahead, and marched towards the cellar door, but Jess paused in the living-room. Harriet Robinson lay on the couch, propped up by pillows, her arms hanging lifelessly by her sides.

"Hello, Harriet," he said kindly. "How are you feeling tonight?"

The old woman moved her lips in a feeble, fishlike motion. Jess walked over to her and patted her hand. "Evy told me about the leak in the basement. We'll fix it up in no time."

"It's this way," Evy interrupted.

Jess smiled sadly at the stricken woman, and turned to Evy. "See you later," he said.

"Give me those," Evy commanded as he approached the door. She gestured towards the wrenches which he held in his hand, and offered him the flashlight in exchange. "You can take a look at it, and I'll hand you what you need."

"Okay," Jess agreed, mildly surprised at the girl's authoritative tone. It occurred to him that she felt confident, being on her own territory. He watched her face as she examined the wrenches which he had handed to her. She ran her hand over their heads and then gripped the handle of the larger one tightly. Jess recalled the awkwardness of his last visit to this house, when he had rebuffed her timid advances in her bedroom. Perhaps her brusqueness was an attempt to dispel the memory of that embarrassing incident which hung between them. Evy lifted her head. "Ready?" she asked.

Jess nodded, and opened the cellar door. The smell which assailed him forced him to step back from the door. "God," he breathed, wrinkling his nose in disgust. "What have you got down there? Dead dogs?"

"Some garbage and stuff. I guess I should clean it out," Evy apologized.

"Yeah," Jess agreed. He thought to himself that at least he knew now why the house smelled so bad. For a moment he looked sceptically at Evy. She was normally so tidy. He wondered if there were a side of her he didn't know. A side that was dirty and careless.

The girl looked at him helplessly. "Maybe you'd rather not help me."

Jess sighed. "No. I'll have a look. But you've got to promise me that you'll get at that basement some time soon. It's not healthy to have food rotting down there. For either of you."

Evy bowed her head in apparent contrition at his scolding. "I will," she promised in a low voice.

Satisfied, Jess switched on the flashlight, drew in a breath, and started down the stairs. He could hear Evy on the step behind him.

"One more down," she directed him. "It's there, on the ceiling to your left."

Jess beamed the light at the pipe which Evy indicated. "I don't see anything," he said, peering up at the rusted metal. "They're not in great shape, but they look dry. Are you sure this is where it was?" He flashed the light on the pipe joints above him, and then shook his head. "I don't see it," he repeated.

The clatter of a falling wrench distracted him. He looked up at the girl.

It took him a few seconds to comprehend what he saw. Evy glared down at him, her white, skeletal face distorted by a sneer which bared her teeth. Above one shoulder she held the larger wrench tensely, prepared to strike.

This is a joke, he thought. She's only kidding. This isn't real. He tried to speak but his throat was constricted.

"What are you doing?" The furious intensity of her eyes incinerated his frantic hope.

Jess's heart froze for an instant and then began to thud wildly. "No," he cried out as he saw her arm start to move, like a scythe, through the air. He raised a clammy hand to shield his face. "Evy, don't!"

She ignored his plea. The last thing he heard was her guttural cry as she swung the wrench down on him. There was an instant of crushing pain. Then, darkness.

15

OWEN hesitated, his hand on the inside handle of the car door. Should he go to the door, or simply honk the horn, he wondered? In the interest of appearing as casual as possible, he finally decided to remain in the car, motor running, and beep.

A few seconds after the second blast the lights went out in the house, and Maggie appeared on the doorstep. The yellow porchlight created an aura around her slim figure which gave her a ghostly appearance. She stepped off the threshold and into the darkness. Owen lost sight of her until she opened the car door and sat down beside him.

"I would have come in," he explained, "but we were running a little late."

Maggie nodded, but did not reply.

"So," he continued heartily, as he turned to back out of the driveway, "I hear you're having a little car trouble. Goddamn cars. You can't rely on them." He straightened his jeep out on the road, and then glanced over at Maggie who sat silently, not responding to his remarks.

"Goddamn nuisance if you ask me," he went on. "This old scout of mine here is pretty good, but when one thing goes, everything else seems to shut down in sympathy. I take it over to Marv there at the Shell station. You know Marv? Great guy. Take your eye teeth any day and tell you 'you look better without them'."

He could sense that she had turned her head to look at him. Owen began to hum an aimless tune.

"Actually," she said quietly, "my car's fine."

Owen ceased his humming and frowned, but he kept his eyes on the road ahead.

"It was me," she went on. "I didn't want to go alone. I was afraid to."

Owen squirmed in his seat and screwed his mouth into an impatient expression. He did not look at her, but continued to peer out at the white line in the road. "That's ridiculous," he said gruffly.

Maggie did not flinch at his observation. "I suppose so," she murmured.

An uncomfortable silence fell between them. Owen cleared his throat, but said nothing. A sigh escaped from Maggie. She kept her face, furrowed with anxiety, turned away from him.

Owen began to hum again, and then stopped abruptly. They rode the rest of the way to the school without speaking.

"America, America, God shed his grace on thee . . ."

A chorus of straining, childish voices perforated the closed windows of the school and then dissolved in the night air as Owen and Maggie pulled up into the parking lot. Owen got out and reached back behind the seat where he had placed his camera equipment.

"God shed disgrace on thee," he boomed out in his *basso profundo*.

Maggie smiled wanly at him.

"Ready?" Owen asked, slinging one camera around his neck and drawing a leather bag up over his shoulder. "Here," he said. "Take these."

Maggie accepted the film containers which he held out to her.

"Hold on to them," he instructed her. "I'll need them later."

Owen began trudging towards the door of the auditorium. He looked back after a few steps and saw Maggie standing rooted beside the car. "Will you come on?" he called back, a note of irritation in his voice.

She roused herself to join him, clutching her reporter's pad tightly in one sweaty hand. "I thought this was a meeting about school business," she whispered as Owen threw open the door of the auditorium. From inside she could hear the young vocalizers launching into their next tune, a poorly co-ordinated round of which none of the words were decipherable.

"Oh, they have a little music recital first. It puts all the proud parents in a mellow mood," he explained. He poked his head in and then entered the back of the room. Maggie slipped in beside him and stood in the shadows. A few feet to her left Maggie noticed an empty chair pushed back against the wall. She quickly sat down in it and lowered her head to examine the blank first page of her pad.

Owen dropped the leather satchel beside her and strode up the centre aisle between the rows of metal folding chairs peopled by parents and other residents of Heron's Neck. He planted himself about halfway down the aisle and held a light meter above his head. Curious eyes around the room turned to observe him as he raised the camera to his face and squinted into the viewer. Familiar with the sight of Owen and his camera at local events, most members of the audience quickly turned their attention back to the choir. Owen shifted his weight as he focused and began clicking.

Maggie raised her eyes from the safety of her notebook and looked around the room. A basketball hoop hung above the heads of the singing children in the room which was ordinarily a gymnasium. The maize-coloured walls were papered with riotous crayon drawings depicting Pilgrims of peculiar proportions and turkeys with brilliant green and purple plumage. The vivid, innocent images made Maggie smile. By contrast the parents were a drab-looking lot, seated upright in their uncomfortable folding chairs, dressed mostly in dull earth tones. Maggie recog-

240

nized some of their plain faces which were upturned in rapt attention towards the children, who stumbled gamely through their song to the accompaniment of a plunking piano which Maggie could not see from her seat at the rear.

She felt a sad fondness for the nameless children as she watched them singing. They concentrated earnestly on the unseen teacher at the piano who led them, but their exuberance caused each little voice to take a path of its own, poking out the choral unity like awkward elbows and knees. And those who sang the loudest, with the greatest zeal, would probably be scolded, she thought.

As her eyes swept the room she noticed that Owen appeared to be gesturing in her direction. She lowered her eyes hastily to her notebook and hoped that she was wrong. Then, unmistakably, she heard him call her name in an impatient whisper.

Maggie looked up to see him nodding at her, and pointing to the leather bag which he had left beside her chair. A few people seated in Owen's vicinity swivelled around to stare at her. Reluctantly, she leaned over and picked up the bag. She dreaded the walk down the centre aisle, and silently cursed Owen for forcing her to leave her seat in the shadows. Slowly she got up and started towards him.

As she reached the passage between the seats, the piano and its player became visible to her.

Maggie recognized the frizzy, blonde head of the woman at the fair who had screamed at her after the boys' accident. Maggie stopped short, disinclined to expose herself by getting any closer. She heard Owen whisper her name again, and looked up to see him glowering at her, jerking his hand impatiently towards her. She looked dumbly from Owen's extended hand to the bag, and then slowly shook her head. She took a step back.

Owen scowled, and stomped over to where she stood. A few people turned around to shoot them disapproving glances.

Angrily, Owen snatched the bag from her and unzipped it. "You're acting like a fool," he said curtly, reaching into the bag and rummaging around. The children's voices piped on, but the piano behind them began to falter to a halt.

Owen found the lens he was fishing for and pushed the bag back into Maggie's arms. He turned to resume his place in the centre aisle. Past his shoulder Maggie looked directly into the eyes of the music teacher, who had pushed back the bench and stood up, and was facing Maggie with a fearsome glare across the distance of the auditorium. The children sang on in their high, nasal tones, but gradually one by one they stopped, as they noticed that the music teacher had abandoned them in the midst of their song.

"Did I disturb you? Sorry," Owen called out,

waving a hand to the front of the room. "Please go on. It won't happen again. Sorry."

A murmur of annoyance travelled around the room, as the audience commented on the interruption. It died down as people settled back into their listening attitudes. However, the music teacher did not resume her seat at the piano. She continued to glare at Maggie, her eyes occasionally darting to Owen. "What are you doing here?" she cried out in a loud, but trembling voice.

For a moment Owen was taken aback by the question, but he responded in a conciliatory tone. "I'm here for the *Cove News*," he said. "I'm taking pictures of this meeting for Tuesday's paper. As I suspect you know," he added smoothly.

The music teacher ignored the suggestion of condescension in his tone. "What about her?" she said shrilly, pointing to Maggie, who stood dumbly in the aisle, watching the proceedings as if it were an accident in the process of happening, and she were helpless to avert it.

"Miss Fraser," Owen retorted, "is likewise here as a reporter, to cover this little event. And we'd like to get on with it so we can get home, if you don't mind."

The woman hesitated for a moment, and then looked defiantly from Maggie to Owen, her mouth set in a hard line. "No," she said.

"What do you mean, no? No what?" Owen said, exasperated.

"I mean no, she cannot stay. We want her to go. You can stay and take your pictures, but she has to go."

"What are you talking about?" Owen cried, over the murmur of surprise in the audience, and the excited whispers of the children, who had not witnessed the public humiliation of an adult before.

"I mean, that she is not welcome here. Do I have to go into it in front of all these children? What that woman did yesterday? At a public gathering?"

"This is unbelievable," Owen sputtered. "I have never heard of such a thing." He turned towards Maggie, as if to commiserate with her.

Maggie stood supporting herself on the chair beside her. Her face was ashen. With a swift motion she hurled the leather bag away from her. Owen rushed to intercept it. Maggie whirled around and stalked out of the room, slamming the double doors behind her.

The music teacher turned back to the children, who were punching and pinching one another, whispering in one another's ears, their eyes wide at the delicious wickedness of the scene. "Calm down now," she ordered shrilly. "We will begin the song again." She sat down at the piano and grimly pounded out three chords on the keys. Her flushed face was mottled with white blotches. The children reluctantly focused their attention on her. She hit the introductory chord with authority.

Owen anxiously pawed through his bag, checking to see if anything had been broken in its flight. "Unbelievable," he muttered loudly as he gathered up his equipment and started towards the door where Maggie had made her noisy exit. A few people tried to shush him as he stomped out. "Don't you shush me, lady," he warned, wagging a finger at a woman who drew back in her seat under his frosty glare. The voices of the children piped his exit march.

As he reached the parking lot he saw Maggie leaning up against the hood of the jeep, her slim frame bent, as if from a blow. He stifled an urge to put a hand on her shoulder. Instead, he opened the door to the back seat and laid his camera bag down.

"I don't know about you," he said lightly. "You seem bent on destroying all my equipment."

Maggie turned around and glared at him. "Thanks a lot. That was great."

"Wait a minute," he protested. "Surely you don't blame me for that ugly display."

"I told you I was worried about it on our way over here," she cried. "I just wanted to sit quietly in the back. But no, you decided to parade me out in front of them. You had to have your bag. What's wrong with you? You couldn't walk back ten feet and pick up your own goddamn bag. You, you had to humiliate me. Drag me up there . . ."

"Hold it," Owen thundered, grabbing her arms which trembled in his grip. "In the first place I had all my meters adjusted to that spot. Which is why I asked you to bring the bag. And more importantly, you can't blame me for what happened here tonight. It isn't my fault."

"I knew this would happen," she went on, jerking herself out of Owen's grasp. "Jess said 'Go to this meeting. Everything will be fine.' I could have told him this would happen. I know what people are like. But no. Jess knew better. And you," she accused him.

"Maggie," he interrupted her tirade. "No one knew this was going to happen. We're civilized people. We don't expect our neighbours to act like Huns. I'm very sorry you had to endure that."

"I expected it," she cried.

"It would be great if people behaved reasonably, but they don't always. They blame you for what happened to those children, not because they have any evidence, but simply because you're new here. You know, your great-great-grandfather wasn't in the crow's nest when Horace McWhirter's ship first bumped into this island." He paused for a second and then mused. "It's a mercy he didn't call it McWhirtersville, isn't it?"

246

"You know about what happened at the Fair," she observed dully.

Owen clicked his tongue in annoyance. "I'm sorry," he said. "I try to ignore most of their silly gossip."

"It doesn't matter," she said wearily. "Everyone knows."

"Now don't take that attitude," he insisted. "You're letting them get to you, and it's not that serious. This will all blow over. Listen, when I first came here they practically used to cross the street to avoid me. You'd think I'd arrived by flying saucer, instead of the ferry." Owen shook his head and chuckled at the memory.

"I don't feel well," she said. "I'd like to go."

"I'm just trying to tell you that I know what it's like."

"I don't want to talk about it," she said.

Owen sighed, and walked around to his side of the car.

"Do you want me to come in with you?" he asked gently when they reached her driveway.

"No."

"I'm sure Jess wouldn't want me to leave you alone."

"Jess wanted me to go to that meeting," she muttered.

"He only thought it would be for your own good," Owen chided her.

"I know," she whispered. For a moment she

was silent. Then she said, "I should have told them all to go to hell."

"You probably should have," Owen agreed.

They sat quietly, each involved in their own thoughts. Finally, Owen asked, "What are you going to do now?"

"I don't know," she admitted. "Sit and stew, probably."

"Why don't I come in? We can have a drink."

"No," she said. "I think I just want to be alone." She opened the car door and stepped out. "Good night, Owen."

Owen watched her in the light of his head-lamps as she walked up the driveway towards her house. "Good night," he said to himself. He shook his head, and backed out towards the road. There was something odd about her. Something so familiar. He wished he could place her. He realized guiltily that he had not pressed her harder about staying for a drink because the events of the night had tired him. Other people's problems usually did. He looked forward to the quiet sanctuary of his house above the lagoon. But as he pulled up to the fork in the road which led to his property, he was troubled by an uneasy feeling. Owen craned his neck to the right to see if any traffic was coming, but the road was completely dark. Suddenly it occurred to him, as he waited, that the porch light at Maggie's house, which had been on when they left, was no longer lit. I should have waited until she got inside, he thought. Made sure she was all right.

Slowly he made the left turn towards the lagoon road. The darkened porch light intruded on his consciousness. He slowed the jeep, and looked back in the direction from which he had come. The Thornhill house was out of sight now. It must have burned out, he told himself. Then he accelerated, and started up the winding road. Gratefully, he realized that he was almost home.

They won't let you be, she thought, as she walked towards her back door. They get an idea about you and that's it. It doesn't matter if you didn't do it. You can cry out to heaven that you're innocent or shake your fist in their faces. It's all the same. They have an idea about you, and that's who you are to them. Maggie felt as if she could barely drag herself along under the weight of the depression which was settling over her.

Lost in her ruminations, it was not until she slammed her shin into one of the steps that she realized the back porch light was out. As she massaged her shin, she looked up in puzzlement at the darkened globe. The house was dreary without the light, but absolutely still. She approached the door and put her hand on the knob, listening cautiously for anything out of the ordinary. All was quiet. I guess the bulb blew, she thought. She turned the doorknob and walked in, groping for the light switch on the wall. Her fingers found it, and threw it. The room remained black.

"Is there anybody here?" she called out anxiously, trying to sound intrepid.

The only reply to her ringing demand was the soft sound of whimpering and tiny yelps coming from beyond the living-room.

"Willy," she called out, "I'm home now." Maggie stood tensely in the doorway for a moment, reluctant to step into the darkened room. In the silence, as she waited, she realized that she could hear neither the humming of the kitchen clock, nor the hum of the refrigerator from the kitchen. She sidled over quickly to an end table and pulled the lamp chain. Nothing happened. "The power must be out," she said aloud. "Goddammit."

But despite the curse, she felt suddenly relieved. Her eyes were adjusting to the darkness by now, and the room seemed to be just as she had left it. She felt her way to the mantel, and located a candle in a brass holder, and some matches. She lit the wick, and then moved the candle in an arc in front of her. There were no signs of disorder. Maggie gave a shaky sigh.

Power was unpredictable on this island. She had heard that often enough. I'd better check the fuse box, she thought. Holding the candle out in front of her, she started towards the kitchen where she located the fuse box on the wall. From the back of the house she could hear the reassuring clamour of Willy's yelping. "All right," she called out to him, as she yanked the fuse box open and peered in at the array of fuses, which looked like an assortment of tiny glass doughnuts. "Just a minute, Willy."

Fortunately, she thought, she had asked Jess to explain this to her one day last week when a fuse blew in the kitchen. Now, if it wasn't a power failure, then it had to be a master fuse, because it seemed to affect the whole house. She held the candle up to them. They looked okay, but it was hard to tell. She reached into the box to unscrew the master fuses. The top one practically fell into her hand. It must have been loose, she thought, frowning. From the back of the house she could hear the puppy's excited cries. "Just let me get this fuse, Willy," she hollered out to him. She examined the fuse intently, and then replaced it in its socket. She screwed it firmly in place.

The lights came on, and the refrigerator began to hum. At the same instant an unearthly howl of agony filled the house. Maggie leaped back, and then ran into the living-room. The terrible cry came again from the back of the house. Maggie ran through the living-room towards the bedroom. As she passed the bathroom door, the stench of burning fur and flesh drifted out.

Maggie stopped short, and stepped into the bathroom. Her heart pounded as she inched forward. Then she froze, and clapped her hands over her mouth to stifle the scream.

In the bottom of the deep, claw-footed bathtub, the tiny puppy sprawled, stiff-legged, in a few inches of water. Willy's raisin eyes bulged out of his fragile skull. The stink in the room was sickening.

"Willy!" Maggie shrieked, and knelt down to reach for the helpless animal. "What happened?" But even as she cried out, she jerked back her hands, her eyes falling on the smouldering electric razor, immersed in the water just inches from Willy's stiffened body. Her eyes followed the cord back to the socket where it was plugged into the wall. With an inchoate cry of fury she ripped the plug from the socket. Sparks crackled out from the fixture.

"What kind of fiend . . . ?" Maggie whispered. She rocked back on her heels, her body trembling uncontrollably. She stretched out her hands towards the puppy's tiny, rigid form, and then quickly retracted them into fists against her shaking rib cage. Her eyes rolled back in her head.

"No," she said. She began shaking her head, her voice rising like a river flooding its banks. "Willy. No." Her bitter lament filled the room, but the puppy heard nothing, felt nothing. He could not see her crouching there, fists clenched, wailing for him.

16

WITH a grimy hand Maggie wiped away the perspiration that had collected on her forehead. She jammed the tip of the shovel into the earth, and then stood quietly, grasping the handle and staring down with dry and vacant eyes at the mound of dirt at her feet. "I'm sorry, Willy," she said aloud. Then she leaned the shovel up against the house, and went inside.

The house glowed warmly in the night but she was oblivious to its comforting light. In her mind her journey had already begun. She found her suitcases in the hall cupboard where she had stored them less than two weeks ago, and dragged them out. She carried them to her bedroom and laid them, open, on her bed. One by one she began to empty the dresser drawers of her meagre belongings and fill the suitcases. It did not take her long. She had not had time to accumulate much.

That's it, she thought to herself. I'm done. For a second she stood there, staring into the suitcases, the sweater she was holding forgotten in her hand. A normal person would call the police. They would say, an intruder has entered my home, killed my dog. The police would take care of everything. The neighbours would be sympathetic. Maggie gave a short, humourless laugh. She looked down at the sweater in her hand as if it were a moon rock. Then she recalled herself to her task. She tossed the sweater into the open suitcase, and snapped it shut.

Wait until Emmett hears about my sojourn here, she thought. All those letters. All that careful planning. What did it matter? It was hopeless, and she could not stay. She wondered who it was that had arranged Willy's cruel death. For a moment her thoughts turned to Grace, but then she dismissed the idea. Even Grace would not be that cruel. Perhaps it was some friend of theirs, or some young punks who had heard what happened to the boys. Maggie realized that it really didn't matter who had done it. Willy's death was like a cross burning. A way of expressing local sentiment. The message was clear. It was a sick thing to do, but what good would it do to say so? Maggie swung the suitcase off the bed, and dropped it heavily by the door.

She ran her eyes over the sparse furniture in the room. It looked as if she had never lived there. She glanced at the bed, neatly made, its pillows side by side. Jess. She had to tell him she was going. He would be furious about Willy, but he would urge her to stay, to keep trying. He would not understand why she couldn't. Maggie walked into the kitchen and picked up the telephone. She dialled the number and waited for six rings, but Jess did not pick it up. As she replaced the receiver, she almost felt relieved. She dreaded telling him about Willy. If only she had checked on him before she turned the fuse. And she was ashamed to admit that she was running away, giving up.

Stay, he would say. Think of us. Maggie shook her head, and rubbed her eyes with her fingers. He didn't know. He couldn't possibly understand. All those years in prison. The relentless abuse. She could not live like a pariah any more. Somehow it had started again. But this time she could walk away. There were no bars or walls to restrain her.

Maggie picked up the phone impatiently and dialled Jess's number again. She would not risk staying here. It was too dangerous. She knew herself too well. Too much pressure. The phone's ringing signal purred steadily in her ear. Where could he have gone, she wondered. She looked up at the clock. It was getting late. "Answer," she urged him aloud. But the phone continued to ring.

She slammed the receiver back on its hook, and wandered aimlessly into the living-room, sitting in each chair, and finding that none of them felt comfortable. She got up and began to pace around the small room. Part of her felt that she should just leave, and call him from the mainland. If she hurried, she thought, glancing at the grandfather clock, she could still make the last boat out for the night. But even as she considered it, she knew that she couldn't do it. Not without seeing him one last time. Perhaps she would even tell him the truth about herself. She probably owed him that. He had believed in her. He had loved her. I should tell him for his own good, she thought ruefully. Teach him a lesson about leading with his heart.

Maggie pushed herself angrily out of the armchair where she had settled again, and returned to the kitchen. She dialled the number again, but she was greeted with the ringing tone. She couldn't just walk out on him without a word. Still holding the phone to her ear, Maggie looked out the window. Just beyond the arc of the back porch light was Willy's grave. She wished she could have buried him over closer to the stream, where she and Jess had taken him to play that first night, but she was daunted by the darkness.

Hanging up the phone, she sat down heavily in a kitchen chair, and examined her hands. They were trembling uncontrollably. She realized, after a moment, that her teeth were chattering. Maggie pushed herself up from the chair and then bent down in front of a cabinet below the sink. There was a bottle of Scotch hidden there. She recalled having seen it when she was cleaning. I need something for my nerves, she thought. She opened the cabinet door and looked in. The tall neck of the whisky bottle caught her eye in the back. She reached in for it. As she did so, her hand grazed a white plastic bottle, nearly tipping it. For a second she hesitated, gazing at the blue and white label which warned that it was disinfectant. She recalled the night that she had poured herself a drink from just such a bottle, and the immediate, searing pain. Maggie frowned. She did not often let herself think of that night when she had tried to end her life.

Now, her hand travelled unconsciously to her throat. She massaged the area absently, her finger probing the spot where the tube had been which sustained her life. It was completely healed now; the only remaining sign was a tiny scar near the base of her throat. Tubes and bottles and bags of blood had restored her to a life which she had finally decided to live. In all the months and years that followed, it had been a struggle to keep going. She could not afford to slip back.

She thrust her fingers in, around the neck of the whisky bottle, and pulled it out. Her eyes searched the room as she poured the Scotch unsteadily into a glass beer mug. She closed her eyes and cringed, as she brought the mug to her lips. Trying to ignore the taste, she swallowed the liquor in greedy gulps. It felt hot, and numbing, going down.

Evy reached into the refrigerator and pulled out

two cellophane-wrapped packages from the middle shelf.

"I might as well do this tonight," she said.

Thin, transparent blood from the chicken parts wound through the creases and folds of the plastic wrapping where the package was sealed, and leaked out over the girl's fingers. She shook the packages over the sink and dropped them on the draining board. "We'll have chicken tomorrow," she announced, and then turned around to gauge the response. "You like chicken," she said.

Harriet Robinson watched her granddaughter with frightened eyes, surrounded by deep circles.

"Right?" Evy demanded.

The old woman blinked, and continued to stare.

Evy peered at her for a moment, and then seemed satisfied, even though there was no discernible reaction to her query. "I know what you like," she said.

She picked up the first package on the draining board, and poked her finger into the plastic wrapping. After several pokes she managed to puncture it, her ragged fingernail sinking into the yellow folds of skin. She gathered up the edges of plastic and tore the wrapping off the chicken parts. The watery fowl's blood ran across her palm.

"Ugh," she grimaced. "I hate this. It's so messy." She picked up the various parts and

258

examined them carefully before laying them on the counter. Then she turned her attention to the other package.

"I got a lot of chicken," she observed. "Plenty of leftovers. Well, who knows," she said, grasping the other package, and turning to her grandmother. "Maybe we'll have company!"

The old woman watched the girl intently.

Evy picked up a knife and used it to poke through the wrapping on the second package. "I know," she sighed. "We never have company."

A rasping sound came from the direction of the wheelchair. Evy wheeled around and eyed the old woman. "What's the matter?" she demanded. Her grandmother did not appear to have budged. Satisfied, Evy returned to her chore.

"I honestly don't see how you can expect me to take care of you, and do everything else I have to do and have company too. I'm only one person," she complained. Taking one half of a breast in each hand, Evy yanked at them. The bones cracked and the two halves separated. She placed the open breast on the cutting board and reached for a butcher's knife. With one swift blow she whacked them apart.

"I know what's bothering you," she continued in a more sympathetic tone. "You know what happened to Jess." She looked towards the old woman for confirmation. Harriet Robinson

259

blinked rapidly, as if trying to clear her eyes of a mote.

Evy removed one half of the breast from the cutting board, and then searched in a drawer next to the sink until she produced a knife with a slender, pointed blade. She placed the knife parallel to the side of the cutting board. Then she lifted a flap of chicken skin between her fingers. For a second she rubbed the skin absently, as if she were judging the quality of a fabric. Then, with an abrupt motion, she tore the skin away from the flesh. The chicken part jerked up, and she clamped it to the cutting board with the heel of her hand. The skin separated from the flesh with a sucking sound, and hung limply in her fingers.

"I know," she went on. "You liked him. 'Hello, Harriet. How are you feeling today.' He was always so sweet to you. He was too sweet," she muttered. "To everybody." She picked up the thin knife and held it poised over the fleshy breast. "Originally I didn't intend for him to be involved," she admitted defensively. She poked the tip of the knife into the ball of her forefinger. A tiny drop of blood squeezed out, but she did not notice it. "But that's what happened." She sank the knife into the fresh meat of the breast, close to the bone, and drew it along. Suddenly she stopped, and looked up sharply at her grandmother, who watched her every move as if Evy were a stirring cobra. At the sudden movement of Evy's head in her direction, the old woman started.

"Listen," said Evy. "I have a bone to pick with you." She laughed at her own joke and then instantly resumed her stern demeanour. "Not really a bone to pick," she corrected herself. "But you do have to promise me something. If anybody asks you anything about . . . you know, downstairs, you better not tell."

Evy peered down at the pocket of flesh she had created with the blade. Then she slipped the knife into it and began to worry it across. "We can't let anyone find out. So if anyone asks you anything, where I was tonight, or anything, you just pretend you don't know anything about it. As far as you're concerned, I was here with you all the time. It's important," she said, eyeing the old woman seriously. "You have to promise." She scrutinized her grandmother's face to see if she understood and agreed. The old woman's fearful gaze troubled her, and she shook her head.

"Don't worry," she assured her. "Nothing's going to happen. No one will probably even ask you anything. There's no way they will find out. Now I've got you worrying over nothing. Believe me, it's almost over. Just a little while longer and we'll be back to normal."

She dropped the knife on the counter with a clatter, and picked up the breast, slipping her fingers impatiently between flesh and bone. "I know you wished it hadn't been Jess. I wished it too. But it had to be that way. It had to be. He brought it on himself. He should never have taken up with her. Anybody could tell just by looking at her what she is." As she spoke her voice rose, and she jabbed her fingers into the chicken breast.

"He was sleeping with her. Just like my father did. You told me that yourself," Evy cried out. She ripped the flesh away from the brittle bones. "Well, that's what he gets!" The bones cracked between her fingers as she squeezed them.

With a strength summoned from every ragged nerve and limp fibre in her ruined body, Harriet Robinson lurched forward, out of her wheel-chair. For a moment it seemed as if she would actually stand, her frail form arched briefly above the leather chair seat that usually imprisoned her. Then she dropped, with a crash, to the linoleum floor of the kitchen.

Evy spun around and stared at her grand-mother, the slick, dripping chicken flesh in one hand, the broken bones crushed in her other palm.

The old woman lay huddled there, her cheek pressed to the cold linoleum, unable to look up at her granddaughter. Her senseless, flannel-draped limbs were splayed out with only her left arm bent crookedly beneath her. She gasped for breath with the nostril and corner of her mouth that were not squashed against the floor. Her eyes wide, she stared ahead at the legs of the kitchen table.

Slowly, Evy turned back to the counter and puzzled over the chicken, as if she could not remember what she had been doing. Then she recollected herself. She picked up another breast from the draining-board and began to wash it off under the tap.

"That's right," she murmured. "You told me all about it. I remember everything you said. He slept with her, and then she killed him and got away with it. She was so jealous of Mummy and me, right? And all she got for it was a few years in prison. That's all. Remember? These days, you can get away with murder, you said. Remember?"

The old woman's body ached as she lay help-less on the floor. Her eyes darted around the room like mice trapped in a maze as her grand-daughter's voice droned smoothly on, reminding her of her own words. She heard the words drip-ping now from her granddaughter's lips into her own ear, like venom from a serpent's fang.

263

17

WITH each desultory movement of the sleeping woman slumped over the table, the empty bottle edged closer to the table's rim. She groaned, and flopped her head over, resting her cheek on her upper arm. The bottle teetered, and then fell to the floor with a crash.

Maggie leapt up, shocked into consciousness by the noise. Confused, and with her heart pounding, she looked around, and then saw the broken bottle on the kitchen floor. She sank back into the chair, aware now of the painful cramp in her side and a throbbing headache above her right eyebrow. She lowered her aching head back on to her crooked arm. The smell of the table reminded her of her desk in grammar school when she had to keep her head down for an enforced nap, unable to sleep because of the suffocating smell of wood and varnish. Now, despite the sickening sensation, she was too exhausted to lift her head.

She turned her head sideways on her arm and stared ahead. Outside the kitchen window the grey, brooding sky was streaked with the palest strands of weak, silvery light. Beside the sink was a glass beer mug still holding about half an inch of whisky. Maggie's stomach turned over as her eyes fell on the glass. Slowly, she sat up, pressing her fingers to her eyes. She turned around and looked at the luminous face of the clock on the wall. It read 5.45. Maggie winced, and then idly kicked at the fragments of glass on the floor.

Her throat was so dry that she found swallowing difficult. A vile taste lingered in her mouth. She looked at the phone. She had called Jess a few times while she was swilling down the liquor in the glass. There was no answer. The last thing she remembered was gulping down a mouthful of whisky directly from the bottle.

"I should clean this up," she muttered, looking down at the hunks of glass on the floor. She leaned over to start picking up the pieces which seemed to be everywhere. The pointed corner of one large piece jutted up, like an iceberg, out of the milk which remained in Willy's bowl. Maggie's stomach rolled over, and nausea suddenly overcame her. She stood up unsteadily, her hand over her mouth, and ran for the bathroom. She reached the bathroom just in time as the whisky surged up, geyser-like, from her nauseated stomach.

The siege of vomiting left her feeling weak, but more stable. She looked at her face in the bathroom mirror with a feeling of unreality. She looked tired, and pale, but not much worse than usual. It surprised her that her face concealed so well the evidence of her night's despair. Practice, she thought wryly.

She pulled the mirrored door of the cabinet towards her, and grasped, with a shaking hand, the bottle of aspirin. She shook out four of them, and swallowed them down with a gulp of water. Then she shut the chest, and shuffled slowly towards her bedroom. For a moment she sat on the edge of the bed, her eyes closed against the weak, grey light of the dawn. She considered returning to the kitchen, and calling Jess now, but decided that he would not want to be awakened, especially since he had been out late. Where, she wondered? Her pillow looked like a cloud to her. Gingerly she lowered her head, and pulled a blanket up over her aching, still fully clothed body. The alarm clock on the table beside her bed was set for 7.00 a.m., but she decided not to pull out the alarm. There was no reason to get to the paper on time. She would just tell Jess she was leaving, and be on her way. You don't have to be on time to quit, she thought. Where had he been all night? She turned the clock face away from her, and closed her eyes. I'll go when I'm ready, she thought. To hell with them.

It was nearly 11.30 when Maggie entered the *Cove News* offices on the cobbled streets of town. The irony of her actions struck her as she placed her suitcases in the hall, just as she had on that first day, two weeks ago. She strode deliberately past the room she shared with Grace and Evy and headed for the door to Jess's office. As she passed by she heard Grace yelp, "Hey, wait one minute."

Ignoring Grace's injunction, she kept on walking until she was in front of Jess's door at the end of the corridor. She began to knock sharply on the door as Grace appeared in the hall and insisted. "Just a minute there. I'm talking to you."

Maggie turned her head and stared coldly at her. "I don't want to talk to you," she said, feeling a thrill of satisfaction at her own boldness. "I want to talk to Jess."

"Well, Jess is not here," Grace shot back. "And furthermore, I would like to know where he is."

Maggie's face sagged. She stared at Grace. "He's not here?" she repeated.

Grace drew herself up indignantly. "Are you trying to tell me that you didn't know that?"

Maggie shook her head, mystified.

"Well, don't look so innocent. I naturally assumed, after what's been going on between the two of you, that he was at your place. Or vice versa. I figured you would show up together, when and if you decided to show up," said Grace pointedly.

"Why didn't you call?" Maggie asked.

"I didn't want to disturb the two of you," Grace snapped.

"Jess wasn't with me. I don't know where he is. Do you mean he hasn't even called?" Maggie asked.

"I noticed *you* didn't call."

Maggie ignored the sarcasm. "Doesn't he usually get in touch with you if he's delayed?"

"Yes," Grace said defensively. "But I told you. I was expecting you to come in together."

"I understand that, Grace. But I haven't seen Jess since about seven o'clock last night," she said earnestly. "I tried to reach him myself but he wasn't there."

"He wasn't?" Grace's indignation began to crumble into ill-concealed anxiety. The two women stared silently at one another. Finally Grace spoke. "It's not like Jess not to call. I'd better try his house." She backed away from Maggie and then turned and hurried into her office.

"What's going on?"

Maggie jumped, startled by the sound of a voice just behind her. She turned and saw Evy leaning against the wall, her head cocked quizzically to one side.

"It's Jess," Maggie mumbled. "He didn't show up for work today."

Evy smiled thinly. "Playing hookey."

Maggie shook her head, and stared straight ahead. "I don't think so," she said.

"How come?" Evy asked.

"He would have mentioned something. He wasn't home last night either."

Evy shrugged.

"I'm sure he's okay," she said. "Jess can take care of himself."

"I hope you're right."

"'Scuse me," Evy mumbled, avoiding Maggie's eyes as she brushed by her and headed down the hall. Watching her pale, guarded face, Maggie suddenly realized that she hadn't seen the girl since the incident at the Fair. A feeling of shame came over her as she recalled her outburst.

"Evy," she said.

The girl stopped and looked back at her.

"I . . . I've been wanting to talk to you about Sunday. Are you okay?"

Evy touched her nostril reflexively. "I'm fine," she said.

"I think I owe you another apology," Maggie began.

"It's all right," said the girl. "You couldn't help it."

Maggie bristled slightly. "Well, that's not really true. I was wrong to blame you for what happened. And for hurting you like that . . ."

"It was a mess," said Evy, as if to dismiss the subject.

"Yeah," Maggie murmured.

"He doesn't answer," Grace announced

shrilly, coming out into the hall. Her concern was evident in her tone.

"Where could he be?" Evy asked.

"Well, I don't know," said Grace, "but I'm not going to stand around imagining a lot of far-fetched possibilities.

Evy sighed in agreement.

"For that matter where's Mr. Emmett? We still haven't heard from him. What kind of a business trip is that when you never tell anyone whether you're coming or going," Grace snorted. "I'm getting the police."

"The police," Maggie whispered.

"Unless you've got some good idea of where he's gone to," said Grace angrily.

Maggie looked at her helplessly. "I don't know," she said. "I can't think."

"Never mind," Grace snapped. "I'm going to tell Jack Schmale. Evy, get in there and finish that work on your desk. We've got plenty to do."

Evy aye-ayed her, and disappeared into the office door.

"You better come too," said Grace to Maggie. "He'll probably want to know a few things from you."

"You're going to the police station?" Maggie asked weakly.

"Certainly," Grace ejaculated.

I cannot go to the police station, she thought. I cannot. She began to feel dizzy at the prospect, and was seized with the sudden conviction that if she stepped over the threshold of the police station she would faint.

"Don't you want to find him?" Grace asked accusingly.

"Of course," Maggie cried.

"Well, come on then."

"Grace, it's just that I don't feel too well. I'm afraid I might get sick," she admitted. "Why don't you call, and ask him to come over here? It would save time."

Grace peered at her. "What's the matter with you? Have you been drinking?"

Maggie seized the excuse. "I did have a drink or two last night, for my . . . for a toothache. It upset my stomach. I may have a touch of the flu."

"All right," said Grace. "I'll call him."

She rushed past Maggie and went back into the office. She picked up the receiver, and began to dial the number of the Heron's Neck police station.

"Riiiii—di, Pagliacco . . ."

A stifled sob pulsed in the tenor's voice. Jack Schmale listened, hands clasped, eyes closed, his face contorted into an expression at once anguished and blissful. It was his favourite moment of the opera. Through his headset, the music poured into his ears.

Surrounded by sound, curtained by his closed

271

eyelids, Jack was transported. He could picture the lonely clown, stage centre, singing his sorrow. Jack had seen *I Pagliacci* during the Metropolitan Opera's Boston engagement two years before. He always planned his vacations to coincide with operatic events. Once, ten years ago, he had even gone to La Scala.

Jack's chin rose in satisfaction as the tenor brought the aria to a triumphant finish. Jack opened his eyes and blinked like a man coming out of a trance. He gazed around the tiny police office which was his working residence. The walls were greying, as he was, and their surfaces were covered with yellowing memos, and posters old and new. The two desks were chipped and scarred, and the windows were thick with grime. The newest item in the room was Jack's portable tape recorder, a treasured anniversary gift from Wilma, his wife, two years before.

In the doorway of the office a young man in a blue uniform and a pink-cheeked brunette loitered. Her little teeth gleamed, white as shirt buttons, as she threw back her head in laughter. The young officer leaned towards her and continued talking. Jack frowned in frank disapproval over the glasses which were slipping down his nose. The music started up again, and Jack conducted it absently with his forefinger as he spied on the couple in the doorway. They seemed totally absorbed in one another, oblivious to his stares. The uneven cadence of flirtatious banter occasionally penetrated Jack's earphones.

Perhaps, Jack thought with a sigh, I'm not setting a good example. He switched off the power on the tape recorder reluctantly, and removed his headset. He turned back to the pair in the doorway.

"Officer Prendergast," he called out.

The moustachioed young man straightened up from the door jamb which was supporting his weight. "Yes?" he asked politely.

"I think you ought to take a run out to the Taylor house. I promised Cyrus we'd keep an eye on it while they were in Bermuda."

The pink-cheeked girl murmured a farewell to the young officer and slipped out the door and across the street to the shop where she worked. Prendergast looked longingly after her disappearing back, and then turned back to face his superior.

"Okay," he agreed. "Anything else?"

"Nothing," Schmale admitted.

"All right. I'm on my way."

"Eric."

The older cop's worried tone halted the young man's departure. "Yeah?"

Schmale cleared his throat. "How's Joanie doing," he asked casually. "Haven't seen her lately."

Prendergast reddened at the mention of his

wife. "She's fine," he said. "She's been real busy with the baby."

Schmale nodded, and then glanced across the street at the window of the dry goods shop.

"Anything else, sir?" asked the young man stiffly.

"No, no," Jack dismissed him. "Better get out to Taylor's."

"Yes, sir," said Prendergast, adjusting his hat on his head.

Schmale shook his head as the door closed behind the young officer. "This is how trouble gets started," he said to the empty room. Sighing, Jack turned back to his desk. He began to peruse his collection of tapes.

The phone at Jack's elbow startled him with its ring. He frowned at the interruption, and placed the box of cassettes back in the drawer. *Turandot* would have to wait. Clearing his throat, Jack picked up the phone and said gruffly, "Police." He was surprised to hear the anxious voice of Grace Cullum, blurting out the news that Jess Herlie had not shown up for work.

"All right, ladies," Jack Schmale commenced, "I would like you to tell me all the facts of this matter."

"I thought," Grace began importantly, "that Jess was with her." She gestured towards Maggie who sat huddled on a nearby chair. "They've been, you know . . ." Grace hesitated, uncertain how to besmirch Maggie's reputation without implicating Jess. "Seen together outside of work," she said finally. "Well, I didn't want to call in the middle of something."

Evy let forth with a slightly manic giggle which earned her stony glances from everyone in the room.

"So," Grace continued, "I waited and waited. Finally, she comes in, and claims she hasn't seen Jess since yesterday. I called his house right away, but no answer. Ordinarily I wouldn't bother you, Jack, but what with no word from Mr. Emmett either, well, naturally I am very worried."

"You did the right thing, Grace," the officer assured her. He turned to Maggie. "What is your name, miss?"

"Margaret Fraser," she mumbled.

Jack Schmale peered at her face for a moment, as if trying to locate a matching card in a game of concentration. Then he shrugged, and wrote it down on the pad he was holding. "And when was the last time you saw Jess Herlie?" he asked.

"Last night," said Maggie softly. "About seven o'clock."

"Where was that?"

"He was . . . It was at my house. Then he went home after that."

The policeman looked at her intently. "So you didn't see him or talk to him after that?"

"No," said Maggie helplessly. "I went out. I tried to call him when I got home but there was no answer."

Jack took off his glasses, folded them up and inserted them in the case on the breast pocket of his shirt. "Well, I think the first thing to do before we get all worked up is to take a ride up there. He might be taken ill or some such thing." He tried to sound reassuring, but his words were unconvincing. Grace and Evy looked at one another. Maggie stared at the floor.

"I'll give you a call as soon as I get back," said Jack, starting for the door. "Meantime, try to recall if he mentioned any plans for today that you might have overlooked."

"No," Grace insisted. "I would have written them down on the calendar."

"Well, sometimes we forget these things," said Jack, zippering up his leather coat and heading towards the door. As he reached the hallway he suddenly stopped short and looked back towards the women's office.

"Whose are these?" he shouted.

The three women crowded into the doorway and saw him holding up the suitcases which had been in the hallway near the door.

Maggie uneasily acknowledged her bags. "They're mine."

Schmale examined them thoughtfully. "Oh, I thought they might be Jess's." Then he looked up at Maggie. "Going somewhere?" he asked.

"I was," Maggie explained carefully. "I was planning on leaving."

"A vacation?"

"No. Moving away," Maggie admitted, feeling ridiculous. "I just wanted to stop here and pick up a few things and tell Jess before I left."

"Leaving?" the cop asked. "Just like that?"

Maggie drew her hands down the sides of her face to steady her expression. She could feel that Evy and Grace were staring at her. "I've been . . . I haven't liked it here," she said. "I wanted to go somewhere else. Jess knew that," she lied.

Jack Schmale pursed his lips and stared at the bags which he had set down on top of one another in the hallway. "Why don't we talk some more about it in the car?" he suggested.

Grace and Evy shot one another a glance. Maggie began to sputter. "In the car?"

"I just want you to take a ride up to Jess's place with me. You wouldn't mind doing that, would you?"

Maggie opened her mouth, but did not speak.

"Can you spare her for a few minutes, Grace?"

"Certainly," Grace acquiesced.

"Come along, then," said Jack.

Numbly, Maggie picked up her coat and followed him.

Despite Jack's warrant that they would talk on the way, Maggie and the officer passed most of the long ride without conversation. As soon as they were in the car, Jack switched on the radio to the classical station and the car was immediately filled with powerful voices singing passionately in foreign tongues.

Maggie was grateful for the wall of sound. The proximity to a policeman made her feel faint with anxiety. The constant creak of leather as he turned the wheel unnerved her. The sound of a pen in his breast pocket scraping against his badge penetrated the music like fingernails crawling across a blackboard. The keys on his belt loop jingled menacingly against the handcuffs which also dangled there. Maggie avoided the man's mild gaze, and watched the now-familiar road to Jess's house run by. Where was he, she wondered? Maggie could see water more frequently now to her left as they neared the spot where Jess's house stood.

"Nice spot up here where Jess lives," said Schmale. "My wife Wilma and I lived up here at Warriner's Point for a few years when we were first married."

"Oh really?"

"Yeah. Good fishing up here. And I could play all my records as loud as I pleased and nobody ever complained." Jack chuckled at the memory. "Except Wilma, once in a while. But, it's really too far from town. I spent my whole time running back and forth."

"It's pretty here," Maggie agreed. "The water view . . ."

"Yup." Schmale turned up the narrow driveway and his car slowly climbed towards the house. "Car's here," he said.

Maggie had already noted the presence of Jess's late-model compact in the driveway. Schmale pulled up behind it and turned off the engine. "Let's have a look," he said, turning his unperturbed eyes on Maggie. He got out of the car and started down the hill towards the jetty and the shed which served as a makeshift boat house. He glanced back to make sure that Maggie was still standing where he left her.

Grey mist from the water below rose up, dank and uninviting. Maggie watched Jack rattle the padlock and peer into the shed window. She turned her head away and looked towards the house. She recalled the first time Jess had brought her to the brightly-lit, cheerful home. "Did every bit of work myself," he said, proudly gesturing towards the woodwork, shelves and newly-plastered walls. "Took me years. Of course I didn't do the curtains. Sharon made them. First year we were here." Jack laboured up the hill and joined her on the walk. "His power boat's there," he grunted. "Let's try the house."

His repeated knock unanswered, Jack Schmale turned the doorknob and went in. Maggie followed behind him. Inside, everything was still.

Jack poked through the ground floor, turning

on the lights and peering into each empty room. Then he returned to where Maggie stood in the living-room.

"I'm going to have a look upstairs. He's not down here."

Maggie nodded and glanced around her as Schmale stomped purposefully up the stairs. "Jess?" he called out.

The living-room was in its usual state of casual disarray, although the few antiques which he had acquired from his parents when they moved off island sat polished and ready for elderly guests of formal town business meetings. A row of plants on the windowsill drooped from lack of water. Maggie drifted through to the kitchen which was orderly, the table cleared, except for the last sip in a mug of coffee which sat on the table. He wasn't here for breakfast, she thought automatically. He drank tea for breakfast, and coffee at night. What she knew about him surprised her. She realized that every habit she had observed, every conversation they had shared, was now indelible in her memory. She could reel it all off, like a catechism.

In the den, the clutter of his books and piled-up papers caught at her with a painful immediacy. It looked as if he had just walked out for an instant. His pipe which she had so recently returned to him lay on its side in the ashtray, as if he had only had a moment to place it carelessly by, before he vanished.

She turned away from the den, and stepped back into the hall. Overhead she could hear the heavy clomping of Jack Schmale's boots, and the faint slamming of cupboard doors. She tried the back door to the porch and found it unlocked. She opened the door and walked out. On a clear day you could see the water below, lapping up against the dock down the hill. Today the fog obscured it in a dense grey cloud, but she could still hear the insistent shushing of the waves.

On the porch was a wicker table, littered with a few empty beer cans, and a soggy copy of the *Cove News*. Beside it an ancient rocker swayed, an old sweater draped haphazardly across the back. Maggie picked up the sweater and ran her hand over it. Her fingers got caught by the frayed hole on one of the sleeves. She clutched the well-worn garment to her chest, and looked blindly out over the land and water now eclipsed by fog. Images of Jess assailed her. The peacefulness of the house only served to exaggerate the dread which was mushrooming inside of her.

"Hey, where are you?" The voice of Jack Schmale rolled down the hallway of the little house.

Maggie started. "Out here," she called back, her voice faint.

Jack Schmale stalked down the hallway and opened the door to the porch. She looked at him questioningly.

"He's not here," the policeman announced.

Maggie nodded. She knew it already.

Jack held up Jess's wallet in his left hand. "Car keys, wallet, watch. All on his dresser. Wherever he went, he didn't mean to stay long."

"There's coffee on the table from last night," said Maggie. She carefully replaced the sweater over the back of the chair, her hands trembling.

"He never mentioned to you that he might be going anywhere?"

Maggie shook her head. "Nothing."

"You better try to remember," said Jack. "He didn't just disappear."

Maggie looked up sharply into the sober eyes of the policeman.

"You may as well take those bags of yours home and unpack them," he observed. "I don't want anybody leaving here for a while. I may have some more questions for you."

"Are you arresting me?" she asked weakly.

"For what?" asked the old cop querulously. "Did you commit a crime?"

"No," Maggie breathed shaking her head.

"No evidence of foul play yet," said Schmale tapping Jess's wallet absent-mindedly against the palm of his hand.

"People will say . . ." Maggie muttered.

"People talk," he interrupted her. "I go by the law. But you just stick around here. I don't want to catch you running for that ferry boat anytime soon."

Maggie nodded and turned away from the fogged-in view. For a moment her eyes rested on the sweater, which hung like a scarecrow's costume over the back of the chair. "Try to find him for me," she said, without conviction.

"I'll find him," Schmale promised grimly.

But Maggie knew, with a certainty that she could not explain, that he would not find him. At least, not for her.

18

THE first thing that Jess was conscious of was a clammy chill which was seeping into his face through his left cheek. He moved his head slightly along the cold, bumpy dirty floor, and an incandescent pain flashed through his skull, leaving him gasping. He lay still for a moment, willing the pain to pass. Then, cautiously, he tried to move his hands.

They were twisted behind his prostrate body, and were so numb that they hardly felt like part of him. He attempted to pry them apart. A tight cord, which did not budge, contained them in their awkward proximity. Although the strand felt like no more than a thread against his insensate flesh, he realized that it must be thick straps which bound him. He tried to jerk his ankles apart and found that they were bound in the same manner.

The pain in his head had returned, but it was now somewhat obscured by the emerging pains lodged in the other parts of his awakening body. Clumsily, he attempted to flex the fingers on his hands. The resultant ache in his stiffened shoulders caused him to cry out, feebly, in protest. His muscles slackened and he lay flat against the damp, dirt floor.

He opened his eyes. His lids felt as if they were lined with particles of glass. He could make out virtually nothing of his surroundings, unable to focus in the darkness.

Jess closed his eyes again, and tried to think. He did not know how long he had been lying there in the darkness. It seemed that it might have been several days. Or perhaps it had only been one. The dank vault in which he lay was silent, and had no light. His moments of consciousness had been few, and disconnected. Jess tried to force himself to remember anything he could. His mind felt as dark and empty as this chamber in which he lay imprisoned.

He allowed his unwilling brain to relax. As he did, an image popped into the darkness. Evy. Wielding a wrench above his head. Her eyes glittering with fury.

He remembered now. But he still had no understanding of it. Why? But before he could analyse the awful deed he was assailed by his physical discomfort. He felt a throbbing in his head, and his bladder ached from the need to urinate. Despite the sickening stench in the room, hunger twisted his stomach. He jerked at his bonded hands in a fit of impotent fury. When was she coming back? On the floor above him he could hear sounds, occasional movements. Then, silence.

Jess raised his torso slightly, to try to move his head into a more comfortable position. His neck felt as if it was ready to snap from resting too long at an unnatural angle. The indignity of his situation enraged him. He did not care how much it might hurt; he wanted to sit up. He needed to lean against a wall, remove his face from the dirt. With a furious effort he began to drag himself towards the wall which he knew was behind him.

A sharp pain in his chest arrested him. A rib, he thought. Broken loose, and sharp, like a sabre inside him. It must have happened when he fell down the stairs. With renewed care he pushed himself back. It couldn't be much further. He could sense the wall, looming behind him. He gave himself another shove. His body met with something behind him, stiff and bolster-shaped.

Jess wiggled his fingers around. Dimly, as if from miles away, he recognized the little remaining sensation in them. Groping behind him, his enfeebled fingers explored the bolster and then stopped. They met the unmistakable shape of their own image.

Jess let out a strangled cry of fear as his fingers deciphered the contours of a human hand. Insensible to the pain, the price in precious strength it exacted, Jess flipped himself over to face the horror.

The corpse stared up at the ceiling, the huge gash on its head blackened, the feet fallen apart, the hands seized up in death.

Agony still lingered on the slack-jawed face,

but the eyes of William Emmett were blank and empty, the ghost of the publisher fled at the startling moment of death.

Despair and incredulity mingled in Jess's distorted wail. "Oh my God. Bill."

He gaped in disbelief at the spectre before him. The body was beginning to bloat in the dampness of its underground tomb. Jess suddenly felt as if he were being smothered by the revolting smell which it gave off. He rolled away from the body and lay on his back, trying to draw in breath through his gagged mouth. He stared up at the ceiling, unconsciously mimicking the posture of the dead man.

She killed him. She killed Bill. Jess tried to absorb this undeniable fact which now assaulted him. He wondered what it meant for him. An involuntary shudder racked his body. He looked again at the corpse and then jerked his eyes away. He felt as if he was falling through space, separated from everything that was solid, that made sense to him. One thought ran through his mind, over and over again. She was mad. She had killed Bill Emmett, and she was mad. With an animal strength born of an exquisite fear, Jess began to struggle against his bonds, twisting and grinding them against the dirt floor, desperately trying to loosen them, even a fraction of an inch, from his limbs.

Suddenly, a swathe of light and an audible clatter electrified his senses. The cellar door was open. Jess could hear scraping and the unconscious mutterings of someone at the top of the stairs. He began to shake his head, as if he could will it back. His eyes were trained on the staircase. As he watched, Evy appeared in the weak bath of light, descending the steps slowly, weighted down by the giant metal washtub which she was carrying.

She came down about three steps, her thin arms shaking visibly from the weight of the large tub. Water lapped up over the edges and splashed on her chest, dampening the front of the sweater she wore.

Evy did not look down at her captive, who lay rigid on the floor, following her progress with wide, unblinking eyes. She turned around and placed the tub on the step above her. Then, slowly, she backed down the stairs, lifting the brimming tub, gingerly, from stair to stair. When she finally reached the bottom, she lifted it up with one last heave, and placed it on the dirt floor of the cellar, not far from where Jess lay. Satisfied, she turned to look at her prisoner.

"Everyone's missed you today," she said pleasantly.

Jess stared from the girl's placid, vacant face to the tub which stood not far from his head. She was going to drown him.

Evy sighed, and sat down on the edge of the bottom step, her body taut. Clearly, she was not resting, but only lighting, like a moth. "They can't figure out where you are. Naturally, I can't tell them."

Evy shifted her weight, and glanced over at Jess. His eyes swivelled automatically towards the corpse of William Emmett, now dimly visible in the dull illumination from the top of the stairs which was filtering down.

"Oh," she said knowingly. "You found Mr. Emmett." Evy shook her head. "I always kind of liked him. Boy, he had a lot of life in him. He didn't go right off. He was moaning and groaning down here. It took him a lot longer than I thought. An old guy like that."

Jess stared at her, his eyes registering all the horror of her matter-of-fact reminiscences of the old man's horrible death. Evy appeared affronted at his look.

"Well, don't look at me like that," she said sharply, getting up. "It's not my fault he was slow. Beside, after what you've been doing, you have no right to look at me that way."

Jess stared at her bland expression in disbelief. He watched her uncomprehendingly as she leaned over him and pushed his hair back from his temples. He tried to pull away, but she clamped a hand down on his shoulder and examined the bruises on his head where she had hit him. The discoloured bump was tender to her touch. Jess winced. Even in the stinking basement her breath had a sour odour as she bent over him.

"That's some lump," she observed. Then she straightened up and looked at him appraisingly. "Yeah," she went on disjointedly, "everybody's wondering about you. They're looking for you. The problem is that they've all got their eye on her now. They're watching her every minute. Now, that's no good. I don't want there to be a lot of fussing going on. Nice and normal. That's how I want it. So I can get at her."

Maggie, he thought. But why? Jealousy? For a moment he remembered Maggie's suspicion. And why did she kill Bill Emmett? Jess felt his brain reeling as he tried to make sense of what the girl was saying. All he could be sure of was that Maggie was in danger. And that his own life might be ended at any moment.

"I'll figure out a way," Evy assured him. "I already got an idea." Evy began to pace in front of him. Jess tried to follow her with his eyes, but she began to circle him.

"You can't figure it out, can you?" Evy taunted him. "You've been just lying down here not knowing what's going on. You thought I liked you, didn't you?" Evy hunkered down and squatted in front of him. "Well, what if I did?" she cried, her voice shrill with anger. "That didn't matter to you. You went off with her anyway. You didn't care. You went and slept with her."

The girl stood up abruptly, and walked over to the washtub. She began to drag it closer to

290

him. Jess watched her straining back as she struggled with the unwieldly tub. Pitted against it, she wore an expression at once pathetic and determined. It was a look he recognized on her. One that had often aroused his pity before. He had never had any idea about her. Never known what terrible thoughts bedevilled her, twisting her mind.

"There," she said. Apparently satisfied with the new location of the tub, Evy straightened up and gazed at it for a moment. Then she turned to Jess. "This is for you," she said.

A sickening sensation of awe and fear churned inside him as he looked into her pale eyes. She was going to drown him in that tub. Hunching over and pulling up his knees, Jess tried to crawl away. Evy started to laugh. Suddenly he felt her arms locked through his elbows, her legs straddling his body. Jess thrashed back and forth, trying to shake himself free of her. She clung to him tenaciously, with a strength that shocked him.

"Hey," she crooned, gripping him tightly. "What's the matter? I'm just going to give you a bath." She dropped him heavily to the dirt floor, and reached for a towel which was hanging from the waist of her skirt.

His chest heaved as he tried to catch his breath, glaring up at her. He felt a giddy relief that she did not mean to drown him. At the same time he shuddered at the thought of her hands

291

touching him. Evy bent over and dunked the towel into the tub. Then she leaned towards him and tried to wipe his face with it. Jess jerked himself away from her. The water splashed out over the edges. Her balance was upset by his abrupt movement. She grabbed at the tail of his shirt, but he twisted away from her, wrenching his torso so hard that he could feel a muscle sprain. She kicked out at him angrily, grazing his side.

"All right," she snarled, "be filthy." She hurled the wet towel at him and it smacked him hard on the side of the face. Then she started up the stairs.

"You don't want me to take care of you. You'd rather be filthy. I should have known that. After what I saw you do with her. Well, that's the last thing I'll do for you. You can rot down here. You can just die as filthy as you are now."

He saw her legs and ankles moving up the stairs. When she reached the top she screamed back down, "Rot down there." She slammed the cellar door shut. Once again, Jess lay in the darkness, gasping for breath, his body alive with pain. He gazed over at the corpse of William Emmett, her last words to him still ringing in his ears.

19

FOR three days the sky had been threatening. Storm clouds rolled up on one another like tanks amassing for an assault, turning the sky over the island to an ever-deepening grey. In the late afternoon the wind had begun its intermittent gusting and whistling. Now, as Maggie stood in the early evening darkness before the silent church at the end of Main Street, she felt the first drops of rain.

Three agonizing days had passed since Jess's disappearance. For Maggie, their torturous unwinding had been like a slow-motion nightmare. Each day she went into the office, only to escape the terrible silence which engulfed her at home. Jack Schmale dropped by every day to fill them in on the search for Jess. Each time she saw his worried face in the doorway, Maggie jumped, her heart thudding with hope and fear. Had he found Jess? Had he not found him? Did he know who she really was?

A thousand times she wished that she had made her past no secret when she first arrived. Now her fears for Jess were compounded by the certainty that if Jack Schmale had uncovered her background, there would be no doubt in the mind of anyone that she was responsible for

Jess's disappearance. But Jack's visits to the *News* offices were marked by no revelations. His terse reports did little to alleviate the gloom and frustration that permeated the atmosphere. Grace's angry mutterings and drawer-slammings were interspersed with fits of weeping. Evy was often too jumpy and distracted to work. Maggie observed them warily. She knew they blamed her. She had overheard Grace talking to Jack.

"What about *her*?" Grace had demanded.

"We've been watching Thornhill's," Jack explained patiently.

"She was trying to run away. Why was she in such a hurry to leave if she didn't know something happened to Jess?"

"Why was she stopping here to say goodbye to him?" Jack replied.

Maggie walked away from the conversation. It didn't really matter what they thought. Jess was gone.

At night, her dreams woke her. Sister Dolorita loomed before her, castigating her, black eyes mad with rage. Bolting from her bed, bathed in sweat, she passed the remainder of her nights in a chair, rocking herself. The mornings found her listless, able to function at only the barest level.

She did not know what had become of him, or why, but she had the absolute conviction that if she had left Heron's Neck that first day, or never come at all, he would still be here, safe from harm.

The wind was more insistent now, and the rain pelted her from all directions. It streamed down her face, and under the collar of the old raincoat she wore, which she had found in a Thornhill cupboard. Her head was bare, and she had no umbrella. For a few moments she stood there shivering, her head bowed to the wrath of the storm. Finally she decided to move.

She looked up behind her at the massive oak doors of the wooden church. Carved into a wooden scroll above the doors were the words "Come Unto Me . . ."

"And I will judge you, and punish you, and see that you have no peace," she said angrily. She turned towards the street, to resume the aimless wandering which had become her pattern for the last few nights. It was better than being alone, in her empty house. There she would doze off in a chair, felled by exhaustion, only to dream of Willy barking, or Jess at the door. For a few moments the light, fitful slumber would be sweet, and then she would suddenly leap up from the chair, reality tearing through the blissful fantasy. She would fall back in her chair, heart thumping, wide awake, with misery at her elbow, like a valet, waiting to dress her in its gloomy garb.

Maggie started down the path towards the street. She reached the hedge and hesitated, deciding which direction to go. A gleam of white from under the bushes caught her eye. She bent down, and retrieved a crumpled mass card, already soggy from the rain. She smoothed it out. The pastel-tinted card bore a prayer, and the image of Jesus, mild eyes turned towards heaven. Looking at it, Maggie was reminded of the pictures in her childhood missal. The edges of the pages were gold, and a thin, purple ribbon was attached to it to mark the pages. It was her most precious possession.

She would sit with it open on her lap, even though she could not read the strange language on its pages. Her father would sit beside her, turning the pages when he turned his own. She liked to sit at the end of the pew and stick her small, white-shod foot into the ruby shadow cast by the stained-glass window, turning her foot and leg pink in its rosy glow. A soothing sensation of peace and safety stole over her now, as she remembered how it once had been, before it had all changed.

Slowly Maggie walked back up the steps and approached the oak doors. Her hands hovered uncertainly near the handle. Then she pulled the door open, crossed the vestibule, and looked in.

Every sound echoed in the hush of the vaulted room. In the dim light Maggie could see the bent heads and huddled forms of a few parishioners, thinly scattered in the narrow wooden pews. She started as a woman near the back rose, dropped to one knee beside the pew, and then hurried up the aisle towards Maggie, still crossing herself.

She brushed by Maggie, her eyes downturned, and closed the outer door of the church behind her. Encouraged that she was not conspicuous, Maggie pulled open the door and slipped inside. She moved to the shadows on the side of the church, and then sat down in a pew not too far from the back. She wondered if the rapid beating of her heart could be heard by the faithful few, crouched there in prayer.

She felt like a spy who had invaded an enemy camp. For a few moments she kept her head bowed, trying to still the sick turmoil which was inside her. The words and rituals of the church, once so familiar, were a foreign language to her now. She could not remember why she had decided to come in.

A harsh, bubbling cough from a man near the front broke the awesome silence. Maggie raised her head and ventured a look around the cavern of the church. Above the altar a desolate-looking Christ hung from the cross. To the left of the altar was a statue of Mary, cradling a placid infant Jesus. The multi-coloured glow of the votive candles and a few dim gaslights provided the only illumination in the nave.

Outside, the wind buffeted the island, and occasionally a branch snapped up against the rain-spattered stained glass in the windows. But sitting there in the silent church Maggie felt snug and vaguely comforted. Her mind wandered back to earliest childhood, when at Christmas time there would be boxes of ribbon candy piled high in front of the statues of Mary holding the baby Jesus, one for each child in the parish.

A sense of longing and sorrow overcame her as she remembered the innocent joy she had felt. Maggie's forehead dropped to her hands, which she had unconsciously folded on the back of the pew in front of her. She stared at her own fingers, locked tightly together, as if they did not belong to her. She was startled to realize that she had assumed an attitude of prayer.

A tremendous gust of wind shook the building and the gas lamps flickered. Two more people got up, perfunctorily crossing themselves and made their way out. Maggie did not look around, but she felt as if she were the last person there.

Maggie licked her lips nervously. Her hands remained clasped as if they were glued together. A draught in the church made her shiver as she slowly fell to her knees on the knee rail. For a few moments her mind was completely blank. Then, haltingly, she began to whisper the words of the Memorare, a prayer for mercy to the Blessed Virgin. Slowly the words came, dredged up through layers of denial and despair. "O Mother of the Word Incarnate," she prayed, "despise not my petitions, but in your mercy . . ."

Strong fingers curled over her right shoulder and squeezed. Maggie jumped and cried out, turning around to face the intruder. She looked up into the bearded face of Owen Duggan.

"What are you doing here?" she asked angrily, ashamed at being caught in the midst of her abject plea.

"I'm sorry to interrupt," he said in a whisper, settling himself in the pew beside her and shaking out his umbrella. "I saw you coming in here. You looked like you needed some company."

Maggie pushed herself away from the rail, and fell heavily on to the wood seat beside him.

"Hey, I hope I didn't come at a bad time," he said. "You weren't having a vision or some sort of ecstatic experience, were you?"

Maggie shook her head and smiled thinly. "No. It's just been a while since I came to church."

"Well, you don't have to overdo it. You've got to take that divine light in small doses at first."

"You think I'm stupid," she said.

"I think it's fine," he demurred. "If it makes you feel better, it's fine."

Maggie nodded, and they sat in silence for a moment. "It doesn't," she said at last.

"Hmmm . . . ?"

"Make me feel better. Nothing could, at this point. Except if Jess . . ."

Owen shrugged. "Come on," he said. "I know something that will. I'll take you out to dinner. I'll bet you haven't eaten."

She looked at him curiously. "Why?"

"Why what?"

"Why are you being so nice to me? For all you know I could be responsible for Jess's disappearance. That's what everybody around here thinks."

"Oh? Did you liquidate him with a wave of your magic wand? No. I don't believe in fairy tales. Poisoned apple pies or witches. Or any of it for that matter," said Owen, glancing around the church.

"You know what I mean," said Maggie quietly.

"Oh, I tend to doubt it," Owen replied, examining his well-manicured fingernails. "You seemed kind of fond of him."

Maggie could feel her face start to crumple. She drew in a breath, and spoke brusquely. "I am hungry."

"Let's go, then."

Owen got up and stood back to let her pass. Maggie walked out of the church. She did not look back towards the altar. Owen followed her out, and closed the door behind them.

A slim figure, dressed in black, straightened up from where she had been kneeling in the shadows at the back of the church. Alone now in the empty nave, Evy walked towards the altar, her face a dead-white oval surrounded by the folds of a black veil. She plucked one of the votive candles from the box where they rested in front of the altar and approached the rows of flickering flames already lit by the faithful. She tipped the candle into one of the flames and lit the wick. Then, clutching the slippery wax shaft in her hand, she walked over to the statue of the Madonna and child and stood before it. She stared into the chipped, rounded face of the Madonna, the chubby, open hands of the infant she cradled. Her own pale blue eyes were impassive. Beads of wax slid down the thin candle and hardened on the skin of her fingers. She stood stiffly, oblivious to the warm wax as it spattered her hands, and the flame, which burned ever closer to her skin. She remained, staring at the statue for a very long time. The candle burned lower and lower, until it licked her skin. She did not seem to notice.

A howling gust of wind punched Owen's umbrella inside out.

"We better make a run for it," he shouted at Maggie, gesturing towards the winking lights of the Four Winds.

Maggie looked towards where he was pointing. "Do we have to go there?" she yelled, looking longingly towards the tiny coffee shop across the street, empty except for a teenaged boy behind the counter. Her voice was lost in the wind. Owen was already striding towards the restaurant on the dock. Wiping the rain from her face, Maggie followed after him.

Owen bounded up the steps and held the door open for her. She passed by him into the warmly-lit foyer.

"Why don't you take off that wet raincoat," Owen suggested, "and I'll hang it up."

Maggie shrugged her arms out of the damp sleeves. Owen took her coat and his over to the coat-rack. As an afterthought, Maggie ran her fingers ineffectually through the wet strands of hair in a vain effort to pat them into place. From inside the dining-room, the hostess, a girl with a long face and dirty-blonde hair braided into a crown, glanced up at Maggie, and then turned her back to her. Owen returned from the coat-rack and took her elbow.

"Let's eat," he said cheerfully.

"The hostess seems to be busy."

"Oh, we'll manage." Owen spotted a table he liked by the window, and started towards it, threading his way through the tables, greeting the few diners who were still in the restaurant. Maggie felt as if she were running a gauntlet of unfriendly eyes, but she stared straight ahead at Owen's back, and slid into the chair which he held out for her.

"This is a helluva night," Owen said pleasantly, studying his menu. "I'm surprised there's anybody here."

Maggie watched him thoughtfully. "It was nice of you to ask me," she said. "I'm just afraid I won't make very good company."

"Better than no company at all," Owen replied, returning to the menu. "Where is that waitress?" Owen looked impatiently around the dining-room for the hostess with the braided crown.

"She didn't seem too friendly when we came in," Maggie observed.

"She never is," Owen muttered. "Oh well, we're in no hurry, right?"

Owen picked up a packet of crackers from the wicker basket on the table and tore it open, crushing a few of the crackers near the top. He reached for Maggie's hand, and dumped several of the little crackers into it. "Have an oyster cracker," he said. "Drink your water."

Startled into obedience, Maggie began to chew on the dry crackers and took a sip from the tumbler.

Owen ripped open another packet of crackers. "So," he said; "How are things at the paper?"

Maggie looked at him incredulously. "They've been better," she said.

"Well, I meant besides the obvious problems."

"We're still publishing," said Maggie. "At least that's the plan. Grace has sort of taken over. Until Emmett comes back." If he comes back, she thought, but let the thought fly away.

"I'd be surprised if she got much work out of you, the way you look."

"I'm tired," Maggie admitted.

"Tired?" Owen snorted. "I'll say you're tired. You're trembling like a leaf. The ice in your glass sounds like wind chimes."

Maggie replaced the tumbler on the table to still the irritating tinkle of the ice cubes. "It's been a bad week."

"Do you want to talk about it?" Owen asked casually.

Maggie avoided his eyes. "What's there to say? You know it as well as I do. Jess is missing. There seems to be some feeling around here that I'm somehow to blame. I haven't been sleeping nights. What else is there?"

"I don't know." Owen regarded her speculatively. "I'd like to know what you're so scared of."

"I'm scared for Jess," Maggie retorted defensively.

Owen waved away her explanation. "Oh hell," he said. "We're all worried about him. But you're as jumpy as a cat, and I don't think it's just about Jess. I noticed it the day I met you."

Maggie gripped the edge of the table and shook her head slightly. "I see," she said. "This is going to be an interrogation. I thought it was a genuine invitation."

Owen thumped on the table with his large fist and scowled. "Listen, Maggie," he said in a low but serious voice. "I don't give a good goddamn what it is you've got to hide. All I'm saying is that you can tell me if you want to. I'm on your side. I think you're all right."

Maggie regarded him quizzically. "Thank you," she said.

"If you want to talk, talk. If not, you can bury your face in your food, and not say a word for all I care. If we ever get served, that is," Owen announced.

Owen sat hunched forward in his chair, his huge frame jutting up from the table like a rock from the sea. His gruffness did not disguise his sincerity. Maggie felt a sudden weary urge to lean against him, to rest the burden of her secrets on him and relieve the loneliness.

He could see that she was about to speak. He watched her diffidently, reluctant to show an interest that might spook her. Maggie frowned, and started to speak several times, but each time she stopped, as if she did not know where to begin. He waited.

Finally she said, "I feel like it is my fault."

Owen did not flinch. "What is?" he asked calmly.

"I don't mean that I know what happened to him, or that I had anything to do with his disappearance," she explained carefully. "But I feel responsible."

Owen waited for her to continue, but she lapsed into silence. "How's that?" he prodded her.

"It's hard to explain. Something happened in

305

the past. A long time ago. Something similar to this . . ." As she spoke the words she felt like a mute whose power of speech had been unexpectedly restored. There were thousands of things she wanted to say that were teeming in her brain, but choosing the words was excruciatingly difficult. The sound of her voice, verbalizing her secret thoughts, was unfamiliar to her ears. "It was terrible. It was a man I loved. I still don't know why, but it has something to do with me. I can't help but feel that . . ."

The halting explanation was difficult to follow, but Owen did not interrupt her. He felt as if she were on the verge of answering the many questions he had about her. His own memory was stirring at her words.

"I was very young when it happened," Maggie said. "But even then I blamed myself. Even though I knew I didn't actually do it I felt responsible. Do you know what I mean?"

Owen took a sip of water and put the glass back down on the table. "What exactly was it that happened?" he asked.

Maggie looked up at him, her face pale, her brow wrinkled in distress. In Owen's mind there was a flash of recognition. It was a trial she had been involved in. He knew it. But which? He stifled the impulse to blurt out his question. Maggie licked her lips, as if she were about to speak.

"I worked for this man. I was in love with

him. But he was married. This was twelve, almost thirteen years ago, now. I was only a young girl at the time . . ."

Suddenly the buzz of conversation in the dining-room stopped, as a young man in a yellow anorak burst through the main door and appealed to the bartender in a loud voice.

"Is Jack Schmale here?" he cried. It was Prendergast, the deputy from the sheriff's office. The diners turned their attention to the intruder. Everyone in the room knew who Jack Schmale was, and this, combined with the urgency in Prendergast's voice, riveted their attention. The waitress emerged from the kitchen, and leaned against the bar. The lights from above made her crown of braids look like a halo.

Prendergast, feeling all the eyes in the room on him, took advantage of the situation to press his search. "Anyone here seen Jack Schmale?" he called out in an official voice. Several of the diners murmured to one another but there was no reply.

Finally a man in a checked coat called out, "Didja' try down the steamship office? He might be checkin' out the ferry situation on a night like this."

Prendergast's forehead cleared as if the thought had never occurred to him. He waved gratefully to the man, and turned to leave. The waitress glided over and put a hand on his arm.

"Hey, Eric," she asked the young officer, "what's up?"

"It's Jess Herlie," he announced importantly, as the continued silence in the room indicated that the diners were hanging on his words. "Guess we've finally found him. His boat just washed up on the North Beach."

"Is he . . . all right?" asked the girl, her voice quivering.

The fear in her voice sobered him like a slap. The young man's solemn reply echoed through the silent room. "I'm afraid not," he said. "Looks like he musta drowned."

20

THE flashing of lights and the squawking of radios gave the deserted North Beach a gruesome carnival atmosphere as Owen's jeep skidded to a halt on the sandy shoulder. Before the jeep had even stopped, Maggie had tumbled out the door and was scrambling over the deep sand of the dunes, stumbling and sinking down into them as she ran.

"Wait a minute. Goddammit," Owen cursed, as he heaved himself out of the jeep and started after her. His bulk moved unsteadily over the mountains of sand. He dreaded what he would find when he reached the beach. The more he struggled to keep his umbrella up over him, the more the wind and whipping rain seemed to mock his efforts. He trudged and slid down the sodden hills. Ahead of him, in the darkness, he could see the arcs of flashlights, helter-skelter across the surface of the sand. The surf was pounding angrily on the shore, teeming up the beach. A knot of men, talking into radios, stood huddled around the wreck of a small boat, its jagged planks toward torn apart by the promontory of rocks it had to cross to reach the shore. A few feet apart from the group of men, Maggie shivered, staring at the wreck of the craft. Her clothes whipped around her like sails come loose from their rigging. She seemed stunned, and unconscious of the rain which beat down on her. Owen hurried towards her, and held his mangled umbrella gallantly over her dripping head and shoulders.

"What's going on?" Owen shouted impatiently at her.

Maggie stared at the broken dinghy which lay on its side on the beach. "I don't know," she said. "I think it's Jess's boat." The flashlight which travelled over the broken craft illuminated the words. "Sharon too," painted across the stern.

"Did they find Jess?" Owen shouted.

Maggie shook her head numbly. "I don't think so."

"Well, maybe the boat just broke loose in the storm," Owen said gruffly. "Here, hold this." He handed her the umbrella, "Somebody around here must know what's happening."

Shoving the handle into her cold fingers with their puckered fingertips, Owen marched over to the group of men on the thundering strand and began yelling to them. Their flashlights roved drunkenly through the sky. Maggie stood rooted in the wet sand, her eyes on the boat in the front of her. The dinghy. She had forgotten Jess even had one. Maybe Owen is right, she thought. Maybe it just broke free. She tried to visualize the dock behind his house. Had he just left it

310

tied there? She remembered him proudly pointing out the power boat in the shed. He'd already put it up for the winter. "The *Sharon*," he had said. "I haven't gotten around to changing the name. Actually I didn't have another name for it. Till now. We'll paint it over in the spring."

Maggie turned away from the broken rowboat and stared out at the angry sea that was roaring against the force of the winds. The ocean he loved. Had it swallowed him? Taken him from her? Become his grave?

Owen trudged back towards her, his head down against the gale. She grabbed on to the lapel of his coat and shook it. She gazed up into his face, her hopes naked in her eyes.

The big man shook his head and began to propel her up the dunes. "Let's get back to town," he said.

Maggie shook her head helplessly at him.

"His gear was in the boat," Owen conceded in a weary shout. "Schmale has it. They already brought the stuff back to town. Come on. It's freezing out here."

The men with the flashlights were beginning to disperse. Several of them were dragging the wreck of the boat up the beach. Maggie stared out at the implacable sea which crashed down on the beach with its angry, unyielding force. Deadly in its raging. Then she closed her eyes, and let Owen lead her away.

"That's the lot of it," Jack Schmale sighed, tossing Jess's torn and soggy jacket on the knapsack and bait box on the chair beside his desk.

Maggie and Owen stared down at the pile of remains.

"Life preserver is gone," Jack observed, "but I don't guess he ever had a chance to make it back to shore. This storm put an end to it."

"It's impossible," Maggie breathed.

The old policeman scratched his forehead and sat down heavily in his swivel chair. "I guess he went out for a little night fishing and ran into some trouble with the boat. It's hard to say what. The sea's a funny place. Anything can happen."

"Well, how come all this stuff was still in the boat," Owen demanded, "and no sign of Jess."

"Oh, he had a footlocker in that little dinghy of his. Most of this stuff was still in it. Even found a couple of cans of beer. I guess he planned to make a night of it. The jacket was stuffed up underneath the bow. It got caught on a nail."

"He'd already put the boat away for the season," Maggie said tonelessly.

Jack shrugged. "He must have changed his mind."

The door to the police station banged open

and Prendergast burst in. "They've got the boat back here," he announced.

"Leave it down at the dock, for tonight," ordered the chief. "We'll deal with it when this weather clears up." Prendergast acknowledged the order and banged back out the door. Jack sighed. "I better call his folks down in Florida. I think I got their number in here." Jack extracted a black phone book from his desk drawer. "I hate doing this," he said.

Maggie walked away numbly and sat down on a bench in the corner of the police station. Jack looked up from his phone book and peered over at her.

"You're free to go now," he advised her.

"I think she just needs to get her wind back," Owen told him, glancing at Maggie's drained face.

"Oh, I didn't mean that," said Jack kindly. "You can rest there as long as you like. I meant you're free to leave the island. If you still want to go."

Maggie looked at him uncomprehendingly and then nodded. "Thank you," she whispered.

As Jack began his conversation with the operator, Owen sat down beside Maggie on the bench. "I could use a drink," he said. "How about it? Come on over to the John B with me."

Maggie shook her head. "I don't want to."

"It'll do you good," Owen urged her. "We can talk. Have it out." He thought briefly of

313

their unfinished conversation in the restaurant. He wondered if he would ever know what she was about to tell him. Probably not tonight, at any rate.

"You go ahead," she said. "I'm just going to sit here for a minute. Then I'm going home."

"Do you need a ride?" he asked.

"No, I've got my car. I think I'd rather be alone. Really."

"If you're sure," said Owen.

"It's okay. Really. Go on."

"Okay. Good night," he said, squeezing her hand lightly. Then he stood up. "Good night, Jack."

Schmale waved absently, as he pressed the receiver to his ear. "Speak up, operator," he insisted. "We've got a terrible connection."

Maggie's eyes rested on the pile of Jess's belongings on the chair. This is how it ends, she thought. Just gone. Love ended, without even a goodbye. Just like every other time. Every other man she had loved. She tried to remind herself that it was not a chain, one death linked irrevocably to the others, but she could not still the whisperings of doom inside her. It was an accident, she told herself. But her mind reeled backwards, out of control. Her father's heart attack, and Roger's murder, and Jess's accident. Death sat on her shoulder, an invisible vulture. Maggie recognized her punishment.

"Hello, Sara?" Jack yelled into the phone.

"Sara, it's Jack Schmale. Yeah, up at the island. Is Marcus there? Well, you better call him . . . Yes. I've got some bad news, dear. Yes, I'm afraid so. It's about your son."

Maggie jerked herself to her feet. She could not bear to overhear the conversation. Without a word to the police officer on the telephone, she walked out the door of the police station. A cluster of men in foul-weather gear stood talking under the shelter of the porch roof. Trying to skirt them, Maggie walked towards the steps with her eyes lowered. "Leave me alone," she muttered. "Just leave me alone." Someone mounted the steps and stopped directly in her path. Maggie looked up into Evy's pale eyes.

The two women stared at one another for a moment. "I heard about Jess," Evy blurted out. "I came right over."

Maggie turned away from her and sank wearily against the railing of the porch. She rested there, trembling from the cold, and hung her head. Evy stood beside her, carefully arranging her old raincoat around her, trying in vain to pull the sleeves down so they would cover her wrists.

"They think he drowned," Maggie said dully.

Evy nodded. "That's what I heard. I can't believe it."

Maggie did not reply.

Evy eyed her warily. "What are you going to do now?" she asked.

"I don't know," Maggie admitted.

A prolonged silence fell between them. Finally Maggie noticed that Evy was struggling to speak. The girl did not meet Maggie's eyes. Her voice was shaky but deliberate. "I'm really sorry," she said. "I guess you feel very badly about Jess. Believe me, I know how you feel."

As weary as she was, Maggie felt a spark of surprise at the girl's words. She studied the wretched face for a hint of derision, but there was nothing but misery written there. She *does* know, Maggie thought. She loved him too.

Tentatively, she reached out a hand and placed it on the girl's frail, veiny wrist. "I know you do," she said. "Thank you."

Evy shrank from Maggie's touch, and quickly assumed a normal tone. "I imagine Grace will be here soon."

Maggie shivered, and shook her head. "I don't want to wait," she said. "I'm going home."

"Already?" Evy asked.

"Right now," Maggie said grimly. She looked out at the shining streets. "It's still pouring."

"Coming down in sheets," Evy agreed. She stood up. "I guess I'll go too."

"I thought you were staying," said Maggie, faintly surprised.

"I might as well go," said the girl.

Maggie nodded. She glanced back briefly at the closed door of the police station. Then she started down the steps. Evy followed close behind her.

"Where's your car?" Evy shouted, tying a plastic rain-hat over her hair.

Maggie pointed towards the *Cove News* offices.

"Come with me. I'll drive you there," Evy suggested, opening the door to her car.

"Thanks anyway," said Maggie. "I'd just as soon walk."

"You'll get drenched," said the girl.

"I already am." Maggie started off in the direction of her car. The street lamps blurred before her tired eyes on the rainswept streets.

Evy watched her departing back for a few moments and then slid into the clammy front seat. All right, she thought. Whatever you want to do is fine with me. She turned on the engine, and backed up out of her space. Then she started slowly up the street in the direction that Maggie was walking. As she passed the bedraggled figure trudging up the road in the rain, she tapped lightly on her horn and waved. Maggie raised a hand listlessly and glanced at Evy's passing car. Evy looked down Main Street as she passed and noticed the old black Buick parked near the corner. Maggie was nearing Main Street on foot. Evy continued on up the road, and then, when she knew her car was well out of sight, she turned left down a long block, and then left again.

Evy circled the block as slowly as she could. When she came around the corner on to Main

Street, she was startled to see that Maggie's car was still sitting where she had been parked. Evy quickly pulled into the parking lot at Lou's Market, and killed her lights.

Why is she just sitting there, Evy wondered? The longer she sat, the more difficult it became. Evy drummed impatiently on the steering wheel. It was a good night to act. The storm was keeping most people inside. She could go about her business unobserved. Now that they had found Jess's boat, made their big catch for the night, Jack Schmale and Prendergast would probably be content to stay inside filling out forms and rehashing the possibilities until the weather cleared. The thought of Jess reminded Evy of Maggie, emerging white-faced from the police station. The news had been a shock to her. Evy was glad of that. Maggie was behaving like she was about to crack, muttering to herself. It was all going to work out perfectly, Evy thought. If only she would get *moving*.

Suddenly, the car she was watching lurched forward, as if propelled by the force of her thoughts. *Finally*, she thought. Evy waited for a moment to start her own engine. The realization that the moment she had waited for was at hand left her breathless with anticipation. Carefully now, she thought. No mistakes.

Evy's car rolled slowly out of the lot where she had parked, and began to trail, at a distance, the old black Buick. Evy automatically prepared

318

for the left-hand turn which led to the road out of town. However, just before the turn for the Midland Road, the Buick swerved right, down the road to the ferry. Perplexed and angered by the unexpected turn, Evy hesitated for a moment. Then, at a cautious distance, she followed.

Maggie debated with herself for a moment, before deciding to leave the keys in the ignition. Who would steal it, she thought? Someone will drive it back to Thornhill's.

She was trying to think of everything, but the agitation she felt made it difficult to focus her thoughts. Her hands twitched as she rifled her pocketbook for the third time.

"Wallet," she said aloud. "Money, address book, make-up case." She touched each item as she named it. There was a steady throb of anxiety in her throat. "Keys," she said. "Leave the keys." With trembling fingers she wrested the jingling house keys from her purse and left them on the dashboard.

"There," she thought. Looking up, through the raindrop prisms which covered the windscreen, she could see the lights of the ferry beaming out across the water as the boat rocked through the waves towards the dock. The sight of the boat steadied her.

She forced herself to take a mental inventory of her belongings at the Thornhill house. She felt compelled to marshal a complete image of what she was leaving behind. It was a meagre picture. Some old clothes. A few books. The objects shifted, spinning in the tumult of her thoughts. Nothing irreplaceable, she thought. Let it go.

Maggie opened the car door, clutching her purse, and stepped out into the storm. The wind shoved her back against the car. She put her shoulder to the wind, and watched the boat come, moving slowly through the stormy swells of the sea. Hurry, she urged it on impatiently. She was oblivious to the water which streamed down her face and neck.

Tonight, I'll stay in a hotel, she thought. Tomorrow, she would go somewhere else. Another town, anywhere but here.

I am so tired, Maggie thought. The image of Jess's face now lost to her for good, crowded into her thoughts. I just need to get away from here, she thought. Start again.

Start again? Doubt hissed in her ear. Rain trickled down her cheeks. She screwed up her face, and covered her ears with her fists. Her mind was made up. A foggy blast of the boat's whistle penetrated her clenched hands. The boat hit the dock with a clunk that could be heard over the roar of the storm. Clutching her coat tightly around her, Maggie began to run towards the lights of the steamship office.

The young man in a grey shirt behind the

counter was pulling down a plastic partition which closed his window as she threw open the door and ran up to him. Maggie began to bang on the plastic. Hesitantly he raised it up enough to hear her.

"I need a ticket for the last boat out."

"Sorry, lady," he said, gesturing towards the dock. "That was it. No more boats tonight."

"But I have to leave."

"Not tonight. Sea's too rough. Tomorrow morning, if the storm lets up." The young man began to lower the plastic shield down between them.

"Wait a minute," Maggie insisted. "There's a schedule right here that says there's one more boat out tonight." She poked her finger at the posted timetable.

The young man shook his head. "Can't help the weather," he said.

"Listen," Maggie cried, thrusting her hands beneath the plastic barrier and trying to force it upwards. "It's very important. It's an emergency."

The young man glared at her. "Let go of that."

"Please," she said, clinging to the shield.

For a moment the young man fumed visibly. Then he turned to a bald, heavy-set man who was seated at a desk behind the counter. "Hey, Tom," he said, in a voice which called for reinforcements, "we've got a problem here . . ."

Maggie turned, and ran outside. A few cars were still issuing slowly from the belly of the boat, as several passengers straggled down the swaying gangplank to the dock. Recklessly she ran towards the knot of crewmen who were shepherding the last passengers out and preparing to close the ship down for the night.

"Wait, please."

The mariners observed the woman running towards them, her arms waving, seemingly unconscious of the rain which soaked her clothes and hair.

She grabbed on to the jacket of one of the men who was directing the operation. "Please," she gasped. "I have to leave tonight."

The swarthy-complexioned man laughed, and his teeth gleamed in the darkness of the night. "Hey, lady, don't you see it's raining?" His bright smile faded as he looked into her eyes. "What's the matter with you?" The other men paused in their work and looked on curiously.

"The timetable says there's one more boat out tonight," she stammered. "I have to be on it."

"I'm sorry, dear," said the sailor, patting her hand, which clutched his sleeve, kindly. "You're gonna have to wait until morning."

"No, I can't," she cried, pulling away from him. "I have to go tonight."

A look of consternation softened his pock-scarred face. "Somebody's sick over there?" he asked soothingly in a singsong voice, pointing over his shoulder towards the mainland. "It'll be all right. These things happen. But we can't go tonight. It's bad out there."

A wild, unreasoning fear shone in Maggie's eyes. "You have to help me," she whispered. "I'll pay you." By now the other crewmen were clustered around them.

"I can't help you," the man explained. "There," he said, relief flooding into his voice. "There's the captain. You tell him all about it."

Maggie whirled around and saw a bulky man in a squashed captain's cap walking towards them. She raced over to the man and blocked his path.

"Captain," she pleaded, trying to keep her voice from rising out of the realm of the rational. "I realize that there is a storm, and that it's a bad night out, but I have to leave this island tonight, and the timetable calls for one more trip."

"I'm sorry, Ma'am. We can't go back out there."

"You have to," Maggie screamed. "You have to make another trip. You can't keep me a prisoner here!"

Taken aback, the man stared at Maggie, whose taut veins stood out on her neck and forehead. Her eyes blazed in furious protest. He raised his hands as if to ward her off.

Turning away from him, Maggie began to run blindly down the slick dock towards the ferry, which was rolling giddily in the outsized waves. Her leather soles slipped and slid on the dock as she stumbled towards it. She had to get on board the boat. She felt that if she could just climb into the vessel she would be safe. She could hear the voices of the men behind her crying out in protest as she ran. She spotted a man still working on the lower deck in the cavernous belly of the boat. If I can just get in there, she thought, they'll have to take me.

"Come back here," they cried.

Ignoring their yells, she scrambled towards the yawning hull. In the darkness she did not see the rope coiled on the dock, which the crewman inside the ship was winding on a pulley. She ran towards the ship's open portals. The whizzing rope caught her ankle and twisted round it. She felt the shocking jerk, and then she fell. Her head smacked against a stanchion. Stunned, she crumpled, arms still extended, to the shining boards of the gangway.

21

MAGGIE was floating. Semi-conscious, she drifted peacefully in a narcotic cocoon. But gradually, through her blissful state, she became aware of an uncomfortable dryness in her mouth. She ran the rough, sticky surface of her tongue over her cracked lips. Her mouth felt gummy, but not relieved, by the gesture. All at once, the cool, nubby surface of wet terrycloth pressed up against her lips. Maggie sucked greedily at the damp rag, and forced her eyes open to see her benefactor.

"Don't swallow the washcloth," Owen scolded her, tugging it away from her.

"Owen," she whispered.

"Hi." The large, bearded man sat back in the chair beside the bed, and dropped the washcloth in a plastic basin on the bedside table. Maggie looked around the room and recognized the pale walls and sterile fixtures of a hospital. Her head ached, and she felt weary.

"What am I doing here?"

"Well, from what I heard, you were injured while trying to hijack a ferry last night.

"You weren't really hurt," Owen went on. "Just a bump. I believe the medical reason for your admission was exhaustion."

"I was trying to get away," she explained.

"So I heard. I shouldn't have left you alone last night. Anyone could see you were wiped out."

"It wasn't your fault. It was just . . . everything that's happened. I just couldn't take it. I tried to run . . ."

"It's been tough," Owen observed.

"Yes."

"You really cared for him."

Maggie nodded.

Owen sighed. "I could see you were hurting. I don't know. I just needed a drink. I had to, you know . . . absorb it."

"I know you did," Maggie said. "Please, don't blame yourself. It was me. I just felt like something terrible was happening to me again. It's the same thing all over again. I fall in love with a man, and the next thing you know . . . Well, I just had to get away from here."

"You were reacting to all the strain," said Owen. "You're worn out."

"I guess you're right. To tell you the truth I'm still exhausted. Although I must have been sleeping for hours. All kinds of dreams. What time is it anyway?"

"You have been. It's five o'clock."

Maggie's eyes drooped closed for a moment. Then she looked up at her guest. "I want to get out of here, Owen. I need to get away from here. Every time I think of Jess . . ." Her voice caught on the name. She cleared her throat and twisted her head on the pillow.

Owen stood up and rearranged the water glass and pitcher by her bed. "I guess they're going to spring you tomorrow morning. The doctor'll be by to talk to you."

Maggie made an effort to compose her face. "Okay," she said.

"Anything I can get you before I leave?" he asked.

"Don't go yet."

"I don't want to tire you. Do you have a way to get home tomorrow?"

Maggie shook her head, and smiled bleakly. "Home," she said.

"Why don't I come get you?" he said.

"You don't have to."

"I don't mind," he said. "I'll call you later on to see what time to come."

"Are you sure?" she asked.

"Yeah," said Owen, pulling on his parka which added an extra layer to his already formidable girth. "Now I'm off."

Maggie watched him as he left the room, holding back the door for the nurse, who was entering with a tray of miniature paper cups filled with pills.

"Here we go," said the nurse. "How are you feeling?"

Distracted by the nurse's bustling, Maggie did

not see her friend disappear, until she looked up and the door was closed behind him.

Owen scraped his boots on the welcome mat, and hung his coat on the rack in the hall. A few slips of paper were piled up on the telephone table beside the staircase. He walked over, picked them up, and began to leaf through them. Just then Mirelle appeared in the doorway wearing her winter coat, a brightly flowered scarf tied around her head.

"Oh," she gasped, and then broke out in a trilling laugh. "I didn't hear you come in."

"I just got here," he replied.

"How's your friend?" Mirelle asked in a suggestive tone.

"Improved," Owen said firmly. "What's for dinner?"

"It's in the oven," said Mirelle, gesturing back towards the kitchen. "It's a casserole. Turn it to three-hundred-and-fifty degrees for forty minutes. It's one you like."

"A surprise?" Owen asked, a trace of sarcasm in his voice.

"Yeah, I gotta run," Mirelle replied happily.

Owen grunted, and returned to his messages.

"Hey," said Mirelle, stopping at the threshold. "You got an important call before."

Owen held up the slips. "Which?"

"It's in there," she said. "Some secretary from

the *Life* magazine. Editor wants you in New York first thing tomorrow morning."

"Tomorrow?"

"That's what she said. Read the message."

"Are they going to do my wild-bird series?" Owen asked eagerly.

"I don't know. That's all she said."

"I'll bet that's it. I should call them back," Owen muttered. He glanced at his watch. "They've probably all gone home by now. Damn."

"I gotta go," Mirelle insisted. "I got a Mother of Mercy Guild meeting tonight."

"Go ahead," Owen murmured, his forehead furrowed in thought.

"Shall I come anyway tomorrow?" she asked.

"I'll have to get on the early boat and then fly from the mainland. Catch the seven-thirty plane," he thought aloud.

"Tomorrow?" Mirelle repeated.

Owen looked up. "Don't bother tomorrow."

Mirelle grinned. "Okay. Have a good trip." She waved goodbye as she backed out the door.

Owen stood in the hall, staring down at the message in his hand. How about that? he thought.

The gentle clacking of blinds being lowered roused Maggie from the stupor through which she had been drifting. She looked around the room and saw the white expanse of the nurse's back as she neatly wound the cord from the blinds around the bracket in the wall.

"What time is it?" Maggie asked groggily.

The nurse did not turn around but continued to busy herself with changing the water and arranging the bedclothes in an empty bed next to Maggie's. "It's almost seven-thirty," she replied briskly.

"All I do is sleep," Maggie complained.

"That's what you're here for," said the nurse, coming around to her bedside and plopping a piece of pale green paper and pencil down on the blanket she had tucked in around Maggie.

"What's this?"

"Tomorrow's menu," said the nurse. "Check off what you want from the kitchen."

Maggie held out the paper and pencil to her. "Oh no. I won't be needing this. I'm leaving tomorrow morning." The nurse eyed her sceptically.

"Really," Maggie assured her. "The doctor was here before . . ." Maggie paused for a second, trying to recollect the visit, and separate it from all the dreams which surrounded it. A young doctor with glasses had visited her. Up close she could see that he had dark circles under his eyes. He had urged her to stay another day, but had finally relented in the face of her determination to go.

"Doctor Sorensen," Maggie said. "The one

with the glasses. He said I could go tomorrow morning."

The nurse picked up Maggie's chart from the foot of the bed and glanced at it. Then she replaced it, and plucked the paper and pencil from Maggie's fingers.

"Okay," she said. "Night nurse will be here soon if you need her." The phone by Maggie's bed began to ring softly. The nurse picked it up and handed it to Maggie. Then she turned to leave.

"Hello," Maggie said hesitantly.

It was Owen. Their conversation was brief, with Owen apologizing for the unexpected trip, and Maggie assuring him weakly that she could manage without his help. She replaced the receiver on the hook, and lay back on her pillow, staring up at the ceiling. Tomorrow morning she could go. Go where? The familiar despair descended, like a fog, over her spirits. The sound of the door to her room opening was a welcoming distraction.

The nurse must have forgotten something, she thought. She looked towards the doorway, and was taken aback to see Evy, advancing to the foot of her bed.

"Hello," said the girl.

"Hi, Evy."

"How do you feel?"

"Better," said Maggie. "Tired."

"I hear you're getting out tomorrow."

331

"Yeah. Have a seat," said Maggie, gesturing towards a chair.

Evy sat down in the chair, arranging her coat and pocketbook in her lap. She glanced around the room, and then back at Maggie who was studying her pinched face.

"How's the food here?" the girl asked.

"Terrible," said Maggie. "What I ate of it."

Evy smiled furtively and nodded.

"How was work?" Maggie asked.

"Oh, we were closed today, because of Jess."

Maggie stared at the foot of her bed.

"Tomorrow there's a memorial service," said Evy.

"Oh."

"Are you going?"

"No, I don't think so."

"You're not?" The girl was incredulous. "Why not?"

"I don't . . ." Maggie's voice started to break. She waited until she could speak calmly. "I'm going to be leaving the island. There are some things I have to do."

"It seems like you'd want to go."

"Well, I don't," Maggie snapped.

"Okay," said Evy with a shrug, "don't bite my head off."

"Sorry," Maggie muttered.

"Doesn't matter," said the girl. She fidgeted in her seat for a moment and then spoke up again. "They took your car back to Thornhill's."

332

"Who did?"

"Cops," said Evy. "I saw them going."

"Oh," said Maggie wearily.

"How are you getting home tomorrow?"

Maggie sighed. "I'm not sure. I guess the island taxi. Owen offered to take me, but he got called out of town."

Evy nodded solemnly. Then an idea seemed to occur to her. "I guess I could come for you," she said.

"I couldn't ask you to do that," Maggie said, dismissing the idea hurriedly.

"I wouldn't mind."

Maggie eyed the girl quizzically. "Why would you want to do that, Evy? I mean, we've hardly been friends?"

"It's up to you," said Evy. "Now that Jess is gone, it seems silly to fight."

Maggie considered her words sadly. Then she leaned forward and peered at Evy. "Don't you blame me for what happened to Jess?" she asked.

The girl looked at her, wide-eyed. "Why should I? He drowned, didn't he? That's what they said. It was an accident."

Maggie fell back on her pillow. "Yes," she murmured. "It was an accident."

"So, do you want me to?"

Maggie glanced at her uncomprehendingly. "I'm sorry, What?"

"To come get you."

Maggie thought for a moment. Then she nodded. "That would be a big help."

"And then maybe you'll go to the memorial service with me."

"I told you. I don't want to go."

"It just doesn't seem right," Evy persisted.

"You wouldn't understand."

"Oh, I know why," said the girl sagely. "You're afraid of seeing everybody. After all the things they've been saying about you."

Maggie stared at the girl.

"But what about Jess," Evy went on. "Don't you want to go for his sake?"

Maggie thrashed her head from side to side on the pillow. "I don't know. I just dread the thought."

"It won't be that bad," the girl reasoned. "You'll be with me. If I'm not mad at you, why should they be?" She stood up abruptly. "Well, I gotta go."

"I'll think about it. Maybe I will want to go," Maggie promised her. "Thanks for coming, Evy. It was nice of you."

"See you in the morning," said Evy, starting for the door.

Maggie sighed, and flopped her head over on the pillow. In the morning. She wished she could leave tonight.

"I'm home," Evy called out, as she slammed the back door shut. She glanced at the kitchen clock.

It had taken her longer than she thought at the hospital. And she still had a lot to do.

She selected a bruised banana from the fruit bowl on the counter and began to peel it. Thoughtfully she took a bite and considered what was next, like a hostess planning a party. She had already got rid of Owen with that fake phone call from New York. Now, at least he wouldn't be getting in the way. She still had a few things to do over at Thornhill's. So that everything would go smoothly tomorrow. And so that afterwards there'd be no doubt in anybody's mind about what had happened.

And, she still had to find her grandfather's pistol. She knew it was still in the house. Her grandmother kept everything. Evy decided that she had better get started.

She tossed the skin into the wastebasket and fastidiously wiped the remaining pulp of the banana off her fingers with a towel. Then, absorbed in her planning, she started through the living-room towards the stairs. A crash from the direction of her grandmother's room arrested her. Frowning, she walked down the hall, and pushed the bedroom door open.

"What'd you do here?" Evy demanded.

The old woman stared up at her with baleful eyes.

Evy entered the room and looked around. Then she saw the old telephone extension, which usually sat on the bedside table, resting lopsided against the table leg, the receiver hooked on the bedframe, the cord caught on the knob of the table drawer. The girl bent down and picked up the phone, replacing the receiver, and moving the phone across the room.

"We really ought to get rid of this," said Evy. "You don't need it any more. You couldn't very well answer it, if it was ringing. I always have to do it. We should get it moved up to my room."

The old woman followed her with her eyes as Evy paced around the bed.

"What happened to your dinner?" Evy asked sternly, pointing to the bed clothes. A tray of food lay at an angle on the covers. the plates and cup had slid down to one end. A corner of buttered toast clung, buttered-side down, to the faded quilt. A large wet stain in which some noodles were stuck spread out across the bed clothes. Scattered and curled in the dark wet circle, the noodles looked like little organisms trapped in a biologist's slide.

"I don't know," Evy sighed, and began to collect the dishes, wiping up desultorily with a greasy, crumpled napkin. "I suppose it's not your fault. I haven't had much time for you lately. When this is all finished, we'll have to figure out what to do about you." Evy leaned over and roughly wiped the corners of the old woman's slackened mouth.

"Now, you sit quietly," said the girl,

smoothing the soggy bed clothes over the heaving, spindly rib cage. "I have things to do."

For a moment Evy stood, lost in thought, tapping her upper lip with her forefinger. "Come to think of it," she said, "you've probably got what I need right here."

Crossing over to the huge mahogany dresser in the corner of the stuffy room, Evy squatted down and began to tug at the handles of the bottom drawer. The swollen wood creaked and made cracking noises. Patiently, Evy rocked the drawer until she was able to pull it open. Then, she sat back on her heels and gazed in at the contents.

The scent of rose sachet issued in a stale cloud from the open drawer. An expression transformed the girl's sallow face as she reached in and gently touched the items in the drawer.

"Oh, look, Grandma," she exclaimed. "All Mama's things." She reached in and gingerly lifted out a silky, quilted bed jacket which she held up to her cheek. Then she ran her fingers lovingly over a grey suède pocketbook with a clasp shaped like a horse's head. Evy replaced each item carefully where she found it, until she came across a lacy white handkerchief.

"Oh, I want this now," she cried, holding the handkerchief close to her breast. "You said these things would all be mine. You told me that when Mama went away to that hospital," Evy reminded her grandmother ruefully. "I need this now." She held up the hanky in front of her to scrutinize it.

"Mama'd put the collection money in it on Sundays. While the priest'd be talking, she'd be holding it, doing like this." Evy demonstrated as she spoke, twisting the pressed white linen into a tightly-packed wad. She let it loose and the handkerchief hung, limp and ribbed with wrinkles, from her hand. "I won't keep it," she assured the old woman. "I'm just going to borrow it."

Laying the handkerchief to one side, she resumed her search through the drawer. She lingered over many of the objects she found, admiring aloud a strand of amber beads, and stopping to gaze at the high-school graduation picture in a cardboard frame, which showed a cool-eyed, thin-lipped face, incongruously crowned by bouncy blonde curls. Reluctantly, Evy replaced the photo in the drawer. Then, she let out a little exclamation of victory as she pulled forth a soft, black sweater with a round neck. "This is what I want," she cried. "And these!" A pair of white gloves emerged next. She placed them on top of the sweater. Then she searched carefully in the drawer, until she drew out a black lace mantilla, which was folded into a wedge at the bottom.

She shook out the veil and examined it for any rents or tears. "It's just like mine," she told her grandmother. "That's why I wanted a black one.

I remembered it on her," she said eagerly. Her eyes softened, recalling a long-forgotten picture. "It looked so pretty on her. Those black lacy flowers on her yellow hair. It always made me think of black-eyed susans." Evy stared down at the veil which had fallen into her lap.

"Why'd she have to go away?" she asked.

The old woman lay on her bed, remembering. Her eyes were raised to the ceiling. Her lower jaw trembled.

"You know why," said Evy slyly. She gathered up her treasures in a little bundle and clutched it to her chest. Then she slammed the dresser drawer shut with an angry shove.

"You told me why. Now you pretend you don't know. Well, I know why." She scrambled to her feet, her knuckles whitening from the pressure of her grip on the top drawer of the bureau.

"Where's that gun?" she demanded, tugging at the handle until the drawer flew open, nearly knocking her backwards. She rifled roughly through the objects in the drawer, until her hand emerged, clutching the old pistol which had belonged to a grandfather she could not even remember. "Now I've got it," she cried. She held the gun aloft in one hand, the sweater, gloves, hanky and veil she had collected in the other.

"She has it coming to her," said Evy. "If it weren't for her, Mama wouldn't be in that hospital. Daddy wouldn't be dead. I wouldn't be here with *you*. Isn't that right? Poor Mama. She got so sick because of it she doesn't even know me now. She has to live in that hospital for ever. All because of that woman. Well, tomorrow she'll get what she deserves. Just like you always told me."

The old woman watched her grandchild with glistening, frightened eyes.

"It's only right," said the girl. "Now, you be quiet up here," Evy ordered. "I have some things to do downstairs."

Harriet Robinson watched Evy's distorted face until she turned away and left the room. Then her eyes travelled over to the telephone which the girl had moved to the desk top by the far wall. It was no use, and she knew it. Even if she could reach it.

She listened intently, staring at the ceiling, as Evy undid the latch and opened the door to the basement. Then she flinched as she heard the echo of the girl's footsteps, going down.

The back porch light was still burning at the Thornhill house. Between that, and the feeble glow of her flashlight, Evy was able to find her way around to the back of the house without tripping and falling. She moved stealthily across the unweeded lawn, testing the doors and windows, which were all locked. The last time she had come, to take care of the dog, they had all been open. She did not really expect to find them so tonight.

For a few moments she stood ruminating in the ankle-deep weeds. Then she picked up the string bag which was hooked on her arm and opened it. She shone the flashlight in on its contents. The light flashed off the silver tie pin with WME III engraved on it in a florid script. She reached into the bag and extracted the worn wallet which she had retrieved from Emmett's suit before she buried it. At the bottom of the bag a gold class ring and a monogrammed cigarette case jingled against the tie pin, and one another. She was tempted, for a moment, to keep one of the objects as a souvenir, but she thought better of it. She had to plant them in the house. Somewhere they could be found after a thorough search. For a moment she was balked by all the locked doors. Then a sudden thought occurred to her. She turned her flashlight on the ground in front of her, and picked her way over to the toolshed behind the house. She pulled open the door, and shone the light inside. There, just to the left of the door frame, a set of keys dangled from a nail driven into the wood.

"They're all alike around here," she thought disdainfully. She slung her string bag over the nail by its cord handle, and closed the door to the shed. She could take care of hiding Emmett's effects in the house in a wink, after she got her other mission done.

Returning to her car, Evy looked in every direction, but the road was pitch black, and utterly silent. Satisfied, she lifted the trunk door, and gazed in at the bulky zippered garment bag which filled the trunk. It was funny. She had looked at that garment bag, hanging in the hall cupboard for years, and never imagined how useful it would turn out to be. She bent over the trunk and reached into it. She heaved the bag out on to the ground. She glanced over in the direction of the embankment by the stream where the old root cellar was. It was a good thing she had remembered. It was too dark to see anything, but she could picture it in her mind's eye. It was a long way to go. With a sigh, Evy decided that she had better begin.

Slowly, she began to drag the bag along the ground through the whispering grasses, jerking and tugging at it when it got snagged on a small stone or a root. It will take a lot of mothballs before we can ever use this bag again, she thought. She moved a little faster now, accustomed to the weight. Good thing I'm strong, she thought. Two years of lifting her grandmother had hardened her muscles. Just a little bit further.

She reached the embankment and began to drag the bag down it. Just as she was nearing the door of the root cellar, her foot landed on a mossy rock. She slipped, gave out a tiny shriek, and let go of her bundle. The bag tumbled down the embankment, landing with one edge of it in the rushing stream. Evy caught herself and regained her balance. Then, she flashed her light down the rocky slope, and felt her way carefully down to retrieve the bag.

Grunting and straining, she pulled it back up the hill, and halted outside the heavy wooden door. With one hand she grasped the iron ring which served as a handle, and forced her weight up against it.

The door to the root cellar flew open. Inside, the damp air was redolent of earth and apples. Evy pulled her bundle inside, and shone her flashlight into the corners of the dark, long-deserted cellar.

"Perfect," she breathed. It saved her the trouble of digging a hole. And worrying that a good rain might uncover it some time. No one would ever bother looking back here. Even if they did, they would still place the blame on the late Maggie Fraser.

She knelt down and placed the flashlight beside the bag. Then, taking in a deep breath and holding it, she gently drew down the zipper. Released by the open zipper, the flaps of the plastic garment bag gaped apart, exposing the putrid, decomposing remains of William Emmett.

22

"HAVING trouble with that?"

Maggie shook her head stubbornly, refusing help. With renewed concentration she tried to force her trembling fingers to finish buttoning her blouse.

The nurse, Mrs. Gray, a cheerful, bland-faced woman, brushed Maggie's fingers away like gnats, and completed the job quickly and expertly. "You're going to be a little shaky," she assured Maggie.

"I'm fine," Maggie insisted. "I'm ready to go." For the twentieth time that morning she looked out the window of her room for any sign of Evy. Then she sighed, and turned back to find the nurse unfolding a wheelchair in the narrow corridor between the foot of the bed and the wall.

"I don't want that," said Maggie.

Mrs. Gray ignored her. "This is for when you leave," she said pleasantly. "Just to the front door." Then she padded out of the room, closing the door behind her.

Where is Evy? Maggie thought impatiently. She regretted having entrusted the girl to come for her. Now she felt constrained to wait. I could have called the taxi and been home by now, she thought. In the time I've been waiting I could have packed. *Home*—how silly that sounded now.

She had been awake since dawn, occasionally taking a fitful nap, but mostly waiting for the moment of her release. It was a grey morning like this, less than a month ago, when she had sat, waiting for another release. An old neighbour, Mrs. Belotti, had come for her at the prison, fed her that night with her family, and taken her down to the basement where she had stored the few possessions she had salvaged for Maggie, after her mother's house was auctioned. Mrs. Belotti had been kind, but anxious. After the first night, Maggie had gone to a hotel for a few days while she got ready to travel. To come here. A feeling of gloom settled over her when she considered the failure of her brief stay on the island. It was all she had counted on in that last year of prison. Emmett had offered a new life to her and she had managed in a few short weeks to ruin it. Emmett—she wondered for the hundredth time when he was going to reappear —God, what would he think of her rehabilitation —well, there was no point in thinking about that now.

Maggie reached down and grabbed her bag which was slumped beside the bed. She found the ferry-boat timetable and checked her watch. There were still two more boats before noon. Maggie glanced worriedly out at the rain. There was a constant grey drizzle, but it was light. Surely the boats were running. They couldn't stop running every time there was a little shower. Once again she got up and walked to the window.

She had not really expected to see anything, and so she started when she spotted Evy, poised by her car, just across the street from the hospital.

The girl was hatless in the drizzle, her white hands clutching a paper bag to her narrow chest. She was looking out for traffic before she crossed, her expression at once intent and somehow distracted. The wind ruffled the spiky ends of her hair, which stood straight up from her head making her appear absurd and wild-looking.

Maggie frowned, and shook her head at the sight of her. An unlikely friend. For a moment she thought of the good-natured Mrs. Belotti with a pang. Just then, Evy looked up, her eyes meeting Maggie's. Maggie flinched, and then forced a jagged smile. Evy just stared at her, and then her eyes fell back to the road. She quickly crossed the street.

In the time it took Maggie to slip on her shoes and retrieve her coat from the cupboard Evy appeared in the doorway of the room.

"You ready to go?" Evy asked.

"I've been ready for hours," Maggie admitted.

"I had things to do," the girl replied defensively.

"Oh that's all right. I'm just anxious to get going," Maggie soothed her. "I've got to ride in that," she added, jerking her head in the direction of the wheelchair.

"I'm used to those," Evy observed. She bent over and expertly pressed on the joints of the chair, testing its readiness. Then she stood up, and produced the paper bag that she was holding under her arm.

"I brought you these. I thought you might want to wear them today."

Maggie emptied the bag on the bed, and frowned as she held up the black sweater, mantilla, and white gloves.

"For the service," Evy explained. "I figured you might want to wear something black."

"Oh." Maggie sat down heavily on the side of the bed. "The service."

Evy picked up the sweater and held it by the shoulders, displaying it for her. "They're having some prayers at the church first; and then they're going on up to the cemetery where Jess's brother is buried."

"I can't bear it, I was thinking that I might not want to go after all," a voice in the back of Maggie's head whispered. "I still have to pack, and I'd like to get a boat this morning."

The girl stared incredulously at her. "You said you'd go," she said.

347

"I said I'd think about it. I'm sorry. I just don't think I can manage it, with the day that lies ahead of me; I'm not feeling that strong, and I still have to travel, and find a place to stay . . ."

Evy hurled the sweater at the bed, where it clung to the blanket and hung haphazardly over the side. "That's just great."

"I'm sorry, Evy. You can still go. You don't even need to drop me. I could get the island taxi."

"Don't you have any feelings?" the girl cried out.

Maggie looked up at her. "Of course I do."

"You don't even care enough to go to say goodbye to him."

Maggie pressed her hand over her eyes. "I don't think I can stand it."

"I don't think I can stand it," Evy mimicked.

"Don't be cruel," Maggie said.

"Cruel. What about Jess? He's dead now. Do you think he'd be having this service if it wasn't for you?"

Maggie dropped her hand and stared at her. "What do you mean?" she whispered hoarsely.

"Nothing," said the girl, lowering her eyes to hood the alarm which surfaced there.

"Yesterday you said you didn't blame me for what happened to Jess. Now you've suddenly changed your tune. It was an accident. You know that. I had nothing to do with it."

"Okay. Forget it. I'm sorry," the girl mumbled.

"Why would I hurt him? I loved him. Doesn't anybody realize that?" Maggie argued shrilly.

"If you loved him so much you'd take the time to attend the service," Evy muttered.

Maggie stared dully in front of her for a few moments. It was true, she thought. It was the last thing she could ever do for him. She had taken his love, even when she knew she shouldn't. And she had lied to him. Even though she knew he had trusted her. She pictured again his gentle, honest eyes. She had been a coward from the beginning. But she could not change what she had done. The least she could do was to be there at the end.

Slowly, she reached over and picked up the sweater. She pushed her hand into one sleeve and then the other, and pulled it on over her head, straightening it out over the blouse. She pinned the black, lacy veil to her red hair, and pulled on the gloves. "All right," she said. "I'll go."

Evy patted the seat of the wheelchair, and Maggie shuffled over to it and sat down.

"We've probably missed most of the church service anyway," Evy reassured her. "We can wait outside if you want and just follow them up to the cemetery."

Maggie nodded numbly. Evy grasped the

handles of the chair behind her, and began to push.

Once, when he was very young, he had gone sledging with his cousin and some other of the older boys. He tramped along behind them, dragging his racing sled, proud to be included. But when the day's fun was over and the grey winter twilight had started to descend, they scampered off and left him there, while he was taking one last run down the hill. He didn't know how to get home. He stood at the foot of the hill in the growing darkness, calling out to them.

"Come back," he was crying. And then, when he knew there was no one to hear him, "Mama," in a small voice. Then louder, his nose running, his face bitten with the cold, "Mama."

Like clear water breaking through a muddy dam, Jess's consciousness returned. His eyes, already open, began to see again. He was lying on his side, his face ground into the dirt of the floor. He realized, to his surprise, that tears had trickled down his face, forming a tiny patch of mud which smeared his cheekbone. Jess lifted his aching head and looked around the cellar. Emmett's pitiful corpse was gone. He remembered now.

She had come down the stairs to collect it. He could not tell how long ago it had been. He had loosened his gag by constant chewing at it and was slurping up water from the washtub when he heard the door open. Quickly he had slid back down to the floor and feigned unconsciousness. She suspected he was awake, and had kicked him in the side several times to see if he would respond. He had remained limp, eyelids closed. Suddenly he felt her fingers, like talons, in his hair. She jerked his head back, holding a fistful of his hair. His mouth fell open. He did not wince, but kept his eyes closed. Then, muttering, she had dropped him, and gone about her grisly business. With one eye open he watched her, as grunting and struggling, she had manoeuvred Emmett's body into some kind of large bag, and began dragging it to the steps, as if it were a sack of refuse. As she started up the stairs, clunking the bag along behind her, Jess had felt his head start to spin and he lost consciousness.

Now he looked up towards the slim band of light, grey and phosphorescent, which hung steadily in the darkness above his head. Occasionally a dark shadow would move across it, and then it would return. It was the bottom of the door. Jess imagined that if he could put his face to that band, he would drink in a stream of cool, fresh air. The putrid smell of the cellar had ceased to nauseate him. He wore it now, like a hood. But the prospect of one clean breath of air was painfully tantalizing.

Used, by now, to the darkness, Jess could see

the many steps which led up to the door. It was the only way out, and it was not far away, yet it seemed as remote as another continent to him. But he knew that he had to try to get out. His extremities were numb, with only an occasional tingle evidencing the remaining life in his hands and feet. He had had no food since she left him down there. She was going to let him die in his dungeon. He wondered if Maggie were still alive. He had to try. He could not just lie there and accept the fact that he was buried alive.

Jess's eyes returned to the glimmer of light. He could also see motes of light flickering through the door itself. Old wood, he thought. Rotten. A trace of hope stirred inside of him. It could be smashed, he reasoned, if it were battered with the hardest thing at hand. With a feeling of despair he acknowledged that his head and shoulder were his only tools. Wearily he slumped back to the earth, his head throbbing from the prospect. Then he lifted his aching head and looked again. He realized that he had to try it. It was better than dying.

With agonizing slowness he summoned all his remaining strength and began to wriggle around the floor to the foot of the stairs. Using his knees and shoulder to propel himself, Jess inched his way over the cold, damp earth. With every few inches he gained he paused, gasping for breath, the clumps of earth sticking to his dry, cracked lips, and clogging his nostrils. His shirt had bunched up almost to his armpits, leaving his torso bare and scraped. The gravel in the floor gouged holes in his bony knees. He sucked in what air he could, and continued on. Finally, after an interminable journey, he reached the foot of the stairs.

Jess dropped his head heavily on the surface of the bottom step. The ragged, splintered surface of the wood snagged him like thorns. He dreaded the prospect of dragging his body across the wooden planks, exposing every inch of his skin to the sharp slivers which would insinuate themselves below the surface to throb there. But the shaft of light which penetrated the rotten door drew him on.

For a few moments he rested, but he did not dare to rest too long, for fear that his consciousness would go again, and he would drift from his purpose like a rudderless boat on an empty sea. He had to concentrate on those steps, and the door at the top.

Inhaling deeply and sending up a silent prayer, Jess hoisted his weight up with the aid of his elbow and threw his head higher. His rear end landed on the bottom stair with a crack, while his head smashed against the front of a higher stair. He balanced there, afraid to breathe for fear of losing his new seat. Slowly he twisted his body, curving his frame against the unyielding wooden planks, balancing off the rickety banisters and forcing himself upwards.

His tedious journey was unmarked by thoughts or doubts or worries. Every fibre of his being was concentrated on the simple progress from stair to stair. His feet and hands, so numb as to be useless, were weights he dragged with him. His body was pierced by splinters and ached in every part. A fog swirled dangerously close to his preciously-guarded consciousness. Jess tried to count, to fight it off, but it was persistent and seductive. He lifted his head and stared at the needle-thin shafts of light which pierced the door. He was so close now that they fell on his sleeves. He forced himself to stay alert.

With a last, anguished push, he reached the top. He put his face to the precious light, and sucked in the air. It was not as cool as he had hoped, not as clean. But it revived him, all the same.

For a few moments he laid his face there, tempted to forget about forcing the door. He would just breathe, and breathe, until someone came. But then the image of the shadow across the bar of light returned to his mind. Evy, opening the door. No one would come. No rescue. He had to try.

Jess pulled himself up until his bottom rested on the top step. The upright position was dizzying, and he leaned his head against his prison door. After a few moments the vertigo subsided. He opened his eyes. He would have to hit the door with all his strength, and hope it gave. Up close he examined the wood, as best he could. As he suspected, it was old and rotted in spots. He looked up towards the area where the doorknob should be. He could see that the door was latched from the outside. Worriedly, he contemplated the possibility of a bolt. Then he shook his head. He decided that a bolt was unlikely in an old house like this. He tried to remember the night he had come here, to look at the plumbing. He searched his mind for the picture of Evy unlocking the door. As he did, another chilling thought occurred to him. What if she were home? What if he managed to break through the door and she was standing there on the other side, waiting for him. The thought made him shudder. He waited until the tremor passed.

The house was quiet. She was probably gone. One way or the other, he had to strike.

He arranged himself on the stair so that when he propelled himself forward he would hit the door with maximum force. He anticipated the pain that would come dispassionately, as if it would be affecting some other man. His one concern was to break through. Jess remembered a TV show he had seen once about karate masters who chopped through blocks of wood. It was said that they imagined their hands on the far side, even as they struck. Jess tried to concentrate.

He leaned his body back, as far away from the door as he could get without falling from his precarious perch. He steeled himself for the pain. One, he counted to himself. Two, three. He hurled himself at the door.

A few mourners were already trickling out of the oak doors of the church when Evy and Maggie pulled up in the car.

Evy gave the misted windscreen a flick of the wipers so that they could better observe the people as they filed out of the church. An elderly man and woman were being helped down the steps by Charley Cullum and another man whom Maggie did not know. "Jess's parents?" she asked.

Evy nodded, staring at the procession which was beginning to disperse as people got into their cars. "I think so," she said. "But we came here just around the time they moved, so I never really knew them."

Maggie wondered fleetingly if Sharon would appear. But let the thought go. What difference did it make now.

The church bell tolled its sorrowful dirge, amidst the sound of starting engines. Maggie could not take her eyes from the doors of the church from where the grim-faced company emerged. The sight of them paralysed her.

Grace Cullum, clinging tightly to the hands of her restless young sons, passed in front of the

356

car. Jack Schmale walked, head down, not far behind her. Maggie looked away from the church portals and saw Ned and Sadie Wilson climbing into Ned's truck across the street.

"There's the Wilsons," Evy observed.

Maggie considered challenging that remark, but wearily let it pass. The hostess at the Four Winds passed by the car, leaning against a handsome, bearded young man in an army fatigue jacket. The girl's crown of braids bobbed up and down with her sobs. Maggie looked dry-eyed, as the young man helped the waitress aboard the back of his motorcycle.

"We'd better get going," said Evy, turning the key in the ignition. "It's a long drive to the cemetery. It's out near your house."

They drove in silence; the only sound was the occasional rush of wind, and the steady squeak of the windscreen wipers. The gloomy procession of cars wound steadily along the island roads, their headlights beaming through the fog. Maggie stared out the water-streaked window at the acres of dark trees, virtually denuded of leaves, which were whipping by. Every branch and rock and fallen leaf reminded her of Jess. The only reason that she did not close her eyes was because she did not want to see his face.

"A lot of people turned out," said Evy. "Especially for such a bad day."

"Yes," Maggie replied unenthusiastically.

"Everybody liked Jess," said the girl.

Maggie only nodded. "Do you think the boats will be running today?" she asked.

Evy gave an exasperated sigh. "Of course. Why wouldn't they?"

"It's wet and foggy."

"That's nothing to them," said the girl. "I'll tell you what's bad. These roads." She squinted hard, and leaned towards her windscreen. "It's hard to see anything."

"Be careful," said Maggie.

Evy shrugged. "It's just over this rise." Within a few moments she had brought the car to a halt just ahead of several others and they both sat, looking down at the valley of headstones, ghostly in the mist. Several of the mourners carried armfuls of flowers incongruously bright, which they set around one of the headstones. Slowly the other mourners began to exit from the warmth of their cars and plod down towards the flurry of sombre activity in the stillness of the cemetery.

"Well, let's go," said Evy.

Maggie hung back. "I can't."

"Come on," said the girl impatiently. "Here, you can use this."

The girl held out a handkerchief towards her, trimmed in a delicate pattern of knotted cotton lace. Maggie hesitated, and then reached for it. She held it near her nose, breathing in the dense, flowery scent. Then she rubbed her fingers

358

together noting the powdery substance on the cloth of her gloves.

"Talcum," said Evy.

"It smells good," said Maggie.

Evy was already out of the car and making her way down the hill. Maggie caught up with her. "Did you bring an umbrella?" she asked.

"I can't remember everything," Evy snapped.

Maggie followed behind her, clutching the handkerchief tightly in her gloved hand. She could distinguish the faces of the others as they neared the graveside. She imagined that she could hear a murmur shaking through the gathered mourners as they approached. Maggie forced herself to look only at the headstone which read, Michael Herlie, 1948—1967. She wondered if Jess's name would be added to the stone, even though his body was still in the sea.

Father Kincaid, the slight, grey-haired parish priest, stepped towards the open grave. His black cassock billowed in the wind. An altar boy in a white robe held an umbrella over the priest's head. "My dear friends," began the priest in a reedy voice. "We gather here, at the grave of Michael Herlie, to bid farewell now to his brother, Jess. Two young men, loving brothers in life, who were struck down in their prime. Now united in death . . ."

The wind whipped his words up and away, like cinders. Maggie could hardly hear him. What did he know about Jess, she thought.

359

Perhaps he had baptized him, ministered to him for years, even married him. And now he was eulogizing him. Everyone there had known Jess longer than she. But she had loved him. His every movement, every word. She had loved to watch him, to touch him, to hear his voice. She should have been content with that. She might have learned to be content, loving him from afar.

This is not your fault, she reminded herself. But you could have let him be, nagged another voice inside of her. But he wouldn't let me, she thought. He would never have been satisfied with "no". The memory of his urgency stabbed her through.

"Ashes to ashes . . ." intoned the priest.

No. Not Jess.

"Dust to dust . . ."

Goodbye. Oh, goodbye.

The finality of the ceremony battered down the wall of her defiant composure. Tears, which she had forced back repeatedly, began to come. They squeezed out, one by one like drops of blood. Her body shook, only partly from the chill. She raised the handkerchief to her eyes, and wiped away the tears with an angry swipe.

"And may the angels welcome him to his home in paradise." The mourners stared sadly at the flower-bedecked gravestone.

Suddenly, an unearthly howl of pain pierced the graveyard. The priest stopped short in his blessing and stared at Maggie who was screaming

360

now, her hands clapped to her eyes. The other mourners stared as Maggie emitted cries like those of a wounded animal. A loud murmur raced through the shocked throng.

"Stop that," Evy pleaded, tugging at Maggie's arm. Looking worriedly around at the other mourners, she began dragging Maggie away from the graveside.

Maggie stumbled blindly along, one hand clutching her eyes, the other grasping Evy's jacket, as the girl pulled her up the hill. "Oh my God," Maggie shrieked.

"We're almost at the car," Evy said. "Hang on." She guided the wailing woman to the car door and then held on to her with one hand as she opened it. The eyes of all the mourners were riveted on the progress of the two women. Evy shoved Maggie gently down into the seat, and slammed the door shut behind her. She quickly ran around to the other side, and slipped into the driver's seat.

"My eyes," Maggie moaned. "Oh God, they're on fire." A thousand burning needles seemed to be stabbing her pupils. Her head felt swollen to the point where it could burst, and her temples throbbed. "Help me," she screamed out in anguish.

Evy wrested the balled-up hanky from Maggie's fingers and examined it. The hanky still smelled of the perfume which she had sprayed on it last night. But the scouring powder was now in streaky tracks along the hanky's surface. The rain had come in handy. It had dampened it just enough so that it didn't matter how many tears Maggie cried. Evy rolled the hanky up again and stuffed it in her purse beside her on the seat. Better remember not to use it, she thought, and gave a silent, mirthless laugh.

"Oh help me. My eyes," Maggie moaned. "I have to go to the hospital." She grabbed blindly at Evy's arm.

"I'm helping you," the girl insisted, shaking off her grasp.

"The doctor. You have to take me. Please," Maggie cried. Evy could hear the weakness and confusion in Maggie's voice even as she struggled.

"I will," said Evy. The car was already moving.

362

23

THE city room of the New York *Daily News* was about the size of a ballroom, filled with enough desks and chairs to make it look like a warehouse for office furniture. Owen threaded his way through the maze of desks, some of them occupied by men and women reading the paper, talking on the phone, or clacking away at typewriters. He moved down the aisles uncertainly at first, until he spotted the man he was looking for. Then he strode up to the reporter, who was hunched over his typewriter, and clapped him on the shoulder.

"Hey, Vance," he said.

Vance Williamson raised his face from the page he was studying and gazed up at Owen through his tortoise-shell horn-rimmed glasses. He pushed a wheat-coloured swatch of hair off his forehead and smiled wanly.

"Hi, Owen." He greeted his old friend as if Owen had merely returned from a break at the water cooler, rather than surprised him with a rare visit from a remote island retreat.

Owen was not put off by the anaemic greeting. He knew the crime reporter's bland façade to be deceptive. Once, over about the fourth scotch in one of their regular drinking sprees in their UPI days, he had declared Vance Williamson to be, "Okay, despite your pedigree". Williamson had indulged in a rare blush which rose from the neck of his button-down collar, Tattersall-checked shirt.

"How's business? The hoods still keeping you hopping?" Owen asked.

Vance tossed his pencil on his desk top and nodded. "Never a dull moment around here. You know that. What brings you to town?"

"A wild goose chase," Owen admitted.

Vance raised his blond eyebrows a millimetre above his horn-rims.

Owen rested his bulk against an empty desk. "I get a call at my house that *Life* wants to see me immediately. I've had this series on wild birds pending . . ."

"Wild birds," Vance scoffed. "This from a man who took the only existing pictures of a mob rub-out in progress in Bensonhurst."

"You city boys are all alike," said Owen. "Action. That's all you think about. There are finer things, you know."

Vance chuckled and shook his head. "You really like it up there," he observed.

"I do," said Owen. "You should come up some time. You can bring your current honey, whoever that might be."

"Barbara," said Vance.

"Barbara? Still? You're slowing down."

Vance shrugged. "She can't get enough of me.

What can I say? So, you came all the way down and they decided not to do the series?"

"It's not that," Owen explained. "They never called. They didn't know anything about it."

"That's odd," said Vance.

"Isn't it."

"Well, at any rate, I'm glad you're here. What'll it be for lunch? Liquid or solid?"

"Maybe a little of both," said Owen. "It's been a long morning."

"Give me five minutes to finish this piece."

Owen nodded, and sat musing quietly as the reporter worked.

"Okay," said Vance, standing up. "Let's go."

"There's one other thing while I'm here," said Owen. "Something's been bothering me, and I want to run it by you, to see if you can make anything of it."

"What's that?" asked the reporter, pushing in his swivel chair below his desk.

"Well," said Owen. "There's a woman who just moved to the island. She's working at the paper. And I know I remember her from somewhere. I think she may have been involved in a trial, or something like that. I think I may have photographed her once. Anyway, she was just on the verge of telling me about it, and then we had some bad news and it all kind of got side-tracked. I've got a feeling she's sitting on some big secret, and it's bothering the hell out of me because I can't remember."

"What was the bad news?" Vance asked.

"Ah, Jess Herlie. He's . . . He was the editor of the paper up there. He drowned in a fishing accident."

"Oh, that's too bad," said Vance. "I remember you saying you liked him."

"I did," Owen admitted. "He was a nice guy."

"So, what's her name?"

"Margaret Fraser," said Owen. "You're the crime man. I thought you might remember."

"Margaret Fraser. Sure, I know who she is."

"You do? Just like that?" Owen was incredulous.

"Well, I'd like you to think I'm a genius," Vance demurred, "but the only reason I know it so readily is that she just got out of jail a month ago, and I was reading a follow-up on her. She was involved in a murder some years back. Upstate somewhere. A married lover, I think."

"That's amazing," said Owen. "I think that rings a bell. I knew I remembered her."

"Mystery solved," said Vance, snapping closed his briefcase on his desk, and pulling on his jacket. "Let's eat."

"Okay," said Owen. He started out of the city room behind the reporter, mulling over this interesting piece of information. "Maybe I could take a look at the clips in the morgue after lunch."

"You probably won't be able to even walk

after lunch, much less read," laughed the reporter.

Owen stopped between two desks and frowned at Williamson. "You think I could take a look at them now?"

Vance shrugged. "Sure. If you want to. Let's go down and have a look."

"In the name of the Father, Son and Holy Spirit. Amen," rapidly intoned Father Kincaid. But the benediction was all but drowned out by the murmuring of the crowd. The priest crossed himself and then turned to the two elderly people, Jess's parents, who stood stoically by, the only ones who seemed to be concentrating on the conclusion of the service.

The priest's obeisance to the parents was the signal the crowd was seeking in order to scatter and discuss the peculiar events of the morning.

Grace Cullum spotted Jack Schmale and Prendergast walking together, each lost in his own thoughts. She thrust the hands of her young sons towards her husband and headed in their direction. The muddy lawn sucked down the little heels of her black pumps as she hurried towards them.

"Jack," she cried out.

Jack motioned for his young colleague to go on ahead, while he waited for the breathless Grace to reach his side.

"What did you think of that?" she asked indignantly.

Jack shook his head. Droplets of rain bounced off the slick plastic covering on his policeman's cap. "I guess she was pretty broken up about Jess."

"Broken up, my eye," Grace shouted. "There's something wrong with her. She's not normal."

"She's strange, all right," he agreed.

"Strange? I'd say suspicious is more like it. Just like that accident of Jess's. I can't believe for a minute he drowned, just like that." She snapped her fingers for emphasis.

"Grace, Grace. We're all sorry about Jess."

"I'm not talking about sorry, Jack. You listen to me," she demanded. "That woman comes here, saying Mr. Emmett told her to come. That was nearly two weeks ago, and we still haven't heard a word from Mr. Emmett."

"I know," Jack admitted tiredly.

"And now, Jess," Grace concluded portentously. "And she carried on at the funeral like a crazy woman. I'm tired of holding my tongue about all this."

"She wouldn't hurt anyone, Grace. Certainly not Jess. She seemed quite fond of Jess."

"People like that don't need a reason," Grace said impatiently. "What do we know about her, after all? She shows up here and things start turning sour. That's what I know. And I think you ought to be doing something about it."

"Evy seems to have befriended her."

"Evy's like a child. She hasn't got the sense to come in from the rain."

Jack squinted up at the drizzling skies, and then looked back at Grace, who was staring at him defiantly. "Well, what do you think I should do? There hasn't been a crime yet, far as I can figure."

"I don't know. Check up on her. Check her fingerprints. For all we know she may be wanted in six states by the FBI. Honestly, everyone on this island acts like the rest of the world doesn't even exist."

"Now, Grace. You're an islander yourself. You know how it is."

"How what is? Are we supposed to be a haven for criminals?"

"Grace, don't get carried away. I'll check on her with the state police. We'll see if they've got anything on her. Although it does seem a bit strange to be checking up on such a sweet lady."

"Oh, for heaven's sake," Grace snorted.

"Have you got something down at the office I can dust for fingerprints."

"I certainly can find something," Grace said grimly. "Let's get down there right now. I've got the keys."

"All right, all right," said Jack.

The cemetery was empty now, except for

Charley Cullum, Who stood at a distance, trying to quiet his unruly sons.

"We can try," said Jack. "But I don't know what you expect to find."

"My God, look at this," Owen breathed as he scanned the file of clips which the morgue librarian had drawn out for him. Vance stood beside him, reading over his shoulder. "Twelve years she was in jail. On a plea bargain."

"She really looks spaced out in those pictures, doesn't she," said Vance, shaking his head.

Owen nodded. "Listen to this," he ordered, and began to read. "The defendant's mother appeared in the courtroom on the day of sentencing, accompanied by a nun, Sister Dolorita of the Angels. When asked by this reporter what she thought about her daughter's sentence, Alma Fraser replied, 'It's God's will. She must pay for the evil things she has done.' Her own mother. Whew . . ."

Owen shook his head, and perused several more of the clips.

"You about finished?" Vance asked, looking at his watch.

"I guess so," said Owen. He began to replace the clips in the folder. Suddenly he stopped, and lifted one out of the pile. As he read it his face began to sag, his forehead creasing into a deep frown. "Jesus, Vance," he whispered.

Vance, who was already signing them out in

the morgue's log book, glanced up at his friend. "What is it? What'd you find?"

"Just a minute," Owen said impatiently. He grabbed the pile of clips and began to flip through them, reading selected paragraphs and throwing them aside. Vance watched his wide eyes and moving lips curiously.

"What is it?" he prodded.

Owen shoved a clipping at his friend. "There's only this one picture," said Owen. "Read the caption."

Vance obediently read. "The victim's wife, shown here with her mother, Harriet Robinson, and her daughter, Evelyn . . ."

Owen put a hand on Vance's arm. "Harriet Robinson," he said slowly, "lives on the island. With her granddaughter, Evy. The girl works at the newspaper there. She has a different name now. Her grandmother's name. But Vance, it's the same girl."

"Yeah. So?"

Owen's normally ruddy countenance was an unhealthy yellowish colour. "So, that can't be a coincidence."

Vance frowned, and shifted uneasily. "I doubt it," he agreed. "But why would this woman Maggie ever want to go somewhere where the dead man's daughter lived."

Owen's mind began to race. He thought about the things he'd heard from Jess, and Maggie. And he thought about Evy. Who acted as if she had no idea who Maggie was. "That's impossible," he said aloud.

"What is?"

"I don't care how young she was at the time. That girl would know who the woman was who killed her own father."

"Of course," said Vance.

"There's something wrong here," said Owen. "Something very wrong. Vance, is there a telephone down here?"

"Right over there," said Vance. "Go ahead."

Owen rushed to the phone and picked it up. After a hurried call to information, he began to dial the island. He tried several numbers. First he called Maggie. The phone rang and rang.

Then he dialled the police station. There was no answer. Maggie was supposed to be leaving the hospital today. Impatiently, he tried her again. "Answer," he cried impatiently. "Answer the goddamn phone."

24

A COLD, grey light suffused the small bedroom of the Thornhill house. The pastel stripes and roses on the aged wallpaper were drained of colour by the gloomy light. The faded outlines of flowers were faint, like pencilled sketches, and only the water stains, near the ceiling, showed up with definition.

The bedside table and walnut dresser in the room seemed sturdy, but stark, unadorned as they were by any flowers, hairbrushes, or crystal bottles.

Bare branches snapped up against the window, their dark shadows shifting on the limp cotton curtains which stood partly closed. In the dimness of the room the curtains appeared to be grey also, although they once were a creamy white.

From the direction of the living-room the chimes of the grandfather clock sounded in the silence, proclaiming that it was afternoon, but the darkness of the stormy day made it seem much later.

The sheets had come loose from the double bed which occupied the centre of the room. The striped ticking, and steel-grey buttons of the sagging mattress were visible in one corner.

The disarray of the sheets testified to the sleeper's restlessness.

Seated on the edge of the bed, her arms wrapped around her chest, Maggie stared blankly out through the narrow opening between the curtains. Her head ached through a dull fog. She reached up and touched a finger tentatively to her eyelids, which were nearly swollen shut. What happened? She had passed out in Evy's car, overcome by the pain. That was the last thing she remembered.

Slowly she pushed herself off the bed and stood up. Her legs felt wobbly beneath her. She wanted to see what her eyes looked like, although she dreaded it at the same time. At least I *can* see, she thought.

A plain, oval mirror hung over the walnut chest. Maggie walked over to the chest and started to look. Then she paused, and reached for the cord on the standing lamp beside the chest. She switched on the lamp. The burst of light was like a dagger in her eyes. Quickly she shut it off, trembling from the pain, tears spurting out from the inside corners of her puffed lids. After a few moments the pain subsided, and she opened her eyes cautiously. She leaned against the chest, close to the mirror, and peered in.

Her vision seemed to swim a little as she strained to see in the grey light, but gradually she was able to focus on her face. She gasped,

374

as her features took shape. The whole area around her eyes was swollen, and even her cheeks appeared to be a virulent, cranberry colour. Her pupils were little more than slits in her face. She touched the area around her eyes wonderingly, recalled the shooting pains at the funeral. Could it have been some kind of nervous attack? She had heard of such things.

She looked at herself again. The black mantilla was still secured to her head, although it was askew from her thrashing on the pillow. She reached up and tried to pry out the pins which held it, but they resisted her, snarled as they were in her copper-coloured hair. She dropped her hand weakly, and clung to the edge of the bureau as a wave of dizziness and nausea passed over her.

Where was Evy? Had they been to the hospital? Had a doctor come and gone? She could not remember his visit. She stared down at her stockinged feet. "Where are my shoes?" she said aloud, and looked helplessly around at the bare wooden floor of the room.

Maybe under the bed, she thought. Painfully, she lowered herself to the floor. It suddenly seemed important to find them. She leaned on her elbows and tried to see into the darkness under the bed. The dust under the bed made her sneeze. Her hand jerked up and hit the bed frame. The sharp little pain was accompanied by a feeling of angry frustration. "I want my shoes," she said irritably. She was just about to reach under the bed again and grope for them when she heard the first noise.

It came from above her head. A rattling sound, like a marble running over uneven floorboards. She sat up sharply and listened.

The house was silent. Maggie drew a breath and waited. The quiet in the house seemed suddenly oppressive. You imagined it, she chided herself. She bent down and ran her hand quickly under the bed.

The rattle came again.

"Who is it?" Maggie cried out. "Evy! Is that you?"

Scrambling to her feet, Maggie stood in the corner of the room and stared up at the ceiling. She shivered, feeling suddenly chilled. It's a mouse, she told herself. That's all it is. As if to explode that comforting theory, a scraping sound broke the silence.

Maggie's flesh prickled. She rubbed her icy hands together and began to edge towards the door of the room. A splinter of wood snagged her stocking, and wedged under the skin of the sole of her foot. She grimaced, but stopped herself from crying out. The scraping sound from the attic had ceased, and the silence descended again.

After a few moment's hesitation, she crept past the bathroom and over the threshold into the living-room. All the drapes were drawn, and the room was sunk in darkness. Maggie's hand hovered near the switch of a table lamp, but, remembering the pain in her eyes from the bedroom light, she decided not to illuminate the room. Instead, she strained to adjust her eyes to the blackness. The ticking of the grandfather clock timed the silence. Outside the wind gave a restive howl.

"Is anybody here?" she called out. Her voice quavered in the dark. There was no answer.

The doorway to the attic staircase was between the living-room and the kitchen. She could see that the kitchen beyond it looked brighter, and she remembered that there was a flashlight in one of the kitchen drawers. Drawing a determined breath, she padded swiftly towards the light. Halfway across the room, she was startled by a thump from above. She jumped, her shin whacking into a chair leg. The chair tumbled back and hit the sofa with a thud. Maggie grabbed her shin and held it. Tears spurted from her swollen lids. She swallowed the curse which rose to her lips.

When the throbbing subsided, she hurried the rest of the distance across the room, and entered the kitchen. She quickly ran to the window and looked out. Her black Buick sat alone in the driveway. Evy's car was gone. Maggie turned back and faced into the room. Her eyes fell on the top drawer of the counter beside the sink. She walked over and pulled it open. The flashlight was there. With a silent prayer she flipped the switch. The light made a yellow circle on the worn linoleum. Maggie gave an unsteady sigh of relief and turned it off. Her eyes travelled around the room and rested on the telephone. Maybe she should call for help. With a wave of despair she realized that there was no one she could call. Owen was gone, Grace would hang up on her. The police? And say what? There's a noise in my attic? The two cops had been at the service this morning. Heard her screaming. And what about Evy? Evy had promised to stay, and then left her alone.

It's probably nothing, she thought. Some little animal, trapped up there. Just find out, she told herself angrily. As she glanced-around the kitchen again, she noticed Willy's dish on the floor. She had not yet had the heart to remove it. She shuddered, and opened another drawer, pawing through it until she brought up a carving knife, with a pitted wooden handle. Grasping it tightly in her sweaty hand, she walked over and reached for the doorknob to the attic stairs. She hesitated a moment, and then pulled. The door opened easily, and the darkened staircase loomed before her.

"Is there anyone up there?" she cried out, trying only half successfully to assume an authoritative tone. There was no reply. A feeling of foolishness overcame her for a moment. That's okay, she thought. If there's no one there, then

378

no one will know that you were sneaking around the house with a knife talking to yourself. Holding the knife and flashlight out before her, Maggie began to mount the steps.

The staircase was old, and creaked with each succeeding step. Maggie's stockinged feet slid on the warped boards as she made her way up. She shone the flashlight up ahead, but even at the top of the stairs she could see nothing but the corners of some old cartons, and an unframed oil painting leaning against the wall beams. A ghostly fragment of cobwebs hung down, and caught the light.

Maggie reached the top step and turned quickly to look into the darkened cavern which spanned the top of the Thornhill house. She could see nothing but the inert shapes of the objects stored up there. It was not a particularly cramped attic. The sparseness of the Thornhills' life seemed to extend to their saving of earthly goods.

Maggie shone her flashlight rapidly around the attic, satisfying herself that there was no one crouched in the far corners. There were several boxes, a shelf of books, the bottom of some dresses and jackets which were not quite covered by a plastic sheet, and a few odd pieces of furniture scattered about. Maggie stepped forward more confidently into the attic, and swept the flashlight around again. Almost all of the objects in the attic were leaning up against the walls, or packed into corners. But in the centre of the room, quite apart from all the other items, was a straight-backed chair.

Maggie focused her light on it, and took a step towards it. She ran the light from the feet up to the seat, and then up the back of the chair, and examined it curiously, from a distance. Then she turned the light on the walls again, giving them a quick scan. As the beam passed over the back wall, a moving shadow caught her eye. She jerked the light back to the centre of the room, in the direction of the movement. She froze, and stared at what she saw in the glare of the beam.

Above the chair, swaying slightly in the close atmosphere, an empty noose hung from the rafter.

A chop of her wrist, from behind, knocked the knife from Maggie's trembling hand. It skittered across the floor and stopped near the leg of the chair. A cold point drilled into the small of Maggie's back.

Maggie screamed, and whirled around. Her flashlight shone full in the face of her assailant. The upturned light cast hollows around Evy's eyes and cheeks, giving her head a skull-like look, but her eyes glittered with a trenchant energy. She jabbed the gun she held tightly clenched in her white hand at Maggie. Her blue veins bulged from the fierceness of her grasp.

"Get back," she growled.

"Evy," Maggie gasped. "What are you doing?"

"Give me that," Evy snarled, grabbing the flashlight from Maggie. She tossed it roughly on the floor, and it rolled over on the uneven floorboards, throwing a drunken light on the two women who faced one another at the top of the stairs. Keeping her gun trained on Maggie, Evy stepped back and illuminated the hurricane lamp which sat on a nearby table. The red globe of the lamp gave the dark attic a hellish glow.

"That's better," said the girl.

Maggie stared in stunned disbelief at the contoured features of Evy's face. A sickening fear filled her throat like bile, and made her start to gag. As if to ward off the awful feeling, she began to shake her head.

"Evy, don't do this. Whatever you're thinking . . ."

Evy poked the gun in the direction of her midriff. "Climb up on that chair," she said in a quiet but menacing voice.

"No. Evy, listen to me . . ."

"Do it," the girl insisted, her voice shaking.

Abruptly Maggie moved backwards. She put her hands up in front of her in a calming gesture as she stepped back. "Evy," she pleaded gently. "We can talk about this. Let's go downstairs and talk."

"Move," Evy ejaculated.

"I'm moving," Maggie assured her. Her every

extremity was filled with an eerie vibrancy of pure fear at the sight of the gun. Evy jerked the weapon recklessly, her eyes hard and disconcerted. An involuntary twitch was visible above her right eye.

Keep talking, Maggie thought. Gently. "Evy, please tell me why you're so angry. There must be some misunderstanding."

"Shut up," the girl growled. "There's no misunderstanding. You're just trying to get out of it. Well, you can't get out of it this time."

She's crazy, Maggie thought. "I'm not trying to get out of anything," Maggie said. "I just want to talk with you. I don't know what's the matter."

Evy laughed. It was a harsh, hooting sound filled with anguish. "I know what you're up to," she said. "You got away with it before. You fooled them. But you can't fool me. I *know* what happened."

"What happened? What are you talking about?" Maggie used all her will to keep her voice calm and even.

"I know what you did," Evy spat out furiously. "You killed him."

Oh God, Maggie thought. It's Jess. She's gone mad over it. Maggie's thoughts spun back to their conversation in the hospital, the veiled accusation, instantly retracted. Her every instinct had warned her that the girl blamed her for Jess's death, but she had dismissed it, lulled by the girl's offers of help. She stared down at the barrel of the gun, and then looked up into the girl's malevolent eyes.

"Oh no," she pleaded, "I swear to you. I had nothing to do with it."

"Don't lie to me," the girl shrieked. "You can't lie your way out of it. You killed my father."

"Your father?" Maggie breathed. The accusation came like a blow, making her feel sick. Was it possible? Jess? Some long-ago island scandal, well concealed. Perhaps he too had kept secrets. Or was it some fantasy that had overtaken Evy's reason? Maggie searched Evy's face, looking for a trace of the features she had loved in Jess. As she stared, a strange and terrible realization began to dawn on her, along with the unformed image of another, long-blurred face. Still, she whispered, "Jess? Jess was your father?" Even as she spoke the words, she recognized, with inescapable certainty, the identity of the girl who stood before her.

"Jess?" the girl said scornfully. "No. Jess was just in the way. Jess was a fool for being taken in by you. I had to make sure that he wouldn't interfere."

"Roger. You're Roger's little girl." Maggie choked out. And then, she felt the delayed impact of Evy's admission. "Oh no. Not Jess. You killed him?"

"Get up on the chair," Evy commanded.

"Oh." A sob vibrated up from Maggie's chest as she gazed at the girl, struggling to recall the child she had heard of, but never seen. "Lynnie," she whispered. "Evelyn." Then she asked softly, "What happened to you?"

"I'm not going to wait," Evy snarled. "If you don't get up there I'll shoot you." The cords in her neck stood out. Maggie was jarred from her paralysed state by the intensity on Evy's face. She turned and placed her hand on the back of the chair.

"How did you . . . How did you know it was me?" Maggie asked, overcome by confusion at the impossibility of the coincidence. Her brain felt like it was short-circuiting. "Did you know I was coming here?" She looked up in confusion at the girl.

"I made you come here," Evy announced, her eyes ablaze with triumphant hatred. "I wrote the letters. Not Mr. Emmett. He never knew anything about them."

Maggie sagged under this revelation. She leaned against the chair.

"Hurry up," Evy cried. "Get up there. It's over now."

Maggie dragged one foot and then the other up on the chair. She stood up shakily. She looked down at the girl, struggling to think of how to reach her. "Evy," she implored, "please listen to me. I don't know how much you know about what happened, but I didn't kill your

384

father. You're too young to remember any of it, but it was just as I told the police. It was all a terrible mistake."

"I know what happened."

"No. You only think you know. It was twelve years ago. I can only tell you the truth. I was a little girl, not much older than you are now. I was mixed-up. I was in love with your father. That was wrong. I know that. But I didn't kill him. I wouldn't have hurt him. You have to believe me." The words tumbled out, full of misery.

"Stop talking," Evy croaked. "I hate your voice. I know what happened."

"No, Evy. I swear it."

"Put on the noose," the girl ordered, waving the gun. "You're going to hang. I figured it all out. Everyone is going to think you hung yourself because you were so sorry for all you had done."

Maggie reached out to touch the running knot. The loop of rope felt like a snake around her hand. "Don't do this," she said. "It's no use."

"Put it on." Evy jerked the gun at her.

Maggie swallowed hard, and took the loop in both hands. Fighting her revulsion, she lowered the prickly rope over her head, holding it away from her neck. "Evy," she said. "You were just a child. You don't really know what happened."

"Oh I do too," breathed the girl, holding the gun on Maggie. Evy nodded her head, and her

385

eyes seemed to glaze over. "I do know. I'm the only one who really knows. I saw things that night. Nobody ever asked me, but I saw things."

The woman on the chair shook her head. "What things?" she asked. "What did you see?"

"I never told," said Evy. "Nobody knows. Just me." Evy's voice seemed to shrink as she spoke. "I was sleeping. I had a cold. I was in bed, with a cold. And I had a nightmare, so I woke up. I was scared. So I called out, but nobody came. I kept calling out and crying but . . . So, I got out of bed, and went to look for Mummy. But she wasn't there. Not anywhere. She said she wouldn't leave me, but I couldn't find her. And Daddy wasn't there. I was all alone. Then I heard the back door open, so I ran in the pantry and hid. I was afraid to look at first, but then I looked. That's when I saw . . ." Evy's voice trailed away.

Maggie could not tear her eyes from the girl's tortured face. "Saw what?" she whispered.

"She still had the knife. She was holding it and talking to herself. And there was blood everywhere. All over her coat and her gloves. She took off all her clothes and put them in the washer. But it was still on her. In her hair. On her face," Evy spat the words out. Evy paused for a moment, the scene vivid before her eyes. Then she droned on. "She didn't know I was watching. When she wasn't looking I ran back to my bed. She told the men who came that night that she was there with me all the time. But I saw her. I saw the blood."

Slowly, Evy lifted her head and looked at the woman standing on the chair, the noose draped on her shoulders. "I saw the blood," Evy repeated, as she stared up at Maggie, transfixed. Under the black mantilla the woman wore, Evy saw golden hair gleaming like a field of black-eyed susans.

The gun stood, forgotten for the moment, in Evy's hand. With one motion Maggie grabbed the rope from her neck, and kicked out as hard as she could.

The gun flew back into the air, and Maggie heard it land on the attic stairs. Evy let out a terrible cry, and snapped to attention. Maggie tried to leap off the chair, but in her stockinged feet she slid, and landed hard on her knees. For a second she rested there, stunned by her fall. Then she spotted the knife, a few feet beyond her, which she had brought to the attic. She scrambled for it, clawing her way across the floor. The handle was inches from her fingers. She reached out to grab it. Her hand came down on the handle. Her fingers curved around it.

Suddenly, the heel of Evy's shoe crunched down on her knuckles.

Maggie cried out in pain, and released the knife reflexively. It spun out of reach. With a swift dive Evy swooped down and retrieved it. Maggie fell back, clutching her throbbing knuckles to her chest. Evy whirled and faced her. She held the knife out, it's point aimed at Maggie's chest.

"No," Maggie whispered. "It was your mother. Not me. You saw your mother."

Evy took another step towards her, her pale eyes glittering with insensible rage.

The aged latch tore out of the wall and the door burst open, snapping back to smash the wall behind it. Jess shot forward, and then fell with a thud to the floor, gasping from the impact and the shock to his lungs of the cleaner air of the house.

For a moment he lay there on his face, his chest heaving, trying to breathe. Then, at a level with his eyes, he saw a pair of slippered feet and blue-veined ankles, twisted grotesquely on the footrest of a wheelchair. With a great effort Jess rolled himself over until he could look up. The old woman stared down at him her eyes colourless and open wide. Her jaw trembled uncontrollably.

Jess licked his lips and tried to speak. "Harriet," he whispered.

As if to answer him, the old woman gave a weak, phlegmatic cough.

"Is she gone?" he asked.

The old woman stared at his sallow, unshaven, hollow-eyed face. She tried to nod, but managed only a jerking motion of her head.

"Harriet," he whispered in a rasping voice. "You have to help me." Even as he said it, he did not know how. He gazed helplessly at the mournful, aged face. She was dressed, as always, in her bed clothes, the ribboned nightgown ludicrous against the tragic eyes, the slack, down-turned mouth. Jess noticed that she had a tray resting across the arms of the chair, and attached to the sides. On the tray was a glass filled with orange liquid, with a straw in it. Jess gazed at it for a moment. Then he looked up into her eyes, wondering if she could understand him.

"Harriet," he said urgently. "I need to get free of these straps. If you could just knock over that glass on your tray, knock it to the ground and break it, I could use the glass to cut them. Can you do that? Do you think you could manage to do that?"

She stared at him for a long moment.

She doesn't know a word I'm saying, he thought.

Then her eyes flickered down to the glass. She shut her eyes, and her frame began to tremble with the effort of making her muscles rigid. It took an agonizing time. She attempted to lift one arm off the armrest, and then fell back.

"That's right," Jess urged her. "Knock it over. Right here. Near me." He watched her apprehensively. There was no way to tell if she would succeed, or when. He would have no warning if the glass fell and shattered. No way to shield his face. He grimaced, trying to keep his eyes open only a slit. "Come on," he cried.

The old woman was breathing in gasps now, willing her arms to move, but they would not. Her torso twisted with the effort. Jess watched her with a growing despair. "Try," he insisted.

She opened her eyes and stared into his. A brew of sadness and fear bubbled behind them. Slowly she lowered her head.

"Please," Jess whispered. "You've got to."

With a sudden motion she jerked her head forward. Her outstretched chin caught the side of the glass.

Jess flinched and squeezed his eyes shut as it fell. The shattered glass flew up. He felt one sliver nick his ear, another gouge his chin. He opened his eyes. A sticky puddle of orange juice oozed across the floor. The glass lay in fragments around him. He looked up at the old woman. "Good," he said.

Even her eyes could not smile. She watched impassively, as he began to manoeuvre his bound hands towards a gleaming hunk of glass.

25

"**I** KNEW it!" Grace's flushed face was triumphant.

Jack Schmale stared at the teletype machine from which he had just received a report on the facts of Margaret Fraser's criminal history. He frowned and looked up into Grace's agitated eyes. "What do you know?" he said.

"I've had a feeling about her from the first day she got here," Grace asserted dramatically. "There was something phony about her. Mr. Emmett, indeed," she sniffed. "Mr. Emmett didn't go around hiring convicts."

"I wonder," Jack mused, "what our friend Miss Fraser knows about the absence of Mr. Emmett."

"Oh my God, Jack," Grace cried out. "Do you think she killed him?"

"Well, I'm not saying that, Grace. We don't know that he's dead. But it sure would have been inconvenient for her if Bill Emmett had walked into the newspaper office and declared that he'd never heard of her and that she had no business being there."

Grace blanched, and stared at the law officer. "Unless she made sure he was never coming

391

back," she said. "Jack, she's a killer. A cold-blooded murderer."

"Well, not quite," Jack insisted. "Apparently it was a crime of passion. She killed her lover. That's a bit different."

"Cold-blooded, warm-blooded. What's the difference? We've got a known killer right here on this island. And two men dead."

"Now hold on, Grace. You know yourself Jess was drowned by accident, and there's no proof of Mr. Emmett being dead. I've been up there to her place, snooping around. There's not a trace of anything suspicious."

"Nothing suspicious!" Grace cried. "Her latest conquest is buried at sea. Now we find out that she killed her last paramour. And Mr. Emmett's missing. Everything points to her."

"I can't argue with you, Grace. It looks bad."

"Bad? Jack Schmale, what are you going to do about this?"

"Well, I think I'm going to go out there and talk to her."

Suddenly, Grace gasped. "Oh my God."

"What is it?"

"Evy," she said. "Evy is out there alone with her. In that woman's state of mind, who knows what she might do?"

Jack stood up and lifted his hat from the coat-rack. "I'm going now," he said.

Grace stood up. "I'm going too."

Jack held up a hand. "Now Grace . . ."

"That child is alone out there with a madwoman on a killing spree and it's partly my fault. If I had insisted on this sooner . . . if I'd followed my nose, none of this would have happened. Oh my God. If anything happens to that girl I don't know what I'll do."

Jack shrugged on his raincoat and did not argue with her.

"I'm going with you," Grace said. She ran to catch up with the police officer, who was already opening the door.

The squad car was parked right out in front of the station house. Jack ran around to the driver's side and got in. By the time Grace had joined him in the front seat he had already started the engine.

"Nasty day," he muttered turning on the heater to try to clear the windscreen.

"Hurry up," said Grace removing a hanky from her handbag and nervously wiping the windscreen in urgent circular motions.

"Give it a minute," said Jack.

"We can't wait," Grace insisted.

"Okay," said Jack, squinting as he backed up. "But I can't see a damned thing." The clunk of the rear end of the car into the bumper of her car which was parked behind him confirmed his statement.

"Watch out," Grace squeaked. "Charley'll brain you if you dent that new car of ours."

Jack pulled out of the space and started up

Main Street. After a few turns they were on the road leading away from town. Jack turned on his low beams to try to pierce the dense fog as they sped along. There was silence in the car except for the swish of the windscreen wipers.

Grace bit her lip, but finally she spoke. "Can't you go any faster?" she said.

"These roads are bad today," Jack explained.

"I hope that girl is all right."

Jack peered anxiously through the windscreen, and pressed his foot down on the accelerator.

The point of the knife weaved back and forth in front of Maggie's face. She did not dare to take her eyes off it. She tried to back away from the menacing blade, but Evy advanced on her, baiting her with the weapon she clutched.

All at once, Evy lunged. Maggie leapt away, but the very tip of the knife caught her upper lip, slicing part way through. Maggie heard the blade rap her teeth. Blood gushed from the small wound, splattering on the floor and her clothes. Evy struck again.

Ignoring her cut, Maggie flopped down to the right, and grabbed the girl's wrist. The sudden movement shocked and unbalanced Evy, and she dropped heavily to the floor. Maggie tried to wrest the knife from Evy's grip. Enraged, Evy sank her teeth into the hand which held her own.

Maggie cried out as Evy's teeth sank through her flesh and clamped around a bone. She

394

wrenched her wrist free from the girl's grasp, and smacked her on the jaw. Evy tumbled backwards, releasing the knife, which shot across the floor and fell between two planks under an eave. She scrambled to her feet, looking for her weapon.

"It's gone now," Maggie cried out, and tackled Evy around the legs. The two women grappled, rolling across the floor, smashing into boxes, and knocking the hanging chair on its side. They gripped each other in a deadly embrace, their limbs straining to control the other's. Suddenly, with a guttural cry, Evy ripped an arm free and struck a sharp blow to Maggie's stomach with her elbow which winded and stunned her. Weakened, Maggie loosened her grasp on the girl. Evy pulled away from her and clambered towards the stairs.

Recovering, Maggie scuttled after her, grabbing at the girl's waist as she bent down over the third stair. As Maggie reached down, Evy turned towards her. Maggie looked into the barrel of the gun.

"Get back," Evy ordered.

Maggie crawled backwards as Evy mounted the stairs.

"Now we'll see," said the girl, training the gun on Maggie. "Stand up."

Short of breath, Maggie struggled to her feet.

"Now, you put that chair back where it was

and get on it," the girl ordered, panting between words.

"Evy," Maggie pleaded, "don't."

"Do it," the girl shrieked. Maggie heard the sickening click as Evy cocked the gun.

Maggie looked from the girl's merciless eyes to the swinging noose. There would be no talking her way out of it. From the corner of her eye she saw a metal lamp base standing about two feet from where she stood. Without pausing to think, Maggie dived down and grabbed for it.

"Stop," Evy screamed, as she saw Maggie's desperate lunge. "No, you don't." She aimed the gun at Maggie's head, and pulled the trigger.

There was a click, and then silence. Evy stared in disbelief at the impotent weapon in her hand. Maggie, halted for a moment by the click, grabbed the metal lamp base, and swung it up hard at Evy.

The corner of the lamp caught Evy on the chin, and the girl spun backwards, and fell on the stairs. She rolled down two steps. Suddenly, a deafening report tore through the silent attic. The girl tumbled the rest of the way down the staircase, her body heavily bumping each step as she fell.

Maggie froze, confused for a moment by the noise. Then she ran to the steps and looked down.

Evy lay in the stairwell, her body contorted, one thin leg sticking out into the downstairs hall.

Cautiously, Maggie crept down towards the twisted form which lay motionless on the steps. Heart pounding, she grabbed the girl's bony shoulder and jerked it back.

Evy's pale eyes were open and wide with shock. Her mouth hung crookedly ajar in a permanent grimace of pain. The waxy complexion looked entirely bloodless. Her lifeless hand still cradled the old gun. A huge, gory blotch spread out across the front of the sweater where the bullet meant for Maggie had ripped into Evy's chest.

Maggie crouched on the stair above her and drew her arms up tightly to her chest, burying her face in her hands. "Oh my God," she moaned. For a while she rocked there, too stunned to move, clutching her arms around herself and keening. She felt a sharp pain in her own breast, and even looked down at herself, filled with the awful fear that she might somehow, spontaneously, start to bleed. All she saw were the splotches of dried blood from her own broken lip. Finally, she pulled herself up and forced her trembling leg out over the body. With an awkward, goat-like leap, she landed in the hall. She knelt down beside the stairs and slumped against the open door to the attic, her chest heaving. Her stomach felt like it was being squeezed. She closed her eyes and tried to take deep breaths.

Evy. It was Evy all the time. Willy. And Jess.

And now she was dead. It was all over. A sense of relief crept over her.

I should get help, she thought. She looked towards the kitchen and the telephone. Then she shook her head. She felt as if her knees were nailed to the floor. There's no hurry, she thought. Evy is dead.

She had killed her. For a moment her feeling of relief was supplanted by a horror of what had happened. Even though she had not actually pulled the trigger, she had struck the blow that resulted in Evy's death.

She chewed on that for a moment and then chided herself. You had to do it. It was self-defence. The girl was trying to kill you. Trying to kill you out of a twisted vengeance for something you didn't even do. It was her mother. Maggie groaned as she mulled over that revelation. It was Roger's wife who had killed him. The wife he had vowed he would never leave. Maggie choked out a bitter laugh, but she could feel tears running down her face. Twelve years in prison. Twelve years of accepting the guilt for a woman who must have been insane. Like her daughter.

Maggie turned her head sideways to where Evy's foot protruded into the hallway. Slowly, Maggie dragged herself up to her feet, and stood there unsteadily. Trembling, with her lips pressed together, she walked over and stood in front of the contorted, bleeding corpse on the stairwell.

She was evil, Maggie told herself. She had to die. But her wrath against the girl would not hold. Maggie kept imagining Evy as a child. An innocent child whose life had been warped by forces outside her control. For years the lonely girl had lived with her secrets and her pain. I know what that's like, she thought. A feeling of genuine pity for the dead girl washed over her.

Bending over the lifeless body, Maggie removed the gun from the twisted fingers, and placed one cool hand over the other in a gesture of repose. Maybe now, she thought, you'll know some peace.

The slamming of a car door jolted her out of her reverie. She heard the sound of feet running up the driveway and pounding on the porch. Maggie groaned with relief. Someone had come. They could help her. She turned to look. The door banged open and Jack Schmale burst into the house, his gun drawn, with Grace right behind him.

He scanned the room and then he saw Maggie, standing over Evy's body holding a gun. Blood was spattered over the two of them. In the next instant Grace saw it too. "Oh my God," she shrieked.

"Drop it," Jack cried, training his pistol on Maggie.

Maggie looked at him in confusion.

"I knew it," Grace wailed. "We were too late. You killed her."

Maggie looked down at the gun in her hand and then at the body in the stairwell. Understanding dawned on her. She looked up helplessly at the policeman and at Grace and shook her head.

"No," she said. "You don't understand. It was an accident. She was trying to kill me. She brought this gun here. This is hers. She was going to kill me."

"Sure, that's right," Jack placated her. "Why don't you hand that over and we can talk about it?"

"We know all about you," Grace screamed defiantly. "We know you were in prison. I told Jack this was going to happen. You won't get away with this."

"I didn't mean . . . I had to," Maggie protested.

"You'll hang for this," Grace threatened her. "We're eyewitnesses. This time you'll pay for it."

"Shut up, Grace," Jack growled.

But his warning was too late. For as Maggie listened to Grace's words, she suddenly understood the position she was in. No one would ever believe her. She had done time for a murder, and now here she stood, holding a gun over the body of a local girl, known and liked by everyone. A girl she had threatened, in fact, at a public fair. There was no way out of it. She was doomed. She stared back at Grace.

"You see," Grace cried triumphantly. "She knows I'm right. She knows she'll get the electric chair for this. You can't kill an innocent girl and get away with it. Not this time you don't. You can kill me too, but you'll never get away with it."

"Don't listen to her," Jack said soothingly to Maggie. "You'll get a fair trial. If you hand over that gun, I'll try to help you."

"Help her!" Grace cried. "She's a killer, Jack."

Maggie looked down again at Evy. A wave of despair engulfed her. You win, she said. You have your revenge, after all. I'm not going back to prison. I couldn't survive that again. I'd rather die.

Slowly, Maggie raised the gun.

"No," Grace screamed.

Maggie lifted the gun and put it against her own temple. She looked impassively at the two in the doorway.

"Don't do that," Jack cried out. "Give me that gun. You don't want to do that. Give yourself a chance."

Maggie almost laughed. A chance. She shook her head, and renewed her grip on the butt.

"Let her," Grace cried. "She doesn't deserve to live. Not after what she's done. Go ahead."

Maggie cocked the hammer, and squeezed her eyes shut. Make it fast, she thought.

"Maggie, no!"

Her eyes shot open at the sound of the heart-wrenching cry. She looked up and saw Jess, bearded and bedraggled, pushing his way past the police chief and the woman in the doorway.

"God help us," Grace screamed.

Jack just gaped.

Maggie blinked at the spectre in front of her. Jess's dark eyes locked with hers. "Maggie, I know what happened. She tried to kill me too. Don't listen to them."

Maggie still clutched the gun to her head. "Where? What happened?"

"She had me in her cellar. Emmett's body was down there. She killed him. Maggie, she was completely crazy. I know all about it."

"You're alive," Maggie breathed. A sad smile formed in her eyes. "Oh, thank God." She lowered the gun slightly.

"We're both alive. It's all over. We're going to be fine."

Maggie's smile faded, and she shook her head. "They're going to put me in jail. I can't go back. I can't do that. I was in prison before. I never told you."

"It doesn't matter," he said weakly.

"You don't understand. I've been in prison before. I lied to you. They're going to say I did it," she cried.

402

"No," he pleaded. "They won't. I'll tell them about Evy. I'll make sure that nothing happens to you. Won't you trust me?"

Maggie looked up at his weary, anguished face. Tears sprang to her eyes. He's alive. You're not alone any more, she thought. It is possible to trust someone. It's time. It's finally time.

Slowly she turned and placed the weapon in her hand on the staircase. She smiled unsteadily at Jess, who smiled back at her. Then he ran a hand over his pale, sweaty forehead.

"You're sick," she said. "Sit down." She rushed to support him as he sank into a near-by chair. He put his arm around her neck. She buried her face in his shoulder. Through his shirt, she could feel his ribs, and his sagging flesh.

"Whew," Jack exhaled loudly. He walked over to the stairs and picked up the gun. Grace followed timidly behind him. In the kitchen, the phone began to ring. "I'll get that," Jack said, although no one was listening to him.

Grace approached Evy's body and looked down on it as if it were some strange ikon in a museum. Then, hesitantly, she bent down and pushed a few strands of hair back off the chilly forehead. She stood up and shook her head. A small sob escaped from her.

"Everything's under control, Owen," Jack's voice boomed out from the kitchen. "Yeah, it's a terrible thing. We'll tell you about it when you

403

get back. We do have one pleasant surprise for you, though." Jack looked out to where Jess slumped in a chair, his arms locked around Maggie who knelt beside him. "It's about Jess."

"I must smell like hell," Jess whispered wryly, stroking the side of her face.

"Like heaven," Maggie said, and held him fast.

THE END